LEON SPARKS

and The Spear of Ares

Books by Sean Tudor

LEON SPARKS

LEON SPARKS and The Spear of Ares

LEON SPARKS

and The Spear of Ares

SEAN TUDOR

Little Ladies Press

First published: 2020

Cover illustrations by Sean Tudor. Planetary image credits (front jacket): Pixabay.com, Wallpaperaccess.com. Interior images (Moon, Mars) based on NASA source images.

A CIP catalogue record for this title is available from the British Library.

ISBN: 978-0-9957363-4-4

Little Ladies Press (an imprint of White Ladies Press)

For further information and enquiries, email the publisher at: info@whiteladiespress.co.uk

For Hannah and Emma (again), and all the fans of the first one.

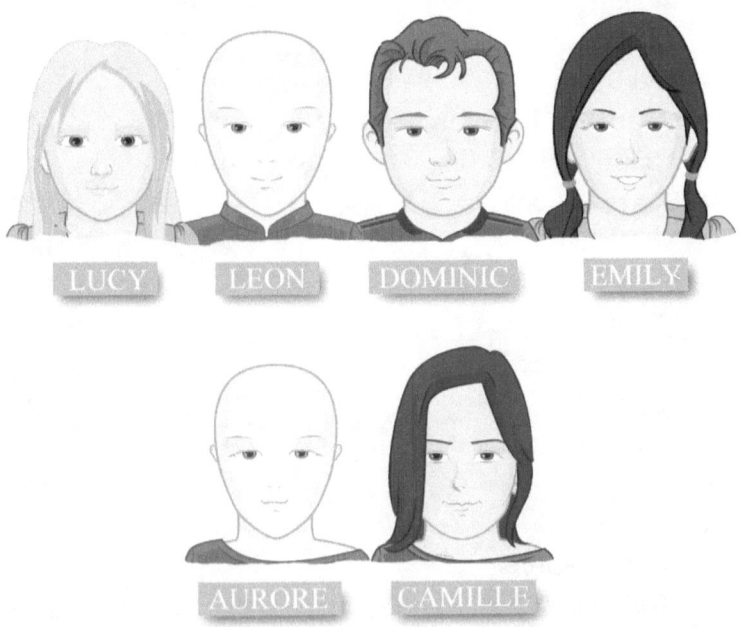

Chapters

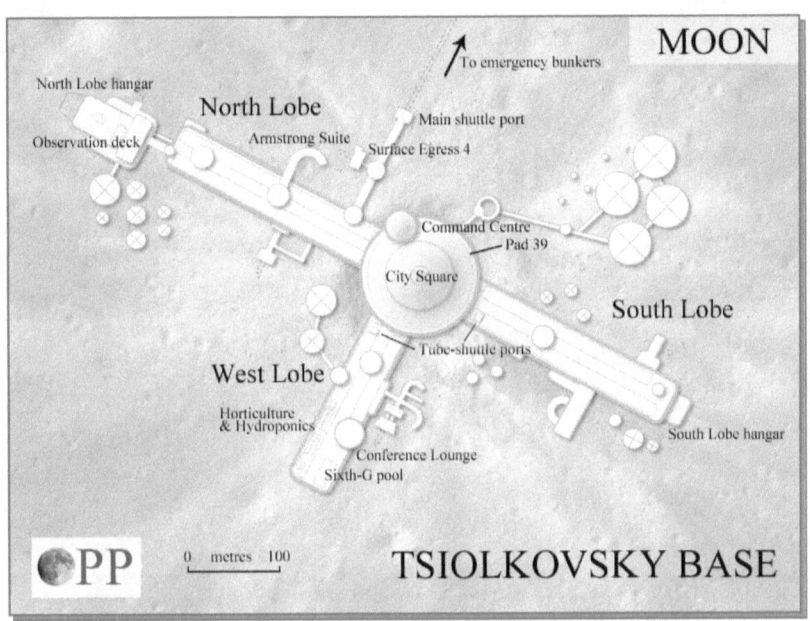

MOON

North Lobe hangar

Observation deck

North Lobe

Armstrong Suite

Main shuttle port

Surface Egress 4

To emergency bunkers

Command Centre
Pad 39

City Square

Tube-shuttle ports

West Lobe

Horticulture
& Hydroponics

South Lobe

South Lobe hangar

Conference Lounge
Sixth-G pool

PP

0   metres   100

TSIOLKOVSKY BASE

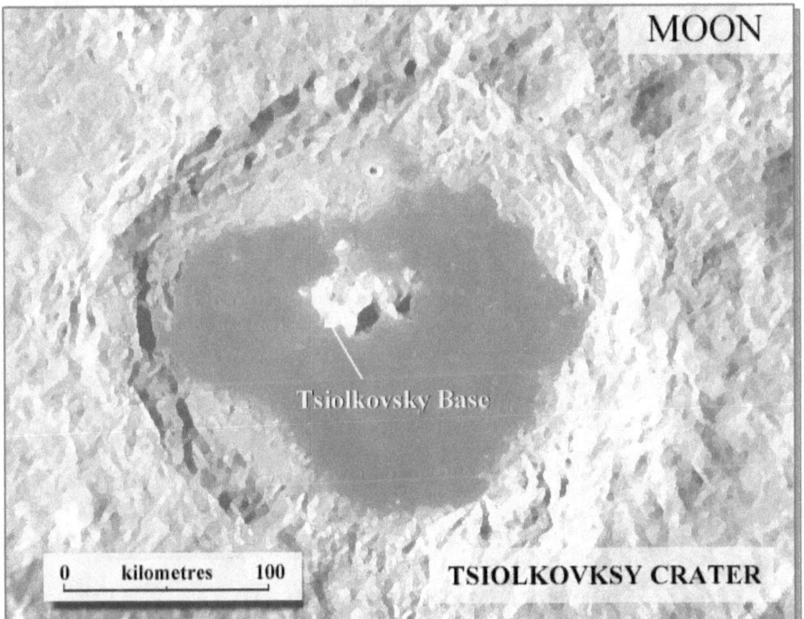

MOON

Tsiolkovsky Base

0   kilometres   100

TSIOLKOVKSY CRATER

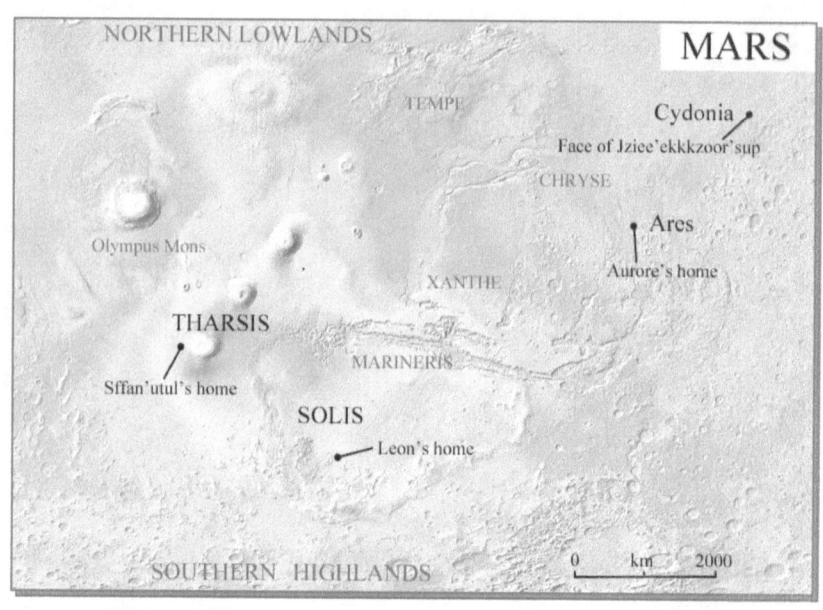

MARS

NORTHERN LOWLANDS

TEMPE

Cydonia
Face of Jziee'ekkkzoor'sup

CHRYSE

Olympus Mons

Ares
Aurore's home

XANTHE

THARSIS

MARINERIS

Sffan'utul's home

SOLIS

Leon's home

SOUTHERN HIGHLANDS

0   km   2000

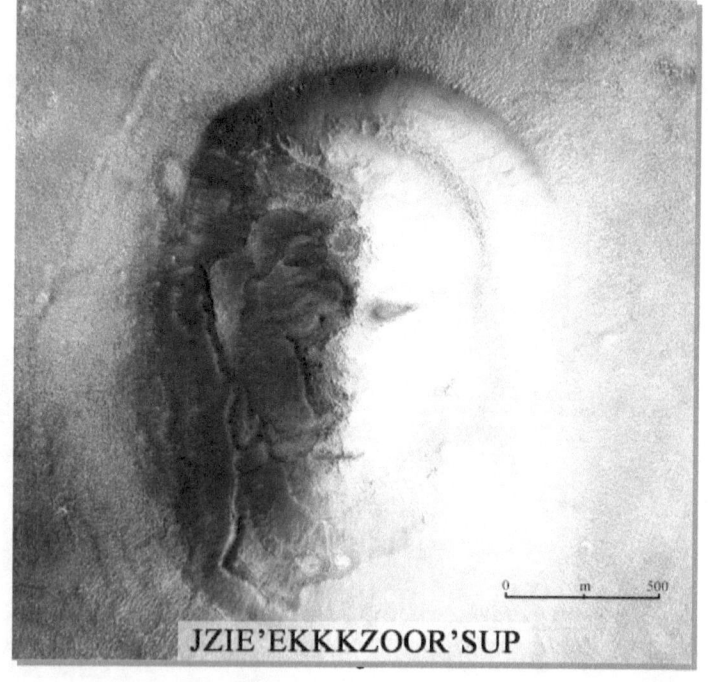

0   m   500

JZIE'EKKKZOOR'SUP

1 · THE MOON

*W*ould you like to come to the Moon?

Dominic stared at the message. The *Moon*? *Was he serious*?

The message was from his friend, Leon. And, yes, he was serious. Leon, you see, was from the planet Mars.

When Leon Sparks walked into Flintworne Junior School for the first time last September, everything had changed – although only a few knew that at the time.

He joined Class 5G (the 'G' was short for Gulliver, Leon's new teacher) and was seated at table 5 with three other children. Their names were Lucy Westbridge, Emily Tiddler and Dominic Addison, and they were to become firm friends.

A year ago, Flintworne Junior School, an ordinary but well-regarded school in southern England, had been one of a selection of schools chosen from around the world to take part in a top-secret interplanetary student exchange programme. A small number of Earth children travelled with their parents to spend some time on Mars, to learn about the ways and culture of the surviving population there. Likewise, a handful of Martian children were placed in schools on Earth to mix with human children in order to learn about Earth customs and how humans interacted socially.

And so, every morning, Leon travelled from the Moon, where he was staying with his parents at a secret American base on its hidden side, to be dropped off early at school by their spaceship as it hovered invisibly over the school. And in the evening, he would be picked up the same way.

To begin with, only Leon's teacher, Mrs Gulliver, the headmaster, Mr Knutt, the school caretaker, Mr Flynn – and two new 'school inspectors', Mr Smiley and Mr Wolfe (who, in reality, were Leon's assigned bodyguards from the Office of Planetary Protection) – knew his true nature. Soon, his tablemates and the classroom assistant, Mrs Miggs, learned this as well.

But others too, including the deputy headmaster, Mr Jones, began to suspect that Leon was rather more than your average human child. When signs of Leon's spaceship's daily visits to the school – strange gusts of wind, an odd whirring sound and unusual lights high in the sky – began to be noticed by the area's residents and reported in the newspapers, agents from a far-off land with designs on the American-led exchange programme and the technologies of the more-advanced Martians developed a keen interest in Flintworne Junior School and its newest student: a pale-skinned, ten-year old boy who always carried a shiny silver briefcase.

When those foreign agents managed to gain access to the school and abduct Leon (sparking a top-level security alert that went all the way to the Prime Minister and the American authorities), Leon's friends, Dominic, Lucy and Emily, found themselves best placed to assist Leon's parents in tracking him down and attempt a rescue.

Their daring adventure – which had involved zapping Leon's captors with a beam of light from Leon's comportal (a special phone-like device that could do all sorts of amazing things) and a hide-and-seek chase through a distant town – ended when Leon was returned safely to Flintworne. But by then it had become clear that, for his continued safety, Leon would not be permitted to stay on at school.

And so, Leon had departed, almost as soon as he had arrived, sadly leaving behind his new friends and teachers, who watched as his spaceship lifted off invisibly from the school fields and shot off skywards, where it flared briefly as a pale green shooting star, and was gone.

That was before Christmas, towards the end of Term One. Now it was the summer holidays and none of Leon's friends had heard from him for ages, despite his parting gift to each of them being a personalised version of a comportal that would enable them to keep in touch.

It was Emily who had seen the message on hers, who then promptly called Lucy and Dominic.

"*The Moon*?" Dominic whispered aloud. "*Epic!*"

He put down his comportal and reached for his mobile phone to call Emily.

"Ems, when did this appear?" he asked. "There's no time on it."

"No," replied Emily. "It wasn't there first thing – I still check it every day. It popped up just now."

"Which probably means Leon's waiting for an answer. What about Lucy?"

"I spoke to her first," said Emily. "She's out with her mum at the minute."

"Oh," said Dominic. "I was going to suggest we get a group chat going with Leon. You can set that up again, can't you?"

"Yes, it's easy," replied Emily.

"OK, how about you and me call him?" suggested Dominic.

"Well, we could. But he can't be serious," said Emily.

"Why not?" said Dominic.

"He just *can't* – we can't just go to the Moon! It must be a mistake. Besides, I thought he was supposed to have gone back home to Mars?"

"P'raps he's visiting," said Dominic.

"Plus, wasn't it forbidden for humans to leave Earth?" said Emily.

"That might have changed," said Dominic, hopefully.

"Well, I don't know about your mum and dad," said Emily, "but mine will be dead against me going. I'm not sure I want to either. It's not like just going up for a short ride in their spaceship. Why couldn't he just come back to Hawlington?"

"Dunno," replied Dominic. "Why don't we ask him?"

"OK," said Emily. "Give me a minute to set up my comportal. I'll send you an invite, then we can call Leon."

At that, Emily was gone. Dominic sat back on his bed. He put his mobile phone down and picked up the comportal. He looked at it while he waited it for Emily to buzz. The outer case had a photo on it of him with Leon and the rest of Flintworne's Year 5 inter-schools football team that was taken after they had won the championship last year. This holiday, which had started with the prospect of six weeks of mostly entertaining himself (apart from visits with his friends and a week's camping in the New Forest) was already starting to look more promising.

The comportal in his hand buzzed. Dominic flipped it over and pressed its sides with his thumb and forefinger. Immediately, a thin blue glow appeared along its edge and a three-dimensional display popped into the space before him. He quickly swiped at a rusty-orange symbol, and a small oval window appeared with Emily looking out at him.

"All set up," said Emily. "Ready?" At her end of the connection, a small head-and-shoulders Dominic replied, "Go."

Emily made a circular motion with her hand and another window appeared beside Dominic's. A small, rather rounded face with a delicate narrowing chin stared back at them. The figure's head was without visible hair, while its small bud-like ears and nose, narrow lipless mouth and large eyes were unusual, and familiar.

"Leon!" they said in unison.

A small curl of a smile formed at the corners of Leon's mouth and his eyes glittered softly. "Hello, Dominic, hello Emily. Is Lucy not with you?"

"She's shopping with her mum," said Emily. "Where have you *been*, Leon? We haven't heard from you for *ages*."

"No, I am sorry," said Leon. "I will explain when we meet. Did you like my invitation?"

"So you're serious?" asked Emily.

"Yes, of course," replied Leon.

"Epic!" said Dominic. "You're there now, on the Moon?"

"Yes," said Leon. "At Tsiolkovsky. We arrived a week ago."

Tsiolkovsky was a secret base built by the Americans that was located in the crater of the same name on the Moon's far side. For some time now it had been used to launch exploratory missions out into the solar system, and had served to host meetings with and accommodate visiting Martian officials.

For Leon, Tsiolkovsky base had been his home all the time he went to school at Flintworne, and twice a day during the thirty-minute trip between the Moon and the Earth and back again, he would peer out of the ship's viewer, or read, on the most exciting and novel school-run one could imagine.

"How could that work?" asked Emily. "Mr Knutt told us that humans, especially children, weren't allowed to leave Earth?"

"Do you remember Mr Smiley?" asked Leon.

"Of course," said Emily.

"Let us say that he has been working very hard to carry on with the programme."

"So you might get to come back to Flintworne?" asked Emily brightly.

"No, that will not happen," continued Leon. "It will... be accomplished in a different manner. So, please check with Lucy, and with your parents – there is room for one parent each – and let me know by Thursday. If you can come – and I hope you can – a pod will be sent on Friday evening to collect you."

"Cool," said Dominic. "Where? Plaxton Fields?"

"No, they are building there now," said Leon. "The school fields. Eight p.m."

"Oh," said Dominic. "OK."

"How long for?" asked Emily.

"A week." suggested Leon. "There is much to catch up on. And to see. Call me if you need to," he said, and he ended the call.

"Well, what do you think?" asked Emily.

"I wanna go," said Dominic. "I'm gonna talk to my dad."

"Let me know what your mum and dad say. I can't see me going, to be honest," said Emily. "No matter how much I'd love to see Leon again."

2

"So what do you think?" asked Emily.

Lucy's reply surprised Emily. "Well, it's Leon, isn't it? I'm sure it'd be safe. Yes," she reflected, "I'd like to go – if I'm allowed to, that is. Why did Leon say he couldn't come here again?"

"He didn't," replied Emily. "Just said it wasn't possible."

"I wonder what we'll need to pack," mused Lucy. "Wonder if you need, like, sun cream, or scarves?"

"Just a space-suit, I should think – and a straw to suck mashed carrot out of a tube," said Emily. Both girls laughed.

"OK," said Lucy. "Perhaps we should talk to Leon again before anyone says anything to our parents. Maybe see you tomorrow?"

"Yes," said Emily. "I'll see if I can come over to yours."

"OK, talk soon," said Lucy.

3

Tea time in the Addison household was generally a communal affair, with all the family gathered around the kitchen table.

Dad, a balding, thick-set man with ruddy cheeks, whose two main interests seemed to be football and beer – his *only* interests, mum had been known to say – always sat at the end nearest the hallway. Opposite him sat Dominic's sixteen-year-old sister, Jenny, who, while often physically in attendance (mum and dad insisted), was never fully present, being ever *soooo* busy dealing with dozens of important messages on her phone or scheduling her frenetic social calendar, that there simply wasn't time to waste on eating properly or conversing with her family.

Then there was Dominic's mum, who Dominic couldn't ever remember actually sitting down to eat with them. Rather she moved continually like a whirlwind between dishing up and washing up, talking, and picking at her own food as she did so.

And finally, there was Dominic himself, who sat with his back to the yellow kitchen wall, pushing roast potatoes into his mouth as a steam engine driver might shovel coals into his firebox.

Finally, he relented, and turned to his dad. "When are we going camping?"

Mr Addison polished off a potato before answering. "Can't wait, eh?" he said. His eyebrows narrowed on his son.

"No, not exactly," replied Dominic. "Just, you know, in case something else came up." He absently pushed the remains of his meal around his plate.

"Like what?" asked his dad.

"Dunno. Like me and my friends doing something."

"Oh," said Mr Addison. "Well, we thought we'd go on Friday."

"Friday?! *This* Friday?"

"Yeah. Only time we can do it really. Thought you knew that." His eyes flicked from Dominic to his wife.

Dominic caught the exchange. No," he said, "I didn't."

He shifted uncomfortably in his chair. He turned to his sister. "Did you know?"

Jenny shrugged. "I'm not going," she said without looking up.

"What's the problem, Dom?" asked Mrs Addison. She shifted uncomfortably, flashing her eyes at her husband.

Mr Addison pushed his plate away. His tongue wormed inside his cheeks, sweeping away any remaining food.

Jenny took this as her own cue to drop her fork onto her plate and pushed her chair back.

"Where are you off to?" asked Mrs Addison.

"Alison's," replied Jenny over her shoulder.

17

Mr Addison waited for her to leave the room, then he turned to Dominic.

"You got a better idea than camping?"

"Maybe," replied Dominic. He looked from his dad to his mum, who had stopped moving and now stood at the end of the table.

"Don't tell me – the Moon?" said Mr Addison.

Dominic's mouth fell open. "How did you know that?" he asked. Then he said, "Wait a minute. You're not laughing."

"No, he's not," said Mrs Addison, who turned away again towards the sink.

"Did you listen in on my call with Leon and Emily? Ah, no, you couldn't, because –"

"Because I was at work," said Mr Addison. "No, actually, your Mr Knutt and Mr Smiley came to see us before the end of term."

"They wha' –" started Dominic.

"Yep. Came to tell us about that Smiley fella's idea to carry on with his contact programme by using the Moon as a meeting place. Your friend Leon was coming back with a bunch of other Martian kids; some of them were on Earth like him."

So... so, we're going?!" asked Dominic.

Mr Addison put his fork down on his plate. "Well, I am." He glanced from Dominic to his wife, who flicked her eyebrows heavenward. He looked back at Dominic. "You can come too, if you like?"

"Yeah? *Yesss!*" exclaimed Dominic. He leapt up, causing the plates and cups to rattle on the table top. "I'm gonna go and pack," he said, making for the doorway, where he paused, turning. "Wait a minute," he said. "What about the others – Lucy, Emily? Did Mr Knutt and Mr Smiley visit their parents too?"

"Yes, they did," replied Mrs Addison. "Lucy's mum and Emily's dad have said they'll go – 'though I can't for the life of me think why. Your dad knows I'm not happy about you going."

"You'll notice she's not worried about *me* going," Mr Addison said with a twinkle in his eye. "Anyway, your mum worries too much. It's perfectly safe – young Leon did it twice a day, and we'll only be away for a week. So, pack your camera, and your sports stuff – yep, they have all the facilities, I'm told. We're gonna have a great time!"

"And your passports," added Mrs Addison.

"Don't be daft," said Mr Addison. "You don't need passports for the Moon."

Mrs Addison shrugged. "Well, you need one for everywhere else," she said, as she collected Dominic's and Jenny's plates and cups.

At that, Dominic was gone. His footsteps clumped up the stairs.

4

Lucy's mum had finally told her yesterday, after they had returned home from the shops.

"You? *You're* coming to the Moon?" asked Lucy.

"Yes, love. Your dad's working, so it'll have to be me, won't it?" she said matter-of-factly.

"But you've never really liked flying, have you?" asked Lucy, still surprised.

"No, but, on reflection, I think I've been missing out," replied Mrs Westbridge, a small woman with pleasantly simple looks beneath a casual mop of blonde curls.

"When I was a young girl, I'd sometimes see the Moon rising on summer evenings and wonder what it'd be like to go there. This was after men had actually landed there, of course, so I knew it was possible. I'd forgotten that – that I'd often daydream of travelling to far-flung places. Somehow, life dulls our dreams – if we let it," she sighed.

"So, when Mr Knutt came round to see your dad and me and outlined their plan – I've never seen him so excited – I surprised even myself by jumping at the chance. Your dad nearly fell out of his chair. Can't get more far-flung than the Moon!"

Now Lucy was with Emily at her house, and it seemed that a similar conversation had taken place there too. Emily's dad, a tall man with short salt-and-pepper hair, was an engineer, who had been fascinated by Leon's parents' spaceship when he saw it on the evening Leon had left Flintworne Junior School. He therefore hadn't needed much persuasion to accompany his daughter on an invited trip to the Moon – even if Emily herself had been reticent about going. But once she realised that Lucy would be going, she finally agreed to the trip – even when *her* mum had stated her opinion on the matter.

Emily had received some further information from Leon about the trip to supplement what Mr Knutt and Mr Smiley had said. The trip would last a week, not counting travelling to and from the Moon, which actually would take only forty minutes or so. The idea was for the Martian children and the Earth children, who had interacted during last year's exchange programme, to get together to discuss and share what they had all learned. There were a dozen children from Mars, including Leon, six of whom, like him, had been placed in schools in different countries and cultures on Earth; while the other six had served as hosts to six Earth children, and a parent each, who had visited Mars to stay with Martian families. And then, of course, there were various friends of all the children, like Emily, Lucy and Dominic, who had been invited to share in the experience. And finally, there were the officials from both sides, including Mr Smiley, who had been assigned to protect Leon at Flintworne, plus a parent for every child in attendance. In all, there would be at least a hundred people gathered there for the week.

"Is it big enough?" Dominic had asked.

"The base?" said Emily. "Yes, it's well, huge. There are around three hundred people who live and work there."

These were mainly Americans, from Earth; plus some Martian engineers and administrators.

The week's programme would include presentations, and discussion groups, and activities (swimming in one-sixth gravity was supposed to be challenging, and fun), and parties.

After tea, Emily and Lucy went to Emily's room and called Dominic, and together they made another comportal call to Leon, this time sharing the good news that they could all come on Friday.

"That is very good," said Leon. "I am looking forward to seeing my friends again. The pod will arrive at eight-thirty, your time. Mr Smiley will be there to meet you."

"You won't be there as well?" asked Lucy.

"No, we are not permitted to come to Earth presently. But do not worry – it does not take very long. I will see you soon."

2 - LIFT OFF

The school was closed for the summer holidays. But this was the time that Mr Flynn, the caretaker, could really get on with some of his groundskeeping and maintenance jobs without fear of disturbance, or of running over the toes of a student who was where he or she oughtn't to be.

Today, Friday – 9 August on his calendar – he had been out in the grounds, on the football pitch (which was without goalposts until the autumn term came around), preparing for the arrival of the pod. The area around the centre-circle of the pitch was now protected by curved banks of camouflaged netting to shield it from view from the surrounding houses. By then, though, it would be dusk and harder to see anything there anyway.

The invited folks – young Leon's friends and parents were to be at the front gates at eight p.m., when he was to let them in and escort them through to the sports wing that overlooked the school field until the pod landed, which he knew would take place at precisely eight-thirty.

Mr Flynn rolled his laden wheelbarrow beneath the canopy that overhung the sports wing and parked it there to await the arrival of the pod. Then he made his way back to his workshop, where he put the kettle on and began to gather the tools he'd need for his next job.

2

Eight p.m. It was time.

Mr Flynn thumbled in a pocket of his overalls for his keys as he walked towards the gates. Young Leon's friends, Dominic, Lucy and Emily – who sometimes visited with Leon in his workshop while he waited for the school to open after being dropped off in his parents' spaceship – waited on the other side of the gates.

He heard a voice say, "Here he is." It was a man's voice, one of the children's dads – and the small crowd shuffled into movement, picking up suitcases and bags and turning to face him.

"Hello Mr Flynn," said Lucy.

"Hullo Lucy. How're you?" He addressed the group. "All ready, are we?" he said as he unlocked one side of the gates and pulled it inward.

"As ready as we'll ever be, I guess," said the blonde lady who stepped through first.

Lucy followed in behind her. Then came Dominic and his dad – "Can't wait," he said.

Finally, Emily and her dad, a tall man who made a small nod of his head towards Mr Flynn but said nothing; not even when he glanced back to see Mr Flynn closing and re-locking the gate – a small action, but one itself indicative that they would not be going back out this way this evening.

3

At 8.25 p.m. the group stepped outside and walked out to the edge of the field. The evening was mostly clear and dry; just the vestiges of sunset remained as a rusty brown stain on the western horizon. Overhead, stars were beginning to appear through the blue-grey of burgeoning night. The planet Mars, distinguished by its flickering reddish tinge, hung low in the southwest.

Soon, a faint star detached itself from the heavens and began to grow steadily. Then it transformed into a white streak that shot across the sky like a shooting star until it was directly overhead, where it faded from view.

But very soon there was a growing sense of electricity in the air and a breeze blew up from nowhere, accompanied by a faint hum. The lights of the sports wing behind them and in some of the surrounding houses flickered, and then something, a dark grey silhouette, descended silently into the field and dropped out of sight behind the camouflage nets.

Beside them, Mr Flynn picked up the handles of his wheelbarrow and began to push it out onto the grass. The others, led by Mr Addison, followed on behind. When they emerged on the other side of the nets, everyone stopped at the scene before them.

Lucy, Emily and Dominic had seen Leon's parents' spaceship on this very spot – and had even taken a ride in it – but this was somehow more mysterious. Before them, on squat tripod legs sat an egg-shaped object, around fifteen feet tall. In the available light, it had the appearance of blackened and burnished copper, struck through with fine veins of blue, which occasionally pulsed with energy. There was a faint crackling sound in the air, like the hissing and spitting of a camp fire, but which emanated a sense of barely-contained electrical force that raised the hairs on heads and necks and arms. Mr Flynn pushed forward regardless, but the others stayed back.

Presently, there was a subdued *whoosh* sound and a seam of light, pale cream in colour, opened in the side facing them, forming the shape of a round hatch. The door itself pushed outwards, as if hinged at the base, and lowered to meet the ground, forming a ramp. In the pale light of the interior there was movement. A silhouette filled the doorway, and a figure stepped out onto the top of the ramp.

"Evening, folks." It was Mr Smiley. He stepped off the ramp onto the grass of the football pitch.

"Wow!" exclaimed Mr Tiddler, Emily's dad, whose name always solicited an unusual look from those who first heard his name and took in his six feet, two inch frame. He tweaked his head to glance inside, and then turned to Mr Smiley. He offered his hand in introduction, "Jeremy Tiddler. Emily's dad."

Mr Smiley shook his hand.

"Are you sure this is big enough?" asked Mr Tiddler. "What's its payload capacity?"

"It'll seem larger inside," replied Mr Smiley, "and is capable of carrying all of us and more. Speaking of which... Mr Flynn?"

He looked past them towards the older man in green overalls and welly boots; check shirt. "Mr Flynn, do you have all you need?"

"I reckon so, Mr Smiley. All loaded in the cargo 'atch."

"Is he coming with us?" whispered Emily.

"Dunno," replied Dominic.

"Good," said Mr Smiley. "Please take your seat, then," he said.

"Make that a 'yes'," said Lucy.

Dominic raised his eyebrows. "You're coming to the Moon as well, Mr Flynn?"

"Yes, lad. I've been looking after some of their gardening needs; fresh vegetables and what not."

"Only so much you can do with hydroponics," said Mr Smiley. "As Mr Flynn has been showing our botanists and horticulturists."

"What's hydroponics?" whispered Emily to her dad.

"Growing plants in water rather than soil," replied Mr Tiddler.

"Yep, well," said Mr Flynn humbly. "I just been treatin' em to a good 'ole mixture of manure and bone meal, with a bit a plant pick-me-up I makes myself."

Mr Flynn moved towards the hatch.

"OK, folks," said Mr Smiley. "Please follow Mr Flynn onto the craft. Leave your baggage on the floor beside Mr Flynn's belongings and find a seat. We lift off in five minutes."

"Here we go again," whispered Mr Addison.

Dominic's dad had been fortunate to have had a brief flight on Leon's parents' ship during Leon's first – and only – term at school.

"Hope you've remembered to bring your passports," said Mr Smiley.

Dominic raised his eyes at his dad.

"Ah, um... *really?*" asked Mr Addison. "We...er, I'm not... er..." he said awkwardly.

Dominic allowed his dad to squirm for a moment

longer before he slipped a hand into a pocket and withdrew two passports, one his, the other his dad's.

"Good job some of us listen to mum," he said. "Come on."

Dominic surged forward and caught up with Emily and Lucy, and the three children boarded together after Mr Flynn.

They stepped into a circular chamber with featureless curved walls that arched into a smooth domed ceiling. The lighting was peachy but subdued, like the illuminated inside of a pumpkin. Jutting out from the wall all around were a dozen plain seats, formed of the same material as the walls themselves. They were identical, except for one, at centre-left of the door, which had an additional arm that extended from the wall, and had a series of circles arranged along it, like the sucker rings of an octopus's tentacle.

The floor was a shade darker in colour and textured with a pattern of finely interlaced and interlocking circles. It rose gently towards the centre, where it formed a low mound.

The three of them placed their rucksacks and cases on the spot marked by Mr Flynn's small tan-coloured suitcase and made for adjacent seats to the right of the control chair.

Mr Addison and Mr Tiddler came in next, followed by Lucy's mum, who made for the seats on the other side of what was clearly the control chair. Mr Flynn had taken the seat nearest the door. Finally, Mr Smiley came in and walked straight over to the control chair. As he sat, he waved a hand over the chair arm and the hatch raised and sealed itself seamlessly into the wall.

"Right, everyone OK?" asked Mr Smiley.

Nods and yeses came back from the guests.

"Good. Then prepare yourselves."

The room's lighting dimmed, throwing the assembled into near darkness.

"No seat-belts?" asked Mrs Westbridge a little nervously.

"You won't need them," said Mr Smiley. He waved a hand over the control arm again and the light changed, becoming a little brighter.

Gasps escaped Mr Tiddler and Mrs Westbridge, who were looking at the walls and floor and ceiling – or, rather, *through* them, as they had become as transparent as glass – all except a narrow ring that ran around the craft under their seats and the circle mound in the middle of the floor.

"What on earth –" began Mr Tiddler.

They could see all around them, the field and camouflage nets, trees, the school's roof and those of houses at the back of the school field. Above, greyish puffs of clouds, glowing at their edges by the back light of a ripening gibbous Moon.

Then there was a slight jolt, similar to that felt when an elevator begins to move, and then they all were looking around and below as the school and their home town of Hawlington fell away rapidly beneath them. Soon, both were swallowed by an inky haze that spread out over southern England as they climbed higher and higher, which was broken only by the golden spiders' webs of towns and cities and the silvery reflection of the Moon's light from the cloud tops and the sea.

As Leon had said, the ride was smooth; unusually smooth. And quiet. The scene outside changed without any sense of motion or noise – no G-forces or sound from engines or the rush of air around the craft; only a low-level hum in the air and the sound of their own breathing.

Then the scene tilted smoothly, and the curvature of the Earth became noticeable. Any trepidation that anyone may have felt at lift-off gave way to buzzing excitement.

"Whoa!" said Dominic, who shifted from side to side, looking up and around and down. They were already much higher and travelling faster than on the children's last trip, when they had remained in the Earth's atmosphere.

"Look! Over there!" exclaimed Mrs Westbridge. She was pointing over the children's heads, where a faint greenish glow hugged the curved contour of the horizon.

"Aurora!" said Mr Tiddler. "How high are we now?" he asked.

"Just passing forty miles; velocity six thousand miles per hour," said Mr Smiley.

Mr Addison looked at Mrs Westbridge and Mr Tiddler. He puffed out his cheeks.

Mr Tiddler shifted in his seat. "*Wow*," he said quietly.

Emily rolled her eyes at her dad.

"How long until orbit?" asked Mr Tiddler.

"A minute or so," replied Mr Smiley without looking around. "Normally we'd go straight out to the Moon. But," he said, looking around and seeming to relax a little, "I thought you'd all enjoy a lap around your home world before we do?"

"Yeah, well, that'd be... epic," said Mr Addison.

Dominic winced at his dad's use of one of his own favourite words. When grown-ups said stuff that they were, well, *too* grown up for, it just came out as embarrassing.

Mr Smiley waved his hand over the control arm. The view tilted again so that the Earth's horizon was brought to eye-level before them, and the Moon shifted to their right.

Below, the charcoal mass of the night-side Earth was just discernable in the ghostly light of the Moon.

"OK," said Mr Smiley. "We're in a parking orbit, 208 nautical miles altitude; 17,600 miles per hour."

Mr Tiddler took a deep breath, shaking his head gently in wonder and admiration. "What a ride," he said.

"The best is yet to come," said Mr Smiley, getting to his feet. "OK, you have eighty minutes to enjoy the view – well, you will in a while when we emerge from the Earth's shadow. Meanwhile, drinks and snacks are served on the middle dais."

He gestured towards the centre of the craft, where a low button-like table now sat. Beneath the dome of its roof sat a tray that held drinks and cakes and other sweet snacks. The children were out of their seats and over to it in an instant. The grown-ups responded less hastily, and it was Mrs Westbridge this time who said, "Er, shouldn't we be floating or something?"

"Artificial gravity," said Mr Tiddler. He looked at Mr Smiley for confirmation.

As if reading his mind, Mr Smiley said, "We still don't know how it works."

"Oh," said Mr Tiddler.

Mr Smiley moved over to talk to Mr Flynn, while the

adults gathered together near the central dais.

Emily, Lucy and Dominic had picked out a drink and a snack and returned to their seats, where they sat and ate and chatted.

On the globe below, the black shapes of land masses were defined against the silver-grey of moonlit oceans. Occasional flashes of lightning lit up cloud stacks like light bulbs. Now and then, one of the children pointed out a feature on the ground they thought they recognised.

Mrs Westbridge watched them briefly, then she said, "Kids seem to take everything in their stride, don't they?"

Mr Addison looked at Dominic, who was already munching his way through a second cake. "They sure do," he said.

"We're not doing so bad ourselves, actually," said Mr Tiddler. "Look at us. Three grown-ups looking out at the same view as the astronauts on the International Space Station, when only fifteen minutes ago we were standing in our children's school field."

"I know," said Mr Addison. "I'll wake up any moment and find that I've been dozing in my armchair – and that's despite the fact that I've been on a short trip before."

"And yet, we've hardly started, have we?" said Lucy's mum. She looked over her shoulder at the bright three-quarter Moon, which still seemed as far away from up here. "I mean, there's really a *long* way to go still, isn't there?"

"No turning back now," said Mr Tiddler.

4

Before very long, the Earth's horizon began to brighten noticeably; at first, as a thin bluish-white line with underlying streaks of yellow and red. Both the children and the adult passengers became drawn to the sight.

"Here we go," said Mr Smiley. "Daybreak."

As if on cue, a yellow disc suddenly broke through the white line on a cushion of red haze, before as quickly exploding into an incandescent yellow-white orb. The Sun flared above the horizon and the blue band of light expanded with it and swept towards them, pushing back the dark veil from the face of the planet below.

Soon they were streaking silently over a sparkling glass orb; over azure oceans and landscapes of ochre fringed with the green of forests and the white frostings of mountain ranges; all draped in the milky puffs and strands and great white swirls of grand weather systems.

Over where the children sat, Emily looked from her dad (who was now talking again with Mr Smiley) to the others and said: "Can't believe my dad. I bet he's asking Mr Smiley all about the ship instead of just looking out the window."

Dominic looked up from the floor, where his gaze had pretty much been glued since they sat back down, to Lucy to Emily and replied, "You haven't looked out much yourself, though, Ems."

Emily shrugged a bit defensively. "Yes, well, I saw it once on IMAX. Besides, it's really high up, isn't it?"

"Yes," agreed Lucy. "I'm trying not to think about it."

"It'll be even higher up at the Moon," said Dominic.

Lucy shot him a disapproving glare, and tried to change the subject. "Well, my mum and Dom's dad seem to be OK, don't they?"

The pair stood at the forward side of the craft, looking out ahead. The Moon had slipped out of sight behind them and the Sun had climbed high, so that they were now bathed in its whitish glare down their right sides, and, on their other by the softer blue glow of the Earth itself.

The sphere of the Earth took up half of their view, a dazzling great topaz marble that rotated slowly beneath them. Dominic stepped down from his chair and stretched out face down on a section of the floor, his hands pressed against it as if peering through the window of a train.

"I've never seen him so quiet," observed Lucy.

"That's one good thing about this trip, then," said Emily. She looked at her friend and they both chuckled.

For Dominic, it was as if he were flying in space, soaring above the planet by himself, like Superman – or like the very first cosmonauts and astronauts.

He lay there for a while, oblivious to anything else – until his attention was grabbed by a bright flash far behind them, on the Earth's trailing limb; a bright streak of light that plunged through the upper atmosphere. In just seconds it was gone; its searingly bright point fizzled out like a firework, leaving only a green after impression on his retinas.

"*Whoa! Did –*"

Dominic turned around. He had been about to say 'Did anyone else see that?', but it was evident no-one had. He'd tell them later.

5

Eventually, the bright scene of the Earth ahead began to fade to purple and violet as shadows lengthened against high cloud systems and mountains below and a dark tide extended beneath them as they re-entered the Earth's shadow.

Mr Smiley called out to gain everyone's attention. "OK, folks. Time to return to your seats, please."

He walked over to his own seat, waving a hand in the process. The mushroom-shaped table in the centre of the craft sank into the floor.

With another swipe as he took his seat, a graphical display appeared over the view of the Earth on the forward section of wall. On it, their position was marked by a pale green dot. A column of figures displayed their orbit height and speed. The dot remained stationary in the centre of the screen as the graphical Earth rotated, bringing another, orange-coloured point in their orbital path into view. They all understood that when the two dots lined up, they would be heading for the Moon.

As soon as everyone was seated, Mr Smiley tapped his chair arm and said, "OK, Tsiolkovsky, this is Pod Nine. Preparing for TLI."

"*What's TLI?*" Lucy whispered to Dominic.

"I think it means we're about to go to the Moon," said Dominic.

"We know *that*," said Emily. "What's does *TLO* mean?"

"TL*I*," corrected Dominic. Before he could answer – if indeed he knew the answer, Emily's dad answered it with his own question to Mr Smiley. *"Trans Lunar Injection*? Same as for the Apollo missions?"

"Huh-huh. If it ain't broke, don't fix it," replied Mr Smiley.

"Affirmative, Nine," came a female voice. It was the first time they had heard a different voice. More than anything until that moment, that voice, in its American accent, brought home to each of them what they were about to do.

"Oh-oh," said Mrs Westbridge, taking a deep breath. "Here we go."

"Can't wait," said Mr Addison, who gave his son a wink across the room.

"Take N-123-Alpha," said the voice.

"Affirmative. N-123-Alpha," replied Mr Smiley. "See you soon."

"Look forward to it," said the voice, now less formal. "See you on arrival."

"Will do. Out," said Mr Smiley. "Now, folks," he continued. He interrupted himself. "You OK over there, Mr Flynn?"

"Yes, lad," replied Mr Flynn, who had kept quietly to himself since boarding, not even joining the others when they snacked. "Jus' looking forward to a cup of tea when we get there."

Mr Smiley smiled. "You'll have it soon enough."

"Right everyone," continued Mr Smiley. "Five minutes until TLI. You'll feel a small nudge of acceleration – even Martian technology can't quite cancel the effects of rapid acceleration, so please remain seated. We'll turn around for you to get the best view."

Everyone sat quietly in expectation as the two

coloured dots came closer together. Several of them looked over their shoulders to see the Moon coming into view again. The graphical display picked it up and a line plotted itself between their position directly to it.

"OK," said Mr Smiley. "Ten seconds."

Unconsciously, the parents aboard all tightened their grip on their chair arms. Mr Addison and Mrs Westbridge tucked their feet under their seats, but even Mr Tiddler found himself holding his breath for the anticipated burst of acceleration. The children, by contrast, sat expectantly, but without tension – although Emily's brow was furrowed in trepidation.

"Nine, you are GO for TLI," came the female voice again.

"Roger, Tsiolkovsky," anwered Mr Smiley. "Thank you. We are GO."

The coloured dots on the forward screen merged. Immediately, there was a small lurch which pushed them forward in their seats. The numbers on the screen began to change, and dramatically.

It was like being shot out of a cannon, but without the sensation of rapid acceleration. They were already speeding through twelve miles per second

Mr Tiddler simply stared at the display, shaking his head in wonder.

Twenty... thirty-two... fifty-four... sixty-six miles per *second.*

"I don't believe what I'm sccing," he said.

"*Whoo-hooo!* This is *ep...* uh, *amazing!*" exclaimed Mr Addison.

Mrs Westbridge said nothing, but she didn't need to. Her expression said everything. She looked like someone starting the steep downward run of a rollercoaster – only this ride had none of the noise and wind and vibration.

"Whoa!!" said Dominic. "This is the *BEST... THING... EVER!*"

Beside him, Lucy and Emily looked at one another with raised eyebrows. They linked arms.

Over beside the door, Mr Flynn was calmly reading his newspaper.

The Earth was shrinking noticeably beneath them (or was it above, or sideways? It really didn't matter in space). Already it fitted comfortably within their view.

Beneath the miles-per-second display on the wall, the same speed was shown in miles per hour: *over two hundred and thirty-seven thousand miles per hour!*

"We'll peak at seventy-seven miles per second for twenty minutes before throttling back for our approach," said Mr Smiley.

"Top speed?" asked Mr Tiddler.

"No," replied Mr Smiley. "The Moon's too close for that."

"240,000 miles is too *close*?"

"Sure. You wouldn't drive at 100 miles an hour to the end of your street. You wait 'til you're out on the freeway for that."

"That's too fast even for the motorway," said Mr Tiddler.

"You get my point," said Mr Smiley. "There are no speed limits in space. There's only too fast and too slow."

He changed the subject. "Right," he said, clapping his hands together. "I heard someone say earlier that they thought we should be floating. Who'd like to float around for a while on the way to the Moon?"

Hands shot up amongst the children. "Me!" "Me!" "Me!"

"Me too," added Mrs Westbridge. Mr Addison tentatively raised his hand. Finally, Mr Tiddler agreed that it might be fun.

"The seat-ring around the outside will remain in normal gravity. Think of it as the pool-side. So, if everyone's ready, here goes," said Mr Smiley.

He waved a hand over his chair arm. Nothing seemed to be any different until Dominic stepped forward and pushed off towards the centre of the pod. His body, then his legs, lifted clear of the floor and he gently floated forwards. His eyes flared wide and his mouth popped open before curling into the biggest smile imaginable. *"Whoooaaa! Epic!"* he said.

Soon the girls and the adults (except Mr Smiley and Mr Flynn, who stayed sensibly on the outer ring) were excitedly flying and cavorting and tumbling and somersaulting in Zero-G.

Outside, the Moon was already the size of a melon, and growing steadily.

3 - TSIOLKOVSKY

The only downside to Tsiolkovsky base, thought Mr Knutt, was that you could never see the Earth from there.

But that was the very point of its existence. The Americans had established it as a tentative scientific outpost in the early 1970s after NASA's Apollo programme had officially closed. But some of the funding continued and was joined by military black budget funds to become what it now was: a fully functional and resourced secret outpost covering fourteen acres of lunar landscape and extending up to a hundred feet below.

When the Martian contact programme grew alongside it in the 1980s, a degree of sharing of information and technology permitted the base to become more or less self-sustaining and the perfect place to host Martian guests under its reduced gravity conditions.

This is where the Office of Planetary Protection was developed and where, now, Howard Knutt, headmaster of Flintworne Junior School in England, was on temporary attachment with the OPP as an education liaison officer to help continue the contact programme between the children of Earth and of Mars.

He stood now, with Leon Sparks, his first Martian pupil, on the observation deck atop the landing complex in the northern arm of the base. A large rectangular and inward-curving window, five storeys up, looked out over the expanse of the flat mare of the basalt-flooded crater. Behind the base, mostly out of sight from here, towered the rugged central peak of the impact basin that reared 10,500 feet above the crater floor, against which the base was constructed.

Through the window, the desolate plain of the basin was touched by bright low-angle sunlight from the west, which laid out long, pitch black shadows behind small craters and other irregularities in its surface. Mr Knutt knew that in the sunlight areas, the surface temperature could be up to 120 degrees centrigrade (twice as hot as Death Valley on Earth), and as low as minus 150 degrees in the shadow areas (almost twice as cold as an Antarctic winter).

Mounted on the wall to the right of the window was a brass commemorative plaque to Konstantin Tsiolkovsky (1857–1935), the father of modern rocketry, without whose research and speculation the Moon base now named after him probably would not exist. Below an engraving of his likeness was inscribed one of his most famous quotations:

Earth is the cradle of humanity, but one cannot live in a cradle forever.

In his time as a science teacher before becoming a head teacher, Mr Knutt had taught this line to a succession of keen-eyed and not-so-keen students. But never had it more meaning for him personally than now. After several weeks on the Moon, the novelty had yet to wear off.

At home, he usually wore a casual jacket and tie. Now he was attired in a regulation one-piece flight suit, courtesy (and at the insistence) of the OPP. It was a design configured to be compatible with a full spacesuit and a little uncomfortable for that, but one he didn't mind at all. In his youth, he had rather dreamt of becoming an astronaut, like the Apollo pioneers who first landed on the Moon. Now, he could regard himself as one – that is, if all you had to do to qualify was to go into space. The title itself was rather grandiose from its outset: Astro-naut. *Star voyager*. It sounded more Buzz Lightyear than fitting for a traveller over the backyard distance to the Moon, particularly one who had earned it effortlessy rather than through skill, long training and no small amount of risk – but he'd take it all the same.

Mr Knutt glanced at his watch, and turned to Leon. "They should be here any time soon."

Leon stared out of the window, looking into the blackness of sky in the east. His reflection stared back at him, but through it there was a pinprick of light. It wasn't a star. It was moving. "I believe this is them now, Mr Knutt."

Mr Knutt stared in the direction Leon was looking. "Oh, yes. Good," he said.

A tiny dot was drawing closer from the right frame of the window. It began to dip lower in a series of steps, becoming brighter as it slowed down. Soon it resolved into a small bauble with a ring of pin-point lights around its base that emitted a soft greenish glow.

Below, outside the window, a circular aperture was opening in the flat roof of the extended building beneath them. Lights twinkled from within. The craft, now properly recognisable as the pod, was moving towards it.

2

"OK, one minute to landing," said Mr Smiley.

Everyone was now back in their seats. No-one said anything. Instead, heads were turned and necks were craned this way and that to take in the varied views all around.

Forward below them was the ever-growing peak at the centre of the crater. Nestled into its side was an array of mounds and slab-lab structures, linked by tubular corridors, and adorned wth dishes and aerials. The pin lights of windows shone from all over the complex structure. Tsiolkovsky base.

They had dropped below the high crater rim, which enclosed the low mare of the 110-mile diameter crater. The crater walls had dropped out of sight, but numerous small craters and the undulations of the landscape were picked out in high contrast by the fiercely bright sunlight. Soon, the central peaks of the crater were stretching skyward above them, smoother than expected and pock-marked with small craters, like huge partially melted mounds of ice-cream.

Mr Addison broke the silence. "I can't believe we're about to land on the Moon."

Then the mountains vanished as the pod descended towards a circular hatch in the roof of the hangar.

3

Up on the observation deck, Mr Knutt and Leon watched as the pod dropped through the hatch in the roof below them.

"Well, Leon," suggested Mr Knutt, "Shall we go down and greet our friends?"

"Yes, Mr Knutt," replied Leon with a small smile.

4

Mr Knutt and Leon stood patiently outside the hangar doors. Standing with them were a number of technicians, both human and Martian, waiting to service the pod.

Presently, the hangar reached adequate pressurisation and the doors slid open with a hiss. The technicians stepped forward immediately, either making their way towards the newly arrived pod or dispersing to wherever they were going. Mr Knutt and Leon followed them through.

The hangar was large, perhaps the length of two football pitches laid end to end, and half as wide again. The walls, which were outward sloping, were corrugated and light grey in colour, and the roof sat high above them – except at the end to the right, where the floor sloped up to meet a set of regular-looking hangar doors.

The pod sat at the back, where it rested on a painted circle on the floor. By now, Mr Knutt was used to the sight of the other vehicles that were also parked in the hangar. At this time, there were two other egg-shaped pods and a larger Martian pod of similar design to Leon's parents' spaceship. And then there were two craft that looked more like conventional Earth design, but far more advanced-looking, and evidently part of a secret American space programme.

They walked forward across the hangar towards the pod, which rested on three short legs. Mr Knutt was amused to see that the feet had signs of some soil and grass clinging to them – a little bit of Flintworne itself that had made it to the Moon too.

Soon, the pod's hatch hissed open and lowered to the floor, and they could see inside. The first to step out of the peachy light was Mr Smiley.

Mr Smiley saw Mr Knutt and stepped over. The two men shook hands.

"Howard," said Mr Smiley. "Good to see you. You settling in OK?"

"Yes, thank you... Jim," replied Mr Knutt. "It's going very well."

Another man appeared behind Mr Smiley.

"Ah, Mr Flynn," said Mr Knutt.

"H'edmaster," greeted the older man.

"I'm not the headmaster here, Mr Flynn. You can call me Howard."

"As you wish... er, Mr Knutt," said Mr Flynn.

"Hello, Mr Flynn," said Leon.

Mr Flynn looked past the two men to see the slight figure of Leon standing there.

"Young Leon," he said. His face lit up in surprise. "How're you? When did ya get back?"

"A few days ago," replied Leon.

"He is going to assist us with the summer school," added Mr Knutt.

"*Summer school?*" said a voice from nearby, a boy's

45

voice.

The group turned to see Dominic, then Lucy and Emily.

Then Dominic noticed who had spoken. He looked up to see the headmaster standing there. "*Hey, it's Mr Knutt!*" he said excitedly to his friends.

The girls looked equally surprised, not least to find Mr Knutt in a one-piece flight suit of sorts rather than his familiar jacket and tie. He peered down at them through his familiar thick-framed glasses. His balding head reflected the bluish light cast by spot-lights mounted high on the hangar's ceiling. He smiled easily, genuinely pleased to see this handful of pupils from his school. Leon's friends.

"That's a very snazzy outfit, Mr Knutt," observed Emily.

"Why, *thank you*, Emily."

"What are *you* doing here, Mr Knutt?" asked Lucy.

"I could ask the same of *you*, Lucy," replied Mr Knutt. He beamed at them. "Actually, I'm here for several months at the invitation of Mr Smiley and the Office of Planetary Protection, to help carry on the schools contact programme. In fact," he said, "it was Leon who first suggested we might use the base here."

Then they noticed Leon standing behind him.

"Leon!" they all exclaimed. They rushed at him, the girls giving him a big hug, while Dominic hovered awkwardly and simply clapped Leon on the back.

"We weren't sure we'd ever see you again," said Lucy.

"It is good to see you all again," said Leon. "I hope you liked the trip?"

"It was amazing," said Lucy.

"And a little scary too," added Emily.

"It was just... just..." said Dominic, who, for once, was lost for words.

"*Epic*?" offered Leon.

Lucy and Emily laughed.

"Well, yeah. But it really was!" said Dominic, and he too chuckled.

"I think you're going to need a new fave word, Dom," said Lucy.

They were joined by their parents. Mr Knutt stepped forward to introduce himself, but of course, they all recognised the headmaster, although it took them a second or two to convince themselves that he was really here too.

Mr Knutt held a hand up. "All will be explained at a briefing in an hour," he said. "Meanwhile, we'll show you to your quarters and you'll have an opportunity for some refreshment before we outline the week's activities. So, if you would follow me –"

"Ah, our luggage is still onboard, Mr Knutt," said Lucy's mum.

"It's quite alright, Mrs Westbridge. It will be transferred to your rooms separately."

As they spoke, they noticed a base attendant loading their cases and bags into a hatch in the wall. As soon as one was set down on a metal tray, it zipped off out of sight, to be replaced by another.

Behind them, two individuals approached from the airlock door. They walked straight up to Mr Flynn.

"Mr Flynn. Glad you could come," said the shorter one. "We'd like you to look at the asparagus crop over in Wing Four, to begin with."

Hold tight, lad," replied Mr Flynn. "I'm not going

anywhere until I've had a cuppa, and a biscuit. 'Ope you boys 'ave got the kettle on."

"We've told you before, Mr Flynn, we don't have a kettle. But we can stop off at the refectory as usual."

"If you mean the cafeteria, lead on, lad," said Mr Flynn. He winked at Mr Knutt.

Mr Knutt smiled. Mr Flynn was more of a natural spaceman than anyone he'd met. "We'll see you later, Mr Flynn."

The party followed Mr Knutt and Mr Smiley through the airlock hatch, which closed after them.

Mr Smiley stopped on the other side. "I've got to get off to catch up with my superiors," he said. "I'll leave you all in the capable hands of Mr Knutt and Leon, and we'll all meet again a bit later."

They bade farewell to Mr Smiley and Mr Knutt led them down a corridor to an elevator, which took them up four levels to base ground level.

"Mr Knutt?"

"Yes, Lucy?"

"If you're going to be here for a while, who will the headteacher be back at school?"

"Ah, yes. That will be Mr Jones."

"Oh, not *Jones*," groaned Dominic.

"Now then, Dom," said Mr Addison. "It's *Mr* Jones, remember. And he did turn out to be a good guy after all."

"And well deserving of his *acting* headteachership this coming year," said Mr Knutt.

5

The elevator doors opened onto a domed space,

perhaps twenty metres across. Doorways and airlocks led off in various directions. Mr Knutt led the directly through it and out into a long rectangular space that resembled an airport gangway. Indeed, it had a travelator walkway just like an airport's. Mr Knutt led them onto it and they kept walking until they reached the very end, where he stopped and turned to address them.

"The formality of a passport check," he said. "Just to show that you are indeed who you say you are."

While they waited in line (there were perhaps a dozen other people ahead of them; all of them looked like technicians or scientists or engineers or officials rather than visitors or tourists like themselves), Mr Knutt outlined the layout of the complex.

There were three main, buildings that stretched out like long low slabs from a central hub, a large dome, which itself was nestled close in to the foot of the central peak of Tsiolkovsky. The building they had just left was the main landing hangar for passenger and freight traffic, which was linked to the outer end of the North Lobe (the main one for the base) by the narrow travelator corridor they had just passed along. The North Lobe maintained normal Earth gravity and conditions (courtesy, in part, of Martian technology).

The other Lobes (as they were called) – the West and South Lobes, had normal lunar gravity (just one sixth of the Earth's) – with the exception that part of the South Lobe, where Martian technicians and visitors were quartered, replicated the gravity, atmosphere and temperature of Mars itself.

Each of the Lobes additionally had spur buildings that projected from them that were populated by laboratories, workshops, offices, sports and recreation areas and accommodations. The West Lobe additionally had a one-sixth G swimming pool.

The North Lobe (sometimes called *Earthlingborough* by the residents, or *Earthborough*, or simply *The Borough*), with its Earth-like gravity, served also as an adjustment zone for personnel re-acclimatising to Earth conditions before returning home; or to re-strengthen weakened bones and muscles after long exposure to lunar gravity.

The central dome held the base command headquarters, plus a plaza (City Square, although it was round) with restaurants and cafés nestled amongst trees and fountains, with some of the best food imaginable on offer, most specially imported from Earth, but some grown here on the Moon. No more astronaut packs of reconstituted powders and pastes.

"Although you can still try some of those, if you wish," said Mr Knutt. "Or you might like the famous Moon beans."

"Huh? Moon beams?" asked Emily.

"Not quite," smiled Mr Knutt. "Beans grown in lunar soil. One of the first foods grown here. They have a rather dry, earthy flavour – or so I'm told."

"So, not a *moony* flavour, then?" teased Lucy.

"No. Oh, I see what you mean," replied Mr Knutt. "Very good."

6

Soon they were cleared through the passport control and Mr Knutt led them down a wide corridor that every so often led off into doorways or other corridors or spaces on either side.

The children walked together, using the time to ask Leon what they were going to be doing during their visit.

"I thought I heard someone say something about summer school?" asked Dominic.

"It is only summer for you," said Leon. "I would term it a space school," said Leon.

"Summer, space, what's the difference? It still has 'school' tacked on the end of it," replied Dominic.

"I'm sure it won't be like summer school at home; like gemming up on lessons and that," said Lucy. "Right, Leon?"

"Yes, Lucy. It will be educational, but also fun. You will have the chance to meet other children, from Mars and from Earth."

"Oh," said all three. It hadn't occurred to any of them that Leon might not be on the only Martian child here.

"So, there will be some classes and demonstrations together, for us all to learn about and get to know one another better. Then there are sports – you heard Mr Knutt talk about the one-sixth G swimming pool. It is where we learned to swim – me and the other Martian children. We had no need of this skill at home. And excursions and –"

"Excursions?" interrupted Emily. "Wherever can we go?"

"You will see. But your dad might find one of them very interesting, Dominic."

Dominic was musing where football might come into it – his dad's primary passtime interest – when Mr Knutt stopped them at the wide entrance to a corridor on their left. Here the structure widened into a dome made up alternately of metal struts and reinforced glass. Through the strips of window, an expanse of the Moon's ashen surface was visible, the interior of a shallow impact crater, perhaps sixty metres in diameter. Arcing around its farthest side, cut into its rim, ran a corridor which joined to a structure, also built into the wall of the crater's rim. Its lighted rooms cast out torch-like beams across the depression towards them, throwing its bumps and powdery texture into fine relief.

At the entrance to the corridor, where airlock doors were presently withdrawn, there was a sign that read 'NL Level 1: Dorm 3'.

Mr Knutt clapped his hands together. "OK folks. This will be your home for the duration of your stay. 'Dorm', of course, is short for 'Dormitory', which for me at least," he said with a smile, "conjures up images of dismal boarding schools, or perhaps military barracks. But I'm sure you will not be disappointed.

"'NL' of course, stands for North Lobe. You'll notice all the sign colours here are blue. In the West Lobe, they are green, and the South Lobe's are red.

"But before we head down and check you in, we'll briefly discuss a handful of 'need to knows'. So please gather around me."

Mr Knutt moved over to wall by the Dorm sign. Below it was a screen which, when Mr Knutt touched it, lit up with a location map of the base. A green dot indicated their current position.

"Number one: 'I'm lost'. If you happen to find yourself separated from one another, you can find your present location on the touch-screen map. There are stations such as this at various points in the base, usually where two or more corridors meet. You can either find out where you need to go by following the map, or by typing or speaking a destination. The computer will direct you to where you need to go. If you need actual assistance from someone, type or call 'Assist alpha' and follow the instructions.

"Two: The base time zone. Tsiolkovsky keeps Coordinated Universal Time or UTC. You may know it better as GMT, Greenwich Mean Time. Lucky you – it means you won't have to make any time adjustment.

"So," said Mr Knutt, looking at his watch, "the time is now 8.55 p.m., as it is at home. If you wish to make a call home, there is a phone in your room. I'm afraid your own mobile phones won't work out here – and if they did, the cost of calls would be considerably more expensive than standard international rates!"

"Next, but definitely not least, number three: Personal Safety. In the very unlikely event of a major emergency, the computer –"

"Major? Such as?" asked Mrs Westfield, concern registering in her voice.

Mr Knutt explained honestly. "Such as a breach in the structure, or a venting of the atmosphere. But in that unlikely event, the computer will attempt to isolate the breach by closing the emergency airlocks nearest to the disturbance."

He indicated the one behind him.

"It will then direct you to the nearest reinforced shelter, where you will await rescue. In most cases, this will be a safe room built into the corridor section where you find yourself.

"In the event, however, of a rapid depressurisation,

your suit – yes, Emily, I'm afraid you will all find your own snazzy suit just like this one in your room, which you must wear for the duration of your stay. In that case – your suit – blue, like this one (the suits are colour-coded to match the resident lobe), will inflate at the fall in pressure, enough to keep your blood from boiling. Here, at the wrists – see this thicker band? – gloves will unfold, which you must slip on as soon as possible, forming a seal around the wrist. Likewise, the collar will open to reveal a hood with a transparent face mask. You will have fifteen seconds to get these on and air-tight. The device on your suit-belt will provide oxygen-enriched air for twenty minutes. Everyone clear?"

There were nods from everyone.

"Replacement packs are available around the base, but be warned that those in the South Lobe are loaded with carbon dioxide, for our Martian guests.

"Lastly, number four. There will be a formal introductory breakfast briefing for all new arrivals tomorrow at 9 a.m. in the Pad 39 restaurant on City Square. Just continue down the main corridor here and follow the signs. Please make sure you are there promptly – not least to get your breakfast preferences ordered in good time.

"OK, that's it, I think. We'll leave anything else until tomorrow – unless anyone has any questions now?"

There were murmured 'no's and shakes of the head and 'no, thank you's'.

"In that case," said Mr Knutt, "I will wish you all good night. Leon here will take you on to your quarters, and I'll see you all in the morning."

Mr Knutt strode off down the main corridor.

Everyone's attention turned to Leon.

"Please, follow me," he said in a small voice.

Leon led them along the corridor to the dorm complex's reception area. This was a large bubble similar in design to the area they had just left, this time with a view back across the crater interior towards the main building. A sign on the wall gave it a more agreeable name: The Armstrong Suite.

By the thick bank of windows stood a low coffee table, an artificial pot plant and a semi-circle of empty chairs that looked out onto the Moon's surface.

And not much else. No people, no sounds of activity or music emanating from elsewhere, as you might expect at a hotel, even late at night; just the faint hum of electricity.

Emily leaned closer to Lucy. "Why are parties on the Moon never a success?" she asked.

Lucy shrugged.

"Because it has no atmosphere!" answered Emily.

Lucy rolled her eyes.

Leon led them to the wall behind, which held an array of shallow slots with name tags on them, including their own. In each of the slots was a thin wrist band, again with their names on them, and in the grown-ups' slots, an envelope too.

"You each have a wristband," said Leon, "which acts as your room key, and as a pass for various areas. Your rooms arc through there."

He pointed to a narrow corridor across the other side of the room.

Mrs Westfield stepped forward and collected her own and Lucy's wristbands. "Thank you, Leon."

Leon smiled back. Beside Mrs Westfield, Lucy tried

to stifle a yawn. It had been a busy and adventurous day.

The others collected their own bands. Finally it was time to part for the night.

"Where are you staying?" Dominic asked Leon.

"We are in South Lobe," replied Leon.

"You're with your parents?" asked Emily.

"Just my mother," said Leon. "My father had to stay behind on Mars."

"Oh, OK. So we may meet your mum tomorrow?" asked Lucy.

"Yes, I am sure of it," said Leon.

Mr Tiddler and Mr Addison also extended their thanks to Leon. Then Mr Addison said, "C'mon, Dom. Let's go and get sorted out. We'll see Leon in the morning."

Dominic shrugged and nodded. He too looked tired despite the huge excitement of the day. "See you tomorrow, Leon," he said. "It's brilliant seeing you again. I can't believe we're actually on the Moon!"

"Me neither," added Mr Addison.

"I think that goes for all of us," said Mr Tiddler. Mrs Westfield nodded too.

"Us too," said Lucy.

"I am pleased you could all come," replied Leon. "It will be an exciting time."

7

When they got to their rooms, they found that all three branched off from another small communal area with comfortable-looking armchairs, a hot drinks machine and a room-service selection panel, and a thick, angled glass window with the same view over the lunar surface as far as the North Lobe main building. As promised, their luggage had arrived, and sat ready for collection from a conveyor platform in the wall.

The rooms themselves resembled a modern hotel's on Earth. Apart from the views from the port-hole shaped windows, the framed photos of famous spacecraft and lunar scenes that adorned the walls, and the blue pressure suits lain out on the couch, it would be easy to imagine you were in one of those.

Even Mr Tiddler was impressed at the standard. "I was expecting something more Spartan, metal boxes and bunks," he said.

Soon they were all settled in, each of the children with their parent per room. They said goodnight to one another, then went in to change and brush their teeth, and finally climbed into their beds for their first night on the Moon.

In Dominic's and his dad's room, Dominic pushed himself up on his elbows in bed. "Where are you going?"

"Just going to call your mum and let her know we got here OK. Then I might sit out and chat to Lucy's and Emily's parents for a little while."

"Aw, can't I stay up a bit longer?" pleaded Dominic. "It is the holidays, and this is really special, isn't it?"

"No, yer mum will kill me if she found out."

"Dad, she's a quarter of a million miles away. How's she gonna find out?"

"Well, it's gonna be a busy day tomorrow, so try to get to sleep, OK?"

"I'll try," replied Dominic. He shuffled down beneath his quilt. "But it won't be easy."

"I know, but do your best, eh?"

When Mr Addison looked in a few minutes later, Dominic was fast asleep.

4 - PAD 39

When they woke up the next morning it would have been easy to believe that the whole thing about the Moon had been a dream, until the night shutters drew back from the windows to reveal the stark lunar surface beneath a black-as-pitch sky.

Everyone dressed in their new pressure suits as instructed and assembled outside their rooms. All looked the part of spaceman or spacewoman, except perhaps Dominic's dad, whose paunchy tummy bulged the suit out somewhat at the front.

"What do you think, Dom?" he asked.

"Looks like it's under a bit of pressure already, dad."

"Yeah," reflected Mr Addison, cradling his girth. "I shoulda tried to lose a few pounds before this trip. Probably shouldn't have had that beer and sandwich last night either."

"Where did you get those?!" asked Dominic incredulously, while at the same time impressed with his dad's ingenuity. "You'd already had your tea, like me."

"Well, I know," said Mr Addison guiltily.

"Oh, it's easy," said Emily. "Over here. I'll show you." She led him to the wall, where there was a panel and a screen. "You can order pretty much any food or

59

drink."

"Really?" said Dominic.

Emily nodded. "My dad showed me. Didn't you see the one in your room?"

"Nope!" said Dominic, shocked chagrined at how he could have missed it.

"You just order what you want from the menu and a few minutes later it's delivered to you, like through this panel."

Dominic's eyes lit up. "This could be my favourite part of the trip!"

"*Boys*," said Emily, raising her eyebrows and looking at Lucy.

"*Dominic,*" said Lucy.

"Oh, Dom," said Mr Addison. "Meant to tell you, I spoke to your mum last night. Just to let her know we got here safely and all that. She told me to remind you to brush your teeth, comb your hair, and make sure you change your underpants every day."

"Dad!" protested Dominic.

"Er, OK," interrupted Mrs Westfield. "Shall we go and find this breakfast briefing? Where's it at again?" she asked, fumbling for the grown ups' information sheet that had been in the envelope.

"Pad 39," replied Mr Tiddler. "I took a stroll down there last night. Five minutes' walk – the graduated gravity down to one-third G in the square makes it feel like downhill on the way there."

2

City Square was busier, and much bigger than expected. It comprised a huge dome, a hundred and twenty metres across by fifty metres high and covered on the outside (according to Mr Tiddler) with a layer of compacted lunar soil, or *regolith*, that helped to protect its inhabitants from extremes of heat and cold, micro-meteoroids and solar radiation.

People of all sorts wearing different coloured uniforms – and among them, unmistakably, a few Martian adults – moved purposefully and deliberately through it.

"This is strange," said Emily, who found herself leaning backwards slightly and sliding forward as she walked, almost as if she was indeed progressing downhill.

"You'll get used to it," said Mr Tiddler, who evidently had adjusted quickly, or he had spent some time practising in the reduced gravity the previous evening.

"The important thing is to try to not go too fast or to turn quickly. Even though you weigh only a third of your normal body weight here, your mass is the same, so you'll keep going if you're not careful. You remember when we've been ice-skating?"

"Yeah, I used to fall over a lot."

"Well, it's a bit like that at first. Start and stop slowly."

Lucy seemed to have gained the hang of it quite quickly.

Lucy's mum was less sure. "Oo-er," she said, as she shuffled forward, looking, well, rather like she needed the toilet. "I'll hang on to the weight loss, but I'm not sure this makes up for it."

Dominic's dad seemed no better adjusted. "I feel like I'm two years old all over again."

Dominic, however, was unfazed. "It's about the

61

same as on Mars," he said. "Leon once told me how I'd have to move if we were there."

Mr Tiddler spoke up. "OK, the restaurant is through there."

He indicated an inner circle of tub-planted trees and plants – palms and evergreens and vines and cacti – in the midst of which was a park-like area and a fountain. The view naturally drew everyone's attention upwards to the domed ceiling, which was in the act of changing from black with pinpoints of stars (which initially suggested it was made of glass) to a bright blue sky with fluffy clouds slowly drifting across it. A background, almost subliminal, sound of rippling leaves and birdsong, plus the mingled aromas of food from some of the eateries, added to the illusion of some idyllic location on Earth.

"Yes, I was surprised too," said Mr Tiddler. "The ceiling is made up of LCD tiles, so the whole thing works a bit like an IMAX screen. I thought it extravagant at first, but it's one way, I'm told, that helps make longer term life here more bearable."

"That's really neat," said Lucy.

"Yes, it is," stated a voice from behind them. It was Mr Knutt.

"It has thousands of scenarios, so one hardly ever sees the same one twice. It generally synchronises with UTC time on Earth, but it can be adjusted as desired. Last Christmas, I gather, they had it snowing, and there were fireworks displays on New Year's Eve and the fourth of July. When I arrived, they had it raining – said it might help me feel more at home, like a typical English summer's day.

"Anyway, how is everyone this morning?" he asked

with a wide smile.

"Great. Slept like a baby," replied Mr Addison.

"Didn't actually, dad. You snored like a buffalo," said Dominic.

Mrs Westfield snickered, while others nodded or said 'fine' or 'good, thanks.'

"Excellent," said Mr Knutt, clapping his hands together. "You're a tad early, but that's fine. Shall we head over?"

Mr Knutt started to walk, but soon became aware that the others weren't keeping up.

"Yes, I'm sorry. I should have mentioned the gravity here. As you've probably surmised, City Square maintains a compromise between the three Lobes to make interchange a little more comfortable."

They passed the closest banks of potted trees. The space beyond was like a small city park, enclosed with greenery. There were benches arranged around a modest fountain that looked like stone, but was probably 3D-printed from some other material, and banks of artificial grass. A few of the base's personnel, some in off-duty colours, sat and read or ate breakfast takeouts.

On the other side of the fountain, in the very centre, was a larger structure, a prism, stood on end and perhaps twelve feet tall, with clean polished faces of white marble. Mr Knutt led them over to it. Mr Tiddler, of course, had seen it himself the previous evening.

"What is it?" whispered Emily. It had a solemn presence that commanded silence and respect.

"This is the Hub Memorial," said Mr Knutt, "It is dedicated to all the astronauts and cosmonauts who lost their lives in spaceflight or training, and to whom an immeasurable debt is owed and without whose contributions Tsiolkovsky base might not have become a reality."

Mounted on the side facing them were mounted several gold plaques naming individuals and crews of various missions, and included Apollo I and Soyuz I, Soyuz II and the Space Shuttles *Challenger* and *Columbia*.

In a low voice, Mr Knutt informed them that the original Apollo I capsule, in which astronauts Grissom, White and Chaffee had perished in an on-the-pad accident in 1967, was actually encased within the memorial.

"They finally made it," Mr Tiddler said quietly. "That's good. As did – as I noticed last night," – he pointed at a smaller plaque, this one in silver, angled atop a small pillar beside the monument – "Jim Lovell, of Apollos 8 and 13 fame."

"Yes indeed," said Mr Knutt. "Commander of the ill-starred Apollo 13. He finally got to land in 2002 when he came here to dedicate the memorial on behalf of NASA."

They paused for a moment longer, then Mr Knutt took a deep breath. "Right, who's ready for breakfast?"

Hands shot up, including Mr Addison's.

3

They emerged on the far side of the City Square into an open space. Immediately before them, the wall of the dome curved up from floor level and over their heads. The simulated sky started some fifteen feet up the wall, level with the faux roof-tops of the restaurants on either side. The lower section held thick windows that looked out over the lunar terrain.

The restaurant, PAD 39 (the sign had an image of a Saturn rocket making up the vertical line of the P, and a plan view of the Space Shuttle in place of the A), was open-plan, with tables and planters of greenery spilling out from beneath its eaves. Several customers sat outside, sipping coffee or nibbling snacks whilst absorbed in perusing tablets or other electronic devices.

Inside the restaurant, at the back, by the windows, there was already an assembled gathering of other children and adults, some human, some Martian. When he saw his friends enter, Leon rose from his chair and came over to greet them.

As they found their seats, the children at one end of the long table, the adults at the other, they took in who else was here. There was Mr Smiley, who they hadn't seen since their ride in the pod. Beside him sat a young woman, blonde and wearing designer spectacles. Next to her was Mr Flynn, looking smart and not entirely comfortable in his burgundy-and-yellow striped engineer's pressure-suit. And then there were a half dozen other humans, three children and three adults, plus two Martians, one adult and one child, both female.

"Where's your mum?" asked Lucy.

"She is in the conference centre," said Leon. "Preparing a lesson. We will see her later."

"*Lesson?*" repeated Dominic flatly.

"Perhaps 'lecture' is a better word," said Leon.

"No, it isn't," replied Dominic.

They sat together, and Leon introduced the other

children, beginning with the Martian girl who sat across the table. It was the first time that any of them had met another Martian child.

"This is Aurore. Like you, she arrived yesterday," said Leon.

Aurore's eyelids flickered and she smiled timidly. She was small, even compared to Leon. Like him (and all Martians), she had a smooth head, large eyes (in her case, green-tinted) that sparkled with intelligence, a small thin-lipped mouth, a mere bump of a nose and tiny bud-like ears.

Leon said something to her in Martian, which sounded high-pitched and squawky. Aurore shook her head.

"Hello, Aurore," said Emily. "My name is Emily."

Lucy leaned forward and offered her hand. "And I'm Lucy. It's nice to meet you," she said.

Aurore looked at Lucy's hand, unsure what to make of the gesture, until the human girl beside her reached out and took Lucy's hand, showing her how it was done.

"Bonjour – ah, hello," she said. "My name is Camille."

Camille released her hand, permitting Aurore to copy the action, which she did with Lucy, and then Emily.

"She does not say very much," said Camille apologetically.

"That's OK," said Emily. "Did Aurore go to school with you in France?"

"Oh, no," replied Camille, who had shoulder-length black hair. "I stayed with her at her home on Mars."

All the while, Dominic had been sitting behind a

cutlery holder that was shaped like the Apollo Lunar Module (the cutlery stood within the widened neck of the docking port), studying the breakfast menu. On hearing 'Mars', his ears pricked up. *"Mars? Cool. What's it like?"*

"What do you mean 'what's it like'?" asked Lucy. "Leon's told you all about it," she said, rolling her eyes.

"Yeah, but I'm asking about where Aurore comes from," replied Dominic.

"It is not very different," said Leon. "Aurore lives two thousand kilometres from my home, near to the northern plains. It is a little flatter than my home."

"Is that your mum, Aurore?" asked Lucy. "Over there, with Mr Smiley and that other lady?"

Aurore looked towards the grown-ups' table. She shook her head. "My mother is deceased," she said awkwardly. "I have come with a guardian. She is with OPP."

"Oh," said Lucy. "I'm sorry."

Camille explained. "Aurore's mother died three years ago. Her father is always very busy, so he appointed a teacher and guardian. Her name is *Skiel'aeljtın* – pronounced *Ski-el-achin* – but we call her Miss Sky. She is the main representative for the programme on Mars."

"Ahem."

They were interrupted by Mr Knutt's voice. He stood at the end of the table, and held a sheet of paper before him.

"Good morning, everyone. I hope everyone slept well? Good, good," he continued without waiting for a reply. "Just a few words before we tuck into a hearty breakfast. Firstly, welcome to the Moon."

He looked at Aurore and the Martian lady, Miss Sky, who sat upright and regally beside Mr Smiley.

"*Earth's* moon, I should say. As you know, we are all guests of the Office of Planetary Protection on Earth, and we have Mr Smiley here, a senior liaison officer for that organisation, and his personal assistant and advisor, Miss Miller, to thank for that."

Mr Smiley nodded in acknowledgment.

"It was Mr Smiley who proposed this base to continue the Controlled Contact cultural exchange programme between the children of Mars and Earth. Needless to remind you, the programme and this facility remain Top Secret."

Mr Smiley nodded in agreement.

"OK. On the end table you'll find a welcome pack and itinerary for the week, which includes a map of the base, and an activities plan. This morning there will be a guided tour, *or* you are free to explore by yourself, if you wish – at least those areas where you are permitted to visit.

"After lunch, you will get a chance to meet the programme's other guests in the conference lounge at the top level of the West Lobe. And after that there will follow a presentation by Mrs Sparks.

"The OPP staff, me included, will be available to answer any questions at any time. Contact numbers are in your itinerary packs. But now, without further ado, please help yourselves up at the buffet bar."

Dominic was out of his chair like a shot – well, as fast as he could in reduced gravity. He hurried over to where the counter and tables were laid out like a hotel buffet breakfast. There were three main sections.

The first was 'Full English & American' where,

beneath a row of warming lights, were laid out stainless-steel trays filled with fried and cooked foods. There were sausages and bacon and scrambled eggs, mushrooms and hash browns, baked beans, fried bread, toast and tomatoes. At its far end, beneath a smaller sign marked 'Astronaut' sat trays of cooked steaks and fried eggs.

Dominic grabbed a serving tray and a plate and was already piling food onto it before the next person arrived – who happened to be his own dad.

Mr Tiddler, who joined the rear of the queue with Lucy's mum, behind Lucy herself, Emily, Leon, Camille and Aurore, wrinkled his brow in bemusement at Mr Addison's zeal.

Dominic moved along the counter, artfully trowelling heaps of food onto his plate. When it seemed he couldn't fit any more on, he moved onto the next section ('Continental') where he paused to look over the selection of cold foods, pastries and cereals.

Here, there were cheeses, cold meats and boiled eggs, plus racks of sliced bread and toast, and pots of butter and marmalade, and jam and honey and syrups for pouring over pancakes and waffles. At the end stood tall clear plastic optics that dispensed cereals with a twist of a handle, and a chilled cabinet with frosted bottles of milk and juices and pots of yoghurt. Finally there were machines serving hot filtered coffee and tea.

Dominic added a side plate of toast, butter and jam to his tray, plus a bottle of orange juice.

Then, before returning to his seat, he shuffled along to have a look at what the Martian section offered – and almost wished he hadn't.

Some of it, it had to be said, appeared perfectly edible. There were various kinds of fruits and vegetables. One type resembled deflated Kiwi fruits; another, dark green gherkins with thick, knobbly skins. A third tray contained flakes of what looked like dried, pressed mushrooms. Other dishes, though, looked distinctly unappealing. Thin flattened strips of what looked like grey pasta writhed slowly about in one tray, while snail-like creatures with long cream-coloured tubes protruding from them, bobbed in clear liquid in another.

Dominic's mouth contorted into an expression of disgust and headed back to his seat.

Presently, Lucy and Emily joined him, Lucy with some scrambled eggs and beans, and a croissant, some jam and a glass of apple juice; while Emily settled for a bowl of muesli and a pancake with syrup. Finally, Leon and Aurore and Camille sat back down. Leon had found some chocolate pudding from somewhere – his favourite.

Dominic was just clearing his plate and got to his feet again.

"Where are you off to?" asked Lucy.

"Going up again," said Dominic.

"But you've had loads," said Lucy.

"Got to keep my energy up," replied Dominic.

"But you will use less energy on the Moon," said Leon.

Dominic shrugged. "Well, I don't feel full," he said.

"Maybe because it's not so heavy on your tummy?" ventured Emily.

Leon nodded. "Yes. You may be sorry later," he said.

Dominic looked from Emily to Leon, then over at the

counter. "Maybe only a *bit* more, then," he said.

"What have you there, Aurore?" asked Lucy, trying to make conversation with the quiet Martian girl.

"They are known in English as..." began Camille.

Lucy winced. Camille had a tendency to answer for her friend.

"Désolée...*sorry*," said Camille. "Aurore?"

Aurore looked up from her dish, to Lucy, then to Camille, and back to Lucy.

"*Je'er an-ijır*, as we call them," she answered quietly.

Camille translated for her. "It means 'ground figs'," she said.

"Oh, Ordonian figs?" said Leon.

Aurore's bowl contained five plump pear-shaped fruits, about the same size as Earth figs, but with wrinkled, leathery brown skin like passion fruits.

Aurore picked up one of the fruits as they watched. She pinched its top, then, with the tips of both thumbs she pressed into it, breaking its skin. An oily brown liquid seeped from the wound. Then she pulled the fruit apart and dropped the two halves back into the bowl, before reaching for another.

The flesh of the fruit was garnet-coloured, with pulpy fibres and pale brown seeds. An aroma not unlike treacle or brown sugar began to permeate the air.

"Hm," said Emily approvingly.

"Would you like to try some?" asked Aurore.

"Er," hesitated Emily. "What does it taste like?" She looked at Leon.

"I do not know," replied Leon. "We do not have them where I come from."

"Oh, they are quite delicious," said Camille.

Aurore had opened the second fruit, so there were now four halves in the bowl. She offered the bowl firstly to Leon, who politely took a half; then to Emily. Emily hesitated for a moment, then said, "OK, I'll try one." Then Aurore offered the bowl also to Lucy and Camille.

Leon took a bite from his piece. His expression showed his approval.

"Leon?" asked Emily.

Leon looked thoughtful for a moment. Then he said simply, "I like it. It is mildly sweet, like bitter chocolate, or carob."

"Oh, OK," said Emily. She brought her own piece to her mouth. And almost immediately recoiled.

"Eugh!" She dropped the fruit onto the table top, and pushed back from the table.

The grown-up leaders looked over from their table. Mr Smiley looked directly at Leon with a quizzical expression on his face. Leon shook his head to indicate that everything was alright. Mr Smiley nodded and immediately went back to his conversation with Mr Knutt and Miss Miller.

"What's up?" asked Lucy. She looked at her own piece, and found herself echoing Emily's actions. Her own piece of fruit bounced on the table, spilling seeds.

"*Maggots!*"

On the table, the seeds were moving, advancing slowly with peristaltic motion away from the fruit, leaving glistening trails of juice behind them.

"No, no," said Camille. "I am sorry, I should have warned you. They *are* seeds. It is a reflex reaction when the fruit is broken open. They seek to find shelter and burrow into the soil to escape the cold and solar radiation."

"So, they plant themselves?" Lucy asked curiously.

"Yes," said Camille. "But these will have been grown in better conditions in underground farms. Aurore showed me one when I stayed with her."

Camille picked up one of the wriggling seeds. "You can eat them. They taste like vanilla."

She popped it into her mouth. "You wish to try now?"

Emily and Lucy both winced, shaking their heads.

"No, I'm good," said Lucy.

4

Through all this, Leon had been studying Mr Smiley across the room. He hadn't appeared his normal, composed self lately. When Leon had seen him, that is. Other than the 'taxi trip' to Earth to collect Leon's friends, as he had termed it, and which he said he'd volunteered for to 'get out of the house for a bit', he had seemed quite distant this past week.

Leon knew that his own father had an important meeting back home on Mars, and Mr Smiley and Miss Miller were to leave to join him there soon. All he knew was that the Controlled Contact programme was something to do with it – which probably explained Mr Smiley's manner.

5

At the grown-ups' table, Mr Knutt asked Mr Smiley when he intended to leave.

"End of the week," replied Mr Smiley. "Should really

be there with Fred now, but, well, I couldn't *not* be here either. Clash of interests."

'Fred' was Mr Sparks's Earth name, adopted on his first visit to Earth in the 1960s, after a popular animated television character. His wife, Leon's mother, was called Wilma.

"He'll be OK. He has our case, and is completely competent, of course," said Mr Smiley. "But I felt it might have been helpful if I were there to address the Council alongside him."

"I'm not quite so sure of that," said Miss Miller, whose first name was Caroline.

Mr Knutt looked from one to the other. He hadn't witnessed any disagreement between them before.

"At least not the full Council," continued Miss Miller. She turned to Mr Knutt. "An assembly of the full Council is virtually unprecedented," she explained. "It meets only in times of planetary crisis. The last time it came together was over a hundred years ago. I doubt humans would be welcome – especially when they are the subject of the gathering."

Mr Knutt scratched his chin. "Oh, really?" he said. "I had no idea. I thought the Contact programme was initiated by the Martians themselves?"

"It was," said Mr Smiley. "And it was – *is* – supported by the majority of the population. But..."

"But?" repeated Mr Knutt.

Mr Smiley sighed. "But... amongst any sizeable group there will always be opposing viewpoints and we can't pretend that the programme is uniformly favoured there."

Mr Smiley looked to Miss Sky, who had thus far sat quietly, occasionally raising a cup to her lips to sip

Earl Grey tea, a much-favoured beverage amongst Martians.

She nodded slowly, considering her words before speaking. Her speech, like many adult Martians, was slower, and less well articulated than either Aurore or Leon, who were accustomed to speaking Earth languages from a much earlier age.

"Ee-et ess true-ie," she said. "T'ere iss mohrch surpporr wirth eour peor-pol. Merny ak-ree th-et co'op-orashun wirth Oear-th ess t'onli wehri-to es-surr ter lorng-toorm sof-vi-vaal ot eour rrass."

It is true. There is much support with our people. Many agree that co-operation with Earth is the only way to assure the long-term survival of our race.

"But there are some," she confessed, "that urge caution; who feel that the process of contact is too rapid, too open; that our kind – although the more advanced, are small in number – and risk acceleration of the extinction of our race by further close contact."

"I see," said Mr Knutt. "And that opposition is sufficient to evoke this extraordinary meeting?" asked Mr Knutt.

"It's not solely about the OPP programme," said Miss Miller. "But essentially, yes, it is."

6

Soon it was evident that most had finished their breakfasts. Mr Smiley got up from his place and left without a word with Miss Miller and the Martian lady. Mr Knutt, now on his own, was getting to his feet and pushing his chair under the table.

At the children's table, plates and bowls had been

pushed back and all the escaping fig seeds had been rounded up. Those not eaten now wriggled feebly amongst the fruit skins of Aurore's bowl. The children, as children often do, chatted together as if they had known one another for rather longer than half-an-hour.

"Well, are you all ready to go?"

The children looked up. It was Mrs Westfield. Behind her stood Emily's dad and Mr Addison. Plus a small lady with dark hair that was slightly grey at the roots and pulled back into a bun. She looked at them through half-moon spectacles, and was evidently Camille's mother.

"Hello, mum," said Lucy. "We are," she said, "but Dominic's feeling a bit uncomfortable."

Dominic looked a little queasy.

"What's up, Dom?" asked Mr Addison.

"Had a bit too much, dad."

"He went up three times," said Emily.

"Yeah, well, you live and learn," replied Mr Addison, a little less sympathetically than even he intended. "You gonna be OK?"

Dominic nodded.

"Else you won't be up for sixth-G swimming later."

Dominic looked at his dad coldly, as if to say, 'Did you *have* to say that right now?'

"Well," said Lucy's mum, "I must say, I'm really impressed with everything so far. Who'd have thought that such a variety of food would be available up here?"

"Something to do with Martian technology, perhaps?" commented Mr Tiddler. He looked at Leon.

"Yes," said Leon quite matter-of-factly.

Mrs Westfield spoke to Leon. "Well, Leon, I see you had some chocolate pudding?"

"Yes," he said. "Mr Knutt." He smiled.

"Of course," said Mrs Westfield.

During his time at Flintworne Junior School, Leon had discovered a liking for chocolate pudding and custard. Mr Knutt had arranged for the school's pudding to be available at Space School.

"He's a great headmaster, isn't he? Thinks of everything."

7

As if on cue, a voice called out from behind them. "Ahem. Well, if we are all ready, we will start our tour," said Mr Knutt.

5 - COUNCIL OF CYDONIA

Mr Sparks stood alone at the head of the cracked processional pathway. A light but icy breeze ruffled his outer cloak and chilled his skin as, head lowered, he paid his silent respects to his destination.

Behind him, within the open entrance of a natural cave, was the transit station he had just emerged from; part of a network of underground tunnels that criss-crossed the planet. Far off to his right, on the eastern horizon, the small white disc of the Sun had just risen amidst a bluish cone of light that was beginning to bleach the muddy sky into a semblance of warmth. Long shadows threw every contour, every rock, every stone into stark relief, accentuating the roughness of the barren landscape, making it seem all the more severe and inhospitable.

High above the horizon to the south, in the still darkened sky, hung the bright points of Phobos and Deimos, Mars's two moons. Phobos, the larger and closer, orbiting at only 3,700 miles above the surface, circled the planet three times a day. Like Earth's moon, Phobos was in a synchronous orbit, so that it always presented the same face to the planet's surface. It formed now a ragged crescent below its tiny companion, Deimos.

The conditions on the surface were harsh, barely tolerable even for Martians for very long, but this was tradition, one that dated back aeons. He would be exposed to them only long enough to reach his destination.

The stepped mesa reared dramatically from the plain before him. Its lower half comprised a massive ovoidal slab of rock, two kilometres in length, whose steep flanks of shadowy brown rock topped out onto a wide terrace. Surmounting this, picked out in rosy terracotta by the sun's first rays, a broad mound rose steadily to take it to its full height of two hundred and forty metres.

The pathway led away towards it, vanishing several times as it followed the undulations of the land, until it arrived at its foot, where an ancient carved archway led into the huge, hollowed-out mount.

Mr Sparks raised his head and took a last studied look at the monument. It had been carved from natural rock by his ancestors tens of thousands of generations before, when Mars was an altogether different and more hospitable world. This and other complexes near here and across the planet's surface were the remnants of their race's once great civilisation, far back in the First Age, when their global society was governed in peace and prosperity by the Council of 360 under the wise guidance of the one whose huge likeness – now badly worn and broken – stared at the skies from the mountain's top.

Mr Sparks pulled a scarf up over his nose and wrapped his cloak around him and set out along the pathway.

2

The stone archway led into a tunnel of red stone that descended at a steady angle. It was faintly illuminated, but from no obvious source and it continued for several hundred metres before it levelled out and then continued on for several hundred more. Finally, it opened out and Mr Sparks found himself inside a huge circular chamber – or more aptly, an oblate spheroid, like the carved inside of a pumpkin.

He had joined it at its mid-level. Below him, it formed a deep basin, where ring after ring of stone-cut benches overlooked a central platform, so that the whole thing looked like a Roman amphitheatre. Midway up, on opposite sides, were two rounded pods, like church pulpits, that interrupted the lines of benches and, likewise, were carved straight out of the rock. The one on the far side was noticeably larger than the nearer one.

The lower benches of the theatre were occupied already by dozens of other councillors, each the representative of a given region of the planetary community, which collectively amounted to little over eighty thousand individuals.

The chamber was subtly divided into two halves. If one were to look closely, it would become evident that the carved benches also differed in design and decoration from one side to the other.

The delegates seated on the far side were dressed in cloaks of inky blue that were overlain with designs in gold and silver. Each pattern design was unique, with symbols of evident meaning and standing to each of their wearers.

By contrast, the individuals on the near-side (and this included Mr Sparks himself) were adorned in gold and silver fabrics, overlain with blue designs.

Mr Sparks's own cloak showed an intricate pattern of shapes and symbols arranged around a circular design that comprised an inner and an outer ring. The outer ring linked two symbols, one a crescent, the other a four-pointed star, so that it resembled the arrangement of the amphitheatre below – with one difference. On the fabric design, there was an additional small star inside the outer ring. As if drawn magnetically, Mr Sparks lifted his gaze to the high dome above him. At its height, the apex lay beyond the illumination of the lower parts of the chamber (as was perhaps intended), so that the design there was visible only by its reflected light, and it was identical to that on Mr Sparks's cloak, complete with the extra star.

He had never before visited this chamber. It was opened only on rare occasions when face-to-face congregation was deemed necessary, and when all three hundred and sixty councillors were obliged to attend to discuss critical planetary matters.

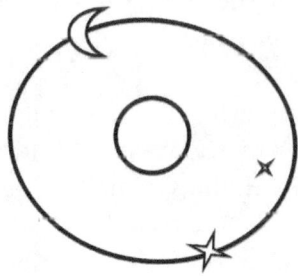

Jim Smiley had wanted to attend with him – or at least

to be on hand should the Council wish to hear his own presentation, but no human had entered this hall since the time misters Schiaparelli, Wells, Verne and Marconi had addressed it as guests of his wife's grandmother (the respected Councillor Kindelbir) over a hundred Earth years ago. It was probably better that Mr Smiley had stayed behind in the Earth system on this occasion.

Mr Sparks sighed. He shook himself from his reflections and started down the steps to find his seat.

3

"Welcome," said the tall councillor. He stood in the stone pulpit on the farthest side of the chamber. He raised his left forearm until it was level with his waist. The blue sleeve of his cloak pulled back to reveal his hand, palm facing downwards. A silver band hugged his wrist. Then he turned has hand over and extended it forward, sweeping it in an arc before the assembly.

He withdrew it and tapped his wristband with his other hand.

"We gather together, friends, at the city of our ancestors... beneath the image of the revered teacher and architect of our peace, to discuss... the human problem."

Mr Sparks turned to the councillor in the seat beside him, an elder by the name of Sffan'utul.

"*Smiall'kes'hep?* High Councillor – *when*? 'The *human* problem?'"

The older councillor – who, unusually for most male Martians, even elderly ones, had a prim pointed white beard not unlike an oriental master's – raised his hand to quell Mr Sparks's whispered questions.

"You have been away for some time, my friend. It has been two months since the decease of High Councillor Skallir'rir. Councillor Smiall'kes'hep was elected in your absence. Much of the North is behind him. Change is in the air. I hope your presentation will be persuasive."

Smiall'kes'hep picked up his speech. He laid out his proposition in a measured, punctuated style:

"We are not a sociable race. But then we do not need to be. And so it is enshrined in our planetary law that this assembly is called only at times of peril for our people. Today, I submit, is such a time.

"It is the contention of this chair that the proliferation of the humans represents a dire and imminent threat to our race."

Murmurs rippled around the chamber. Smiall'kes'hep raised a hand. The sounds abated.

"Hear me. We have tolerated the humans for too long. They have been permitted to make rapid advances in science and technology and now have the capability to leave the confines of their planet.

"Now their drones orbit our world. At the behest of High Councillor Skallir'rir, we did not react. Their *crawlers* traverse our terrain. And still we have not reacted.

"But their philosophical and moral development has not kept pace with their material progress. They have grown in such numbers that they despoil their own world, and now speak openly of colonising *ours*."

Further murmurs came from the assembly. He waited for the sound to subside, making use of the pause.

"We have previously heard from our esteemed colleagues of the men and women of their race that stand for peace and goodwill and co-operation. But since we accommodated the first of them in this chamber over sixty of our years ago, as a race, the opposite has been true."

He waved his hand and a three-dimensional display like a hologram appeared over the central platform of the auditorium. It began to show the worst excesses of human activity on Earth.

"Their planet has been continually ravaged by warfare, conquest, famine and disease. They pollute their very environment with waste products and radiation to the detriment of all life.

"I put it to you, friends: do you believe they will not bring this... *malady*... to infect *us*?"

On the north side of the chamber, and around Smiall'kes'hep, dozens of delegates touched their wristbands, which began to glow dull red in colour; at the same time, a discordant, low frequency wail of noise spread out across the amphitheatre.

The elder councillor beside Mr Sparks touched his own wristband. A shrill, sonar-like ping went out and bounced back from the walls of the chamber. Eyes turned towards him as he struggled to his feet.

"Sffan'utul of Tharsis," he said in introduction.

Smiall'kes'hep nodded. "The floor gives way to the eminent Councillor."

"Thank you," replied Sffan'utul, who nodded graciously.

He sighed and spoke slowly in his address: "High Councillor, eminent colleagues of the North and the South," he began. He focused his attention on

Smiall'kes'hep.

"High Councillor, sixty-two of our years ago, your predecessor stood where you now stand to share the necessity for us to work together with the enlightened minds of Earth for our mutual survival. I was present at that assembly, which was called by my late good friend, the renowned Councillor Kindelbir.

"It was she who recognised the threat we pose to ourselves by our own insularity. I need not remind this assembly that our global population then was a hundred and forty thousand. It is now eighty thousand. We cling to survival in underground pockets on a world that is hostile to its own sentient life. We all know the reason for this.

"It is true that humankind hinders its own development. It may even be destined to follow our own world's path to self-destruction. But with some guidance, it may be possible for them to avoid this, and we in turn to benefit from the assistance and resources offered by Earth to assure our own future.

"With this in mind, once humanity had attained a sufficient level of scientific and intellectual maturity, Councillor Kindelbir was authorised to attempt contact with some of Earth's brightest and imaginative minds to begin this process. The initiative that was established at that time survives today as the Controlled Contact programme between our two worlds that promises continued benefits for the peoples of both Earth and Mars. Together we are stronger than the sum of our parts.

"I therefore urge all gathered here today: do not bow to prejudice or be hasty in your rush to judgment. Be patient, be wise. Hear, then, my esteemed colleague,

Councillor Shieekk'ssup'pl of Solis, who comes from Earth with a new address from the humans."

Sffan'utul looked to Mr Sparks before he re-tapped his wristband and retook his seat.

Mr Sparks made a nod towards his colleague. Then he tapped his own wristband and started to rise from his seat.

Instead, Smiall'kes'hep gestured for him to sit down again. Mr Sparks looked to Sffan'utul with some uncertainty and sat back.

Smiall'kes'hep spoke. "Sffan'utul, we hear you out of respect for your age and long service to our world. But you have been blinded by your close association with the humans.

"I ask you: who benefits chiefly from this 'Controlled Contact'? Who benefits from the incautious sharing of Martian technology? In exchange for what? For *what?!* Earl Grey *tea*? *Television*? *Poisonous foods*?"

Sffan'utul tapped his wristband again. "It is true that I have had a long interest in the humans," he said. "With respect, High Councillor, since the time when you yourself were barely a babe out of arms. I reject the idea that I have been blinded by my experience. Rather, it has opened my eyes to its possibilities."

"What do *we* gain from this calamitous alliance?" demanded Smiall'kes'hep.

"Survival, High Councillor," Sffan'utul replied calmly.

"*Survival?!*" stormed Smiall'kes'hep. "It is a flawed notion that we need the humans to survive. On the contrary, we have everything to lose from our association with them. Their planet's most powerful tribes overrun indigenous peoples in conquest, exploitation and genocide; they swarm across its surface like the locusts of their world, consuming everything before them, leaving devastation behind. Like them, they are a plague; an infestation."

"We are the older race, technologically and ethically superior to the humans. But we are few. They are many. We must *not* permit them to become our technological equals, at risk that they become our masters, our conquerors. Our *ending*."

The cacophony of noise from the benches around him filled the air again. Amidst this, Councillor Shieekk'ssup'pl, more familiarly known as Mr Sparks, rose from his seat. He tapped his wristband, the cue for someone to speak, and the assembly fell quiet again. This time, Smiall'kes'hep did not prevent him from speaking.

"Councillor Shieekk'ssup'pl. Welcome. Please," he said, inviting Mr Sparks to address the assembly.

Mr Sparks bowed his head. "High Councillor; esteemed colleagues," he said. "My intention in coming here today is to respond to some of the unfounded fears – and I do call them *fears* – about our contact with humans.

"My wife and I have been proponents of the Controlled Contact programme for many years. My wife's grandmother was Councillor Kindelbir. My own son, Shieeekkksssup – known better to some of you by his Earth name, Leon Sparks – was one of the first of our exchange students. Some of you will also be aware that, when on Earth, he was abducted from school by factions with designs on our technology.

"And so, I accept that there are risks in dealing with

humans. But there are risks for them also in interacting with *us*. Most humans are not ready to accept our existence, less so an older, technologically superior race sharing the same system. We represent a threat to their political, economic and ideological systems. And so there will be wariness and distrust and fear, from both sides.

"But we believe the benefits outweigh those risks, and it may be essential that both planets accept them.

"*We* can help them to survive. *They* can help us to learn to become social creatures again; to draw together to help prolong our own race; to help us re-build this world."

Mr Sparks spread his arms and looked up at the decorated dome above them.

"This chamber has not been used in generations. Our technological abilities mean we have unlearned how to communicate directly. And so, I am grateful that the call for this assembly was made – thank you, High Councillor – even if its subject is the programme of which I have spoken. But lest it be thought that my representation of the humans is of my own construction, I submit to this assembly that James Smiley, a senior officer of the OPP is poised, on invitation, to come to Mars to address us in person."

"The OPP?" said Smiall'kes'hep. "This is the *Office of Planetary Protection*?"

"Yes," replied Mr Sparks, knowing full well that Smiall'kes'hep knew this already, and where he was heading with this.

"The organisation established to protect Earth and other bodies of our system from biological contamination?"

"Yes," said Mr Sparks quietly.

"How ironic," said Smiall'kes'hep. His words gained added weight from the brief silence that followed. Then he spoke again, looking at Mr Sparks with altogether more focus and seriousness.

"And he represents all the humans?"

"Not all. But –"

"Then he can make no difference," said Smiall'kes'hep abruptly.

"High Councillor –" began Mr Sparks.

"Thank you, Councillor," said Smiall'kes'hep.

"But High Councillor –"

"I said *thank you*, Councillor," repeated Smiall'kes'hep. He straightened, addressing the whole chamber.

"The floor is open to debate, or recess, as you prefer. The vote will take place in three solhours."

He turned and stepped down from the North pulpit and was gone from sight.

4

Mr Sparks and Councillor Sffan'utul stood at the chamber's tunnel entrance. Neither had wished to return to his seat. The full assembly had come back together and High Councillor Smiall'kes'hep stood again in the North side pulpit.

"Please cast your vote," said Smiall'kes'hep.

Around the amphitheatre, the hundreds of delegates touched their wristbands. The light level of the chamber swelled as each lit up in one of two colours. Those who remained in favour of continued Controlled Contact glowed green. Those against flared

red. It was soon apparent by the rosy glow that the reds were outshining the greens. Most of these lay on the northern side of the chamber, including Smiall'kes'hep's own; plus a surprising number amongst the southern delegates.

Smiall'kes'hep stood unmoving throughout.

Finally, there was a dull clang of a sound that indicated that all votes had been registered. A panel on the front of Smiall'kes'hep's pulpit lit up red.

"It is decided," he said.

6 - ABOUT TURN

Everyone had agreed to stay together for the tour of the base, which was led by Mr Knutt.

In the South Lobe, they went as far as the airlock to the Martian section. The glass sections of the closed doors permitted them to look into the corridor and complex beyond. The light was subdued, gloomy orange in hue, to replicate the conditions on Mars itself. The glass and metals of the door were cool to the touch, reflecting the colder atmosphere inside, where carbon dioxide was the major constituent of the air. Leon explained how he and other Martian children and adults had to wait a full five minutes to pass through the airlock, which had to adjust for air changes and temperature differences on either side.

From there they headed back through City Square and onto West Lobe, where they visited Mr Flynn, who was working in the horticultural and hydroponics section. They found him in a long glass-roofed extension, effectively a huge greenhouse. Large rectangular trays of dark soil covered most of the floor space, while banks of terraces climbed the walls at either side at forty-five degree angles, making maximum use of the space. It was noticeably warmer and more humid in here. Vegetables and fruits of all kinds bloomed in the one-sixth G. Overhead, grapevines climbed on poles and netting. Above them, hung from the underside of the roof, large banks of lights (not presently switched on) served when the base entered the long lunar night.

Mr Flynn, back temporarily in his familiar green overalls, was halfway down the central aisle, where he was hoeing a cleared section of soil. When he saw them coming, he put down his tools, wiped his hands and brow with his sleeve and stepped back onto the path to meet them.

"Mr Flynn," said Mr Knutt.

"Mornin', he'dmaster; everyone." He couldn't drop the habit of addressing Mr Knutt as headmaster.

"So, Mr Flynn, would you care to share what your contribution to the space programme has been?"

"Course, he'dmaster. As you can see, growing vegetables, the natural way. None of that hydroponics palaver in here.

"As you can see, all these vegetables are growing in proper soil – that's Moon dust mixed with compost from vegetable matter."

Mr Flynn bent down and picked up a handful of soil. He showed it around the group, which had gathered around, children in front, adults behind. It looked quite like soil on Earth, charcoal brown, with lots of small fragments of crushed rock and sharp, glassy particles that glinted in the light.

"Course, you can't jus' grow things in Moon dust. It's sterile. Needs a bit of encouragement to get started. But after a while, with extra nutrients, and light and water and warmth, it's like growing in volcanic soil – not that there's much of tha' where I comes from.

"In this gravity, we can grow produce twice as fast

as on Earth; so we gets enough to keep the base in fresh veggies."

2

By the time they left Mr Flynn, it was lunch time, for which they headed back to City Square. Then, afterwards, it was up to the conference lounge at the top level of the West Lobe.

The lounge was a large open-plan space, tastefully arranged with comfortable-looking seats and couches arranged around wavy sections of leaf-green carpet. Water coolers, hot-drinks dispensers, potted plants and units holding tablet computers were sensibly placed within easy reach of the seating areas. The lighting was subdued, which naturally drew the eye towards the large high-def widescreen monitor mounted on the front wall, on which a graphic of a slowly rotating planet Mars played. On the lounge's far side, curved banks of thick glass windows looked out towards the foot of the crater's central peak.

Already there were a number of people, children and grown-ups seated there. Most were human, although there were a few Martians amongst them.

"Over here, please," said Leon, and he led them to an arrangement of couches that formed a central arc facing the screen. "I reserved them."

Mr Knutt looked at his watch. "Er, the presentation by Mrs Sparks, Leon's mother, will commence in twenty minutes, and will last for approximately an hour. Its purpose – as you may have surmised from the screen – is to teach us something of Mars's history and customs. Mums and dads are welcome to stay – or you may prefer to step out to the observation deck for drinks, or return to your quarters."

He gestured towards the back of the lounge where, through smoked glass windows and door panels, they could see a similar space.

"The rear lounge – where Martian children can learn a broad history of Earth and *its* customs. Not that they need it, really. Martian children are far more informed about Earth than we are with Mars – but it helps to fill in some of the cultural gaps and prepares both parties before they come together to share classes over the next few days. In our case, Leon, Aurore and Camille will stay with you."

Behind Mr Knutt, Dominic (from where he had already planted himself on the central couch) rolled his eyes again at the mention of classes.

A red light flickered at Mr Knutt's side. He reached for the pager clipped to his suit belt, looked at it; frowned; then he said, "Will you excuse me," and strode off the way they had come in.

Mrs Westfield and Mr Tiddler looked at one another, then around at the seating arrangements.

"Shall we?" suggested Mrs Westfield.

"Sure," said Emily's dad.

Mr Addison, meanwhile, walked over and sat next to Dominic.

"What are you doing?" asked Dominic.

"I want to hear the presentation."

"Alright, but can't you sit over there with the other parents?" replied Dominic.

"Why?"

"Kids sit with kids. Dads sit with other dads and mums."

"Well, OK, if you like," said Mr Addison. He got up to move.

"No offence, Dad, OK?"

"None taken, Dom."

As soon as Mr Addison left, Dominic nodded to the other children to come and sit together.

"How is your mum, Leon?" asked Lucy. The last time she and Emily and Dominic had seen her was on Leon's last day at Flintworne, when they had tearfully said their goodbyes to Leon, whom they weren't sure they would see again.

"She is fine, thank you," replied Leon. "She was very pleased to have been offered an opportunity to teach with the programme. Her knowledge of our history made her a logical choice for that. So, we came back together. I think you will find her presentation very informative."

3

Mr Knutt stepped out of the elevator into the main corridor of West Lobe. Mr Smiley was waiting for him. His expression was serious.

Mr Knutt raised his eyebrows questioningly.

Mr Smiley sighed. "We have a problem," he said simply.

"Oh," said Mr Knutt.

The pair started walking together.

"Well?" said Mr Knutt.

"In my office," said Mr Smiley.

4

When they arrived at Mr Smiley's office, there were others already there. There was Caroline Miller, and Aurore's guardian, Miss Sky. And there was another officer, whom Mr Knutt hadn't met before. Mr Smiley introduced him. "Karl Winsom, OPP negotiator."

"Howard Knutt."

"Yes, sir. A pleasure, sir."

They all sat around the table. Mr Smiley wasted no time imparting his news.

"We've just heard that the Martian Council has ended Controlled Contact."

Whatever it was Mr Knutt was expecting, it wasn't this. "What? *How* –"

"But that's not all," said the other man. "I'm afraid it's more serious than that. The Council leader is pushing for Mars to withdraw from human contact. Period."

"I don't understand," said Mr Knutt, who was clearly confused and taken aback.

"We're about to talk to Fred Sparks."

"From Mars?"

"Huh-uh. Comportal link."

Mr Smiley waved his hand over a pad on his desktop and the wall-mounted screen before them lit up. A moment or two of static settled into a steady black screen over which played some odd-looking symbols, which then gave way to the crisp image of Mr Sparks. He too was accompanied by another individual, a noticeably older Martian.

"Fred," said Mr Smiley.

"James. Good."

"Fred, briefly, on our side, you know Miss Skiel'aeljtɪn, Caroline Miller, and Mr Knutt, headmaster of Flintworne."

"Howard Knutt. Yes, of course." Except it came out as *Hawudd-nut*; almost like *hard nut*, which might have been amusing in other circumstances.

"And this is Karl Winsom, a negotiator and linguistics specialist with the OPP."

Winsom greeted Mr Sparks in Martian, which he did without apparent difficulty, considering that the human larynx or voice box wasn't built for it.

Mr Sparks nodded in appreciation.

"And with me, James, is someone known to you and to Skiel'aeljtɪn: Councillor Sffan'utul."

"Yes indeed. Greetings, Councillor."

Sffan'utul nodded.

"Right, Fred. Update us please."

"Since my earlier message, James, the situation has deteriorated."

Mr Sparks took a deep breath.

"The Council has decreed that withdrawal of all Martian subjects should take place immediately. All Martian technology in the hands of humans is also to be accounted for, withdrawn or destroyed."

Mr Smiley visibly swallowed. Mr Knutt appeared stunned by what he was hearing. Only Miss Sky looked on implacably.

"You have two sols to evacuate – by 1200 hours, 12 August UTC. By order of the High Councillor and the General Assembly."

Miss Sky spoke: "How is this possible, Councillor? How can the entire assembly have turned so quickly? I have received no notification as principal representative of the programme."

The elder Martian at the other end opened his mouth to speak. He spoke only in Martian. The comportal display automatically displayed a translation. "Your deputy is in discussions with Smiall'kes'hep's officials. She will contact you directly in time."

Mr Smiley spoke again. "OK. What else do we know about this Smiall'kes'hep?"

Mr Winsom answered. "I met with him a year ago, when he was a back-bench official. He was quiet, taciturn, but polite – quintessentially Martian, I'd say – no indications that he aspired to hands-on power, although he clearly commanded the respect of his peers for his wisdom and political experience.

"Then High Councillor Skallir'rir died, creating something of a vacuum, and he became the leading candidate to take his place."

Sffan'utul nodded. "Yes. In many ways, he was the logical choice to lead the North. His family claims descent from one of the twelve ruling families from the time of Jziee'ekkkzoor'sup, with a long history of political influence. But it was not foreseen that he might begin so aggressive a course as he has now taken. Nor that he would gain widespread support, even amongst our numbers."

"Excuse me," said Mr Knutt, "The North?"

"My wife will explain it to you, Howard," said Mr Sparks. "Meanwhile, James, I wish you to inform her about what has happened. Make preparations, please, but for the moment I suggest you carry on as you are. Sffan'utul and I are continuing to talk to our colleagues and the moderates on the other side of the assembly."

"That'll be for the OPP to decide at higher level. Miss Sky and I will talk to our superiors on Earth after this."

"As you wish. I shall report again as soon as possible."

"Councillors, thank you," said Mr Smiley.

The connection was broken.

Mr Smiley turned to the others. He sat back. "Well, what do you all think?"

Caroline Miller was the first to speak. "With all respect to Fred Sparks, I believe we should wait for an official bulletin from the OPP. While we were listening, I checked for any news on this. Nothing."

"OK," agreed Mr Smiley. "Let's monitor the situation. I'll brief my superiors in Washington. Until we have evidence to the contrary, it's business as usual. Agreed?"

Heads nodded around the table.

"Including tomorrow's plans for my newest group?" asked Mr Knutt.

"You'll be the best judge of that, Howard. But presently, I don't see why not, do you?"

"No," said Mr Knutt.

"Thanks, Howard." Mr Smiley looked at Mr Knutt expectantly.

"Oh, of course," said Mr Knutt. He got up to leave.

7 - SPACE SCHOOL

Mrs Sparks strode into the room. A hush immediately descended, as if a strict or respected teacher has entered the classroom.

Mrs Sparks was tall, slim, and dressed in a long black gown. She took her place at a lectern before the large monitor on the wall behind her. When she looked up, her eyes, large and deep, simultaneously projected a penetrating intelligence and gentle compassion.

Lucy and Emily looked from her to Leon and back again.

"We-yel-coom, evfery-ywon," greeted Mrs Sparks.

Welcome, everyone.

She spoke slowly, and in a broken accent that made it initially hard to follow, but after a while during which their ears 'tuned in', everyone found they could follow her without too much difficulty.

Before Mrs Sparks had even begun her presentation, Mr Knutt quietly joined them and found a seat with the children's parents.

Mrs Sparks continued. "This afternoon, we are going to cover a brief history of the planet Mars – as you call it on Earth."

Behind her, on the screen, the 3D graphic of Mars began to rotate a little faster. The two moons of Phobos and Deimos picked up their pace in their orbits circling the planet.

"In our language, we call our home world *Oztzıldıj*, which translates approximately as *fire star*. In some of your languages and mythologies, it is *Mars,* or *Ares*, after the god of war. While Mars experienced conflict in its distant past, our race has been at peace for many thousands of years."

Mrs Sparks waved her hand over the lectern and the moon Phobos lit up.

"We have two small moons; in your language, Phobos and Deimos, named by American astronomer Asaph Hall after the sons of Ares. Phobos – meaning 'panic' or 'fear' – we call *Su'umka'r*, the hawk. Its brother, Deimos, we know as *A'yrk'yrok*, the kite."

She waved a hand over the lectern again, and a smaller, star-like symbol appeared on the screen, in an orbit inside that of Deimos.

"Once there was a third moon, smaller even than Deimos, a captured asteroid that we knew as *Ti'aransc*, the sparrow. It no longer exists. We will come back to it soon."

Mrs Sparks waved her hand again and the monitor screen began to zoom into the planet. It descended through the atmosphere, through clouds, until it slowed above a broad landscape that appeared quite different to the Mars of today. There were still peaks and valleys and large craters, but there were also wide vales of green vegetation and lakes and rivers, and a sky that was purple rather than the faint rust colour it is now famous for.

"Such was our planet many millennia ago. Our race is a very ancient one. When people on Earth were hunting and gathering in small groups and dwelling in caves, our civilisation was at its peak. It spanned our own world and had ventured out to other planets."

Mrs Sparks spoke deliberately, without boastfulness or pride. If anything, it was with an air of sadness as the screen behind her began to display images of a culture that was extensive, advanced. Great buildings and statues thrust skywards from lush parklands, where trees and fountains flourished and people gathered together or walked along shady promenades. Overhead, aerial vehicles whispered busily along in all directions. And above them, Mars's three moons were just visible in the late afternoon sky.

It was not clear if they were watching some kind of advanced computer graphics, or somehow, actual images from Mars's past. All eyes in the audience – particularly those of the adults present, who seemed less able to take new or surprising information in their stride – were transfixed by the images.

"Our planet once supported a population of six hundred million. We outgrew an early period of intertribal conflict, when the seven ancient ruling families of the northern hemisphere and the five families of the South were brought together in truce under the great peacemaker, *Jziee'ekkkzoor'sup,* the first High Councillor and father of our race.

"But it was but a short march of years following the death of Jziee'ekkkzoor'sup that our planet suffered one of its greatest calamities, from which our race has not recovered."

Mrs Sparks moved her hand, and the display zoomed out to show Mars in context within its region of the solar system. Beyond Mars, between its orbit and the orbit of the gas giant, Jupiter, lay the asteroid belt, where bodies larger than mountains hurtled about, colliding, breaking into yet more fragments.

"From its position in the solar system, Mars is at greater risk than Earth from impacts by space rocks from the debris field beyond our planet.

"Unlike on Earth, where meteoroids burn up in the atmosphere, the thinner atmosphere of our planet permits many to reach the surface. Approximately two hundred impacts of moderate size take place every year – which is one reason why we continue to live underground today.

"But even on Earth, the rock may be of sufficient size and composition and velocity to survive deep into the atmosphere."

The display changed again to show old sepia photographs of a flattened forest; then colour video of an intensely bright spear of light streaking across a morning sky.

"Examples from Earth in recent times include the superbolide events in Tunguska in 1908, which destroyed a large expanse of forest in Siberia; and the Chelyabinsk meteor, a rock twenty metres in diameter and mass in excess of twelve thousand tonnes, exploded with high energy over central southern Russia in 2013. And only –"

"Hey," exclaimed Dominic. "I saw something like that hit the Earth yesterday, before we left orbit!"

Lucy and Emily frowned at Dominic, both at his loud intervention and for his claim. He hadn't mentioned this before now. Mr Knutt and his own dad were amongst those now looking his way in puzzlement.

Mrs Sparks interrupted her presentation. She

peered at Dominic. He was surprised to find she remembered his name.

"Very good, Dominic. Indeed, an event is recorded at that time over the South China Sea. There have been no reports of damage or causalities."

Mrs Sparks straightened. "Fortunately, such events on Earth are quite rare. And very large events, in which an asteroid survives to strike the surface, are even rarer. But when they happen, they are truly devastating, and can have planet-changing effects.

"Thirteen thousand of your years ago, an asteroid or a comet collided with Earth's northern ice sheets. It unleashed huge destruction on a flourishing global culture, of which only remnants survive and are recalled in your myths and legends of a great deluge which only a handful survived."

The grown-ups in the room looked at one another in surprise. This had never featured in the history books.

"And so it was also on Mars, much longer ago. Our calamity was greater still, and was, in part, of our own making. It involved Ti'aransc."

The screen changed view again, this time to display a visual representation of what Mrs Sparks began to describe.

"We had become technologically capable of deflecting threatening asteroids away from our planet. We had proven this time and again by the use of engines that generated unimaginable power. So when Ti'aransc's orbit became unstable, the Council ordered an attempt to stabilise it or send it back out to the asteroid field.

"But something went wrong. Ti'aransc spiralled into our planet. The combined force of its impact and four exploding zero-point engines sent shock waves around our planet, unleashing untold destruction. Virtually the entire surface population was decimated. The explosion disrupted the planetary magnetic field and blasted a large portion of its atmosphere into space. What remained became clouded with dust and choked with the toxic fumes of volcanoes that were triggered by the impact, so that the Sun was not visible for a generation.

"The explosion altered the orbits of Su'umka'r and A'yrk'yrok, and coated them with the death blood of our world.

"Starved of solar radiation, our biosphere died. In the cold that followed, water vapour condensed out of the thin atmosphere, and our once great lakes and rivers froze into the ground. The oxygen produced by our plant species became bound to the iron compounds in the soil, turning our planet's surface into an arid red desert beneath a blush sky. What remained was an atmosphere dominated by carbon dioxide and the heavier gases.

"Such was the ruined world witnessed by the small numbers of survivors that emerged after the cataclysm.

"They – a few thousand – were forced to seek shelter underground. Since that time, we have existed in this manner. The old cities became ghosts, subjects of mythologising, as you have on Earth about your great antediluvian civilisations – Atlantis, Lemuria."

"*Anti- what?*" whispered Dominic.

"Before the deluge – the *Great Flood*," Lucy whispered back.

"Over time," continued Mrs Sparks, "our bodies

have adapted to higher levels of carbon dioxide, which is broken down in our respiratory cycle – so, like plants, we breathe in carbon dioxide and exhale oxygen.

"And we recovered, slowly. We ventured out again, and we watched as Earth's peoples flourished into great global civilisations.

"And," she said forlornly, "we felt guilt and shame when we failed to prevent the cometary strike that overwhelmed them in a manner that echoed our own fate."

"And so, our ancestors placed a sentinel satellite in permanent orbit about your planet to monitor and to shield its people from a similar future threat."

The screen changed to show altogether more pleasant scenes, of underground houses and complexes, of domes with plants growing in them and underground tanks of water.

Mrs Sparks continued. "On Mars, our ancestors had retained their technical knowledge, and it was this that helped our race to survive. But we were scattered around the planet, and our small communities became insular. We stagnated socially, and it became almost impossible for us to properly rebuild.

"So when it was realised that the humans had recovered well and had progressed to a primitive technical age, it became clear that there was much they could teach us about society and cooperation."

The screen changed again and a kindly looking elderly Martian lady looked out at the audience.

"My grandmother, Councillor Kindlebir," explained Mrs Sparks.

Lucy leaned towards Leon. "Your great

grandmother?"

Leon nodded.

"*Obviously*," whispered Dominic.

"My grandmother," said Mrs Sparks, "sought an audience with the Council, to seek permission to contact Earth.

"Rarely did the councillors come together to meet. There has not been a system of government as you know it on our planet since before the cataclysm. We have a system of leaders, 360 in number, preserving the traditional number of district councillors of old, even though many of the districts exist now only in memory.

"The Council had not met for two hundred and fifty years. There was resistance, but a Council majority agreed to a limited, exploratory programme of controlled contact."

Someone in the audience – not from Leon's group – stifled a yawn. Others fidgeted in their seats.

Just like real school, thought Dominic glumly.

Mrs Sparks looked up. She smiled kindly. "There is not much more today."

But Mr Knutt and the other grown-ups were captivated by this unknown history. Leon and Aurore, of course, knew it already. Even Camille had more of an understanding from her own stay on Mars; while Lucy and Emily sat politely attentive.

The images on the screen changed again – this time to half a dozen craft leaving Martian orbit, bound for Earth. A faint greenish haze surrounded them as the streaked away from their planet.

"It was 1896 by your calendar. Our orbiting sentinel had begun to detect a capability in electromagnetic communications. In America, Mr Tesla had already invented the principles of radio, but Mr Marconi was achieving the first successful transmissions in England. But this was too primitive to permit interplanetary communication.

"My grandmother therefore led an expedition. She was accompanied by her assistant, Tek'tu'jan. There were twelve other pilots and crew members. They chose the United States of America for their initial survey, as it showed the best indications of technological development.

"At first, they surveyed from afar. The historical evidence was that humans were volatile, hostile. But as the mission progressed and sightings of our craft attracted no significant interest, my grandmother decided to draw closer. She authorised closer observations to be made across the country to permit the humans to become acclimatised to our presence – as we had from time to time in Earth's history. Occasionally, a pod landed, usually for the replenishment of provisions.

"Meanwhile, the mission had begun to identify individuals to consider for direct contact. In the United States, these included the inventors, Mr Nicola Tesla and Mr Thomas Eddison, the astronomer, Mr Percival Lowell, and the writers, Mr Gustavus Pope and Mr John McCoy."

The screen changed to show photographs of the five men.

"And elsewhere, they had identified others: the visionary writers, Herbert Wells and Jules Verne, the astronomer, Giovanni Schiaparelli and the inventor Guglielmo Marconi."

Again, the images on the screen changed in pace with the lecture.

"But then something went wrong, a tragic incident that brought the mission to a premature end. During the second phase of visits in the United States early in 1897, a pod that was surveying at low altitude was attacked with ballistic weapons. It was damaged; it could not gain height and crashed, killing the two occupants. One was Tek'tu'jan, my grandmother's assistant."

In the audience, Leon and Aurore exchanged looks. Aurore looked up at Mrs Sparks, who made momentary eye contact with her before bringing her attention back to her lectern.

"Saddened, and criticised for the incident," continued Mrs Sparks, "my grandmother withdrew the mission."

Mrs Sparks looked up again.

"But she did not give up. She returned, alone, shortly afterwards on an unauthorised solo mission to establish peaceful contact. This time she chose Europe and the visionary writers, philosophers and astronomers of the time, who she hoped would be able to spread the idea of benevolent contact amongst the human population.

"Some had begun already to write about contact with Mars. There was Camille Flammarion, and Hugh MacColl, both in France; and in Germany, Kurd Lasswitz, and in Northern Ireland, Robert Cromie.

"But my grandmother settled on England first, where she made contact with Herbert Wells, whom, as a popular writer in the English language, she believed would be most influential to promote her message.

Plus, she had learned that the Italian inventor Guglielmo Marconi had taken up residence there.

"My grandmother met Mr Wells one afternoon in a tea room near his home. That meeting is much celebrated on our planet, as their discussion not only marked the start of what would eventually become the Controlled Contact programme, but it took place over a pot of Earl Grey tea. That beverage was to become much favoured on our planet after Mr Wells brought a gift of Earl Grey tea and chocolate during his first visit to Mars."

In the audience, eyes darted about, especially amongst the grown-ups. Even Mr Knutt raised an eyebrow in surprise. He knew that Leon's great grandmother had met H. G. Wells, but it hadn't occurred to him that he may have travelled to Mars, making him possibly one of the first ever astronauts.

"The speculative fiction of the time that described contact with Mars was generally negative. My grandmother wished that Mr Wells – or Bertie, as he was known to his friends – would write a positive message of contact, portraying our true intention. But, following a second visit to our planet a month later, during which he stayed for two weeks and met many notables and was given the freedom to research and learn about our history and culture, he returned to Earth and, without explanation, wrote *The War of the Worlds*, portraying Martians as aggressive invaders.

"My grandmother was confused and upset by Bertie's actions, but she continued to try other means of fulfilling her mission. In 1899, she exchanged radio messages with Mr Tesla, the first interplanetary communication using Earth technology.

"This resulted in a fresh, sanctioned visit to Earth in the year 1902. She returned to Mars with Mr Tesla, Mr Marconi, plus Mr Eddison, Mr Schiaparelli, Mr Lowell, Mr Cromie and Mr Lasswitz. Mr Verne was not approachable, and whilst my grandmother made a conciliatory visit with Mr Wells, he declined to return to Mars with her.

"The party was politely received by the Council – which was the last occasion that it assembled before the present time. But the damage had been done. Mr Wells's work, in particular, set the idea of closer contact back many years. And while my grandmother kept in contact with Mr Tesla and others, she died without seeing what her efforts have ultimately yielded: today's Contact Programme."

Mrs Sparks looked up from her lectern. The screen fell dark behind her.

"Thank you," she said. "This concludes today's presentation. Does anyone have a question?"

As is often the case, stillness hung over the audience before several hands were finally raised.

One of them belonged to Emily. "What happened to Mr Wells on Mars that made him write his book that way?"

Mrs Sparks nodded gently. "That is a good question, Emily. I'm afraid my grandmother did not speak of it."

Mr Tiddler was next: "Most of these gentlemen are famous for their contributions to our science and technology – Marconi, Eddison, Tesla. But were they selected for their brilliance, or are their inventions a consequence of their visit to Mars?"

"Another good question... Mr Tiddler."

Mr Tiddler raised an eyebrow, impressed that

Leon's mother should know who he was even though they had not formally met.

"Both. Each stood out for his evident talent, but it is true that some of their later inventiveness may have been inspired by their visits to Mars."

Mrs Sparks switched her attention to a third raised hand. It belonged to Aurore, who surprisingly had found her voice:

"What happened to your grandmother's assistant, who died on her first visit to Earth?"

Mrs Sparks's eyes narrowed on Aurore. Her air of kind-heartedness and composure faltered for the first time.

"Her remains were eventually recovered and returned to her family on Mars."

She attempted a small, kindly smile. There was an awkward pause that was not lost on the grown-ups as Mrs Sparks looked from Aurore to her own son, and then around at the audience.

"Well, if that is all, the next presentation will be at the same time tomorrow afternoon when we will look at the development of the Contact Programme with the Office of Planetary Protection."

There was a brief round of applause, led by the grown-ups.

Mr Knutt stood up. "Thank you, Mrs Sparks, for your enlightening presentation. It's good to know that the threat from asteroids, while real, is thankfully rare, but also something our Martian friends are assisting us with."

Mr Knutt looked at his wristwatch. "Right, thank you everyone. I believe it is now time for our younger guests to head over to the one-sixth G swimming pool.

Miss Sky will lead the way."

The audience began to get up and leave. Mr Knutt stepped forward to speak to Mrs Sparks.

In the children's group, Emily was first to her feet.

"Well, that was cheery," she said.

They started together towards the exit.

"Phew," said Dominic. That was worse than Mrs Gulliver's maths lessons."

"Don't exaggerate, Dominic," said Lucy.

"I'm not," he replied. Then he noticed Leon beside him. "Oh, sorry. No offence – your mum and all that."

"It is alright," said Leon.

"Actually, it was really interesting," said Lucy. "I didn't know that Mars was quite like Earth."

"Yes, a very long time ago," said Leon, wistfully.

2

The one-sixth G pool was located at the lowest level of West Lobe, inside an underground dome. It was only half the length of an Olympic-size pool, but what it lacked in size it made up for in novelty. Ingeniously, it was set on a natural slope of the underlying surface, so that when underwater, there was a view through thick glass out onto the lunar surface. From the outside, it might look like an aquarium, with humans darting past instead of fish.

Gentle swimming felt much like on Earth, but it was when one either splashed or jumped in that the difference was really noticeable. Every splash travelled higher and stayed in the air longer. And when surfacing after swimming underwater, it was possible to boost higher out of the water, a little like a dolphin rising for a fish treat.

The children spent an hour in the pool, supervised by Miss Sky and a pool attendant. Even Leon and Aurore found that they enjoyed the experience now that the children from Earth were here, all of whom were far more proficient swimmers than they. There simply was no such luxury as a pool for recreational purposes on Mars.

Lucy and Camille helped Leon and Aurore to learn the basics of various swimming strokes, while Emily swam lengths or dived to peer through the windows, and Dominic did splash bombs off the single low diving board (until Miss Sky told him off).

And so, they swam or dived or paddled and played water polo, until finally that unspoken moment arrived when everyone had had enough and tummies began to rumble and they left the water.

3

When the children met up with their parents again, it was at a restaurant in City Square for their evening meal – a different one this time, *Sputnik*.

Mr Knutt was there, although throughout the meal, he seemed a little distant. But the children were in good cheer, having worked up a healthy appetite from the swimming and (after a small snack) some one-sixth G gymnastics in an adjacent trampoline gym.

The parents were in a relaxed mood too. They sat with Mr Knutt and Miss Sky and Mrs Sparks, who had joined them for the first time, and were by now completely at ease on the Moon, whose brightly lit surface was visible through the thick curved windows at the end of their table. They scarcely looked that way as they ate and drank and chatted.

Finally, Mr Knutt got to his feet, and came over to the children's table.

"Well, I hope you have all had a good day?"

A Mexican wave of nods raced around the table. Mr Knutt smiled.

"Good. I'm sure you are looking forward to the next exciting instalment of Mrs Sparks's Space School class tomorrow? Gosh," he reflected. "That's a bit of a mouthful, isn't it?"

Another wave of nods started, which faltered when it reached Dominic, who scrunched up his face. Lucy dug him in his ribs with her elbow.

"But before that, tomorrow morning, we have something very special lined up for you."

Dominic's expression changed instantly. He sat up attentively.

"You are going on a field trip."

All the children except Leon looked at one another, abuzz with curiosity.

Leon leaned closer to Dominic. "The excursion I told you about yesterday that I said your dad might enjoy," he said.

"Oh," replied Dominic. "Are parents coming too?"

"Those that wish to, yes," answered Mr Knutt. "I have just discussed this with them, and all of your parents – including Mrs Bazinct, Camille's mother – have indicated that they'd like to. Those from Earth, that is. Miss Sky and Mrs Sparks have declined – but I'm sure you will all look after Aurore?"

"Yes, we will, Mr Knutt," said Lucy.

"Thank you, Lucy. Now, you'll need to be at the

North Lobe hanger soon after breakfast. The pod will leave promptly at 9 a.m. Mr Smiley has said that anyone even a minute late will miss it.

A voice from behind Mr Knutt interrupted them. Mr Knutt glanced back to see Miss Sky waiting for him. He acknowledged her with a nod and turned back to the children.

"Oh," he added. "You will need a packed lunch. Please order one from your room service facility this evening."

Finally, he turned to Miss Sky.

"Miss Sky, what can I do for you?"

"About Aurore."

"Yes?"

"Perhaps she should not go on the excursion tomorrow."

Mr Knutt looked at her quizzically. "Nonsense," he said. "She will be fine."

"But... as her guardian, I am not sure she will find it very instructive."

Mr Knutt's generally buoyant manner faltered. "Oh?"

"She is familiar with the fledgling efforts of your space programme from the archives."

Mr Knutt overlooked the unintentional slight. "I see," he said. "But then she may just as well have learned about us entirely out of the archives, don't you think? That is the whole point of Controlled Contact, is it not?" He smiled kindly.

"Yes, of course," replied Miss Sky. She nodded and backed away.

Mr Knutt looked after her for a moment before going on his own way.

8 - NEIL.A.LIEN

After breakfast the next morning, the children and their parents assembled outside the North Lobe hangar.

Mr Tiddler looked at his watch. "So much for being here promptly at nine."

"I'm sure they'll be here soon," said Mrs Westfield.

But ten minutes later, there was still no sign of Mr Knutt, Mr Smiley or anyone else.

The children occupied themselves as only children can where no mobile phones are in sight. Lucy and Emily led off with Rock, Paper, Scissors, which clearly was beyond Aurore.

"I can follow the logic," she said, "but what are its objectives, parameters, application?"

"It has no purpose. It is just fun," replied Leon. "It will come to you."

Finally, Mrs Westfield spoke again. "Perhaps we should call someone?"

"Don't suppose anyone has Mr Knutt's number?" asked Mr Addison.

"We won't need it," said Mr Tiddler. "Just find a comms station and say 'Assist Alpha' – remember?"

"Oh yeah," said Mr Addison.

"I'll go," said Mr Tiddler.

As soon as Mr TIddler left, the hanger doors parted

behind them, and out stepped Miss Sky. She stopped before the assembled crowd. She furtively looked around, taking in who was present, before appearing to relax. Her eyes found Aurore.

Aurore spoke to her in Martian. Miss Sky shook her head, replying in their own language. Then she turned to the grown-up humans.

"We've been waiting out here," said Mrs Westfield. "Are they on board already?"

"No," replied Miss Sky. "Not yet. I am not sure who is coming. Mr Smiley has called a meeting in his office this morning."

Cries of 'aw' came from the children.

"I am sure someone will be along shortly," said Miss Sky. "Please excuse me. I must go."

Before departing, Miss Sky turned again to Aurore. She handled her a lunch bag and said something quietly to her, again in Martian. Aurore nodded.

Leon looked quizzically from one to the other.

Presently, Mr Tiddler came back. "I was told they'll be here very shortly," he said.

It was another ten minutes, though, before, finally, Mr Knutt and Mr Smiley appeared around the curve of the corridor.

Mr Knutt had the lead. "Ah, good morning everyone. I'm sorry we're running a little late." He glanced at Leon and Aurore.

"Is there a problem?" asked Mr Tiddler.

"No. Just some communications issues," said Mr Smiley. The team is working on it. Nothing to concern us. We'll get on as planned."

"So, if everyone is ready," picked up Mr Knutt. "We'll board the pod and get on our way."

2

The pod lifted off and zipped through the overhead hatch of the hangar. Mr Smiley waved his hand over his armrest and the walls became transparent. The base was shrinking below them, and the peak of Tsiolkovsky itself already resembled a mound of sand.

It was strange to be back outside. On the base it had been remarkably easy for everyone to forget that they were on the Moon. Here now, they were reminded how far away from home they really were, and how alien and forbidding their surrounding environment was.

The pod lifted skyward. Mr Smiley guided it upward on a trajectory that took it on a suborbital arc westward around the Moon.

"Some of you may have guessed our itinerary for this morning," said Mr Smiley from his command seat. "For those who haven't, we are going to visit some of the iconic Apollo landing sites."

There was a buzz around the cabin.

"Most of you weren't born when these events took place. Hence the idea that they did not happen at all, that they were staged by NASA to give the impression that American won the space race to the Moon, has increased in popularity in recent years."

Dominic glanced at his dad who, before now, had been one of the doubters. Mr Addison nodded back. He was past that now.

"Today you will see for yourselves that they are wrong," Mr Smiley said simply. "In thirty minutes we'll descend to approach the first site – appropriately, the first landing, Apollo 11."

A ripple of excitement went around like electricity.

"Yesss!" said Dominic.

All of the grown-ups looked just as excited. Mr Tiddler, who had been born a few months after the first landing, appeared quite emotional.

Just then, someone cried *"Look!"*

Forward, in their direction of travel, a bright sliver was prising itself clear of the Moon's limb. Rapidly, it broke loose from the monotonous muddy-grey, pitted and pock-marked surface that rotated below them, to jump clear, revealing a bright blue and tan marble covered in wispy swirls of clouds.

The Earth. Home. It was startlingly bright, and actually about the size of a golf-ball at arm's length.

Gasps escaped almost everyone aboard. Even for those who had witnessed Earthrise dozens of times, like Mr Smiley, it lost little of its grandeur.

Mr Knutt spoke up. "Imagine what it was like for the first humans to see this – as it was for the crew of Apollo 8 on Christmas Eve, 1968. I remember it well," he said, "although I was a young boy at the time."

Soon it was time to descend. As they did so, the horizon flattened out and the terrain below became steadily smoother – still pock-marked by craters, but generally they were smaller and shallower pits that marked a gently undulating landscape.

"Mare Tranquillitatis," announced Mr Smiley. "The Sea of Tranquility. ETA five minutes."

Everyone was now on the edge of their seat, peering intently ahead for the first signs of the famous landing area."

"Are we going to land?" asked Emily.

"No, we aren't permitted to do that, Emily," said Mr

Knutt. "But we'll get close enough to get a clear view without disturbing the site."

"We're approaching on the same trajectory as Neil Armstrong and Buzz Aldrin on 20 July, 1969," said Mr Smiley.

"Wow!" said Mr Tiddler quietly.

All eyes now were scanning the surface ahead.

It was Camille who spotted it first. "I see it!" she said. There was a tiny glint ahead, a reflection from something, a pin-prick on the surface next to a modest crater.

"Well, I never," said Mr Addison, almost to himself.

"OK, we're slowing," said Mr Smiley. "We'll stop a quarter of a mile away – although we won't be spraying dust the way Eagle did a half century ago."

The pod came to a halt as Mr Smiley said, approximately four hundred metres from the landing site, and around ten metres above the surface. It hummed perceptibly, which became noticeable as everyone fell quiet. Even from this distance, the remains of the lander, the scorched descent stage, sat like a flat octagonal table, in the centre of a radial pattern of streaks.

The moment seemed to command silent respect. This was it – the actual spot that men from the planet Earth first set foot on the surface of another heavenly body. It took a while for that to sink in.

Dominic was the first to speak. "There you go, dad."

"Yeah, Dom. I took it all back, you know, as soon we got to the Moon. But this is the final proof for sure."

Mr Tiddler turned to Mr Smiley. "Did either Armstrong or Aldrin come back to visit – y'know, like

Jim Lovell?"

"Not that I'm aware," replied Mr Smiley.

"Did you know that 'Neil. A' spelled backwards is 'A.lieN'?" said Emily.

Several of the group raised eyebrows, including Mr Smiley. It was an odd coincidence.

"Well," said Mr Addison, "it's rumoured that aliens – er, sorry," he said, suddenly aware of Leon's and Aurore's presence. "Well, there are rumours that the landing was watched by spaceships that weren't ours, that sat on a nearby crater rim. It's said that NASA stopped that report from going public."

"Another one from the conspiracists – albeit those with a little more imagination," said Mr Smiley.

"Actually, it is true," said Aurore. "A Martian ship was sent to witness the event – but it remained out of range of detection."

Mr Smiley seemed taken aback. "Is that so? Why didn't we know this?"

"I do not know," replied Aurore innocently. "It is in our archives."

"Leon, did you know this?" asked Mr Knutt.

"No, Mr Knutt," said Leon. "I did not." Again, he regarded Aurore questionably. He had studied the archives before coming to Earth and could recall nothing about this.

"OK, folks," said Mr Smiley. "You have ten minutes to take it all in while we cycle around the site.

"Then we'll head out over higher ground to Apollo 16, across to 14 and 12, and return via Copernicus Crater and Apollo 15, and finally, the last landing site, 17, before returning to base.

The trip to the Apollo 16 site took only twenty minutes over rugged and heavily cratered highland terrain. Here was the familiar base section of the lunar lander, but this site was surrounded by evidence of a great deal more activity. The footprint trails of astronauts Charlie Duke and John Young were still there, plus there was their lightly dust-covered rover that they had used to drive farther afield over the lunar surface. Unlike the Apollo 11 site, the flag was still standing, although it was bleached white by the unbridled solar radiation.

From there, they proceeded westward on another short suborbital hop to visit the Apollo 14 and Apollo 12 sites.

It is quite odd how quickly humans can become rather blasé to events or situations where a degree of familiarity has set in. Just as public interest began to wane in the Apollo missions themselves into the early 1970s, the children's interest, at least, began to wane a little with every site.

From Apollo 12, their route took them north across Oceanus Procellarum towards Copernicus, a huge ninety-kilometre wide impact crater. The transit time was ideal to take a spot of lunch. The children enthusiastically grabbed lunch bags and settled down on the floor of the central hub of the craft. It was like sitting on the back of a fast moving boat, but instead of waves passing beneath them, the transparent floor around them showed ever-changing patterns of light and shadow formed by areas of interspersed plains and battered uplands. Through the upper section of see-through wall at the rearward side of the cabin, the Earth hung like a bright globular lampshade.

Leon dipped into his bag and was pleased to find a wedge of chocolate cake. He peeled back the wrapper and started on it.

"Aren't you supposed to eat your pudding last?" commented Lucy.

Leon shrugged. His expression said '*Does it really matter?*'

Dominic, who was already halfway through his first sandwich, jumped to Leon's defence: "And who wrote the rules on that?" he spluttered.

Camille sat next to Aurore. She took out a small tub of mixed salad and glanced over at her friend. "So, what did you bring? Oh, what's that?" she asked.

Aurore was looking at a note she had withdrawn from her own lunch bag. At Camille's attention, she said, "Oh, it is nothing." She folded it over and dropped it back into her bag. In its place she picked out a flat green triangle that looked a little like a tortilla chip and began to nibble at it nonchalantly.

Mr Smiley pulled his own lunch pack to his lap as he monitored their course over the landscape. He retrieved a flatbread wrap (it was chilli chicken and salad) and took a bite. Just then, a voice – a male voice – piped up on the comms system.

"Pod Nine, this is Tsiolkovsky. Do you read?"

Mr Smiley waved his hand over his armrest. "This is Nine. Go ahead."

"Jim, this is Winsom." He didn't sound his usual calm self.

"Karl, what's up? Any news?"

"Better go to headset, Jim. Something's definitely

up."

Mr Smiley looked over at Mr Knutt, whose face was also showed some concern. As did those of the other adults on board.

Mr Smiley pulled a thin headset ring from around his collar over his head. When its speaker buds sat over his ears, he said again, "Go ahead."

"Jim, there's been nothing from Fred Sparks. Or from anyone Mars-side. It seems that all comms systems are down. And the Martians have left."

Mr Smiley sat up in his chair. He automatically waved his hand over his armrest and the pod slowed down. He looked around the cabin. The children were occupied with their lunches and inter-chat. The adults, meanwhile, had picked up that something was wrong, and were looking his way. He tried to avoid eye contact with any of them. Mr Knutt came over and silently mouthed 'Problem?'

Mr Smiley nodded and waved him back.

He spoke quietly into the microphone. "What do you mean, they've left? Who? When?"

"Most of them, except Wilma Sparks and a few others. The last pod left about ten minutes ago. They all appear to be setting out on a Mars trajectory."

"Skiel'aeljtın?"

"Gone. With the others."

"Have you spoken with HQ?"

"Yes, same there. They don't know why; nor can they make contact with Mars. Not sure what's going on, but I think you'd better get back here."

"Yeah," said Mr Smiley. "On our way."

He was about to end the communication when Winsom's voice spiked again. "Wait! We're picking up

125

some incoming!"

"What?" asked Mr Smiley.

"Looks like a meteoroid swarm."

"And we're just seeing it *now*?" asked Mr Smiley incredulously. Earth technology wasn't as advanced as the Martians', but it could detect most near-Earth rocks of a given size.

But there was no reply. A buzz of static flared over Mr Smiley's speakers. He winced. He waved his hand to cancel it. Then he turned to address everyone.

"Folks, I'm sorry, but please return to your seats. We have to return to the base immediately."

"What is it?" asked Mr Knutt.

"Maybe nothing, but caution dictates." Then Mr Smiley leaned closer to Mr Knutt and whispered. "Fred and everyone are offline, and the Martian contingent has departed."

"Oh?" said Mr Knutt.

4

Mr Smiley put the pod into an automated sub-orbital return mode. Then he called up a display that showed the Moon, which he expanded to take in the Earth and near-Earth space. His eyes widened. So did those of many around in the cabin. Tracking perceptibly towards both the Earth and the Moon were seven objects of various sizes. None of them looked small.

"Computer, ETA for first arrival," said Mr Smiley.

"Specify location," said a voice the others hadn't heard before. It was female and carried a slight Martian inflection.

"Earth, then the Moon."

"Earth," replied the computer right away. "First impact estimated in ninety-seven minutes; eastern seaboard United States. The Moon –"

"*Impact*?" said Mrs Westfield.

Suddenly the atmosphere in the cabin grew more tense.

"The Moon," continued the computer. "Impact in ninety-three minutes."

"Location?" commanded Mr Smiley.

"First impact: Mare Crisium."

"Next?" said Mr Smiley.

"Moon; Tsiolkovsky crater. Ninety-eight minutes."

Mr Smiley's face paled. He waved his hand and the display collapsed. The computer voice could now only be heard through his own headset.

"Estimated blast magnitude?" he said quietly.

"Based on estimated object size and mass, and velocity of 16 kilometres per second, yield estimate is 35.2 megatons. Crater generated: 844 metres in diameter; ejecta spread: 8.2 kilometres."

He waved his hand again, and said, "Karl, do you read?"

"Here, Jim."

"Are you seeing the radar data?"

"Yes, we're looking at it. I've started evacuation of all non-essential personnel to the shelters."

"Good," said Mr Smiley. "What have we got in terms of evac craft?"

"Yeah, that's a problem. There's the XL-67 Cargo and the resident shuttle in North hangar. The shuttle in South Lobe is out of commission. And then there's you."

"That's it? For two hundred and forty people?"

"Afraid so. The shelters are the only way. You'll need to get back here asap."

"Yeah. I suppose an abort to Earth is out of the question?"

"No way. The first event there will be in the North Atlantic, off the coast of Florida, followed by one in the Western Pacific; both surviving entry. The second one, Jim – it's estimated at 240 metres; 882 megatons on impact. Both coasts of the United States, Japan – darn, all the Pacific nations – are preparing as best they can for major shocks and tsunamis. Trust me, you don't want to be re-entering the atmosphere when those babies come in. And they're not alone, as you've probably seen."

"OK, Karl. Get on with it. I'm taking over here on manual. We'll aim to be back there within twenty minutes."

"See you then. Over and out," said Winsom.

9 - ATTACK

The pod landed back at the North Lobe hangar. It was met by Karl Winsom and Caroline Miller. Mr Smiley wasted no time in getting everyone off and getting up to speed with the latest information as they walked.

"Any idea why the Martians departed without saying a word?"

"No," replied Caroline. "We're thinking it could be related to the edict given by High Councillor Smiall'kes'hep."

"But what about the asteroids? Coincidence?"

"Hard to say at this point," said Mr Winsom.

"OK, this one headed for us – any idea where it's predicted to hit?"

"Pretty close," said Mr Winsom. We should be just outside its ejecta range, but that's difficult to be certain, of course."

"Well, *that* seems less like a coincidence," said Mr Smiley.

"Hm," conceded Mr Winsom.

"And you've heard nothing from Fred Sparks?"

"Not a thing," said Caroline. "Wilma's in the command centre. She wants to talk to you."

"Of course. OK, get these folks to the main shelter,

then meet me in my office. We have one hour."

2

Caroline Miller led the children and their parents down the main corridor.

"We have emergency bunkers built into the mountain of Tsiolkovsky itself. We'll take the North Lobe tube-shuttle directly there. You'll be perfectly safe. It's built to withstand an event such as this."

She tried a smile, but none of the parents were having it.

"*What is going on*?" demanded Mrs Westfield.

Caroline stopped in her tracks. The shuttle port lay ahead. She turned to face them.

"I'm sorry. You deserve an explanation, but there is not much time. Please, as soon as we get to the shelter…"

"No. *Now*," insisted Mrs Westfield.

"OK, OK," said Caroline. "We are tracking an asteroid heading for this location. It is a possibility that the base is in danger. We need to seek cover urgently."

"Say that again," said Mr Tiddler.

The children looked on, alarm written on their faces. Mr Knutt stepped in. "Ah, children, why don't you come this way? Give your parents a few minutes?"

He led them forward along the side corridor that led to the shuttle port, from where a shuttle train ran underground to the bunker facility. They entered a node area, a cross roads space in the corridor, where signs pointed to a surface airlock to their left and to a power relay station to the right. Here, in this circular area, were couches and vending machines. Mr Knutt encouraged the children to sit while their parents hung back to talk to Miss Miller.

As he understood it, there was the best part of an hour to go until the first meteoroid arrived at Tsiolkovsky. The crater itself was huge – around 110 miles across. It was likely that it would impact a long way from here, but there was no point in taking chances.

Mr Flynn. Where was Mr Flynn?

Mr Knutt stood up, and almost immediately there was a dull *boom*, like a muffled explosion. Simultaneously, the building shook and he was knocked off his feet. The lights blinked off as a concussive wave threw him and the children across the node, where they landed in a heap. Raucous klaxons began to sound as a gasping, hissing sound filled the air. Emergency lighting flickered on to accompany the angry red pulses of the klaxon lights.

Atmospheric breach.

Mr Knutt lay on his side. He felt something warm and wet trickle down his face. *I'm bleeding*, he thought.

He struggled to look up. Through his daze, he could see through the curved windows something like black rain falling all around onto the lunar landscape, coating the visible parts of the base with dust and fragments of regolith.

He became aware of the emergency air-lock doors either side of him closing to contain the pressure drop; just as he had a sense of bodies scrambling away back in the direction of the North Lobe's main corridor.

With the pressure drop, his own suit had activated,

and now it was inflating around him. His wristbands and collar band had released their contents and someone now was helping him to get the face visor and gloves on. As he breathed the first of the suit's supply of oxygen, he looked up to see that it was Leon, who was already fully into his suit. Leon helped him to sit up. He nodded. When he had recovered sufficiently to speak, Mr Knutt asked, "The others?"

"All OK," replied Leon.

"Good. What happened?"

"I am not sure. A meteorite, I think. There is a new crater outside. The explosion has destroyed the entrance to the shuttle port ahead. The pressure doors have closed on that side and behind us. The grown-ups have escaped back to the main part of North Lobe."

"So we're trapped here?" asked Mr Knutt.

"I am not sure," replied Leon. "Come on, Mr Knutt. Try to get to your feet. We need to get out of here. We are losing atmospheric pressure, and these suits will not last very long."

Mr Knutt nodded again. He leaned forward onto his knees, and then used the wall to his side to pull himself up. He was pleased, at least to see that all of the children were waiting for him, all in their suits as they had been briefed on their arrival.

"Is everyone alright?" he asked. It came out muffled and barely audible over the klaxons' grating sound. All of the children, eyes wide through their masks, nodded.

He turned to the airlock doors behind him, the way they had come. He stepped closer and peered through. To his right, he could see that the wall of the corridor had been torn open. Rocky debris had spilled through a three-foot hole where a window had been.

Down the corridor, on the other side of another set of emergency doors, he could make out movement. Then he realised that there were people there. It was Caroline Miller and the children's parents, all thankfully safe too. Miss Miller saw him and gestured to the wall beside her. Then she pointed at him and repeated the gesture. He looked around and saw a comms panel. One of the buttons was lit.

He became aware of Leon by his side. Mr Knutt looked at Leon, who nodded. Mr Knutt pressed the button. The sound of the klaxons died.

"Is everyone OK?" asked Miss Miller.

"Yes, yes," said Mr Knutt. He looked around. "We are all OK. Thankfully."

Leon and he could both hear the voices of the parents saying things like 'Thank God,' and 'What do we do now?'

"What happened?" asked Mr Knutt.

"We're not sure," said Miss Miller. "It seems a smaller undetected meteoroid was ahead of the pack. Now, we've got to get moving in case there are others."

"We appear to be trapped between two pressure doors," continued Mr Knutt. "Now, I know that normal procedure is to find the safe room and wait for assistance. But under the circumstances, I'm not sure that will necessarily happen... in time," he said.

"There's a leak of atmosphere coming from somewhere – not large, but..."

He forced a smile, although he was doubtful anyone could see it. "I don't suppose the doors can be overridden?"

"Not from the inside," replied Caroline. "But listen. You're in a node section. That means you have options. I'm assuming that if your atmospheric pressure is largely intact, those are either undamaged, or their emergency airlocks are engaged. The corridor on your north side is short; it leads to an exterior service hatch. That's your best option. There are usually one or two LEVs – that is, lunar excursion vehicles – on the ramp. We call them bugs. You'll need to get into one of them. You should all fit – just. There will be life-support for all of you for up to four hours.

"But please listen carefully. We're hearing that the main corridor of North Lobe has also been breached, behind us, in the direction of the main hangar.

"Mr Smiley advises that you drive all the way to the hangar and board the pod for the short hop to the ancillary hangar at the end of South Lobe. There are bug hatches and tube-shuttle stations in both West Lobe and South Lobe, but we think it'll take too long to drive all the way around North Lobe to get to them. From the South Lobe hangar, Leon and Aurore will lead you through the Martian section to its tube-shuttle. It's near to City City Square. We'll wait for you there. But hurry. There's not much time."

"Wait," said Mr Knutt. "I'm not a pilot. I can't fly the pod."

"No," said Miss Miller. "But Leon can. Or Aurore."

Mr Knutt looked at Leon. "*You can?*"

Leon nodded. "And I can drive the LEV," he said calmly. "I spent one day with a maintenance crew when we stayed here in term time last year. I can do it."

"Leon," said Caroline. "Can you fly the pod to South

Lobe?"

"Yes," answered Leon. "Or I could fly it back to Earth?"

Mr Knutt raised his eyebrows.

"No," said Miss Miller. "There is no time. Earth is in danger too. Just bring it around as soon as possible. Now, all of you, get going. Try to let us know when you're in a bug. Good luck."

3

Miss Miller ended the call.

"This way," said Leon. He immediately led Mr Knutt back to the others.

"Follow me," he said to them all.

"Where are we going?" asked Lucy.

"Are we going to die?" asked Emily. Her voice sounded strained.

"Not if I can help it," said Leon. He smiled at Emily.

She tried to smile back through her misty visor.

"Come on. We are going to find a way out of here."

Dominic was unusually quiet. He and the others followed Leon down the short side corridor sign-posted as NL-SE 4. They soon came to a T-junction with a regular sliding door. It was fully lit here; a good sign. The power supply was uninterrupted. Nevertheless, Leon looked through the door's clear panels before pressing a button to open it. It whooshed open. To the right, there was a short stub of corridor leading to laboratories and workshops, and a thick window that looked out onto the lunar surface. Debris littered the visible part of the surface, and they could just see the damaged exterior of the corridor section that led to the shuttle port.

Miraculously, this part of the complex appeared untouched. Leon led them to the left and there before them were three red-panelled hatches and a sign above them that read 'North Lobe – Surface Egress 4'.

Leon quickly moved forward to the central hatch. Set in each of its two sliding doors was a triangular window. There was another in the wall to the left of the hatch. He looked through the two door windows and moved to the third, which looked out to the exterior.

"Check the others," he said.

Dominic stepped forward, followed by Mr Knutt.

"What are we looking for?" asked Dominic.

"One: that there is a bug there. Two: that it is not damaged," replied Leon.

Soon it was evident that the one on the right had a cracked front screen. Leon stepped towards the middle one. He typed a code into the panel keypad, and the hatch doors parted, followed by two grey inner doors that belong to the LEV itself.

The inner space was about the size of the interior of a large transit van. Up front, there were two seats, with a broad U-shaped steering wheel before the one on the left. Behind them, two more seats; then after these, a series of fold-down seats around a wide aisle that might be used for carrying equipment.

They all hurried aboard. Leon climbed into the driver's seat and powered up the bug. All systems came on immediately. A relief. Mr Knutt took the front passenger seat, and everyone else found a seat behind.

The hatch doors closed, and Aurore looked wistfully back. She seemed bewildered. No-one had mentioned her guardian, Miss Skiel'aeljtın. Their parting words earlier had involved Miss Sky telling her to find her immediately on their return from their Apollo excursion.

Mr Knutt led the way on removing his suit's visor hood and gloves. As soon as the connection was broken, its oxygen feed was cut off.

Leon pressed a button on the bug's dashboard, and they all felt it release from the dock. The lights flickered for an instant as it came under its own power. Mr Knutt was about to ask Leon if his feet could reach the pedals when he realised that it *had* no pedals.

"Everything OK, Leon? Know where we have to go?" asked Mr Knutt.

Leon nodded. He was concentrating on driving the bug off the ramp and onto the lunar surface. Once they cleared the end of the maintenance wing, they came into the full glare of the sunlit surface. The forward screens automatically adjusted their tint to compensate. A little way ahead was a bright new crater, perhaps thirty metres across. Rays of debris fanned out from it, and already the caterpillar treads of the bug were negotiating the uneven surface, while Leon steered around the numerous blocks that were a foot or larger in size. Some of these had caused the significant damage to parts of North Lobe.

Behind them, Dominic had revived sufficiently to offer to drive the bug for a bit. Mr Knutt turned him down, then called for him to be quiet as a voice came through the dashboard.

"Leon. This is Jim Smiley. Do you read? Over."

Mr Knutt looked at Leon, who pointed to a button on a panel nearest Mr Knutt. Mr Knutt pressed it.

"Howard here, Jim. We're on our way."

"Good. We picked up your motion. I've sent Caroline Miller and the children's parents onto the West Lobe tube-shuttle port. They'll be able to transfer to the shelter from there. I'll be staying on here with Karl Winsom and some other key staff. We need you to get around as soon as possible."

"Yes," said Mr Knutt.

"But," said Mr Smiley. "I should tell you that we can't locate your Mr Flynn. He hasn't reported to a shelter, and he's not in the horticultural wing in West Lobe. We're assuming he's at his quarters, but we can't be sure."

"He's not answering?"

"No. There's a contained breach between Dorms 4 and 5. He was quartered in 5. If he's there, he won't be able to get through to City Square and one of the shelters. He may be injured," added Mr Smiley.

"In that case, we need to try to find him," said Mr Knutt.

"There might not be time, Howard," said Mr Smiley quietly. "The asteroid's ETA is now at forty-six minutes. It's going to be close. You need to be in the shelter within forty at the latest."

"We'll bear that in mind," said Mr Knutt. But already his thoughts were on Mr Flynn. "How long to the hangar?" he asked.

"At your pace, twelve minutes. You need to pick it up," replied Mr Smiley.

"I am going as fast as I dare," said Leon from the driver's seat.

"I'll drive!" offered Dominic.

"No you will not!" said Emily firmly.

"And there's no closer docking station?" asked Mr Knutt.

"Ah, no. You'll need to use the hangar station. Now, be safe. And *hurry*."

4

Leon steered the bug around the edge of the new crater. It had been formed by a meteorite of perhaps a few tonnes, and was a sobering reminder of the scale of threat the larger asteroid posed.

In the distance, some three hundred metres away the long slab-like main building of North Lobe (which they were now travelling parallel with), the roof and communications dishes and spires of their destination, the hangar, were visible. Mr Knutt looked through the windows along the side of the building as they passed. There was no sign of life or movement. Somewhere in there was Mr Flynn, possibly injured. They couldn't leave him behind.

Could they? Must they? He pushed the thought from his mind.

"Are we there yet?" asked Camille from the back.

Mr Knutt realised he had neglected the children somewhat during this crisis. If the situation hadn't been serious, Camille's question might have raised some laughter, the classic question posed by many a child during a long car journey. He turned to face them all.

"About five minutes," he said as calmly as he could muster. "Now, I want you to know that everything is going to be alright. Leon is doing a fine job of getting us to the hangar safely. You probably heard that we appear to have misplaced Mr Flynn. Once we dock, I want you all to board the pod with Leon. *I* will go to look for Mr Flynn. Leon will wait for no longer than fifteen minutes, when he will seal the hatch and get the pod over to South Lobe. There he will guide you through the Martian section – you'll all need your face masks and gloves back on for that – and to the tube shuttle there that will take you to where your parents will be waiting. Is that understood?"

All of the children nodded.

"Leon?"

"Yes, Mr Knutt," replied Leon.

"Hopefully, I'll be back with Mr Flynn before then and we can all go together."

"I'll come with you, Mr Knutt," said Dominic.

"Me too," said Lucy.

"Absolutely not," said Mr Knutt.

"But if he is injured, you might need some help," said Dominic.

"That's possible," conceded Mr Knutt. "Very well, you stay close to me."

"OK," both replied.

5

Mr Flynn pulled off his headphones and yawned. Unusually for him, he had taken an extended rest period this afternoon, and after a Ploughman's sandwich and a pot of tea for his lunch, he had kicked back on his couch to catch up on some podcasts of *Gardeners' Question Time*. Now, he found himself waking to soft static playing in his ears, and a sense of disorientation that sometimes arises after an unplanned mid-day nap.

He swung his legs off the couch and scratched his head. He still had his non-regulation green gardener's overalls on, and dirt under his nails.

Age startin' t'catch up on yer, Flynn, my lad, he thought.

He got to his feet and wandered towards the tinted windows of his quarters, which looked out northeast from North Lobe.

Shower and change, then go see how those avocados are getting on.

His attention was distracted by movement; something passing from right to left outside, a floor below him. He peered out the window to see a maintenance LEV kicking up dust, which settled quickly behind it. He became aware of the sizeable crater to the right of his window, and frowned.

Was that there yesterday? Must 'ave been. Don' know 'ow I missed that, he thought. *Not that I've spent much time in 'ere.*

He stepped away from the window and made for the bathroom. *Time to get cleaned up an' back to work.*

6

Leon reversed the bug onto the docking bay at the hangar and made it secure. He pressed a button and the rear doors opened with a small hiss, followed by the base airlock doors.

"Good job," said Mr Knutt.

"That was brilliant, Leon," said Lucy.

"Thank you," said Leon, who was clearly relieved to have arrived safely.

When they emerged from the LEV station into the main hangar corridor, it was clear the situation had altered in the short space of time since they were last here. There was no-one else about. Most of the equipment and lights were running as normal, but something was different. Perhaps it was just the absence of people, but there was a ringing, ominous stillness, a quiet tension in the air that was almost palpable.

Mr Knutt looked at his watch. They had thirty-two minutes. Less actually, considering that was when the asteroid was expected to strike.

"Right, everyone, gather around. Leon, please lead Emily, Camille and Aurore to the pod and make it ready. Lucy, Dominic and I will check Mr Flynn's quarters. We'll be back as soon as possible.

"What if you're not back in fifteen minutes like you said?" asked Emily.

"Perhaps now give us five more?" said Mr Knutt with a small smile. "But beyond that, Leon, I'm sorry, but it falls to you to decide what's best. But risking the rest of you will *not* be acceptable. Now, everyone, *go*."

Leon led the others towards the hangar, while Mr Knutt strode off in the opposite direction. Lucy and Dominic struggled to keep up with Mr Knutt's long stride, and settled instead on a half-run. Pretty soon, Dominic decided he might as well run the rest of the way, and he suggested to Mr Knutt that he go on ahead. After a moment's hesitation, Mr Knutt nodded.

7

Mr Flynn stepped out of his quarters. The door closed

automatically behind him. To his right, right where he'd left it, was a trolley laden with fruits and vegetables that he'd picked earlier and intended to run down to the restaurants in City Square when they reopened. He spun it around on its castors and pushed it out towards the main corridor of North Lobe.

8

Mr Smiley answered his comms unit. "Yes, Karl. What's the latest?"

Karl Winsom had remained in the base command centre overlooking City Square when Mr Smiley left for his office. Wilma Sparks, Leon's mum, was with him. Between them, they had been trying to determine what was happening on Mars and regarding the sudden departure of the Martian scientists and diplomats (including, disappointingly, Miss Sky). Plus, critically, about the incoming cluster of meteoroids.

"A couple of things. Neither good," answered Mr Winsom.

"Fire away," said Mr Smiley resignedly.

"OK, firstly, we've established contact with Fred Sparks."

Mr Smiley sat up. "Well, that's good. Isn't it?"

"Yes. And no," replied Mr Winsom. "Wilma?"

"With comportal communications nullified," reported Mrs Sparks, "it occurred to me that my husband would seek any available means to contact us. It seems he found my grandmother's original equipment that she used to communicate by radio with Mr Tesla in 1899. We scanned for a range of frequencies, and detected some of his repeated transmissions. Since then, we have established contact. How long this will remain so is uncertain. We have evidence also that the Sentinel has awakened and is altering its orbit."

Mr Smiley was taken aback. "*When*?" he asked.

The authorities on Earth had been aware of the alien satellite for some time, but all attempts to analyse it or communicate with it had failed. It had seemed inert, dead; although no-one had been able to explain how it had maintained its orbit.

"About the time we started to communicate with Fred," said Mr Winsom. "It's widening the radius of its orbit. Naturally, we can't be sure if there is a connection. Nor can we ascertain whose side it is on."

"*Side*?" asked Mr Smiley.

"Jim, the comms silence, the Martian evacuation, the meteoroid swarm – they're all related. We're under attack!"

9

Dominic arrived outside Mr Flynn's apartment. He was pleased that he wasn't breathing hard – thank his football training for that – and he had arrived far ahead of Mr Knutt. He pressed the buzzer and waited for a moment. Nothing. He tried again. A moment later, still nothing. No sound, no indication of life from within. Finally, he made a fist and hammered on the door.

"Mr Flynn. It's me, Dominic Addison. Are you in there?"

"No, lad. I'm 'ere," came a voice from behind him.

Dominic spun around, almost fainting.

"What's all the fuss about, lad?"

Dominic took a deep breath. "I, er... where have you been? We've got to get out of here."

"I forgot me 'edphones, didn' I? Wanted to listen to me gardening programmes this afternoon while I did some prunin'."

He paused. "Get out of 'ere? What on Earth for?"

"It's Mr Knutt; no, well, it's all of us. There's an asteroid coming and we've got to go. *Come on. Quick. There's not much time.*"

"Hold tight," said Mr Flynn. "Go where?"

"To the tube-shuttle at South Lobe. An asteroid's going to hit us in – well, *really* soon! We've come to rescue you."

Mr Flynn stood there, scratching his head. "Well, I never," he said. "Where's the h'edmaster?"

Another voice answered. "Over here, Mr Flynn."

Mr Flynn looked up to see Mr Knutt and Lucy coming towards them.

"Blimey," said Mr Flynn, taking in Mr Knutt's appearance. His hair was dishevelled and there was a sore-looking red gash on his forehead with smears of dried blood below it and down his nose and cheek. "Beg your pardon. Wha' 'appened to you, h'edmaster?"

"Never mind that now, Mr Flynn," said Mr Knutt. "Dominic is completely right. We have to leave right now. We need to get back to the pod immediately."

"But the quickest way to the shelters is straight down to the Square –"

"It was," said Mr Knutt. "Until sections of the building, including the route to the North Lobe shelter, were damaged a little while ago by a meteor strike. We can't get through that way. So please, follow us."

145

Mr Flynn still looked perplexed, but he said, "Whatever you say, h'edmaster." He took hold of his trolley.

"What are you going to do with that?" asked Lucy.

"If we're goin' t'be in a shelter for a while, we're goin' to need a bit of fresh fruit. No point it goin' to waste."

10

Mr Smiley called Karl Winsom and Mrs Sparks from his office.

"Karl, Wilma, you can give me any updates when we're all together. Now, it's time for you to get out of there. Get to the shelter. I'll meet you there. I just need to check in with Howard Knutt and the children."

11

In the command centre, Karl Winsom turned to Mrs Sparks. "Go on ahead."

"You are coming to the shelter?" asked Mrs Sparks.

"Yes, but I need to do something first," he replied.

"What is it? I could help."

"We need to stay in touch with your husband. I need to secure his radio link and patch it through to the shelter comms."

"There is no time," said Mrs Sparks.

"He's our *only* source of information from Mars. If we *are* under attack, every bit of news might be vital. It won't take long. Please go."

Mrs Sparks hesitated for a moment, then nodded. She turned and made her way to the exit. She glanced back to see Mr Winsom disappearing through the doors on the opposite side.

12

"How long?" asked Emily.

No-one had to ask what she meant by that.

"Eighteen minutes," said Mr Knutt.

Over the comms system, Mr Smiley's voice reached them. "How are you doing, Howard?"

"We're just leaving. We have Mr Flynn."

"Glad to hear it, on both counts. See you soon. Godspeed," said Mr Smiley.

The pod rose cleanly through the roof hatch of the hangar. Once outside, the walls of the pod turned transparent. Perhaps it might have been better had they been set otherwise. Leon guided the pod in an arc towards the South Lobe. The journey would be a short one, minutes at most until they were back on the surface. Below, to their left, was a stark, fresh crater with bright streaks radiating out from it, so that it shone back in the dazzling sunlight like a star. Some of the streaks ended at the buildings of North Lobe. The damage was evident even from up here.

"*Phew*," remarked Mr Flynn, seeing it for the first time. "Anyone hurt?" He looked at Mr Knutt. "Apart from your good self?" he added.

"Thankfully, a few minor injuries only," said Mr Knutt. "As far as we know."

The pod levelled out and even now was beginning its shallow descent towards the smaller hanger building at the end of South Lobe. It had been used primarily for the berthing of Martian spacecraft, and was where most of the departing pods had left from this morning.

Mr Knutt addressed everyone. "Please get your suits ready with visors and gloves again. The hangar's atmosphere may be Martian in composition. Leon and Aurore excepted, of course."

Most of the children began to fiddle with their suits. Mr Knutt looked at Mr Flynn, who was dressed in a clean, but distinctly non-regulation set of overalls.

"Ah, I'm not sure what we're going to do about you, Mr Flynn."

Mr Flynn looked a little sheepish. "Um, summit will work out, h'edmaster."

When he looked around again, Mr Knutt noticed that Camille hadn't moved at all. She was staring through the roof of the pod. Her complexion glowed like porcelain in the brilliant sunlight.

"Camille, you too," he said.

"What is that?" she asked without moving her head.

Mr Knutt followed her gaze. Several of the others, Mr Flynn included, followed her gaze.

At first, the glare of the Sun made it difficult to see anything, but after a moment or two, a pattern of bright star-like points became evident. Mr Knutt's initial thought was that they looked like the Seven Sisters, a star cluster more formally known as the *Pleiades* – except these were surrounded by a gaseous green glow. And they were moving; the two brightest ones perceptibly against the backdrop of a few visible stars.

Then, suddenly, something streaked by at a steep downward angle before them. In was gone an instant, but replaced almost immediately by a rising spray of debris, of rock and metal and the gaseous plume of an explosion.

"Good heavens," said Mr Knutt, the words escaping his mouth.

Leon reacted quickly. The view tilted dramatically as he rolled the pod away from the blast. "Hold on, please."

"Well, that's that," said Mr Flynn, who was staring down at the base.

"Mr Flynn?" asked Mr Knutt.

"It came down in the angle between West Lobe an' South Lobe, h'edmaster. Looks like the South 'angar's taken a hit, and some o' the structure around City Square. Oh, an' West Lobe, where the hydroponics labs are," he sighed.

"So we might not be able to land?" asked Lucy.

The strain showed on her face. Beside her, Emily was wide-eyed and visibly trembling. Tears welled in the corners of her eyes. Camille and Aurore sat quietly together, while Dominic was doing his best to remain stoic.

Leon waved his hand over the command armrest. The walls of the pod lost their transparency, except for the forward portion of wall. He called up a graphical overlay that showed their position in relation to the base and the Moon. It also showed the lead asteroid and a number of smaller objects accompanying it that the base's sensors hadn't detected. One of these smaller fragments had evidently just struck the base. Another was about to impact somewhere else in Tsiolkovsky crater.

"What do we do now?" asked Dominic.

"Pod Nine, are you there? Leon? Howard?" It was the base. Mr Smiley.

Leon answered. "Yes, Mr Smiley. We are safe. For now."

"Thank goodness. We detected another strike. Are you damaged?"

"No. We avoided it," answered Mr Knutt. "We are turning now to come back around, but it appears that parts of the base sustained some damage."

"Yes, we're detecting that from both West and South Lobes, and the hub."

"Where are you?" asked Mr Knutt.

"I'm in the shelter. Wilma Sparks is here, and all the children's parents. We're missing one, though. Karl Winsom. Can you see where the hub got hit?"

"One moment, we're just coming back over the base now," said Mr Knutt. "Oh," he said.

"What are you seeing?" asked Mr Smiley.

Mr Knutt swallowed. "The outer ring of the hub between the two Lobes is destroyed. And the command centre has taken a hit."

There was a moment of silence over the communications. Finally, Mr Smiley said, "Copy."

Then he said, "You'd better land as soon as you can. I have a lot of anxious faces here looking this way."

"Ah, that might be a problem, Jim. It looks like South Lobe has sustained some serious damage."

There was another pause before Mr Smiley spoke again. Finally he said quietly, "Leon, can you make cislunar space?"

"I can get us into orbit," said Leon.

"Not orbit," said Mr Smiley. "When the big one hits, it'll throw up a lot of debris. Earth is off the agenda too, for now. You need to get into the space between the Moon and the Earth and ride this out. Can you do that?"

Leon answered right away. "Yes, but –"

"Then do it," said Mr Smiley.

10 - SENTINEL

"Please, everyone, do not leave your seats," said Leon. He waved his left hand over his other armrest and a small blue hologram of a sphere formed above it. Leon placed his hand over it. He rotated it and immediately the pod shot spaceward. The base and Tsiolkovsky crater fell away below them. The acceleration was noticeable.

"How long do we have, please, Mr Knutt?" he asked calmly.

"Fourteen minutes," answered Mr Knutt. "Is that long enough to get far enough away?"

"Oh yes," said Leon. He glanced over at Mr Knutt. "But we are going to get closer."

"*Excuse me*?" said Mr Knutt. "Now, Leon, this is not the –"

"Leon, you're crazy, mate," said Dominic, who had been uncharacteristically quiet for far too long. "We can't stop that thing."

"Please, Leon, just get us somewhere safe," pleaded Emily.

"No, we cannot stop it," replied Leon. "But we may be able to divert it."

"But Leon –" began Lucy.

"Look," said Leon. He drew their attention to the

screen graphic, which now showed the incoming asteroid in relation to the Moon. He waved his hand and its trajectory became marked by a line – red behind it for the path it had followed, and yellow forward of it to its projected impact on the Moon. It ended at the centre of Tsiolkovsky crater – more precisely, at the base itself.

"Do you see the kink in the red line?" asked Leon. "That is a course correction. It is being *guided*. Recall my mother's lecture. Mars long ago had the technology to affect the course of asteroids near our planet. All Martian children learn about the First World and the cataclysm that changed it, which has passed into legend. No-one believed that kind of technology might still exist today. But this is the evidence for it."

"And this," he said. He called up another image, of a green dot streaking away from the asteroid trailing a glowing green tail. And another, of the asteroid that was approaching Earth. This too had a similar object flying away from it. "Zero-point engines." he said plainly.

"What's your plan, lad?" asked Mr Flynn.

"We try to nudge the asteroid off course. Now that it has been released. Our force-field will protect the pod. A small diversion may still mean it misses its target. *But it must be made soon.*"

"Leon," said Mr Knutt. "A laudable idea, but it sounds too dangerous. Mr Smiley –"

"Mr Knutt," said Leon. He had never cut the headmaster off like this before. "The asteroid is targeted precisely at Tsiolkovsky base. If we do nothing, a direct hit will release energy approaching that of the most powerful hydrogen bomb ever developed by humans. Nothing will survive." He looked at Mr Knutt without blinking. "The shelters will not protect them."

There was a round of gasps. An involuntary yelp escaped someone.

Mr Knutt stared back at Leon. He nodded slowly. "Then we must try," he said quietly.

Leon wasted no more time. He ran his hands over the armrests in a blur of actions. The graphics on the forward screen altered rapidly. He spoke as he continued to work. "Everyone, please keep your arms clear of your legs. I'm about to strap you in. Prepare for rapid acceleration."

Everyone, including Mr Knutt and Mr Flynn did as they were instructed. Wide bands of what looked like smooth, shiny metal or plastic curled out from the undertray of their seats and fastened together seamless over their occupants' thighs.

The graphical display plotted a course out of lunar orbit on a long parabolic path that overshot the asteroid before curving back round to come up behind it.

"Ready. Three-two-one," said Leon.

The acceleration was swift. The closest it could be compared to (for those who had had the experience) was a fast-starting rollercoaster; one that takes your breath away at the same time as leaving your stomach behind and your head in a spin. Most of the children, and Mr Knutt, held on to their seats. Only Leon, Aurore and Mr Flynn seemed to take it in their stride.

My dad would love this, thought Dominic. *Better than anything at Blackpool.*

Then it struck him that if this didn't work…

His eyes became moist, and pushed away the thought.

At their velocity, the pod flew past the asteroid in seconds. To those aboard, it might have seemed they had missed it, but Leon immediately reduced speed and they felt the pod turn in a wide arc and soon the asteroid, with the Moon behind it, came into view. Leon closed the distance to it, matching its velocity. They could now see it for what it was: a large, roughly ovoid mass, coal black, and covered in rocky debris, like a huge sooty lump that tumbled slowly end over end.

"Ah. This might be a little tricky," said Leon. "Aurore, can you assist?"

Aurore, who had been sitting quietly beside Camille, seemed surprised to be asked, but she tapped her seat and its lap restraints released. She stepped over to the command seat.

Leon spoke to her in Martian. She nodded and replied, and Leon made way for her to access the primary armrest controls. She looked at the forward screen and made some adjustments, which were reflected in a change in the graphical overlay. After a moment she said, in English, "It is done."

Leon explained what was happening. "I have never performed such a manoeuvre before. My knowledge and experience is mainly from theory and simulators. Aurore is especially gifted in physics and spatial geometry. She has configured the pod to match the rotation of the asteroid as best we can."

He took the controls again. The walls became completely transparent again as Leon nudged the pod closer to the asteroid.

"We have eleven minutes," said Mr Knutt soberly.

Leon did not reply, but moved the pod until the asteroid loomed above them. It was perhaps seven times their length; thousands of tonnes in mass. At a given point, Leon waved his hand and sat back. The rest, it seemed, was down to the pod's computer and Aurore's programming.

"Our force-field has been configured to cushion us from what we are about to try," said Leon.

The pod moved closer until a pale green glow appeared on the asteroid's underside. The glow was joined by orange, red and yellow sparks where the pod's force-field came into contact with the surface. There was a small jolt and they felt the pod's engines (or whatever powered the craft) draw more energy as it pressed into the surface of the asteroid. After a few moments, the pod backed away a little, then it repeated the action. It did this several times more. Each time it pulled back, a cloud of smaller rocks and dust was drawn off the surface of the asteroid.

Finally, the operation was over. Leon took over control again and backed the pod away from the asteroid. Immediately, the asteroid began to shrink.

"That should be enough," said Leon. He looked over at Aurore, who had returned to her seat. She nodded.

"It looks like it's still heading for the Moon," said Lucy.

"It is," said Leon. "But it should not now impact close to the base."

"How far away?" asked Dominic anxiously.

Leon waved his hand over his armrest and a line extended from the asteroid to a point on the rim of Tsiolkovsky crater. It was approximately sixty miles from the base.

"Is that enough?" asked Emily.

Leon nodded. Then he swiped his hand again. Almost immediately, a voice came over the comms system.

"Leon, Howard. *Finally!*"

It was Mr Smiley.

"Where have you been? We lost contact."

"That was me, Mr Smiley," said Leon. "You might have tried to dissuade me and there was no time to be lost."

"What –"

Mr Knutt interjected. "Jim, it's Howard. There is no time for discussion. In eight minutes, the asteroid will strike the eastern rim of the crater. You should be out of immediate danger. "As you probably know," he added quietly, "it had aligned itself for a direct hit."

The children, including Leon, looked at him.

"Yes," said Mr Smiley. We learned of the course change from Karl Winsom. We'll talk about that when you get back here. "But, great job, Leon. Meanwhile, I'm sorry to report that Karl Winsom didn't make it."

Mr Knutt straightened. Mr Winsom. He didn't know him very well, but he had seemed like a decent chap.

"I'm sorry," said Mr Knutt.

"Yeah," said Mr Smiley. "OK. Now –"

They were suddenly interrupted by a brilliant flash of light and a wave of static interference that broke up their communications. After a few moments, contact was re-established.

"*What on Earth was that?*" asked Mr Knutt.

"I believe it is the Sentinel," said Leon.

"Copy that," said Mr Smiley.

"Has it exploded?" asked Dominic.

"No," replied Mr Smiley. "It's still there. Oh, and it's changing orbit again. The lead Earth-bound asteroid is gone. Leon, are you able to confirm?"

Leon adjusted the display. "Yes, Mr Smiley. We are seeing a debris field there."

The screen graphics showed a slowly dissipating cloud of particles near to the Earth.

"I believe most of it will burn up on entry," said Leon.

"Great. Wow, that thing really works! Your mother has more to say on this, when you can get back here, or safely to Earth. But for now, please stay at a safe distance. And keep an eye on everything, huh? We'll talk in a short while. Over and out."

At that, Mr Smiley was gone.

"What do we do now?" asked Lucy.

"Nothin', besides sittin' tight an' waitin', wouldn't you say, h'edmaster?" suggested Mr Flynn.

"Indeed, Mr Flynn," replied Mr Knutt.

2

Other than the sound of breathing of those waiting and the whirr of fans, the entire shelter was silent.

It had been cut two hundred metres into the central peak of Tsiolkovsky and extended fifty metres beneath it. It was completely self-sufficient, with power, resources, a command and communications centre, and accommodation to sustain a population of three hundred for up to two months. A fast underground tube-shuttle system linked each Lobe to the shelter.

It now housed two hundred and twenty five people,

including the children's parents, Caroline Miller and, of course, Mr Smiley, most of whom were gathered in the mid-level lounge area – the only space large enough to accommodate them all. A number of personnel remained on the base, either trapped there, or engaged in repair and recovery operations.

Everyone now awaited the impact of the asteroid.

"Twenty seconds," said Mr Smiley.

As the seconds counted down, even the sound of breathing quietened. Zero came and went, and nothing had changed. Another ten seconds passed.

"Brace, everybody," said Mr Smiley.

Mrs Westfield looked puzzled. She turned to Mr Tiddler. "What's happened?" she whispered.

"It will have hit already," he said. "The shock wave will take some seconds to arrive. Get ready."

The parents instinctively moved closer together. Mr Addison looked more serious than perhaps he had ever been – or at least, since Dominic and the other children were cut off from them during the evacuation and their narrow escape when the second small meteor had hit the base.

For each of them, of course, there was the worry about their children, but also for their spouses and families and friends back home on Earth, which was still threatened by at least four other sizeable asteroids.

Then it arrived, the primary shock wave from the impact. Like in an earthquake, the building around them jolted and shook and reverberated as the wave passed through the bedrock enclosing the shelter. As it met the airspace within the shelter itself, a deep, booming rumble filled the air, so that it was felt and heard simultaneously. Several people were thrown from their feet, as anything loose – chairs, cabinets, mugs of coffee – twisted or jumped or tipped over. Chips of concrete and plaster popped from the walls, and strung lights swayed with the movement.

After a few moments, the effect passed and sighs of relief filled the room. No-one dared voice what many were surely thinking – that a direct hit would not have been survivable.

"Everyone OK?" asked Mr Smiley. It was soon evident that, apart from a few instances of cuts and bruises, everyone in both the shelter and the base were alright.

"OK," said Mr Smiley. "There'll be some aftershocks, but that should have been the worst of it. Let's get back to work."

He turned to Caroline Miller. "Let's re-link with the OPP for a status update, and see if we can get back out to the base and organise whatever evac is necessary."

Caroline nodded, but before leaving, she said, "What about the children's parents? Shouldn't you say something to them?"

"I will," he replied. "Just as soon as I've spoken with Howard Knutt. If the South Lobe hangar's out of commission and Earth is off limits, they'll have to come back to North Lobe and take it from there. Meanwhile, I've got to try to re-gain contact with Fred Sparks." He looked over to the door, where Wilma Sparks waited patiently for him.

"OK, Howard, how are we doing?"

"Well, Jim, we are doing fine. How are you all?" asked Mr Knutt, aware of the eyes of all the children on him.

"Glad to hear it," replied Mr Smiley. "We're good. Shaken but not unduly stirred. A few minor injuries only. But you can tell the kids that all their parents are OK. Just worried about them, naturally."

Dominic, Lucy and Emily breathed sighs of relief. Camille looked like she was about to cry. Lucy moved over to comfort her when it appeared that Aurore was oblivious to her friend's feelings. She herself sat calmly and silently.

"That was quite a wallop. Must have looked impressive from up there," continued Mr Smiley.

"You have a fresh new crater in your neighbourhood. We will show you the video at some point," said Mr Knutt.

"Yeah, good," said Mr Smiley. "Now, what can you tell us from your vantage point?"

"Leon will update you," said Mr Knutt.

"Hello, Mr Smiley," said Leon.

"Hullo Leon. What you got?"

"Well, the Sentinel appears to have destroyed another asteroid. It looks like it missed another. I think it entered somewhere over the western Pacific.

"Copy. The OPP has confirmed it came down a hundred miles off the coast of Japan, where it has triggered major quakes and tsunamis in Japan and around the Pacific basin. The other one was projected to strike in the Gobi region of Mongolia; aimed, we believe, at China's Jiuquan Satellite Launch Centre. Evidently the Sentinel is focusing on taking out those posing the greatest threats – the probable ground strikes. It seems it can't stop them all."

"Perhaps we can do something?" suggested Dominic, who was beginning to bounce back to his old self after their successful mission.

"It is possible," said Leon. "There are two major ones left. If the Sentinel can destroy one, we may be able to intercept the other?"

"Er, that's a definite 'no', said Mr Smiley. "There's a chance you'll be in the way of the one it targets."

"But we –"

"Just get back here, Leon. Land back at North Lobe and wait there for someone to come along. And 'well done' again."

4

Across space, in high orbit about the Earth, the Sentinel patiently awaited the last of the cluster of asteroids. For millennia, it had silently, dutifully defended Earth against such invaders, emerging from its long sleep to intercept them. Then it would fall dormant again until such time it was needed again.

The Sentinel was self-powered, self-sustained. It had existed without detection by the humans until the beginning of their last century, and until this time, its function and the reason for its presence in its silent, perpetual polar orbit around their world had been unknown. It had resisted all attempts to analyse it, to communicate with it.

But now, it had revealed itself as a protector rather

than a potential foe. As the two remaining large asteroids closed in, it again began to glow from within, an icy green patch that spread outward from its core to flood its ancient darkly crystalline body with light. The intensity of the light increased until, suddenly, it was discharged. A plasma-like bolt, like green lightning, shot out across space and into the body of the forward asteroid. It held across five thousand miles of space until the vast rock began to glow like a red hot coal. Something behind it – no, *two* somethings, which themselves emitted a greenish glow – departed from the two asteroids and veered off into space.

The first asteroid exploded into a million fiery fragments that soon faded and died.

The Sentinel pivoted to target the second asteroid. But while it was formidable, it was of ancient design and not built for fast or nimble action. Before it could recharge for a second energy bolt, the two zero-point engines that had guided the asteroids, appeared as if from nowhere. One zoomed in and attached itself to the Sentinel. Immediately, it flared with power, pressing against the Sentinel, trying to force it down from orbit.

The Sentinel reacted, turning and released its energy at the second engine. It connected and immediately there was a searing explosion, greenish-white, that expanded rapidly, like a mini supernova. It overtook the Sentinel and the second engine. There was a second huge explosion that masked the Earth itself. When they subsided, the second asteroid, the zero-point engines, and the Sentinel, were gone.

5

Down on the Earth's surface, the Sun was joined momentarily by a second star. It flared brightly in the day sky, overtaking the Sun in intensity and casting a second set of shadows. It faded quickly, to be followed by streams of meteor trails that radiated from a point where its bright centre had been.

6

"Leon, come in. Are you still there?"

"Yes, Mr Smiley," replied Leon.

"What happened?"

"It appears the Sentinel has been destroyed," said Mr Knutt.

"*What?*"

"It exploded. But the second asteroid appears also to have been destroyed in the process."

There was a sound of a deep sigh over the comms. Finally, Mr Smiley said, "Well, that's some consolation. Get back here as soon as you can. I'll meet you at the bug terminal at North Lobe."

Leon didn't answer. Mr Knutt looked at him, and he seemed distracted with the controls.

"Leon?" asked Mr Knutt. "Is everything alright?"

Leon again failed to answer right away. He continued to move his hand over the armrest controls. Then he looked up at the screen graphical display and then at Mr Knutt. His brow was furrowed in a manner that Mr Knutt had not seen before, even through the current crisis.

"Is something wrong?"

Leon nodded. "I have lost control of the pod."

"What's that?" said Mr Smiley's voice.

"I am no longer in control of the pod," repeated Leon.

"You're out of control? Are you damaged?" pressed Mr Smiley.

"No," replied Leon. "It appears still to be under control. But not mine," he added.

11 - MARSBOUND

"*Mars?*" said Mr Smiley. "How can you be heading for Mars?"

"That is what our course projection shows," replied Leon.

"And what does Aurore say about it?" asked Mr Smiley. He didn't care that he voiced this on open comms. She had, after all, re-programmed the controls to divert the asteroid.

Aurore looked up calmly at the sound of her name. "I did only what I was asked to do," she said.

"She did help save us all," said Leon.

"Yeah, OK," conceded Mr Smiley. "But something's not right. Check it out, please – both of you – while we try to figure it out from this end."

2

Mr Smiley was with Mrs Sparks in the shelter command centre. He did not have to say anything. She had heard it all.

"What do you think happened?" he asked her.

"I do not know. The trajectory is deliberate. That is all we can say at this time."

"Is it possible that someone – Aurore, perhaps –

could have re-programmed it; or is operating the pod remotely? More importantly, are they capable of regaining control themselves?"

Mrs Sparks shook her head. "I do not think so. Leon has studied pod systems, but from an operational standpoint. I do not know Aurore's capabilities – she clearly is gifted at programming, but this would be beyond most Martians, of any age or ability. To answer this, we must contact my husband."

Mr Smiley absent-mindedly rubbed his chin. "What about Skiel'aeljtın?"

"Skiel'aeljtın? An administrator," answered Mrs Sparks. "I do not think she would have that capability. And there are the questions of motive and opportunity."

"Hm," said Mr Smiley. "But she left the base secretly with the other Martians. Why would she leave Aurore behind – especially if she knew what was coming? And how can we ignore *that* coincidence? Don't you find that surprising?"

"Yes, but all Martians were ordered to leave by then."

"But to abandon a child in her care?"

"Perhaps she had no choice."

"Maybe," said Mr Smiley, "But you did. You stayed. Perhaps she put in place a contingency?"

3

Onboard the pod, Leon and Aurore stood at the command chair. On the screen behind them, the Earth and Moon were shrinking perceptibly. Overlaying them, a complex of symbols flickered and changed as the two Martian children reviewed the programme settings.

Mr Knutt waited patiently on the sidelines while they worked. Unconsciously, he tapped his toes inside his shoes.

Finally, Leon reported their findings. "Nothing. It all appears to be as it should – except that we cannot control the pod."

"And we're heading for Mars. Some kind of return-to-base override, perhaps?" asked Mr Knutt.

"I do not know," said Leon. "It is possible."

"Hm," said Mr Knutt. "And how long until we get there?"

"At our current velocity, twenty-four point seven hours."

"Right, right," mused Mr Knutt. "Erm, perhaps you and I should keep working on the problem, Leon. The rest of us, I think, would be advised to try to get some sleep. It's been a long day – or least it seems like it."

Dominic looked at his watch. "But it's only half-past-three – by the time back home."

Mr Knutt raised an eyebrow and sighed. "Is it really?"

"Is there anything else to eat?" asked Dominic.

"*Dominic*," said Emily, aghast.

"Well, is there?"

"There's all tha' fruit and veg I brought along," said Mr Flynn. "Good job too. It's in the pod's 'old. You can help yerselves to that, if yer like."

"Uh, no thanks, Mr Flynn," said Dominic. "I was thinking of a sandwich or a bar of chocolate or something."

"There are some provisions aboard," said Leon.

"Emergency supplies mainly. Most of it will be Martian food, but there will be something that you can eat."

"We'll have a look at that," said Mr Knutt. "But, it may be sensible if we ration what we have – until we can determine if we can get back, or another source of food becomes evident. For now, please, do what you can to rest."

"Mr Knutt."

"Yes, Lucy?"

"Er, is there a toilet onboard?"

Mr Knutt's eyes widened. Another good question. And a very practical one. "Ah, Leon?"

Leon looked at Aurore, then back to Mr Knutt. There was a twinkle in his eye. "Well, Mr Knutt. As you might recall, Martians do not... wee. So –"

Mr Knutt pursed his lips. "Ah, yes. Of course. Well, er... "

"But we still have need of toilets, just like on Earth. So, yes, the pod has one." He pointed to a panel in the wall behind. "It is through there."

Mr Knutt visibly relaxed. The children laughed. Mr Flynn chuckled at the headmaster's momentary discomfort.

"Well, thank goodness for that. Thank you, Leon."

4

Mr Knutt stood looking at their rearward view. Already, the Earth and Moon had diminished to mere points in the glare of the Sun.

It makes one begin to realise just how large our solar system is, he thought.

Looking around at the children, he was happy to

see that they seemed to be taking it all in their stride. That was good.

As for Mars, it was home, of course, to Leon and Aurore, and Camille had visited it before. The other children perhaps viewed the prospect as a grand adventure, despite the recent danger – and it might have been for him too but his worry over what they might be getting themselves into. And then there was Mr Flynn. Solid, reliable, unflappable Mr Flynn, who was catching a nap, arms folded across his chest. He was glad to have the Flintworne school caretaker along.

5

"How are we doing?" asked Mr Smiley.

Mrs Sparks was looking at her comms panel. "I sent a message fifteen minutes ago. If he is there, I expect a reply in approximately twenty-four minutes. That is the best we can expect without comportal technology."

"OK, we need to know how to re-gain control of the pod – *before* it reaches Mars. And the latest he knows about what's happening over there. Especially if there are any other asteroids coming our way."

"I will try. But it is very limited only with primitive radio equipment. The first messages have been in Morse Code. I am hoping he can find a better way, else it may take a long time to exchange information – longer than we may have."

"Yeah, I know. Thanks Wilma. I'll talk to the OPP to find out what they know. Plus," he said, "I need to report what's happened to Karl Winsom. Meanwhile, we need to get some transport up here and see if we can get the base operational again."

6

Fred Sparks returned to his laboratory. Most Martian families had laboratories where Earth people might have garages or lofts or garden sheds. His computer sat amongst a jumble of antiquated equipment, alien in appearance, which his wife's grandmother had long ago collected and modified to communicate on equal terms with Nikola Tesla and Guglielmo Marconi and other pioneering scientists on Earth. And so, she had assembled quite a collection of primitive spark gap transmitters and simple vacuum tube radio devices as they were invented on Earth, and had used them to keep in contact with Earth for some years following her visit. On her death, all of her research materials had been placed in storage. When Mrs Sparks had begun her own researches into the history of Martian-human contact, she had taken them out to study her own grandmother's contributions in that area.

After the conference at Cydonia, he had returned home to monitor developments from there. After their joint communications with Mr Smiley and his wife on Earth's Moon, Councillor Sffan'utul had returned to his own home.

It was not long after that the edicts had begun to be issued by the Council. Firstly, the call for the withdrawal of Martians from Earth, which included a ban on Martian ships departing for Earth. Then there was the really shocking action, of blocking comportal communications, thereby removing the ability to communicate instantaneously over long distances.

The Controlled Contact programme had relied on Martian comportal technology for its communications. Now, he could see that that had been a mistake. Human comms would have been useful, even considering the time lag between Mars and Earth. But no such backup had been instigated. And so, he had resorted to find what options remained.

And so, Councillor Kindelbir's archaic hobby equipment now lay strewn across his laboratory's central benches, where he had attempted to interface them with his Martian computers. That hadn't worked – to begin with – and he had resorted to the extremely simple, but effective, method of transmitting a looped message by radio in Morse Code via a makeshift aerial set up on a nearby knoll outside his home.

That had eventually been answered, and he had learned of the Martians' evacuation and the asteroid swarm descending on Earth and the Moon.

Since then, there had been radio silence. Three solhours without a word, without knowledge of what might have befallen his wife, his son, his colleagues and his friends on Earth and the Moon.

He spent that time trying to configure a better way to receive and send messages without the need to be in attendance all the time. Finally, he had managed to get the computer to read and simulate the signals from the vacuum tube set, so now he could compose and see messages on the computer's 3D virtual display.

At last. There was another message from his wife. Correction, two. The first read:

Safe here, in evac shelter, but Karl Winsom lost. Sentinel re-activated and pulverised all but one asteroid aimed at

Earth. Guided by zero-point engines Two impacts on the Moon – Crisium, and one at Tsiolkovsky. Sentinel itself destroyed.

And the other:

Leon and friends with Mr Knutt in pod – diverted asteroid targeted at base. Now without control and on way to Mars. Is there a way to override? Any further news?

Mr Sparks sat back from the computer. *The Sentinel gone? Zero-point engines?* They were not supposed to venture outside of Martian space without authority. And now his own son and several Earthlings were being brought to Mars against their will.

He typed quickly in reply:

Gratified you are safe. No more news; comportal network shut down widespread. Smiall'kes'hep.
   Pods have a safeguard mode for emergency rescue situations. It can be set to activate when they detect no input from the crew – such as when the operator may be injured. The pod will initiate an automatic return to base. But it is a little-known function, and disabled by default. It needs to be activated, and can usually be overridden simply by re-taking active control. That it cannot suggests it has been tampered with.
   I will review the design of the pod and revert with instructions. Can pod comms be calibrated to communicate directly with Leon?

It would be nearly another solhour before he could

expect a reply. He changed the display on his computer to call up the working manuals for the pod.

7

On the Moon, Mr Smiley had ordered a partial re-population of Tsiolkovsky base. He had advised the children's parents to remain in the shelter until they could be sure that any immediate danger had passed.

He now sat in his office at the base, assessing its overall status. It had sustained heavy damage to the outer hub ring between South Lobe and West Lobe, and breaches in all three Lobes. But it could have been worse. Much worse. Repair crews were already engaged in each Lobe and the atmospheric breaches contained. Plans were underway to evacuate the guests and any injured and non-essential personnel back to Earth as soon as practical.

Meanwhile, he had something else that was nagging at his attention.

8

Onboard the pod, most of the children had fallen asleep. They lay on the floor of the pod inside the central circle, huddled together like puppies.

Leon remained awake. He had adjusted the pod's skin transparency to fully opaque, so that now the cabin had a subdued level of light. He was still examining the pod's systems for any way to re-take control.

Mr Flynn had come out of his nap, giving Mr Knutt a chance at forty winks. But try as he might, he was too hyped to relax. Instead, he sat quietly, wondering what lay in wait for them on Mars.

9

Mrs Sparks and Caroline Miller entered Mr Smiley's office.

"Sit down," he said.

"What is it?" asked Caroline.

"Want you to take a look at this," said Mr Smiley.

The screen on the wall lit up. It showed what looked like security camera footage from the hanger in North Lobe. The view was from a high-level widescreen that captured most of the hangar. The airlock doors to the corridors were to the right. On the left, stood the pod that Mr Knutt's schoolchildren had arrived in, and at the rear of the hangar sat the two Earth craft, the XL-67 and the smaller shuttle.

There was no activity. The only indication of passing time was given by the camera's time coding, which showed the seconds ticking by.

"And?" said Caroline.

"Keep watching," said Mr Smiley.

On the screen, the hangar doors parted, and in marched a figure, a female figure. It was only small on screen, but Mrs Sparks said immediately, "Skiel'aeljtın."

"Yes," said Mr Smiley. "This was this morning, before the Apollo excursion."

They watched as Miss Sky crossed to the pod. Her head turned right and left as she proceeded, no doubt on the look-out for any hangar crew. She carried something in one hand – a bag?

"What is she doing?" asked Caroline.

When she reached the pod, Miss Sky took something out of the bag, something small, and waved it against the skin of the craft. Then she stepped back. The pod's skin parted and the door unfolded from it. Miss Sky hurried inside.

"What on Earth?" said Caroline again.

Mr Smiley switched views, to a camera closer to the pod.

Noting the time on the screen, Mrs Sparks spoke. "Three hours before she left with the others."

Mr Smiley said nothing. As they continued to watch, it wasn't long before Miss Sky reappeared at the pod's entrance. Once out, she reversed her actions of a few minutes before and strode away from the pod, clutching the same bag.

"That looks like a lunch bag," said Caroline Miller.

"The kids all had one," said Mr Smiley. "That one, I believe, belonged to Aurore."

"I'm guessing you're not suggesting that she only went in there to hand Aurore her packed lunch?"

"You're very astute. As always," replied Mr Smiley. He permitted himself a small smile. He had worked with Caroline Miller for some years.

"No, she was there for some other reason. Whatever it was, it didn't take long. And I'm guessing that she carried something into the pod in that bag, that later had something to do with the pod's behaviour."

"So, assuming you're right, two questions," said Caroline. "One: where did she get this device or knowhow? Two: why would she go to that trouble, when she left shortly after with the others anyway?"

She bit on her lower lip, in thought. "It was Aurore,

wasn't it? She didn't plan to leave her behind?"

"Hm-m. I think it was a back-up plan. She probably planned to leave with Aurore as soon as the pod returned from the Apollo field-trip, either with the other Martians, or by themselves in the pod. With the asteroids on their way, she must have known it would be cutting things fine. As it was, when the other Martians began to leave, she was forced to make a choice. Activating the pod's auto-return was her insurance policy. Aurore could sneak back onboard as soon as she could. Or, if they were still out on the field-trip, she could leave knowing that the pod would be away from the base when the asteroids were due to strike. Then the auto-return would deliver Aurore and the rest of us to Mars – and even I would be unable to prevent it. Clearly, though, she didn't anticipate the smaller meteoroids either."

"OK," said Caroline. "That seems plausible. But, if Skiel'aeljtın knew about the asteroid attack, why, as the OPP's principle Martian representative, didn't she warn us? It doesn't make sense."

Mr Smiley looked to Mrs Sparks. "Wilma..."

Mrs Sparks looked up: "Skiel'aeljtın is Councillor Smiall'kes'hep's daughter."

10

Three hours had passed since they had set out for Mars. There really was no need for Leon to occupy the command seat. The pod was flying itself. Everything he had attempted to wrest back control had failed. The only value the seat now had was for communicating with Mr Smiley. And *that* was becoming more difficult with increasing distance. At their present velocity, they were getting farther away from Earth by eight-and-a-half million miles every hour. By now, messages would take over two minutes each way, and it was already more practical to resort to typed messages and replies. The last one had been an hour ago, a brief check-in by Mr Smiley. There wasn't much to do. And so, Leon had settled down to catch some rest while Mr Flynn kept watch.

12 - AURORA

Mr Smiley and Caroline Miller visited the children's parents at their quarters in North Lobe, where they had been permitted to return when the all-clear was given.

"Any news?" asked Lucy's mum. "Are they alright?" She looked drawn and fidgety.

"Yes, they're fine, Mrs Westfield," said Caroline. "*Really*," she reassured her. "And now we have been able to link Mr Sparks into the communications. As they draw closer to Mars, he will be able to voice-link to them to guide and assist them. We now know that the pod was pre-programmed to return to its original departure point. Mr Sparks believes that is located in the planet's northern hemisphere, at *Ares Vallis*. He will attempt to be there to meet them."

"*Attempt?*" asked Mr Tiddler.

Mr Smiley stepped in. "He'll do his best. I can't promise he'll reach there in time – or at all, given the situation. As you're aware, much has changed on Mars. A conservative faction amongst the northern delegates of the ruling Council has assumed control, led by Councillor Smiall'kes'hep. We can't be sure of the full situation due to a communications blackout. What we do know is via Fred Sparks.

"All we can say presently is that your children and Mr Knutt and Mr Flynn are accidental passengers. We are confident that they will be received and treated courteously on arrival and returned to you safely as soon as possible.

"Now," he said. "NASA, the OPP and other nations have all their available space telescopes on alert for any other asteroids and presently, there is no new danger. So... you have a choice. You can go home. Or you can stay here. Either way, we'll keep you apprised of developments. OK?"

There were nods from everyone.

"Just let Caroline know what you want to do."

"We'll stay," said Mr Tiddler. He turned to the other parents. "Yes?"

"Yes," said Mrs Westfield, "Without question."

"Absolument. *Absolutely*," said Camille's mother.

"And that's a 'yes' from me," said Mr Addison. "Although I'd like to be able to call my wife, if that's possible?"

"Fine, OK. And Mr Addison, we'll see what we can do – for all of you, if you wish."

2

As they walked away, Caroline Miller turned to her boss. "You didn't mention Skiel'aeljtın."

"No need for them to know at this point," said Mr Smiley. "It doesn't change the immediate scenario."

"No," said Caroline. "But isn't *Ares Vallis* – the Valley of Ares – Councillor Smiall'kes'hep's ancestral district?"

"Uh-huh."

"I take it you haven't told Mr Knutt or Leon either?"

"Correct. No way to do that without the risk of alerting Aurore."

"*Aurore?* She's just a child. You don't seriously believe she could be part of this?"

"That remains to be seen. But she showed astonishing ability programming the pod's manoeuvres. Even Leon gave way to her on that."

"Which happened to save us all."

"True. But she hasn't appeared particularly concerned at Skiel'aeljtın's departure, leaving her behind," said Mr Smiley.

"Isn't that just her character?" said Caroline. "She was always very quiet and reserved."

"Perhaps," said Mr Smiley. "Let's see if there's anything from Fred."

3

At his home on Mars, Fred Sparks sent his reply to Mr Smiley and moved into what on Earth would be called the kitchen. Unlike on Earth, though, this space had no cooking appliances. It was fairly sparse. In the middle of the space there was a simple oval table with chairs arranged around it, which looked like they had grown out of the floor itself. Behind these was a large curved window, thick and angled, that stretched from wall to wall and framed a view overlooking a shallow valley. A rim of hills formed the horizon. The Sun was somewhere overhead to the west, casting lengthening shadows across the rusty valley floor.

The entire inner space of the house had been cut into the rock of an outcrop, so that the roof of the house was a thick layer of sandstone. The top of the outcrop had been levelled to accommodate two landing platforms. The family pod – a larger ship than the one carrying Leon – sat up there now, its conical base resting in an inverted cone that led to the building's interior. At its lowest level, the complex held water tanks and an underground vegetable garden.

Mr Sparks moved to the table, in which were set a number of panels, a different symbol inscribed on each. He pressed one panel, then another. A brief flare of amber light appeared around their edges, soon followed by blue, after which they slid open to reveal a different dish. He removed his food and placed them together in the place that faced the window.

No sooner had he sat, a small hatch near the floor in the wall to his left levered inwards. It resembled a cat-flap. A small head appeared, followed by a long scaly body. Soon, the entire creature was inside. From its appearance, on Earth, it would be called a lizard. It was pale grey and about as large as a puppy.

"Hello, Shheikspule."

At the sound of its name, the creature tilted its head to look at Mr Sparks with its large black eyes. Shheikspule was the family pet, Leon's *doglet*, as he once described it for his friends.

"Did you find anything interesting out there?" asked Mr Sparks.

He didn't expect an answer, but *kes'eldriji* were creatures of intelligence, at least as clever as dogs or cats on Earth. Shheikspule tilted his head back again and scuttled over to a spot below the windows. There he tapped the floor three times with a clawed forepaw. Moments later, it parted and a dish appeared filled with a mixture of dried, spiky crustacean-like creatures, grey in colour like raw shrimps, and elongated sandy-coloured grubs similar to crane fly larvae.

Judging by how hungrily he began to eat, Mr Sparks guessed not. Normally, Shheikspule would spend much of his time outside, foraging for roots and sandworms. Since Leon had left with his mother for Earth's Moon, though, he had stayed close to home.

Mr Sparks returned to his own meal, a selection of vegetables and a kind of soup. He ate quietly as he thought through what he must do in the hours ahead. The pod, with his son and his friends aboard, would be arriving in less than twelve solhours. He had been in contact with Sffan'utul, who had agreed to go with him to meet them – if they could. The landing spot was in the heart of Smiall'kes'hep's territory. That was clearly intentional, taking Aurore directly home, and where he suspected Skiel'aeljtın would now be waiting to meet her.

Skiel'aeljtın. Their principal representative within the Office of Planetary Protection, who had fled without a word before the asteroid attack on the Earth system and now was nowhere to be seen or heard. No wonder his wife had expressed her sense of betrayal at Skiel'aeljtın's actions, which had resulted in one man's death on the Moon and several thousand thus far on the Earth itself. And for their own son, who was now being forcibly returned to Oztzıldıj.

There was no further news about the situation. Sffan'utul could only confirm that news of the events on Earth did not appear to have been publicly shared on Oztzıldıj.

Mr Smiley had shared Skiel'aeljtın's suspicious actions in the pod hangar in his last transmission, which included a description of the device (from an enhanced image) of the item she had removed from a bag before boarding the pod.

He had just sent his reply. If the device had been attached to the pod's drive core, as he suspected, it could not be removed while under power. Leon and the others would have to wait for the pod to stop and power down before they could remove it and regain control. He had listed the locations within the core that Leon should search first if he could.

Meanwhile, his thoughts were turning to Leon's companions. Their environmental suits would protect them only so long on Mars. Critically, their oxygen supply would not last very long. He would have to adapt some bracelets for them.

When on Earth, Martians wore adapted bracelets on their wrists that contained replaceable phials of liquid that helped to de-oxygenise their blood. He would have to prepare something similar for the humans that reversed the situation – that broke down Mars's carbon dioxide atmosphere into breathable oxygen.

Firstly, he would need to clear some bench space. He looked over at his lab worktops. Kindlebir's antique devices could be returned to storage – he had now replicated their function through his computer and could now communicate directly with Mr Smiley, and now with Leon as their pod drew closer.

He waved his hand over a sensor on the side of the bench and began to disassemble his grandmother-in-law's equipment. Moments later a rectangular panel opened in the floor nearby and out came a platform with a metallic-grey trunk on it. It stopped at waist height.

Mr Sparks went over to it and waved a hand over it. The lid parted and its halves slid down its sides. He began to carefully carry over and re-pack the radio equipment for its return to storage. When he had finished, he was about to close the lid when he noticed a panel in the end wall of the trunk that had come away a little. He didn't recall seeing that before. He bent to investigate it.

The panel had shifted up perhaps four millimetres from its bottom edge. There appeared to be a cavity behind it! He tapped his wristband and a small light appeared which he used to peer inside. There was definitely a cavity there. And there was something inside!

He quickly checked inside the trunk, in case he had merely been looking inside. No, the wall was complete and slightly angled downwards, so that a small space was created between it and the outer wall. Now more than a little curious, he turned his attention again to the outside. The panel looked like it originally slid up and down. That function appeared to have stopped working. He fetched a blade-like instrument and inserted its point into the thin space. By levering it at either side, the panel lifted slightly with a slight creak. His other task was momentarily forgotten as he raised it as high as he could. Then he had to go and find another implement to increase the gap. The panel creaked and groaned some more as it edged slowly upwards. Finally, it was high enough to reveal what was inside.

Mr Sparks paused to examine the contents. There

were three memory prisms, two of somewhat different design, longer and yellowed compared to the other one; plus a collection of objects from Earth: a pocket watch, a small leather-bound notebook and a sleeve of yellowed papers, a few faded photographic prints and a book. Immediately he saw that the facing photograph was of H. G. Wells.

He reached in and withdrew the photos. He shuffled them slowly front to back: H. G. Wells; a photograph of Mr Wells with a young Kindlebir taking tea together; Nikola Tesla; Mr Marconi?

Next he retrieved the papers and the book. The book was H.G. Wells's *The War of the Worlds*, an original 1898 version. He put them aside and shifted his attention to the notebook and papers. Some of the letters were in the cursive handwriting of a human correspondent. To him, they were quite unintelligible. Again, he shuffled them until one, in particular, caught his attention. It was a newspaper clipping, in which one word stood out.

Mystery Airship Crash

Aurora, Wise County, Tx. April 18, 1897

Residents of the small Texan town of Aurora had a rude awakening yesterday morning when, at about six o'clock they were astonished to see the mystery airship...

Aurora. Aurore? A coincidence? He read on:

... that has been seen across the country. It passed slowly and at low altitude over the north side of the town, where it collided with a farmer's windmill and crashed to earth. Shortly afterward it exploded with terrific force, scattering debris widely about.

Amongst the wreckage were found the damaged remains of the pilot, which showed sufficient distinction to human anatomy to suggest he was not a resident of this world, and to which signal service officer Mr T. J. Weems offers his opinion that he was a native of the planet Mars.

The wreckage has inspired much curiosity amongst the townsfolk, who have been viewing it and gathering samples of the strange metal of which it was constructed.

The funeral of the pilot is due to take place in the town cemetery at noon today.

Mr Sparks carried the papers to his workbench. He put the clipping aside and examined the others. There were several about Nikola Tesla and Guglielmo Marconi. One, dated 1934, reported Tesla's claim to have invented an energy beam weapon that he called 'teleforce', but which would become popularly referred to as a 'death ray'. Then there was a part of a newspaper serialisation from Garrett P. Serviss's novel *Edison's Conquest of Mars*, dated 13 January 1898, which described Edison's invention of a disintegrator beam to combat the Martians. Wells's own novel had had the Martians as the wielders of a death ray superweapon in their conquest of Earth.

Was there a connection here; between this small collection of items? Why had Kindlebir hidden them away?

Mr Sparks returned to the trunk and withdrew the memory prisms. He closed the trunk and went back to his bench. A wave of his hand sent the trunk back to storage.

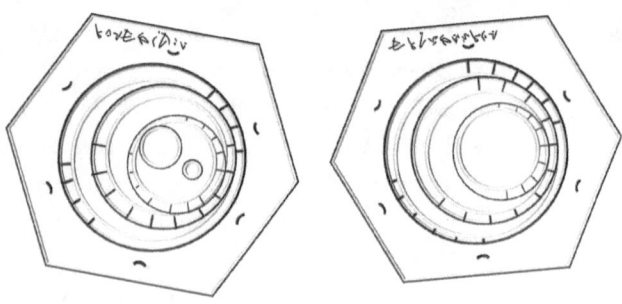

He picked up the newer-looking prism, a crystal about five centimetres in length, similar to a quartz crystal, clear and unblemished. One end was pointed; the other, flat. He rotated it to view the flat end. There was a small inscription there, the unique symbol signature of Kindlebir. He put it down and examined the others. He frowned at these. They too were inscribed, but with characters and symbols he did not recognise. And instead of completely smooth sides, they were embossed with a number of small bumps, rods and triangles. He put them down and picked up the first prism and placed it in the holder of his computer. A blue beam immediately connected with it and it began to glow with a greenish-blue light that swirled within the crystal like eddying fog.

On the holographic screen that popped up on the screen space above it, Martian text appeared that flowed in pace with Mr Sparks's reading. Soon it was flying by as he became engrossed in what his wife's grandmother's diaries had to tell him.

4

Mrs Sparks sat at her computer terminal at

Tsiolkovsky Crater. Her husband had evidently managed to configure the primitive radio systems to enable transmission of images. She now sat staring at one such image, the first newspaper clipping that he had managed to scan and transmit to her. It now sat on her computer screen.

Mr Smiley looked over her shoulder.

"Yes, I know this story. One of the incidents in the airship flap of 1896–1897. As you know, everything space-related was about Mars back then. Of course, I didn't know your grandmother's connection with it until we met. Or that there was more to it – Tek'tu'jan and so forth.

"But Fred seems to be suggesting that there may be a connection between Aurore and the place of Tek'tu'jan's crash – beyond just the coincidence in name?"

"Yes," replied Mrs Sparks.

"How could that be?"

"I do not know," said Mrs Sparks. "But there is more to Tek'tu'jan's story than even he knows. My grandmother shared this with me before she died, which I have discussed with no-one else – not even my husband. But I will share it with you now as it may be relevant."

She sighed. "The reason my grandmother was especially mournful over Tek'tu'jan's death was that she was with child at the time."

"Oh," said Mr Smiley.

"My grandmother knew this before they left for Earth. She advised her to stay behind, but Tek'tu'jan insisted on going. Grandmother could have forced her to stay. But she did not.

"But that is not all. Tek'tu'jan survived the crash. She stumbled from the wreckage, stunned and injured, but not fatally, it is believed. She took refuge in the barn, which offered protection when the pod exploded. A while after, dazed and unable to breathe, she emerged and staggered towards a group of humans – I believe they were called *cowboys* – who were among the first to investigate.

"Tek'tu'jan surprised them. She reached for one to save herself from falling. But the men, shocked at her appearance, reacted in fear, and they attacked and killed her."

"Oh my," said Mr Smiley.

"An autopsy revealed that the foetus lived; a boy. Martian babies have reserves of dense fats and oxycarbon that can sustain them for a few days. A wet nurse was found to attend to him, but he became sick and ailing.

"My grandmother learned of the incident and went in search of her assistant. She found and recovered the baby, but Tek'tu'jan had been buried with the pilot's remains. Her fate was quickly covered up.

"So, my grandmother returned with the baby to Mars, where he was handed to Tek'tu'jan's family."

"So," said Mr Smiley, "You think she kept the newspaper copy out of guilt, or as a memorial of some kind?"

"No," replied Mrs Sparks. "The items my husband has found are very selective. I believe they are connected; that they are intended to tell us something that was too sensitive to reveal in her own time."

13 - OZTZILDIJ

"Right everyone. We are three hours from Mars," said Mr Knutt. "We need to ensure our environmental suits are working. Mr Sparks has made us some wristbands, a little like the ones that Leon and Aurore wear on Earth, which will provide us with a source of oxygen. He will bring them with him to meet us.

"But... and it is a 'but' – we are not sure what kind of reception we shall meet when we land, so we need to be prepared. Outside of the pod, you will not be able to breathe the atmosphere. You each have been given five replacement oxygen packs. That's just a hundred minutes of capacity. Make sure you keep them with you.

"Anyway, we know now that we are being brought to the planet's northern hemisphere, to a place known as the Valley of Ares."

Camille stole a look at Aurore, who showed no reaction. It was not lost on Mr Knutt, or Leon.

"Have you any idea why we are being taken to your home district, Aurore?"

Aurore looked up at Mr Knutt. She shook her head.

"Camille?" asked Mr Knutt.

Camille's face flushed red. "Non. No. I er, spent

three months there, where I stayed with Aurore and went to school. That is all."

"OK. But Mr Smiley and Mr Sparks believe the pod was programmed to do so by Miss Sky before she fled the Moon. Do you know anything about this?"

Again, Aurore shook her head innocently.

"Fine," said Mr Knutt. "I am sure we will find out more once we land."

2

"What is it?" asked Mr Smiley.

"My husband is trying to assemble what he can from my grandmother's diaries in the time he has," replied Mrs Sparks. "It will not be possible to know everything now without comportal connection. But he believes he has found something important. It may help to explain what is happening now on our planet."

"Like what?"

"I believe there are some clues in the items she has left for us."

Mrs Sparks called up images of the book and the newspaper clippings.

"It never made sense to me that Herbert Wells returned from Mars and immediately set to writing *The War of the Worlds*. Grandmother always maintained that they had 'fallen out' over that. But it was never clear what their disagreement really was about.

"Then there is this."

An image appeared of a book cover. It was titled *Edison's Conquest of Mars*.

"The book version was published in 1947, bringing together the parts published separately in the *New*

York Journal in 1898. Mr Edison was not involved in it. After his return from Mars, he made a short personal movie called *A Trip to Mars*, then did nothing else related to it. But the author, Mr Serviss, portrayed him as an inventor of anti-gravity propulsion and a particle beam weapon that he used to defeat the Martians on their own planet.

"Together, these items share the themes of advanced weaponry and war with Mars. Much of it is fiction, of course. But recent events begin to suggest a kernel of truth to them."

"Hm," said Mr Smiley. "Except for two things. One: there is no history of hostile actions by Mars – peace has reigned there for millennia. Two, it's still not clear where the Aurora incident fits into this."

"That is true," said Mrs Sparks. "None are officially recorded."

"But Wells, being the first, and possibly the closest, of your grandmother's contacts – you think he was blowing the whistle on something he uncovered on Mars?" asked Mr Smiley.

"That is beginning to look likely," answered Mrs Sparks.

3

Mr Sparks sent a final message to Mr Smiley and Mrs Sparks.

I am sending this to you only. We cannot risk the pod holding this information in its memory when it lands. You will understand why.

Kindlebir meant it for you, my wife, to find after her

death. She wrote you a letter. You will find this as a following message.

 I have copied the data from your grandmother's diaries to our computers. I was not able to do so with the older prisms – they are not compatible with our systems. I have replaced the prisms and other artifacts in their trunk. But we cannot act on this information without the comportal network.

 I leave soon to go to Sffan'utul before we go together to Ares. Before I depart, I will contact Leon and Howard Knutt with instructions.

 I hope to be able to contact you again soon.

Shieekk'ssup'pl / Sparks

Mrs Sparks exchanged glances with Mr Smiley. She took a deep breath, visibly preparing herself for the message her grandmother had left her. She selected the message file and clicked to open it.

The message was in the language of the Martians. Mrs Sparks began to read. Her thin lips moved as she silently traced the words. At several points she flinched. Then she collected herself, and turned to Mr Smiley.

"Can you read?" she asked.

"Only slowly," he replied.

"Then I shall translate."

She took another deep breath, then began:

Kımb'bul'bir. Precious one.

 There is much I wished to tell you, but could not while I lived. It was not the time, and you were too young.

 It is my hope also that you do not find this message

before you have gained the maturity and learning to accept it – that, in spite of all you have learned, what I have to tell you is the truth.

Our history is not as it seems. It has been my life's burden to carry this knowledge; and it lies heavy on my heart to leave it as my legacy to you, with all the difficulties it may present.

But truth is truth. Our people deserve to understand how they have been deceived, and be empowered to remove this foul corruption from our society. I refer to an ancient and pernicious force that has controlled and undermined our society since the time of Jziee'ekkkzoor'sup. It exists at the highest echelons of our society, with the councillors and leaders of our world.

And yet it took men from Earth to make this apparent to me. Herbert Wells was the first to suggest an alternative history of our race. He came to Oztzıldıj believing that he had found his utopian society – one based on peace, equality, justice and provision for all. But in attempting to understand what made it so, he discovered instead that it was not.

To my everlasting shame, I could not accept what he told me. A human correcting me about Martian history! It was only after he left and I felt compelled to look into his discoveries, that I came to accept the truth – and what he came to write in his book was close to it.

A small but influential clique amongst us has long secretly controlled the destiny of our world in preservation of its own interests. It has held a deep animosity towards all that might threaten its position.

You should know that Ti'aransc was no accident. It was the desperate act of the northern factions that had attempted to reassert their dominancy after the decease of Jziee'ekkkzoor'sup. When they were poised to fail in their struggle with the South, Ti'aransc was brought down upon them. Most of the survivors were from the North, the principal families amongst them.

But they miscalculated. The destruction was far greater than they anticipated. It resulted in the deaths of millions and the end of our great civilisation.

But when a global civilisation first arose on Earth and became capable of spaceflight and reached out to the planets, that technology was evoked again – like a long spear thrust out to strike at Earth.

And so, Earth has long been regarded with two minds, with amiable interest by the majority, and with suspicion and fear by a few.

The Sentinel was eventually set in place by the peaceful majority, and peace *has* been the prevailing state in our world since that time. But Earth now grows strong again, and the benevolent leadership of Skallir'rir will not last forever. I fear, even as I write this, that the dark centre of our society makes its plans against them.

The evidence resides in the two prisms left with these diaries, and with the rest of the hidden archives behind the face of Jziee'ekkkzoor'sup, which Bertie discovered during his time here. He stole them away, eager for me to view them. I did not try until much later, and then I found they could not be read with our technology – only that still functional at Cydonia, where I dared not venture. Fortunately, his letter and his notebook describe his discovery. These too I leave for you.

As you know, precious one, Bertie's departure saddened me, but his book may have forestalled a terrible reprisal. It caused uproar on our planet – the man who had brought us Earl Grey tea and English manners portraying us in such a savage manner! And yet, the distance it imparted between Martians and Earthlings, leading to official contact ending completely within a few years, surely bought some time.

But that time is running out. I leave you my life, its works, and the keys to unlocking a better future for our people. More even than that, I leave you my enduring affection.

"Hm, nice letter," said Mr Smiley. "But, darn, why didn't she just tell us where this archive is? Did Fred send a copy of Wells's letter or his notebook?"

"No," replied Mrs Sparks. "I am sure it will be included with the prism data."

"Which we can't receive until we can regain comportal comms. OK, see if you can get Fred to send it to us now, separately."

"He will probably have left by the time the message arrives."

"Uh-huh, but let's try anyway."

"Of course," said Mrs Sparks.

"Oh, Wilma. One more thing. What was that about a reprisal? What for?"

"Yes, I noticed that. I assume it related to Tek'tu'jan."

4

Leon waved his hand over the armrest and the walls became transparent.

"Whoa!" exclaimed Dominic. "I didn't think we'd be *that* close."

Outside, Mars dominated the view, a great rusty ball that glowed dimly in the reflected sunlight.

Although their speed had reduced on their final approach, it still grew perceptibly larger by the minute.

"Mr Flynn."

"H'edmaster?"

"Do you any of your fruit left? I think it would be wise if everyone ate something before we get there."

Mr Flynn left his seat. "I'll takes a look, Mr Knutt."

"Thank you. Now, if anyone else has any food left, now would be the time to eat up or share if you do not want it."

The children pulled lunch bags closer. Dominic scrunched his face up at the sandwich crusts in the bottom of his bag. Emily found a piece of fruit cake, still in its wrapping, that she didn't want and offered it to Dominic, who took it without hesitation.

"Sorry, Leon, no chocolate cake, I'm afraid," she said.

"That is OK," replied Leon.

"Aurore has some," said Camille. "She does not like it. Can Leon have it?"

Aurore nodded. Camille tossed the bag to Leon, who thanked her before opening it. In the bottom was the untouched piece of cake. And a screwed-up ball of lemon coloured notepaper.

He unwrapped the cake and started to eat while he unravelled the paper. There was a written note on it. In Martian script. He immediately stopped eating. He glanced at Aurore, then at Camille; then at Mr Knutt. No-one looked back.

It was a short note, with a simple message:

On your return, report immediately to me. If I am not there, go back and re-board the pod. Do not be seen. Tell no-one. Wait

aboard. The pod will bring you home to Oztzıldıj, where I will
meet you

When he looked up again, Aurore was looking in his
direction and, in particular, at the note in his hand,
now aware of what Leon had found. Their gazes met
awkwardly, Aurore unsure what Leon would do; Leon
himself unsure what *he* should do.

The comms system crackled and the moment was
interrupted by an unexpected call. It was Mr Sparks.

"Hawudd. Leon. Yuse he-yed setzpliess."

Howard. Leon. Use headsets, please.

Leon put his headset on. From somewhere, he
produced a set for Mr Knutt too.

"Hello... *Dad*," said Leon.

Like most Martian children, Leon was
unaccustomed to addressing a parent or any grown-up
informally. Several months on Earth, exposed to new
friends and their interactions with their own parents,
hadn't changed things quite that much. But he – and
his parents – *were* trying.

"Son," replied Mr Sparks, just as awkwardly. "Now,
both, please, attend carefully. I soon leave to come to
you at Ares. As you have surely surmised, the pod is
under programmed control. It is highly probable this
was arranged by Skiel'aeljtın using a device she
installed in the pod's hyperdrive core. It cannot be
removed while the drive is operational. But Leon, as
soon as the pod stops, you must access the core and
remove it. Do you understand?"

"Yes, father," Leon said without questioning.

"It will be located in sector 60 or sector 90. You
should be able to remove it without effort. Then hide it.

Do it as quickly as possible on arrival, before the hatch opens. Ensure that Aurore does not see you."

Mr Knutt frowned. He couldn't help glancing at Aurore, then at Leon, who he noted didn't seem surprised.

"I will come with a colleague, Council Sffan'utul of Tharsis. We trust that you that will be turned over to us. However, if we are prevented from seeing you, then you must attempt to escape, in the pod. It will respond to your commands and you must do what otherwise I had in mind to do myself. You must travel to Su'umka'r and –"

"*Su'umka'r?*" whispered Mr Knutt.

"Howard, please, do not question," cautioned Mr Sparks. "Just utter 'yes' to confirm, or 'no' if you do not understand or disagree."

"Yes," replied Mr Knutt, who felt embarrassed to be corrected.

"Su'umka'r is the name of our largest moon, the one you call Phobos. Su'umka'r is the symbol of the North. Ours, representing the South, is the smaller moon, Deimos, which we know as A'yrk'yrok. They have always been regarded as territories of the respective hemispheres.

"Su'umka'r has upon it a beacon that is used for planetary defence and communications. It seems to be the source of the comportal interference. It is against our laws to impede or track one another. It is imperative that the beacon is disabled and the comportal network reactivated.

"The majority of our people will be unaware of events at Earth, and remain ignorant of their own true history – which, Leon, your great grandmother's diaries reveal. It is time it is told.

"A copy of her diaries and the content of the prisms will be automatically sent to your mother once the comportal network is reactivated. The prisms are in Kindlebir's repository here in our home. In the event that I am not with you, you must come here to retrieve them and take them to Sffan'utul. Do you understand?"

"Yes," said Leon quietly. By his tone, one might have thought his father had just asked him to tidy his room rather than prepare to steal a pod and fly to an asteroid moon to disable some advanced technology.

"Ah, Fred. Why can you not do that yourself?" questioned Mr Knutt.

"It is too dangerous right now, Howard. Diplomacy first."

"Understood," replied Mr Knutt.

"And Leon."

"Yes, father?"

"If you are there, please feed Shheikspule."

Leon's brow wrinkled at this, but again he calmly said, "OK. I will."

"I hope to see you very soon," said Mr Sparks.

And then he was gone.

5

They had forty minutes until landing. Mars grew ever larger outside.

While everyone else looked busy preparing for arrival, Leon stared at the piece of paper in his hand. He closed his fist around it as he became aware of Mr Knutt.

"Leon," he said in a low voice, his back to the others. "Can you do what your father asked?"

"Yes, Mr Knutt," said Leon quietly.

"Is it dangerous?"

"Once the pod has stopped, it will be safe."

"And you know precisely what to do?"

"Yes," replied Leon. "The core is similar to our own pod's. It will not take long."

"Why do you think he wishes us to prepare to escape? Does he believe we will be in danger?" asked Mr Knutt.

"He will know what is best in the situation in which we will find ourselves," replied Leon.

Mr Knutt smiled. "You're a very loyal and modest person, Leon. He has much confidence in you."

Leon smiled thinly. "Thank you, Mr Knutt."

Mr Knutt started to step away. Then he said: "Oh, Leon, one more thing: why do you think your father didn't want Aurore to hear what was being said?"

Leon felt his fingers tighten around the note in his hand. "I am not sure," he replied.

14 - ARES

Mr Sparks ascended to the top level of his home, a space of simple, clean design beneath the rocky outcrop. A window at the rear looked out onto the flattened space of the roof and, beyond it, to the higher outcrop on which he had set up his primitive radio transmitter.

A wave of his hand in the room's centre would take him up into his pod, which was docked above. But through the window this time, there was something to distract him. On the flat roof space sat another pod, of smaller design, and standing before it were three individuals dressed in dark one-piece outfits and knee-length over-cloaks that flapped limply in the slight Martian breeze.

Mr Sparks sighed. The Council Guard. Their appearance was not unexpected, but their timing could have been better – like, *after* his departure. He opened the small silver briefcase he had brought with him and withdrew a smaller flat case that he tucked into a pocket inside his cloak. Then he stepped towards the hatch and waved a hand. It opened and two of the guards stepped forward.

There was no customary greeting, the usual gesture of respect between adults.

"Councillor," said one. "We are instructed to bring you to Ares."

Mr Sparks looked from him to the other. "What is the reason?"

The first guard turned to look at the aerial sitting up on the hill behind. "You have been communicating with Earth."

"You have been monitoring me."

He said it as a statement rather than a question. "That is against our laws!"

"A new ruling of the Council, Councillor – as you well know."

"My wife and son are there," said Mr Sparks. "Their safety has been threatened by Smiall'kes'hep's illegal actions!"

"They should have left when instructed," the guard retorted curtly.

One of the guards stepped past Mr Sparks.

"Where is he going?" asked Mr Sparks.

"Routine," replied the other.

"This is highly irregular," said Mr Sparks. "I will be raising a formal complaint with the Council."

"That is your prerogative, Councillor. Now," said the guard, "come with me."

2

The pod dipped through the thin clouds and levelled out over the rugged dusty terrain. On the far horizon, the terrain softened into dry valleys, craters and the edge of a flat plain.

"Valley of Ares," said Camille.

"You recognise it?" asked Lucy.

"Oui. Yes."

"Can you tell where we are going to land, Leon?" asked Mr Knutt.

"No. Perhaps Aurore may be able to tell us?" he said.

"Aurore?"

"There is a pod port at the mouth of the valley. It is likely we go there."

"OK, thank you, Aurore," said Mr Knutt. "Mr Flynn."

"H'edmaster?" replied the older man.

"I suggest you and I are the first ones out."

"As you wish, h'edmaster."

"Now, everyone," said Mr Knutt. "Please activate your environmental suits."

All of the children apart from Leon and Aurore did as instructed.

"Now, seats everybody," said Mr Knutt.

3

A new voice appeared over the comms. A female voice; familiar, even speaking Martian.

"Aurore. This is Skiel'aeljtın. Prepare to land."

Mr Knutt's mouth fell open. He looked at Leon, whose nod confirmed what he was thinking. The communication had come through the comportal channel. The pair of them shot glances at Aurore. Camille also turned to look at her friend.

Aurore looked at Leon and Mr Knutt. Then she answered, also in Martian.

"Yes, Miss Sky. But I am not alone."

"We know. Please inform your friends to remain on

the pod while suitable environmental conditions are prepared for them. Out."

"Translation please, Leon," requested Mr Knutt.

Leon did so.

"Is the comportal network operating again?"

Leon checked his own comportal. "No," he said.

"Then how –"

"There are reserved channels," said Aurore.

"Have you been using yours all along?" asked Leon.

"What's that?" said Mr Knutt.

"No, I have not," said Aurore.

"I believe Aurore may have something to tell us," said Leon. He looked at her.

Aurore seemed composed. "It is nothing. I was instructed to reboard the pod after we returned from the field excursion. That is all."

"And you didn't think to tell anyone?"

"It became irrelevant," answered Aurore plainly.

"Then you must have known that Miss Sky was leaving with the others?" challenged Camille, clearly upset at her friend's actions.

"No. It was if I could not find her."

"But you knew the pod would bring you back to Mars?" said Mr Knutt.

"Yes."

"And us with it," said Emily.

"You were not part of the plan," admitted Aurore.

"And that plan was to try to *kill* us all?" snapped Dominic.

"I did not know about that," said Aurore. "*I* helped to save Tsiolkovsky."

"But loads of people have died on Earth," said Emily. "You might have been able to help save them!"

Aurore fell silent.

Mr Knutt spoke up. "What is done is done. I do not believe that Aurore could have known about the asteroid attack. We cannot be sure at the moment that Miss Sky and the other Martians could have known either. There are clearly events happening on Mars that are bigger than any of us. I suggest we remain calm and prepare for what awaits us when we land."

Mr Knutt took a deep breath and sat back. Nevertheless, he looked at Aurore with some uncertainty. There was more here than met the eye. And hadn't Fred Sparks already warned him and Leon to be wary of her?

4

Mr Sparks looked out from his cell at Ares. It had been called a *guest room*. It was comfortable, well furnished; he had been offered adequate refreshments and all courtesies had been extended. But he was not free to leave, and he was yet to find out formally what he was being held for.

A wall-spanning window at one end framed a view over the plain beyond. Down there stood the pod port, a complex with a capacity to accommodate sixty or so pods of various sizes. Several pods – from this distance, represented by bright dots in the late afternoon sky – were either approaching or leaving. One of them, he knew, would be the pod carrying his son and his friends.

5

The dimming sky, deep pink turning to purple and festooned with the faint pin-pricks of stars, combined with the golden lights around the pod port complex below to look like a scene out of Hollywood.

Skiel'aeljtın looked dispassionately through the window as she awaited the arrival of the pod. She had shed the pressure suit that had been de rigueur on Earth's Moon, and was attired in a graceful sapphire-blue gown that was delicately embroidered with gold thread.

Below her, outside, on the forecourt of the landing area stood two uniformed guards, one by a shuttle sled.

Presently, a bright star appeared above the horizon. It grew steadily as it dropped down and approached steadily and silently. Finally, it reared up in Skiel'aeljtın's view as it came near to overhead and then descended steeply, its feet extending to bring it softly to its landing on Mars.

6

"Full stop?" asked Mr Knutt.

Leon nodded.

Mr Knutt flicked his eyes to direct Leon to access the drive.

Leon immediately left his seat and went to the rear of the cabin. Mr Knutt and Mr Flynn moved to their prearranged position in the centre of the craft, blocking a direct view of Leon by Aurore.

Leon moved quickly to a trapezoidal shape marked

on the floor behind the pod's central hub. He waved his wristband across the shape and it slipped silent aside. A faint green glow painted the edge of the aperture and Leon's legs as he lowered himself into the space. Soon he was out of sight.

7

In the narrow space below, Leon moved as quickly as he could around the central disc of the propulsion drive, which resembled a huge, flattened and multi-lobed lemon squeezer.

It was offline, but it still pulsed and crackled with latent energy. He tried to ignore the crawling sensation that crept over his skin as he edged around it.

Leon read off the sectors that were marked around a ring that was suspended over the core. He came first to sector 60. Nothing there. He looked over the lobe again before continuing on towards sector 90.

At first, it again appeared that there was nothing there. Then Leon noticed a small protuberance on the lobe's far side, carefully hidden near its base, where it began to curve back into the body of the disc. It was about half the size of Leon's fist, gunmetal grey in colour, and sleekly shaped like a computer mouse. Leon reached out with some trepidation. He took hold of it and felt the transmitted vibration of the disc. It came away easily as he lifted one end, weakening its magnetic contact.

8

Above, in the cabin, the lights flickered momentarily.

Everyone looked up and around – except Mr Knutt and Mr Flynn, who maintained their cool demeanour. Aurore looked around and moved her head from side to side, as if to peer past the grown-ups. Was she missing seeing Leon?

9

Leon looked at the object in his hand. It looked and felt like an inert piece of metal, only a fraction of the expected weight. He closed his hand around it and made his way back to the hatch. Soon he was back in the cabin and the hatch aperture became solid floor again. He walked over to Mr Knutt, who stood with his back to him, hands clasped together behind. Leon touched the device to Mr Knutt's hand and Mr Knutt took it from him without looking around. Just as deftly, Mr Knutt passed it to Mr Flynn, who secreted it away in an inside pocket of his overalls.

"Pod Nine, prepare to be debark," came a voice in broken English over the comms.

"Visors on, everyone," said Mr Knutt.

"A suitable atmosphere has been prepared," said the voice.

"Nevertheless, please keep your visors on until we're sure," Mr Knutt said to everyone.

"Now, Mr Flynn, what are we going to do about y –"

A hissing sound indicated the door seal had been breached. A moment later, the door opened and they found themselves looking not out to a Martian evening, but into a short tunnel.

"Permit me, h'edmaster," said Mr Flynn.

Mr Knutt nodded and Mr Flynn stepped gingerly

out into the tunnel. It was no longer than ten feet in length and led into another compartment. He sniffed the air. Hm, it was perfectly breathable.

Mr Flynn edged forward. The tunnel took his weight and he found himself looking into the chamber. There were a number of seats arranged either side of a central aisle. Beyond these, a curved window set before two forward-facing seats, one of which was occupied. The figure turned and their eyes met.

"Wely-ie-commmb," said the guard. As he spoke, he raised his left hand and turned it over so that it was palm-up and extended it towards Mr Flynn in the customary Martian greeting.

Mr Flynn, who had never managed to replicate the gesture, returned a quick, self-conscious wave. "'Ow do, lad," he replied.

"Pliess beisz-eetid." *Please be seated.*

"Jus' a minute. I'll be gettin' the others firs'," he said.

Mr Flynn walked back up the tunnel to the hatch of the pod. The end of the tunnel formed a perfect seal around the door.

"Mr Flynn?"

"Looks like a bus of some kind, h'edmaster. One driver. Tol' me to take a seat."

"No-one else? No Miss Sky?" asked Mr Knutt.

Mr Flynn shook his head.

"Right," said Mr Knutt. "What is there to stop us taking off again, under our own control?"

"They got the 'atch open and tha' tunnel attached now. Don' think we 'ave much choice now, h'edmaster."

"No, indeed, Mr Flynn."

Mr Knutt led everyone off the pod and soon they were being transferred to the main building of the complex.

He looked out of the window. Despite the probable danger they were in, he found it quietly exhilarating to think they were actually on Mars. *Mars*. It had been an impossible dream realised to find himself in space; then at the Moon. Now, through happenchance, on the Red Planet.

The vehicle reversed onto a docking bay, the click of locking bolts announcing their arrival, and Mr Knutt was shaken out of his musings.

This time, Mr Knutt led the way. They emerged into a wide corridor. Behind them, on either side, large windows looked out on the pod port. Pale purple light from the setting sun filled the space and washed over the figures before them. There were five altogether: four guards and, standing in front of them, Skiel'aeljtın herself.

She looked at the humans with their protective masks on – all except the older human, who was breathing quite easily.

"You have no need of the environmental protection here," said Skiel'aeljtın. "The atmosphere has been constituted for you."

Mr Knutt put his hand out again in caution. Then he noticed Mr Flynn beside him, who seemed quite at ease without a visor. He'd forgotten about Mr Flynn's predicament. He relaxed and removed his own visor, and indicated that everyone could follow suit.

"Miss Sky," said Mr Knutt plainly, and with as little emotion as he could muster.

"Mr Knutt," replied Skiel'aeljtın graciously. "Welcome to Mars. Even when your presence was unintended."

"Yes," replied Mr Knutt. "It was just Aurore you were interested in bringing back, wasn't it? I hope our presence hasn't overcomplicated matters for you."

"We shall deal with it," said Skiel'aeljtın. She turned and found Aurore. "Welcome home, daughter."

Heads turned and eyes widened amongst everyone in the Earth party. All eyes fell on her. Aurore looked around apprehensively, finally into the eyes of her friend, Camille.

"Is is true?" asked Camille.

Aurore had told her that her mother was dead. Aurore answered her friend by composing herself and walking over to Skiel'aeljtın and bowing her head. "Mother," she said.

Skiel'aeljtın reached out and touched Aurore lightly on the head. She said something quietly to her in Martian. Only Leon knew what she said: "Asıl'el'tassz. Come. You have done well."

Skiel'aeljtın turned to the others.

"Quarters have been prepared for you. There you will wait... while it is decided what to do with you."

"I assume you mean to return us to Earth?" said Mr Knutt curtly.

"That remains to be seen," said Skiel'aeljtın. "Contact with Earth is prohibited. It is complicated."

"Actually, I think it is quite straightforward. We were brought here against our will. We have children who are separated from their parents. I demand that we are returned as soon as possible."

"You are in a position to demand nothing, Mr

Knutt. You will do as instructed, or we will not be responsible for your well-being." said Skiel'aeljtın. Her tone had changed in an instant.

Mr Knutt was taken aback. He softened his own tone. "Miss Sky, what happened? You were held in high esteem within Controlled Contact."

"You have a saying on your planet: Keep your friends close, but your enemies closer."

"Enemies?" said Mr Knutt. "That's what we are to you? What about Wilma Sparks. You and she were friends, were you not? How could you do this to her?"

Skiel'aeljtın smiled thinly. "There, you see. This is the problem. Her name is *Kımb'bul'bir*, not some comical Earth name."

Mr Knutt frowned. "I'm sure nothing is meant by it – just a means of familiarity..."

"It demeans us," retorted Skiel'aeljtın. "Contact with Earth demeans us. Earth is toxic: its people, their numbers; its very atmosphere. Our ancestors had a better way."

Mr Knutt was still in shock at Skiel'aeljtın's venom. "You mean by attacking anyone or anything they perceived to be a threat?"

"My father tried quietly to warn our people for years. When High Councillor Skallir'rir died, he decided it was time for more open talk. And when that failed, direct action."

"One moment," said Mr Knutt. "Your father is *Councillor Smiall'kes'hep*?"

"*High* Councillor Smiall'kes'hep," corrected Skiel'aeljtın.

The implications sank in with Mr Knutt. *And Aurore is his granddaughter.*

"We have the right to defend our race," continued Skiel'aeljtın.

"Even when it involves murdering thousands of innocent people?"

Skiel'aeljtın waved dismissively. "Propaganda," she said.

Aurore looked up at Skiel'aeljtın. She spoke in her native tongue. "I heard this, mother. Is it true?"

Skiel'aeljtın looked down at Aurore, and she replied in Martian. "The human exaggerates. But hard decisions – sacrifices – sometimes have to be made, little one."

Leon stepped forward. He spoke in English. "Mr Knutt does not exaggerate. Nor does he lie!"

Dominic stepped next to Leon. "Those asteroids were fired at Earth. And the Moon. Our parents are there. They could have been killed!"

"Well, thankfully they were not," said Skiel'aeljtın.

"Only thanks to Leon," said Lucy.

"With Aurore's help," added Camille.

"Oh? Is that so? Well... well done. Well done, both of you," said Skiel'aeljtın with an air of false sincerity. "Leon? Your proper name is Shieeekkksssup, is it not? Or do you respond more readily to 'Leon'?"

"My friends call me Leon," he replied. He looked around at them.

"My father," said Leon. "Councillor Shieekk'ssup'pl. He was going to be here to meet us..."

"Was he now?"

"Is he here?"

"He has... been delayed," said Skiel'aeljtın.

Mr Knutt looked at Mr Flynn. Their eyes met. So, Fred Sparks was being held.

"But," said Skiel'aeljtın. "Let us not stand here," she said in a more conciliatory tone. "Where are my manners? You have had a long journey. Allow me to show you to your quarters. You will find there refreshments. Tomorrow we shall talk some more."

The guards left Skiel'aeljtın's side and positioned themselves to form a box around them. With a nod from Mr Knutt, the party followed Skiel'aeljtın and Aurore along the corridor.

15 - ESCAPE

Their quarters were surprisingly pleasant: well furnished, well-lit (compared to the more dismal natural light of Mars) and well-provisioned. In the central lounge area, where large windows looked out over the pod complex and the setting sun (now turning grey-blue on the horizon), was a seating area with a low table laid out with food and drink – mostly food from Earth, Dominic noticed hungrily. Only the presence of the guard outside the main door served as a reminder that they were not fully welcome guests.

Mr Knutt examined the food, trying a morsel himself (which was surprisingly good) before permitting the children to tuck in while he and Mr Flynn inspected their accommodation.

The central lounge had four small rooms leading off it, each just large enough to contain two simple beds.

"Well, Mr Flynn. What do think?" asked Mr Knutt.

"All looks very comfy, h'edmaster."

As he spoke, Mr Flynn turned his back to the doors to the bedrooms, which fanned around the lounge, to face Mr Knutt in the centre of the room. The main door was hidden from his view by Mr Knutt himself. Mr Flynn brought his right hand palm upward and splayed his gnarled fingers. He touched his palm at its four corners with the forefinger of his other hand and gave a slight nod in the direction of an upper corner of the room.

Mr Knutt nodded slowly. He too had noticed the small silvery spheres that were probably cameras of some kind.

"I thought they was banned from spyin' on each other?" said Mr Flynn.

"True," said Mr Knutt. "We'll have to assume things have changed."

He glanced over to the table, looking for Leon, who stood by himself, a small plate of a green vegetable of some kind in his hand. He appeared thoughtful, distracted. Camille also, without her friend, sat quietly apart from Dominic, Lucy and Emily.

"Leon," said Mr Knutt.

Leon looked up. "Yes, Mr Knutt?" He put his plate down and walked over.

"Leon, your father. Have you any idea where he might be now?"

"No," said Leon. "Just that he was to have met us here."

"And we have no way to contact him?" said Mr Knutt.

"Not without a working comportal," replied Leon.

"Hm," said Mr Knutt. "I guess we are expected to remain here, at least for now."

"An' if not, there's that fella outside to make sure we do," said Mr Flynn.

"Yes," said Mr Knutt. "It does appear that way."

2

The door opened and Mr Sparks looked around to see

Skiel'aeljtın and Aurore enter the room. He was surprised to see anyone, let alone Skiel'aeljtın herself. And this must be Aurore too. He raised an eyebrow – or at least an eye ridge, as Martians didn't have eyebrows.

"Skiel'aeljtın," he said simply.

"Councillor," replied Skiel'aeljtın.

"Have you come to permit me to go on my way?" asked Mr Sparks.

"Not at this time, Councillor."

"Then when will that be? I remind you that I am a *Councillor* –"

"Who is suspected of sedition –"

"*Sedition*? A crime against the state? *Whose* state is that? Smiall'kes'hep's? What is the nature of my 'crime'?"

"That will be presented at a hearing of the Sedition Committee in due course."

Sedition committee?

Mr Sparks was momentarily speechless.

"Simply, I am here to save time," said Skiel'aeljtın. "Where are the real prisms?"

Mr Sparks feigned ignorance.

"Prisms? Explain."

Skiel'aeljtın moved to the window, her back to him. "The ones you replaced with blanks in Kindlebir's repository in your home?"

"I do not know what you are talking about," said Mr Sparks.

Skiel'aeljtın turned to face him again. "Of course you do," she said coldly. "But no matter. We shall soon break through your computer encryption and –"

"That is against our laws."

Skiel'aeljtın smiled thinly.

"– and then we will know the depths of your plotting."

Mr Sparks deliberately changed the subject, to one that was also of genuine concern to him. "Where are my son and his associates?" He looked at Aurore, who stood quietly by the door.

"They are safe and are being cared for," replied Skiel'aeljtın.

Mr Sparks turned to Aurore. "*Are* they, Aurore?"

Aurore nodded.

"Do not talk to her," said Skiel'aeljtın.

"I wish to see them."

"In time," said Skiel'aeljtın. "If you co-operate."

Mr Sparks softened his own tone. "I will consider it. If I am not permitted to see them, I will ask if you could relay something from me?" He reached inside his cloak.

Skiel'aeljtın watched him curiously. "What is it?"

Mr Sparks withdrew a thin clear case. It looked like plastic, but was probably something more advanced. "Oxygen bands. For the humans. Their environmental suits have limited life."

Skiel'aeljtın hesitated. Then she took the package from him.

There were seven silver wristbands inside, and three packs of liquid phials. One of the wristbands was different, having a bluish inset, like a sapphire set in a ring. All the rest had red ones.

"They have no need of them," said Skiel'aeljtın. "The air in their accommodation replicates Earth's."

"*Please*," said Mr Sparks, as close to pleading as he would permit himself. He glanced again at Aurore. "A precaution. They are innocent. Just children, and their teacher."

"I will consider it," said Skiel'aeljtın.

3

Skiel'aeljtın and Aurore entered their own quarters. Skiel'aeljtın threw the case onto a table.

"We are not taking it to them?" asked Aurore.

"No. They have no need of them."

"But without –"

"The humans are of little concern, little one. They will be soon be processed along with any other humans still on Oztzıldıj, and from there our contact will end. Think no more on them."

"Processed? They will be returned to Earth?"

"That I cannot say," said Skiel'aeljtın.

Aurore was stunned.

"But... mother. Camille and I are *friends*. She stayed here with us; learned about us. *I* stayed with her on Earth. You too spent time on Earth and on their Moon. How can you say this? All that means nothing?"

"Asıl'el'tassz, understand. This was for a purpose, to serve the long-term interests of our people. The humans are dangerous; inferior. They threaten our very existence. Something had to be done. The OPP programme permitted us to study them from within, to understand their capabilities, their ambitions. And their weaknesses.

"This was my task – and to determine how to disable the Sentinel. In that, alas, I failed, and that had to be achieved another way.

"So, wring from yourself all signs of emotion – another disease of the mind brought by the humans. Discipline yourself with the reason and logic with which you were reared. And accept that all of this is necessary and right."

4

Once everyone had eaten and drank something, they sat together in the lounge area. The children looked tired. It had been a long and quite traumatic couple of days. But Mr Knutt was curious to find out more about their predicament. He focused his attention on Camille, whom he thus far had not engaged with very much.

"Camille," he asked. "Aurore – when you stayed with her on Mars, or when she stayed with you on Earth, it was never mentioned that Miss Sky was her mother?"

"No," replied Camille. "It was said that her mother had died several years ago."

"And who told you that?"

"Miss Sky. And Aurore."

"Aurore too?"

"Yes," said Camille. She looked away for a moment, her eyes moistened.

"I'm sorry, Camille," said Mr Knutt. "But this may be important."

He gave Camille a moment, then he asked, "And Miss Sky – how was she introduced to you?"

"Excuse me?"

"What was her title or role?"

"Oh," said Camille. "She was – how you say – a

nanny? And a teacher."

"And she led Aurore to lie about their true relationship, even to claim her mother was dead. Why?"

"I do not know," said Camille.

"No, of course not," said Mr Knutt. "Just thinking aloud. Now, at the same time, Miss Sky had become the chief Martian representative of the Office of Planetary Protection. Someone was sure to find out sooner or later. Would it matter that she also had a daughter?"

Leon finally spoke. "Martians are very private; therefore not usually inquisitive about one another. But Miss Sky may have had a reason to prevent it being known that Aurore was High Councillor Smiall'kes'hep's granddaughter."

"My thought too, Leon," said Mr Knutt. "Camille, another question: who chose Aurore's Earth name?"

"Yes, I know this," answered Camille. "It was Miss Sky. Aurore told me that her Earth name had been given to her when it was known she would be coming to France. Aurore is not uncommon as a girl's name there."

"'Scuse me, h'edmaster," said Mr Flynn, "I may be getting' a bit slow in my 'ead as well as limb in me ol' age, but what exackly are you gettin' at?"

"My apologies, Mr Flynn," said Mr Knutt.

As if to underline Mr Flynn's impatience, Dominic let out a yawn, and was followed by Emily trying to stifle her own.

"Right," said Mr Knutt. "This will not take long. Then we can all get some rest. Leon, I believe you and I are on the same wavelength on this. Would you care to elaborate?"

Leon sat forward. "Yes, I considered this after Aurore spoke after my mother's presentation this week. It was the first time I had seen her so bold. I have not known her long, but she is usually very quiet."

"Is that your experience too, Camille?" asked Mr Knutt.

"Yes. She did not waste words."

"So," said Leon. "I looked up the incident in which my great grandmother's assistant died. And I discovered that her pod crashed in a small town in the United States of America. It is called Aurora."

"Oh," said Lucy and Camille together.

"Is that true?" asked Emily.

"Yes," said Mr Knutt. "Aurore is the French version of Aurora. It would seem to be more than a coincidence. It is likely that Miss Sky chose it on purpose."

"But why would she name her daughter after a place where someone died?" asked Lucy.

"I believe it was intended as a veiled attack on my mother," said Leon.

"How come?" asked Emily.

"For her work with the OPP," replied Leon. "And because her grandmother really started the Controlled Contact programme. Plus, she was held by some as responsible for the death of her assistant, Tek'tu'jan."

"Which might suggest a political motive. Or perhaps a personal one," said Mr Knutt.

Mr Knutt sighed. "OK, everyone. I suggest it's now time to get some rest. We are going to need to keep safe and alert. The children can take three of the bedrooms. Mr Flynn, you take the other. I'll catch some rest out here."

"But h'edmaster..." began Mr Flynn.

"No, Mr Flynn. I insist," said Mr Knutt.

The children looked at him. "Off you go, then," said Mr Knutt.

The children began to get up. "Leon, could you stay back a minute?"

Leon nodded.

The other children made their goodnights, leaving Leon with the two grown-ups.

"Sit down again, Leon."

Leon did as he was told.

"Leon," said Mr Knutt quietly. "You know our situation better than any of us. We need you to guide and advise us. Before we landed, your father said that if he was not here to meet us, we should attempt to escape?"

"Yes," said Leon.

"Which indicates that he expected that we might be held captive?"

"Yes," said Leon again.

"We must therefore assume that he is being held somewhere himself?"

"Yes," said Leon a third time.

Mr Knutt took a deep breath. He had rather hoped that Mr Sparks would be here; that they could have left with him, and then soon been on their way back home. Now, it seemed he must contemplate a risky escape and a dangerous mission with a handful of schoolchildren.

"What is the chance that you and I could get back to the pod and attempt to fulfil your father's instructions?"

"Excuse me?" said Leon.

"Can we get to the pod and get to Phobos without being apprehended?"

"But h'edmaster..." interrupted Mr Flynn.

"Mr Flynn, it will be far safer if Leon and I attempt this. You will stay with the other children."

"So, Leon. What do you think?"

"If we can get to the pod – assuming it is still there and is not guarded – it might be possible. But I do not know what to do when we get there."

"Well, for that I will trust in your father's confidence in you. I don't believe he would send you if he felt it could not be achieved, or that it would place you in significant danger."

"You can't just leave us here, Mr Knutt?" said Emily.

Mr Knutt, Mr Flynn and Leon all turned to see Emily and Lucy standing in the doorway to their room.

"Emily, I have a duty to keep you safe," replied Mr Knutt.

"Mr, Knutt, in case you haven't noticed, we're on Mars. It's not like we're at Flintworne now. We should stick together."

It was Dominic, who now stood in the doorway of his room. The door next to his slid open and Camille stood there too.

"I agree," said Camille. "We all stay. Or we all go."

Mr Knutt pushed his glasses back on his nose. A genuine predicament. He couldn't, with any conscience, leave any of them behind. Nor could he and Leon take them all without further risk.

Much as he would hate to admit it, Dominic was

right. They weren't at Flintworne now, and strictly he wasn't their headmaster right now either. The situation was as it was, and they would have to do their best. Together.

"Hm. I guess that's decided," said Mr Knutt. "Mr Flynn, Leon, we need to think about how to get past our guard and to the pod station. Without being seen or apprehended."

5

On Earth's Moon, Mr Smiley was with Mrs Sparks.

"They should have landed by now. Any news?"

"No," replied Mrs Sparks.

"And nothing from Fred either?"

"Nothing."

Mr Smiley nodded slowly. "I've spoken with HQ. They do not have even a single pod that we could use to go ourselves. The most advanced Earth technology would take weeks."

"We must assume that they are preoccupied. I... hope it is with my husband's plan."

6

No time like the present. Everyone was tired, especially the children. But there was no point in delaying things until a better time. There wasn't one. The children sat quietly around the seating area while Mr Knutt and Mr Flynn spoke quietly about their plan.

They had covered over the ceiling cameras, if that was what they were. If they were, they would probably have only a short time before someone came to investigate. The only snag would lie in getting Mr Flynn to the craft without an environmental suit.

"OK," Mr Knutt said quietly. "We know that Martians are intelligent; advanced. But I bet they haven't watched many action movies. So, on my mark, we will attract the guard's attention by hammering on the door. Hopefully, he will come in to investigate, and Mr Flynn and I will overpower him while you all escape. We will follow you."

"But, Mr Knutt..." said Emily.

"You must do as I ask, Emily," said Mr Knutt. "I'm told that humans are generally stronger than Martians due to our gravity. Now..." he said.

He was interrupted by a soft thump. He looked at Mr Flynn, who cocked his head to indicate it had come from outside the room. Leon stepped towards the door, but Mr Flynn put a hand out to stop him.

Mr Flynn reached out to the door. It suddenly slid aside. There, on the floor of the corridor outside lay the guard, apparently unconscious.

Mr Flynn looked around, perplexed at what he was seeing.

"What is it?" asked Mr Knutt.

Before Mr Flynn could comment, he heard "Aurore!"

He turned back around to see Aurore stepping into the room over the fallen guard.

Camille got to her feet. "Aurore!"

Aurore looked at her friend and gave her a small smile.

"You have to get out of here. *Now*," she said.

"Aurore, what happened?" asked Lucy.

"I stunned the guard. There is no time to explain more. You must leave. Immediately."

Aurore walked over to Leon. She reached out with her left hand and said something to him in Martian. Leon answered her and raised a hand to hers. Their wrist-bands touched, and the dim lights on both brightened and flickered for a moment.

Aurore then handed Leon something. It was the transparent case that Mr Sparks had given to Skiel'aeljtın. "They are from your father."

Leon's eyes widened. "You have seen him?"

"Yes. But he too is under guard. I saw him with my mother. He gave these to my mother to give to you. But... but she has refused," she said awkwardly. "There are oxygen bands for the humans. And a spare band and phials for you. Now, go."

"Come with us," said Leon.

"I cannot," said Aurore. "Please do what you must."

"We will try," said Leon.

Aurore turned to the others. This time she spoke firstly in French to Camille, then in English to the others. "Good luck."

7

Within a few minutes, following Aurore's directions, they had made it safely to the transfer station – and without anyone falling over in the lighter Martian gravity.

But two problems now presented themselves. One, no vehicles. Two, another guard.

They huddled back around a corner before the guard spotted them. At least they didn't look so conspicuous now without their environmental visors. The bands that Leon had handed out fitting easily and without pain or discomfort, and they provided a steady stream of concentrated oxygen that passed through the skin and into the bloodstream. They breathed normally and didn't notice that their oxygen was coming from another source. The only downside was that the thinner atmosphere made their throats drier and their voices sound squeakier.

Mr Knutt whispered to the others. "Right, we'll try the same plan as before. Leon, you go forward and talk to the guard; distract him. Mr Flynn and I will sneak up on him and disable him."

This time, there were no protests.

"One. Two. Three. Go," said Mr Knutt.

Leon strode out, moving to the left of the broad windows that looked out over the pod port. As he intended, the guard spotted him and began to move in his direction.

When they were sure they would not be seen, Mr Knutt and Mr Flynn emerged and moved as quickly as they could across the space. The children watched as their former headmaster, who was tall and normally quite formal, and Mr Flynn, in his familiar green groundskeeper's overalls, lumbered after the guard.

"Oh, I do hope he knows what he's doing," said Emily.

"I wouldn't bank on it," said Dominic from his hunched position in front of them.

Out in the lobby area before them, the guard was talking to Leon. He had his hand covering a comportal at his waist, like a highway cop on Earth or an old western gunslinger.

Mr Knutt and Mr Flynn were tip-toeing up on him from behind. Once they got close enough, Mr Knutt raised a hand, poised for it to fall like an axe in a karate chop.

Back in the huddle, Emily gasped.

The guard, sensing someone behind him, whirled around and whisked out his comportal, faster than anyone could have suspected. Mr Knutt brought his arm down, but instead of chopping the guard at the base of his neck as he intended, he caught the guard's arm. The comportal flew from his grip and clattered across the floor.

Just as quickly, the guard shoved Mr Knutt with both hand in the centre of his chest, toppling him over backwards and into the arms of Mr Flynn, who, even in the lower gravity of Mars, was unable to hold him and the two collapsed in a heap.

Meanwhile, Dominic was already moving, scampering across the floor towards the guard's comportal. Catching what Dominic was doing, Leon hurried in front of the guard to prevent him going after it. The guard grabbed Leon and roughly spun him away, sending him to the floor.

But Dominic was already there. He grabbed up the comportal, turned it and aimed it at the guard. He squeezed the sides of the comportal to fire it, as he had been taught with Leon's last year. Nothing. It didn't work. Dominic stared at it aghast. He looked up. The guard was leaning towards him to take the comportal back. Then he stiffened momentarily and fell limply forward, landing beside Dominic, unconscious.

Mr Knutt stood over him, massaging his right hand.

"Well, that worked better than I anticipated," he said.

The other children hurried over.

"Oh, Mr Knutt, that was amazing!" said Emily.

"They don't call me Hard Knutt for nothing, Emily," he replied with a wink. "Well done, Dominic, Leon. Mr Flynn, are you OK?"

"Yes, Mr Knutt. I'm alright."

"Good. Let's get out of here."

8

The pod was a quarter of a mile away. They had found their way outside and now they ambled in the evening gloom across the expanse of the pod port towards it, being careful not to stumble in Mars's lower gravity. Every once in a while, someone looked back to see if they were being followed.

"Bloomin' 'eck, it's cold out here," said Dominic. "When's the Sun coming out?"

"It is out," said Leon. "It hasn't set yet. It's over there."

Dominic looked towards the horizon. A feeble bluish-white dot hung there like a dim light bulb.

Mr Knutt had advised everyone to fit their face visors for the transit. Only Mr Flynn was without one. Mr Knutt was concerned for him and had offered his own visor, which Mr Flynn had refused. A dusting of frost from his exhaled breath coated his nostrils and lips. Mr Knutt helped him to move on as quickly as they could.

9

The pod sat on its tripod legs perhaps a hundred feet away. Mr Knutt almost sighed in relief. There was no-one guarding it. Wait. No. A figure appeared from around its left flank. Mr Knutt almost wilted. He wasn't sure he had another karate chop in him, not out here in the cold and with Mr Flynn helped along on his arm.

Before Mr Knutt could do or say anything, Dominic nudged Leon and the pair of them walked out towards the guard. Leon led the way, Dominic right behind him. As before, the guard spotted Leon and cautiously moved towards him.

The others heard the guard address Leon in Martian. Leon replied. Then, suddenly, Leon dropped down and Dominic, behind him, stunned the guard with the comportal he had taken from the other back at the complex. Then he turned and waved the others over.

Leon raised his wristband to where the pod door should be, and immediately it began to push out and unfold from the skin of the craft.

Soon everyone was aboard and taking their seats. Leon waved his hand over the command armrest and the door closed back up.

Mr Flynn, fortunately, appeared no worse for wear.

"Ready for take off," said Leon. With another wave of his hand, the craft lifted skywards. Leon made the walls transparent as they climbed high out of sight of the pod port.

Leon waved his hand again and the interior light flickered.

"I am drawing extra power to cloak us from detection," said Leon.

"I didn' think this pod could do that, lad?" said Mr Flynn.

"It is not a natural function of this design," said Leon. "But it is possible to sustain a cloaking field for a short period – in case they attempt to track us."

"Where are we headed, Leon?" asked Mr Knutt.

"To my home, Mr Knutt. We may need some things from there. Plus, my father may have left further instructions for us. Then, if we must, to Su'umka'r."

"Won't they guess we will go to your home?" asked Lucy.

"It is likely," said Leon. "Except –"

"Except that I mentioned Su'umka'r – Phobos – in front of Aurore on our way to Mars," said Mr Knutt. "It is possible she told her mother before her apparent change of heart."

"Yes," said Leon. "That is my hope."

16 – SHHEIKSPULE

Leon brought the pod down on the spare docking spot on the roof of his home. Already he could see signs of trouble. The family pod stood there, lit underneath by three spot-lights – which meant his father had not left here by choice. And the hatch to the roof space was open, revealing an illuminated interior that spilled a pale blue light over the flat roof space.

Once the pod's hatch was open, Leon said, "I'll go first."

Mr Knutt didn't try to stop him. Leon knew his home, and there was no present sense of danger. Nevertheless, he said, "Stay here everyone, until we can be sure that the coast is clear."

Mr Knutt emerged from the house a minute later to give the all clear, and everyone entered the building and followed Mr Knutt down to the main living level.

The scene was chaotic. Surfaces had been cleared of their contents and strewn across the floor. A metal trunk had been emptied of its contents and sat upside down on the floor. Its base had been cut open and was also empty. Leon stood in the middle of the room.

"They have taken my father's computers," said Leon. "He looked at the broken trunk on the floor. "And my great-grandmother's belongings."

"Oh, Leon, I'm sorry," said Lucy.

Leon shrugged. "What is done is done. Let me show you around."

"Ah, Leon. Do we have time for that?" asked Mr Knutt.

"I need to gather some things, Mr Knutt. Lucy, Emily and Dominic may wish to see some of my home – Camille too? – while I am about it?"

"*Yes, please*," said Emily.

"I'll come," said Dominic.

"I will stay here," said Camille.

"Me too," said Lucy.

"Mr Flynn?" said Leon.

"Yes, lad?"

"Would you care to see our vegetable garden?"

Mr Flynn looked at Mr Knutt, who nodded.

"Well, if we have time…"

"Be as quick as you can," said Mr Knutt.

"Much of it is hydroponics," said Leon.

Mr Flynn stood up straight. "Hydroponics? Hm, alright, lad. Lead on."

Leon led Emily and Dominic to the rear of the room and they disappeared into a short corridor that led further into the rock outcrop. At its end, there was an elevator, which they took to the complex's lower levels.

2

They stepped out into a round room, off which branched three further spaces. In front of them, the hydroponics garden and laboratory. To their right, another corridor. And behind them, the archive room.

"Please, go ahead," said Leon. "I will be just a moment."

Leon disappeared into the corridor. Emily and Dominic followed Mr Flynn into the garden room.

When Leon caught up with the others, they were still in shock at the scene. Leon too reeled at what he saw. Many of the plants had been pulled out of their tanks and from soil trays by their roots and were scattered about the room.

"It's the same next door," said Emily.

"Lot of broken stuff in there," said Dominic.

"I'm sorry," said Emily.

"Do not apologise," said Leon. "It is not your fault."

"No, but the damage…" said Emily.

"They was lookin' for somethin'," said Mr Flynn.

"Yes," said Leon. "And they found it – that is, they found where it was hidden. My great grandmother's trunk."

"That was it – upstairs?" asked Emily.

"Yes."

"Is that what we came here for?" asked Emily.

"Yes. And some provisions," said Leon.

"What 'ave you got there, lad?" asked Mr Flynn.

Leon unfolded the blue fabric he had draped over a shoulder. "For you, Mr Flynn."

He handed it to him. "An environmental suit – OPP issue. A spare kept here by Mr Smiley. You can change through there," said Leon, indicating the corridor he had just come from. "Dominic and Emily can help me gather some food, and we will see you back upstairs."

3

Mr Knutt, Lucy and Camille had tidied the living space. Camille had left to find a toilet, while Mr Knutt had gone back to the pod for something.

Lucy sat by herself at the table. Presently, she heard a soft creak coming from over by the window. She looked up. Her eyes lit up. "Aww."

Just coming through a small hatch below the wide window was a small, pale grey creature. It had skin that looked scaly but also pliantly soft like chamois leather. It lifted its black eyes towards Lucy and immediately recoiled, withdrawing one foreleg through the hatch.

"It's alright," whispered Lucy. "It's OK. I won't hurt you."

The creature looked up at her like a puppy. Its thin mouth, which curved gently upward at the corners, seemed to smile at her.

"It's Shheikspule, isn't it?" she said quietly.

The creature flicked its head to one side at mention of its name."

"Shheikspule!"

Both Lucy and Shheikspule looked over to where the voice had come from.

It was Leon, with Emily and Dominic and Mr Flynn.

Leon rushed forward. Shheikspule waddled towards him, waggling its tail, and raised his forelegs to rest against Leon's knees. Leon bent and fussed him between his eyes. Shheikspule's eyes rolled back and he purred like a cat.

"Hello, hello," repeated Leon until Shheikspule calmed down and began to take a wary interest in the humans, who were joined by Mr Knutt and Camille. On seeing Shheikspule, Camille came forward to crouch down to fuss him with Lucy and Emily.

"And who is this handsome little creature?" asked

Mr Knutt.

"His name is Shheikspule," said Lucy.

"He's Leon's doglet," said Emily. "Leon showed us a picture of him last year in school. We didn't think we'd ever get to meet him, though. He's cute, isn't he?"

"Yes, I imagine so," said Mr Knutt. "Hm, Leon, isn't it about time we got on our way?"

"Yes, Mr Knutt. I just need to check something first."

"What is it?"

"If we came here, my father asked me to feed Shheikspule."

"Yes. Alright. That shouldn't take long?"

"No," replied Leon. "But the point is, we do not *have* to feed Shheikspule. He generally looks after himself by foraging outside. If he does eat prepared food, it is dispensed automatically when he wishes."

"So why did your dad ask you to feed him?" asked Dominic.

Leon walked over to a point on the floor near the window. Shheikspule followed him, looking up at Leon and then at the floor expectantly.

"I believe he wanted me to do this," said Leon. He tapped the floor three times with the toe of his shoe. There was a brief pause before the floor parted and up came a tray. On it was a clear package. Mr Knutt raised his eyebrows.

"What's that?" asked Emily.

Leon picked it up, and held it out for them to see. It held three crystal prisms and a wad of papers. "My great grandmother's diaries and papers."

"Your father must have known that his computers would be taken. An ingenious solution," said Mr Knutt.

"Wha's that?"

Mr Knutt turned to see Mr Flynn join them. He was tugging at the trouser legs of his borrowed blue environmental suit, which were too long for him. Draped over a shoulder were his green overalls.

"You are just in time, Mr Flynn. Leon's great grandmother's papers. I gather they contain important information about Martian history that has been long hidden."

"Oh, is tha' right?" said Mr Flynn, unaware of what this was all about. He had in his hand the device Leon had removed from the pod's drive back on Mars and handed to him. He looked at it, then unzipped an outer pocket of his suit and popped it in there.

"Mr Sparks indicated that they must be taken to a fellow councillor, Sfa.. ah..."

"Councillor Sffan'utul," said Leon.

"Yes. Thank you. Do you know where he is?" asked Mr Knutt.

"Yes," said Leon. "But first we must try to disable the beacon on Su'umka'r."

"What are you talking about?" asked Dominic.

Leon answered him. "There is a structure on the moon Phobos that my father believes is the reason the comportal network is offline. We need to find a way to disable it."

"Oh, that sounds easy..." said Dominic.

"Would it not be better to get some help first?" suggested Camille.

"There is no time," said Leon. "It will not be long before Miss Sky finds out we are missing and starts a search for us."

"Alright," said Mr Knutt. "What will we need?

Leon?"

"I do not know, Mr Knutt. I was hoping that Mr Flynn might have something we can use."

"Mr Flynn?" said Mr Knutt.

"Ah, h'edmaster, well, I 'ave some garden equipment and some cablin' an' stuff in the pod's 'old tha' may come in 'andy. But I assumed we'd use um... a laser beam or somethin'?"

"The pod does not possess weapons," said Leon.

"I have this," said Dominic, who held a comportal in the air.

"Where did you get that?" asked Lucy.

"That guard I stunned. It's his. I brought it with us."

Mr Knutt sighed. "OK, Dominic, please be careful where you point that. But yes, it might prove useful.

"Right, we do not know what we will encounter, but we must at least try to do something. We may be lucky. But it will probably be dangerous. It might also be better if we didn't all go on this one."

"Mr Knutt." It was Emily. "Are we really going to have that conversation again?"

Mr Knutt paused for a second. Then he said, almost to himself, "Your parents will never forgive me. Come on."

4

They hurried to the pod. Leon sat back in the command chair and called up the graphics screen as he plotted their course into orbit for Su'umka'r.

He had handed the package to Lucy. Now he asked her to spend the time reading through the printed material for anything of significance. He turned to Camille.

"Camille, when you stayed with Aurore, did you ever use data prisms?"

"Yes, of course," said Camille.

"Then you may be able to read these into the pod's memory so we can all view them?"

"I will try," said Camille.

17 – SU'UMKA'R

The journey to Su'umka'r didn't take long. Thankfully, it was also uneventful. Leon had half expected Miss Sky's people to have posted a pod to defend the moon. But there was no sign of that.

The moon grew large on the forward screen, a huge pock-marked potato with a dusty red skin.

"Where is this beacon? What do you know about it?" asked Mr Knutt.

"I do not know," replied Leon. "I did not know about it until my father told us."

"I do!"

"*You* know about the location of this beacon, Dominic? How?" asked Mr Knutt.

"Yes, how would you know about it when Leon doesn't?" posed Emily.

"It's on the Internet," replied Dominic. "I've read a lot about Mars since... well, since we've known Leon."

Mr Knutt exchanged glances with Leon.

"They call it the Phobos Monolith. It's really big, like a triangular block of flats, hundreds of feet tall."

"Are you *sure*?" asked Emily.

"Course I'm sure. A photo was taken by a Mars probe years ago. You can read about it on Wikipedia. It's near a crater called... er, *Sticky* or something.

Always remembered that 'cos it's sticking up."

"*Stickney?*" said Leon.

"Yeah, that's it," said Dominic.

"We call it *Tum'sur'k*. The hawk's beak," said Leon.

"Is it easy to find?" asked Mr Knutt.

"Yes, it is the largest feature on Su'umka'r," replied Leon.

"Good. Well done, Dominic!"

Dominic shrugged, as if to say 'it was nothing', but secretly he was beaming.

"OK," said Mr Knutt. "Let's get closer and have a look."

Mr Knutt turned to Lucy and Camille. "How are you both getting on?"

Camille seemed familiar with the pod's facilities. She had found a spot on one of her chair's arms where she could insert the memory prisms. "One has finished uploading, Mr Knutt. But the other two do not fit."

"Alright," said Mr Knutt. "We'll have a look at the one we can. And you, Lucy?"

Lucy looked up from the sheaf of documents she held. "Well, some of them are newspaper cuttings, about someone called Tesla. And there is one that describes a flying saucer crash – at a place called Aurora."

Simultaneously, Camille turned her head towards Lucy and Mr Knutt said, "There it is again – the incident found by Leon. Anything else?"

"Yes, a letter," replied Lucy. "An old one, written in ink. It's a little difficult to read – I've managed to get the gist of the first few paragraphs. It's a letter to Kindlebir from 'Bertie' – something about a hall of records?"

Leon looked around sharply. *"Hall of Records? Jazu'ul'ard'zahl?"*

`"What's that?" asked Dominic.

"The fabled lost history of our world," said Leon.

"What else does it say?" asked Emily.

"I don't know," said Lucy. "I need to keep reading. The notebook also seems to be describing the same thing."

"Good," said Mr Knutt. "Keep on it, Lucy. We'll come back to them when we can. Leon's great grandmother must have left them for very good reason. For the moment, we must concentrate on the task ahead.

"Leon, how long?"

"Three minutes, Mr Knutt."

"OK, let's get ready," said Mr Knutt.

2

The pod crested the outer rim of Stickney crater and coasted over a broad sloping plain that was littered with coarse debris.

Their destination stood in relief against the black sky. Even from this distance, it looked artificial, a great rectangular tower with an angled top, like the sharp end of a chisel. Its surface, rippled and polished, reflected the Sun's rays like dirty ice.

"Whoah," said Dominic. "That's big."

"We are still half a mile away," said Leon. "It is sixty metres tall."

"Wha's tha' in old money, lad?" asked Mr Flynn.

"Around two hundred feet," replied Leon.

"I don't suppose your dad told you how to disable this thing?" asked Emily.

"No. He did not," replied Leon truthfully.

Leon brought the pod to a stop fifty metres away from the monolith, which filled the screen before them. He made the pod's skin transparent and its full height became evident.

Some twenty metres beneath the pod, the surface of Phobos was littered with jagged rocky debris and dust. The area around the base of the monolith was disturbed, pushed back in a ridge, almost like it had been forced into the surface rather than constructed. The monolith's surface was smooth, with gentle undulations, and translucent, like melted smoked glass.

"Where's the plug?" joked Mr Flynn.

"Yes indeed, Mr Flynn," said Mr Knutt. "Leon, again we're in your hands. What do you suggest?"

Leon was quiet for a moment before answering. "Perhaps we can try to push against it with our force-field – as we did with the asteroid. Perhaps we can push it out of alignment, or topple it?"

"Hm," said Mr Knutt. "It depends how deep its foundations are? Is there anything else we could do?"

"I cannot think of anything," said Leon.

"Anyone else?"

"I could try shooting at it with my borrowed comportal," suggested Dominic.

"But wouldn't we have to open the hatch to do that?" asked Lucy.

"I do not think there will be any cause to go outside," said Mr Knutt. He looked at Leon, whose expression suggested that this wasn't entirely out of the question.

"Ah, OK," continued Mr Knutt. "So it looks like we

will attempt to nudge it. Leon?"

"Yes, Mr Knutt. I have the same programme ready that we used on the asteroid."

Leon manoeuvred the pod to near the top of the monolith. He stopped it just below where it began to taper to a blade-like edge.

   In the centre of the rectangular face was the first feature they had seen – a circular depression, perhaps six feet in diameter, in the middle of which was a small projection made of what looked like clear crystal. The transmitter itself?

Mr Knutt had seen it as well as Leon. "Could it be aligned with Mars?"

"It is possible," said Leon.

"Let's give it a go," said Mr Knutt. "Brace, everyone."

Leon moved his hand over his armrest and the pod began to move, slowly, towards the monolith.

Everyone held their breath.

The pod began to hum as Leon increased the power to the force-field. He nudged it forward. Presently, they all felt some resistance and a faint greenish-blue glow began to fill the cabin.

Then they seemed to be drifting backwards.

Leon increased the power again and they drove forward again. The glow outside brightened, then backed down as they were again forced backwards. Leon made another gesture and the pod surged forward, more forcibly than he had originally planned. The glow became much brighter. Again the pod slowed before, suddenly, it was thrown back.

Several of the children yelped in surprise as the pod tumbled end over end away from the monolith. Through its transparent walls, the moon's horizon was flipping over and over, showing alternately its coarse surface and the black sky. They were coming perilously close to crashing on Phobos.

"Leon!" called Mr Knutt as he gripped his chair arms. "Leon..."

The G-forces of the spin were beginning to overpower the pod's gravitational dampeners.

Leon didn't answer. Calmly, he tried to wave his hand in controlled motions to try to stabilise the pod's spin and its trajectory. They were heading for some higher ground behind, with a very real possibility that they might crash. Maybe the force-field would help cushion their impact...

After what seemed like minutes, but in reality was only a few seconds, the horizon seemed to be going around less rapidly, until Leon managed to slowly regain control and level it off in relation to the cabin. Simultaneously, he applied force to slow their backward motion until, finally, they came to a dead stop just metres above the surface.

They were now several hundred metres away from the monolith.

"Phew," said Dominic. "That was worse than Dragon's Fury!"

"What is this?" asked Camille.

"It's a theme park ride, in England," said Emily.

"Is everyone alright?" asked Mr Knutt. He hardly waited for an answer before saying, "Leon, what happened?"

"When I increased the strength of our force-field, it pushed back with greater force with its own. But..."

"Yes?"

"But when I scanned it before we got closer to it, it

showed no signs of having any force-field of its own."

"It sounds like a defence mechanism," said Mr Knutt. "This may be more difficult still."

"We are going back there?" asked Camille.

"We must," replied Mr Knutt. "But clearly we will have to try something else."

3

Skiel'aeljtın sprang to her feet. *"What do you mean that they have escaped?!"*

Aurore looked up from her place at the viewer but said nothing.

The guard officer cowered before the daughter of the High Councillor. "I discovered their guard outside their quarters. He was stunned – level two strength. He does not remember who shot him."

Skiel'aeljtın looked from the guard to the table in her quarters. The pack of phials she had taken from Councillor Shieekk'ssup'pl were gone. She looked at Aurore, who felt her mother's eyes on her back but she did not turn.

"And where are they now?" she asked the guard.

The guard tremored before her. "I do not know. They overpowered the port guard and took the pod. It cloaked on lift-off."

Skiel'aeljtın's eye-lids blinked rapidly. Her thin lips pressed together and a greenish flush of anger rose to her cheeks.

"Have the negligent guards arrested. Now, find out where they went."

"Yes, mistress," replied the guard.

Once the guard had left, Skiel'aeljtın turned to

Aurore. "Now, daughter, you and I must talk."

4

Leon touched the pod down at the foot of the monolith, close enough to avoid a long scramble over the loose, rocky surface, but far enough away to avoid another repellent attack.

"So, our only plan now is to shoot it with the comportal?" asked Mr Knutt.

Leon and Dominic both shrugged.

"Alright. We'll all need our pressure suits on. And I suggest only a few of us go outside. The gravity is almost non-existent here. We do not want anyone floating away."

"Me, you and Leon, Mr Knutt," suggested Dominic eagerly.

"I was rather thinking of Leon and myself," said Mr Knutt.

Dominic frowned gloomily.

"But I'm a better shot than anyone here," protested Dominic.

"That is true," said Leon. "But it is not a matter of accuracy this time, but safety."

"Eh?" said Dominic.

"It seems to have a strong defensive capability," said Mr Knutt. "A bit over generous with respect to Newton's Third Law," he added, almost to himself.

"Huh?" asked Dominic.

"It means that it is likely to shoot straight back," said Leon.

Dominic looked at Leon uncertainly.

"Perhaps I should do it?" said Leon.

"H'edmaster?" said Mr Flynn. His eyes met Mr Knutt's.

They stepped aside to speak quietly together.

"Shouldn' we, y'know, as the grownups, be takin' the risks an' such – instead of the children?"

"I'm afraid, Mr Flynn, that unless you or I know how to shoot a comportal, we will not be much use. Leon is the one for the job."

Mr Flynn nodded. "Whatever you say, h'edmaster."

5

Mr Knutt and the others watched from the open hatch as Leon, who was perched on the end of the ramp, adjusted a setting on his suit's belt.

The monolith towered above them, like a great oblong mirror. They sat approximately fifty metres from its base. The moon's surface was littered with rocky debris, rough boulders of every size jammed together and covered with red dust.

On Earth, Leon's anti-gravity undersuit had helped him to compensate for Earth's gravity, and even to float above the surface. Now, he was about to use it to float over the rocks and prevent himself from drifting away.

"I am ready," announced Leon into his headset.

"OK, Leon, be careful," said Mr Knutt.

"Good luck, Leon," called out the girls.

Leon made a small turn on his belt with one hand. He leant forward and lifted off the ramp. He floated forward slowly, his booted feet trailing behind him, pushing him towards the monolith.

The comportal was capable of firing over this

distance, but Leon had calculated it would be more effective at closer range. Besides, if the monolith *did* fire back, it would be better to be away from the pod.

From the vantage point of the pod, Leon shrank to the size of a pea. The true size of some of the boulders, and of the monolith itself, became apparent.

Leon positioned himself behind a boulder that was as tall as he was. He carefully braced himself against the rock. Looking down, he saw a small cavity made by three smaller rocks. He wedged one foot into it to anchor himself in position. Then he took out the comportal and carefully aimed at the middle of the monolith. He took one deep breath, and fired.

At the pod, the others saw a fine bluish-white beam strike the monolith. Immediately, a greenish-blue glow began to grow around the end of the beam. It lasted a second or two longer, then the beam and the glow vanished.

Leon straightened and peered over the shoulder of the boulder. Well, it hadn't shot back; although its force-field had intercepted the beam. Leon set himself to fire again, this time for a longer contact.

The beam flared out again. Leon held it as steadily as he could, trying to keep it focused on the same spot. The monolith's force-field again began to glow where the beam struck it. The coloured patch spread and grew in intensity.

Then it seemed to stop, and then to contract. The colour of the glow began to change to yellow, then orange and finally to red. It shrank to a dot, right behind the head of the beam. Then it exploded outward, sending a searing white beam in Leon's direction. Before he could react, the rock beside him was cleaved in two. Debris flew out in all directions, narrowly missing Leon. The side nearest him tilted, sinking towards him. Leon found himself pressed downwards. His foot sank further into the cavity. The large rock stopped moving. Relieved, Leon tried to remove his foot. He couldn't. He was trapped.

Behind him, the pod looked like a toy. The figures gathered in the hatchway looked impossibly small. Leon spoke into his headset. Nothing. Not even static.

He looked down again at his trapped foot. He tried tugging at it, taking care not tear his suit. It didn't budge. If anything, the rocks gripped tighter like a fist around his ankle.

He looked back at the pod again, which was partially hidden by the rocky field between them. And waved. And waved again.

6

"He's alright," said Lucy. "I just saw him wave."

"But he could be hurt," said Mr Knutt. "That was quite an explosion."

Mr Knutt tried his headset again. "Leon, can you hear me?"

Nothing. He looked hard in Leon's direction, trying to determine his condition.

"I think we are going to have to go over there. Mr Flynn, I believe it's up to me and you. What do we need?"

"Yes, h'edmaster. I'll look in the equipment 'atch."

"What do you mean?" asked Dominic. "Shouldn't we get over there and find out if he's OK first?"

"Saves time," said Mr Flynn. "Saves yer goin' back

for somefin' you might need."

Mr Flynn made his way slowly down the ramp. It was all he could do in the slight gravity to prevent each footstep from launching him clear of the surface. Finally, he stood on lip of the ramp and paused there for a moment.

"Be careful, Mr Flynn," called Emily.

Without turning, Mr Flynn held his hand up.

Finally, he extended his left foot and planted it as firmly as he could into the dust and fragmented rock of Phobos's surface.

Despite his concern for Mr Flynn, and for the plight of Leon, a thought popped into Mr Knutt's head, paraphrased for the occasion: *That's one small step for a school caretaker, one giant leap for...*

It was a shame that Mr Flynn hadn't thought of something to say, as he was in all probability the first human to set foot on a foreign moon.

Mr Knutt gingerly followed Mr Flynn onto the ramp. Soon he was on the surface and catching Mr Flynn up.

Fortunately, this side of Phobos was in sunlight, else it would have been an impossible prospect to carry out this mission.

Mr Knutt edged around the pod, where he found Mr Flynn already with the auxiliary hatch open and rifling through an assortment of equipment. Soon he had what he was looking for. He brought out a crowbar, a long metal pole and a common garden rake. On his belt, he wore a holstered mallet, and strapped around his forehead, a head torch.

He looked around to see Mr Knutt. Without saying a word, he handed the rake to him.

"OK, let's go get young Leon," said Mr Flynn.

For an older man, Mr Flynn – who was in his sixties – was surprisingly nimble, adaptable and resilient. He led Mr Knutt back around to the ramp with all the ease as if he had lived on the moon for weeks.

When they arrived back at the ramp, they found Camille alone in the hatchway. Her discomfort and concern showed through her visor.

"Camille?" said Mr Knutt.

"It was Dominic. He could not contain himself." She nodded in the direction of the monolith.

Mr Knutt stared after her gaze. Then he detected movement. Three tiny figures, one out in the lead, were stumbling over the surface. He felt his lips tighten.

"*Foolish!*" he blurted, more in frustration than anger.

"I am sorry, Mr Knutt," said Camille. "I could not stop them." Her expression looked strained with worry.

"It's alright, Camille. It's not your fault. But we can do without heroics and risks of injury. Or worse," he said. "I'm beginning to think that I have not been a very effective teacher."

Mr Knutt sighed. "Alright, Mr Flynn, let's get after them."

7

Dominic moved out ahead, leaving the girls trailing. In his haste, every footstep threatened to launch him forward, and his breathing sounded in his ears. His wristband was hidden beneath his gloves; he couldn't tell how long he had before his oxygenating capsule would need changing.

But he was almost there. Leon was just a little way

off now.

Every now and then there was small flash of bluish light. Dominic knew what it was. Leon was activating his boots, which were capable of generating gravity-compensating force. He assumed that Leon was trying to force himself free.

He thrust forward and very soon found himself overbalancing. He struck a foot out against a rock and then found himself soaring across the moonscape until Phobos's weak gravity drew him down and he crashed in a bouncy, dusty tumble.

"Oooh," exclaimed the girls. But before anyone could say or do anything, Dominic was back to his feet and scrambling gingerly towards Leon.

8

Dominic was shocked to find Leon positioned awkwardly beneath the overhang of a large fractured boulder, his body twisted and one leg trapped in a rocky hole.

Leon looked up at Dominic's arrival. Dominic spoke to him, but Leon shook his head and tapped the side of his visor, to indicate he couldn't hear. He looked at his trapped foot and shook his head again.

As Dominic set to work to try to help Leon, Lucy and Emily arrived and soon joined in plucking at debris around the rim of the hole and tugging on Leon's trapped leg to get him out.

"Be careful you don't tear his suit," said Lucy.

The rocks at their feet weren't like weather-rounded ones on Earth. They were dark and coarse, like volcanic ejecta.

Dominic picked up the comportal that lay on the surface beside Leon. He showed it to Leon, who shook his head again. Dominic raised it as if to aim it at the monolith, but Leon stopped him. Through his visor he mouthed the words 'Doesn't work'.

Undeterred, Dominic aimed it a small distance away and squeezed it to try to activate it. It flared briefly like a dim bulb then fell dark again. He dropped it to the surface. Broken.

It wasn't long before they were joined by Mr Knutt and Mr Flynn. After a quick assessment of the situation, Mr Flynn shooed the children out of the way. He then took the rake and looked around the area immediately surrounding Leon. Lighting his way, he stooped to wedge the head of the rake beneath the rock that overshadowed Leon. Then he moved to its other end and pushed it under a rocky outcrop, so that the shaft lay clear of the surface by a couple of inches. He took the crowbar and mallet off his belt and knelt down. "H'edmaster, if you will?" he said.

"What is it, Mr Flynn?"

"I need you to 'old me down as best y'can," replied Mr Knutt.

"Excuse me?" asked Mr Knutt.

"Hook yer toes under the rake and press down on me shoulders," instructed the older man.

Mr Knutt did as he was told.

"Kids, 'old onto Mr Knutt to steady 'im; on his left side outa me way. One of you get set to pull Leon out."

Lucy made her way over to Leon, while Dominic and Emily stood beside Mr Knutt. They tucked their feet under the length of the rake, which Mr Flynn had fixed a couple of inches above the surface.

Mr Flynn positioned the crowbar so that its point was pressed vertically into the rocky surface. He then took the mallet and hit the curved end of the crowbar. With each blow, silent in the vacuum surrounding them, the point pushed deeper into the surface. And each time, that forced tried to lift Mr Flynn upwards. Only Mr Knutt, anchored by his feet, and the children holding onto him, prevented Mr Flynn lifting off. Soon, the curved end had been hammered into place over the wooden shaft of the rake.

"A bit of extra insurance," said Mr Flynn, puffing as he got to his feet.

He stepped over to where Leon waited patiently. Mr Flynn used his head torch to peer into the hole where Leon's foot was trapped. There wasn't much room down there. He patted Leon on the shoulder and looked into his eyes.

"OK, lad?" he said, aware that Leon couldn't hear him, but he carried on anyway. "We've got to find a bit of room down there for this." He held up the metal pole.

Leon nodded.

Mr Flynn lowered it into the hole. He got down to reach into the hole, checking with his hand that it wasn't in contact with Leon's foot, but lodged under the rough lip of the largest rock that pinned Leon's right foot beneath it.

"Now," said Mr Flynn, this time to everyone. "We can't lever the rocks without us being anchored down. So get ready to 'old on again, to me and each other."

Mr Flynn now had the metal pole angled quite steeply out of the hole. He moved over to its end, which hovered over the horizontal rake, and positioned himself with his feet lodged under and his hands clutching the end of the pole at his eye level.

"Now, after three. Get ready, Lucy. One... two... three. *Go*."

Mr Flynn pulled firmly down on the end of the pole. Mr Knutt kept a hand on his shoulder, helping to increase the force on the lever. After a moment of nothing seeming to happen, the end of the pole began to sink, slowly at first. Then, suddenly, it gave, and it dropped several inches at once, and Mr Flynn lost his grip on it and fell back onto his bottom. He therefore missed what the others saw.

At the hole, a plume of rocky fragments and dust sprayed into the air and Leon, with Lucy pulling on an arm, lifted clear of the hole, his foot finally free.

When Mr Flynn sat up, he heard Mr Knutt say, "Oh, well done, Mr Flynn!"

"Yes, well done Mr Flynn," called Lucy excitedly.

"Well, tha' went better than I expected," said Mr Flynn. "Is the lad alright?"

Leon stood on the surface, looking no worse for wear.

"I think so," said Lucy.

"In tha' case, I think you should all get back to the pod," said Mr Flynn.

"Indeed," said Mr Knutt. "Enough foolhardiness. Wait a minute. You too, Mr Flynn?"

"I jus' wanna take a closer look at tha' monolith, h'edmaster."

"Is that wise, Mr Flynn? You've seen what it can do."

"Well, I wasn' plannin' to shoot anythin' at it. Jus' try an' see if we missed anythin'."

"Erm, I'm not sure that's a good idea. But I do not believe that Mr Sparks would have sent us on a futile errand. Be careful and come back to us as quickly as you can."

"I'll do tha', h'edmaster."

Mr Flynn picked up the metal pole and began to use it as a staff as he picked his way forward towards the monolith.

"Where's he going?" asked Dominic.

"Taking a closer look at the monolith," answered Mr Knutt. "He will not be long. I hope. For us, our time is up. Let's get back to the pod. Slowly. Carefully. Someone assist Leon. And... no more mishaps, please."

9

Skiel'aeljtɪn studied her daughter. "*Su'umka'r?* How certain are you of this?"

"I heard Mr Knutt repeat it in conversation with Mr Sparks."

"Sparks," said Skiel'aeljtɪn. "*Fred Sparks,*" she repeated disdainfully. "You mean Councillor *Shieekk'ssup'pl?*"

"Yes," Aurore said quietly.

"So!" said Skiel'aeljtɪn. "His plan thwarted, like a coward he sends his son and his Earth friends to attack the guardian? *Ha!* They will find it is more than capable of meeting any attack. But no matter."

Skiel'aeljtɪn took out her comportal. She waved over its surface, and a three dimensional display took form above its surface.

"What are you going to do?" asked Aurore.

260

Skiel'aeljtın made several gestures over the device. Then she waved a hand over it to collapse the display.

"They shall be brought back," she said. "Now, daughter, while I am gone, I need you to reflect carefully on your actions and decide whether your allegiance is to me and your people, or the humans and their kind."

10

Mr Flynn stood before the monolith. The pod was far behind him, but he didn't feel alone. He had often spent late nights and early mornings attending to lonely tasks in the grounds of Flintworne Junior School. He put the metal pole down and removed his tool belt, eager to avoid having too much metal about him as he edged closer to where he sensed the monolith's force-field began.

At home, he had become familiar with the force-fields generated by Martian pods. The monolith was clearly a much larger and more powerful construction, but perhaps it would behave the same way and permit an unarmed human to pass through the barrier?

As he reached out, he could feel a tingling sensation begin in his fingers and start to travel up his arm. Unlike the force-fields generated by pods, this one didn't yield so readily. In fact, the more he pushed into it, the more it seemed to push *back*. Soon, it was evident to him that it would use his own strength against him, and he decided to give up. In any case, there was nothing visible on the monolith to suggest a control point or a point of weakness. It was a great obdurate surface like a slab of thick slab of smoked glass.

Mr Flynn turned away and bent to retrieve his tool belt. Phobos could keep the metal pole. If he had been of Mr Knutt's mind, he might have stuck it into the regolith and tied a handkerchief around it as a flag. He looked at the pebble-sized rock fragments at his feet. On impulse, he picked one up then turned to face the monolith again. With an underarm flourish, he tossed the rock towards the force-field. It seemed to slow down as if caught by a band of invisible elastic, and then shot back out again. Mr Flynn found himself ducking instinctively.

"How are you doing, Mr Flynn?"

Mr Flynn replied through his headset. "All done 'ere, h'edmaster – which is to say nothing can be done. I'm on me way back now."

He turned and started on his way back to the pod. He hadn't been going very long when he felt a buzzing sensation.

For a moment, he was puzzled. *The monolith's force-field? But how?*

Then he realised it was coming from the leg pocket of his pressure suit. He stopped and tentatively reached into the pocket and drew out a small device.

Of course – the thing Leon removed from the pod's drive. He had all but forgotten about it since Mr Knutt quietly passed it to him on their arrival on Mars. When, later, he had changed out of his regular overalls, for some reason he had transferred the device to a pocket of the pressure suit. Then it had looked a featureless piece of metal. Now, in addition to vibrating, it glowed dimly with greenish light.

Mr Flynn raised an eyebrow as he stared at it. He

looked up to see the pod not too distant now. He looked again at the device in his hand and, even before it began to click and pulse with new activity, he had decided what to do with it. It had been planted stealthily to control the flight of the pod; to bring them to Mars. It was no use to them and it would be better to rid themselves of it. Without turning, he tossed it firmly over his shoulder and continued on.

11

The device tumbled end over end, hardly falling or slowing in the faint gravity. It had enough momentum to reach the monolith, and when it came to where Mr Flynn had encountered its force-field, it passed right through without hindrance and latched onto the monolith's surface.

Mr Flynn halted unsteadily in his tracks. He turned around. Something was different. He wasn't sure what it was, but there was definitely something up. Then he felt it – a low rumbling that was transmitted through the moon's regolith to his feet and on upwards along his spinal column to his brain. He shook his head. The monolith seemed to be vibrating. Pulses of faint green light spread out from a point low on its facing side like a ring of ripples from a cast pebble. Then the central point began to glow brightly. It grew until it filled the monolith. Then it abruptly collapsed, leaving the monolith dark and inactive again.

Mr Flynn wasn't going back to check on it, but he felt sure that the force-field was now gone and the monolith itself deactivated. On his way back to the pod he retrieved his garden rake, using it to keep his balance. Soon he arrived back at the pod's ramp and was safely inside. Leon waved a hand to close the hatch and repressurise the interior. Soon it was OK for everyone to remove their visors and breathe easily again.

"What happened?" asked Emily.

"I think I broke it," said Mr Flynn.

"Mr Flynn, you are a master of understatement," said Mr Knutt. "What did you do?"

"Well, I don' exackly know, h'edmaster. I'd jus' tossed tha' thingummy you handed me – y'know, the one that brought us to Mars – I tossed it over me shoulder, an' after that the monolith thing started to go up the wall. Maybe jus' a coincidence."

"I do not think so," said Leon. "I believe the device was designed to work within powerful force-fields and to override the programming of the system it is attached to. I believe that Miss Sky was probably trying to override our pod control. In any case, it has cleared the comportal interference."

"Good," said Mr Knutt. "But that might also mean that she knows where we are. Leon, firstly, sorry, I didn't ask how you were?"

"I am fine, Mr Knutt."

"Good. Now, can you take us to Councillor Sffan'utul?"

"Yes, I am programming it now."

"And your father?"

"I have tried. Nothing," replied Leon. "But it may now be possible to contact my mother and Mr Smiley."

"Oh," said Mr Knutt. "Perhaps we may try as soon as we believe it is safe to do so?"

Leon nodded. "We are ready," he said.

"How long?" asked Mr Knutt.

"If we do not draw attention to ourselves – we can cloak and hide behind Deimos part of the way – fifteen minutes."

"Alright everyone. Seats please. Off we go again," said Mr Knutt.

As soon as everyone was seated, Leon guided the pod up and away from Phobos. With the action, their orbital velocity slowed and Phobos surged ahead beneath them.

"Now, Camille," said Mr Knutt. "Shall we have a look at the prism tapes? And Lucy, what about Mr Wells's letter?"

"Yes, I have read it all," said Lucy. "And we have copied it to the pod's memory."

"Good. Leon, see if you can send it to your mother and Mr Smiley. Then let's hear it," said Mr Knutt.

18 – SFFAN'UTUL

S kiel'aeljtın had returned to her quarters. The lights were down and she stood before the window that looked over the pod port. The light from her comportal display reflected from the windows, and as she spoke she glanced up at the light that was Su'umka'r as it perceptibly climbed the vault of the sky.

"When did you know?" asked her father, High Councillor Smiall'kes'hep, whose figure was framed by the comportal's three-dimensional projection.

"A solhour past," said Skiel'aeljtın.

"And only *now* I learn of this? The council is stirring, asking questions."

"I instructed our guards to find them. They were cloaked. It is likely they continue to cloak themselves."

"Until they use their comportals. They must de-cloak for that. Monitor all communications. We must know where they are and who aligns against us," said Smiall'kes'hep.

"But –"

"This is a critical situation, daughter. A coterie of humans led by renegade home-worlders has managed to overcome Su'umka'r's guardian. We must know what they are likely to do next. You interrogated Shieekk'ssup'pl?"

"Yes. I have just come from there."

"And?"

"He gave nothing away, but he intuited that something was amiss. He seemed quietly pleased."

"He shall not be so when we intercept his son. And make it known that the renegades are being sought in connection with an act of gross sabotage."

"Yes, father," replied Skiel'aeljtın.

2

"I have been expecting you."

"Councillor Sffan'utul?" asked Mr Knutt.

"I am," replied the elderly Martian. His speech was slow, precise. He made the customary gesture of greeting, which Mr Knutt and Leon both returned.

The councillor stood in the entrance to his home, which was cut into the cliff face behind a wedge-shaped spur that projected from it. In effect, they had landed in Sffan'utul's front yard, which was bare but for a handful of dry-looking woody stemmed plants that grew out of cracks in the rocks. It was still dark; the only light from the Sffan'utul's home and the pod itself.

"You knew we were coming?"

"Yes, master Dominic," replied Sffan'utul.

Dominic was impressed that this venerable Martian knew his name.

"There is much speculation about you now that the comportal channels are open. I am intrigued: how did you defeat the guardian?"

"The what?" asked Dominic.

"The beacon on Su'umka'r."

"As they say on Earth, a happy accident," said

Leon. "Is there any news of my father?" he asked, trying to quell the tremor of emotion in his voice.

"Not yet," replied Sffan'utul. "Although I and several colleagues have made inquiries. Now, please come inside. There is much to discuss, and I fear we have little time. They shall be searching for you, and my association with your father is well known."

3

Sffan'utul's house was Spartan in character. The walls were bare rock, although smoothed to an attractive finish; the décor simple, with the exception of recesses containing banks of crystal prisms and an intricately cut pink crystal sculpture of a Martian lady.

"My late wife," explained Sffan'utul. "Can I offer you all refreshment?"

"That will be welcome," said Mr Knutt. "If we have time?"

"It is well to take little time to talk, to plan," said Sffan'utul calmly. "Please be seated."

"I wouldn' say no to a cup of tea, if you 'ave some?" said Mr Flynn.

"Of course. I have Earl Grey. And also some Darjeeling, Green tea, or a little Moroccan Mint?"

"Ah. I don't suppose you 'ave any P.G. Tips?"

"*Pee-gee-teeps*? No, I am afraid not."

"No, well, worth a try," said Mr Flynn. "In tha' case, I'll try the Moroccan Mint."

"Ah, yes. I'll try that too," said Mr Knutt.

"And for the children, I have some *kaiyd'ais'yn*?"

Leon explained: "It is like lemonade, but with a little cinnamon. I drink it at home."

The other children nodded enthusiastically.

Sffan'utul waved a hand over the arm of his seat. He uttered some words in Martian. Then he sat back.

"Now, to business. Let us share our news before we formulate a plan to free Councillor Shieekk'ssup'pl, and to do what we can to unseat this upstart, Smiall'kes'hep."

4

"Of this I was afraid," said Sffan'utul. "Our people will be saddened at the wanton destruction of life. What evidence do we have?"

"If the comportal network is back up," said Mr Knutt, "we may be able to contact Mr Smiley on Earth's Moon for more information."

"We have the visual recordings made by the pod," offered Leon. "It will show the attacks on Earth and at Tsiolkovsky."

"Good," said Sffan'utul. Please make a prism before we send the pod away."

"Send it away? Where to?" asked Leon.

"To Earth. Its departure will serve two purposes. It may persuade our foes that you have fled Mars. And it will provide a pod for Mr Smiley and your mother to return here."

"But what will we do without it?" asked Lucy.

"We will use this information to confront Smiall'kes'hep. I will recall the council to Cydonia and travel there in my pod. They will not suspect that you accompany me."

"There is another reason for us to go there," said Mr Knutt. "We believe we have been left clues by Leon's great-grandmother as to the secret history and governance of your world by a self-serving elite. And references to a lost hall of records."

Sffan'utul raised an eyebrow – well, an eye ridge, for there was no hair on the upper part of his face, or his head, although he sported a fine white beard on the point of his chin.

"We have a copy of a letter written by Kindlebir to Leon's mother. In it she mentions a letter she was left by H.G. Wells about his discovery of a repository of ancient records beneath the face of... excuse me, *Jzieeekkkzoor-sup*? We have his letter. And a notebook he kept while he was here."

"Indeed?" said Sffan'utul. "I met Mr Wells on several occasions while he visited us as Kindlebir's guest. An interesting and far-sighted man."

"Yes," said Mr Knutt. He produced the letter, unfolded it, and handed it to Sffan'utul.

"It is written in the cursive style of handwritten English. If this presents any difficulties, I can perhaps read it aloud?" suggested Mr Knutt.

Sffan'utul stared at it for a moment. Then he handed it back to Mr Knutt. "Please," he said.

Mr Knutt cleared his throat and began to read:

June 8, 1897

My dear Kindie,

By the time that you read this, I will have returned to Earth. I shall never return.

I leave you my heartfelt thanks for your kindness and hospitality during my visits to your planet, and for your friendship in both worlds.

Scarcely could I have imagined just two months ago that you and your people might actually exist, less so that I might be singled out for your attention and to have had the opportunities and experiences it has afforded.

You know the reason for my departure. An unpalatable truth can be hard to countenance. But be assured that I ascertained that it was the truth before I confronted the great Kindlebir (and I mean that sincerely) with an alternative history of her own race.

In so doing, I accept that I betrayed the trust and have forfeited the friendship of my host and sponsor. For that I ask your forgiveness. But I offer no apology. It is my hope that, one day, you will understand.

Alas, it now falls to this missive to urge you to investigate for yourself. I appreciate the difficulties, and the dangers, that this presents; more so, once yourself persuaded, in persuading others of its truth. But nothing may be more important for our respective peoples.

Enclosed with this letter are two prisms I removed from the hidden archives of Jyiee'ekkkzoor'sup, that great sphinx in the deserts of Cydonia, which hides treasures surpassing Earth's mythical books of Thoth.

Read them; use them, and the hundreds that remain. You know the way in, Kindlebir. You know the inscription. Nothing is sacrosanct if it guards a deception. History is gathering on itself to repeat the dreadful actions of the past. Act, please, before it is too late.

Yours most faithfully,
Bertie

Mr Knutt refolded the letter and placed it on a table. Beside it, he placed the prisms they had found with the letter. Councillor Sffan'utul glanced at them. He looked pensive.

Then he said, "I am afraid I am as much to blame as my late dear friend Kindlebir. Mr Wells brought the inscription to me after Kindlebir declined to translate it. There are few who can. It is in a very ancient form of our language, inscribed in but one place in the ruins of the destroyed city of Cydonia, and attributed to Jziee'ekkkzoor'sup himself.

"Translation into our modern language fails to preserve the elegance of its poetic meter. In English, an even cruder approximation can only be made. As follows:

> The wise hearken to my words
> In hearing, they enter into knowledge
> In knowledge, they encounter truth
> In truth, they are set free

"It would seem that Mr Wells interpreted it literally. I believe it confirmed something he already suspected. Something, actually, that a few of us knew as a legend: that the effigy of Jziee'ekkkzoor'sup was also the location of Jazu'ul'ard'zahl, the ancient Hall of Records."

"And he broke some kind of taboo by going there and finding it?" asked Mr Knutt.

"So it would seem," said Sffan'utul. He eyed the prisms that now lay on a table in his home.

"No-one knows the burial place of Jziee'ekkkzoor'sup. It is forbidden in our culture, on pain of death, to disturb his remains. It is possible that they lie within that sacred place."

"So," said Mr Knutt, "until Wells came along, no-one could verify whether the legends were true or not?"

"No," replied Sffan'utul.

"And by violating that space, Wells had no choice but to leave, regardless of what he found?" said Mr Knutt.

"Yes," said Sffan'utul. "I am sure that Kindlebir will have been appalled by his action – enough certainly to have strained their relationship. But, worse still, if it became openly known, it may have placed him and Kindlebir, and me, in mortal danger. And risked even more," said Sffan'utul. "As it may even now," he added.

"As it was," said Mr Knutt, "he *did* find something, which he felt he had to share with Kindlebir, even at risk of offending her and placing her in an impossible position."

Sffan'utul considered his words carefully. "She will have been acutely aware of the implications. At the same time, as a historian, I believe that, privately, she could not have helped but be fascinated by Mr Wells's discovery.

Sffan'utul sighed. "Oh, Kindlebir," he whispered. "How you must have been torn by that knowledge."

"As for myself," he said, "I cannot pretend that I had no inkling of what Mr Wells was considering when I helped him with the translation. Like Kindlebir, perhaps I should have declined. But he was a clever and resourceful man. I later consoled myself with the thought that he would eventually have found a way to decipher it.

"At the time, I was young, and bold and inquisitive

and little inclined to question the means of advancing my own knowledge and standing. Like Kindlebir, I possessed a keen interest in our ancient history. And here was someone, a human, unbound by our traditions and cultural limitations, who promised an answer to one of our unanswerable questions!"

Mr Knutt nodded. "But Wells's motivation was not simply to verify the existence of a lost archive. He evidently had cause to suspect that the official version of your planet's history was a sham – a far cry from the utopian society that he at first believed he had found here. What could have led him to that conclusion, and then to seek his proof at Cydonia?"

Sffan'utul again looked thoughtful. "I believe it may have come about from simple logical deduction. Kindlebir had shared with him a good deal of her knowledge of our past. She, of course, had introduced him to the Council at Cydonia, and undoubtedly about the distinctions between the peoples of the North and those of the South."

Mr Knutt nodded. "In Kindlebir's papers there is mention of the 'Council of Seven'. Evidently, *all* of the ruling northern families survived the holocaust of Ti'aransc. But *none* of the southern families."

"That is true," admitted Sffan'utul. "Our history records the northern leaders tried to warn their southern counterparts, but not in sufficient time. Ti'aransc came down in the southern hemisphere. There were few survivors."

"How many of the North's ruling families survive to this day – or at least to Wells's day?" asked Mr Knutt.

"Three. Three remain."

Mr Knutt turned away from Sffan'utul. It wasn't he

who answered. It was Leon.

"Leon?" asked Mr Knutt.

"Three of the original families are represented still on the Council."

"How do you know this?" asked Mr Knutt.

"His mother," answered Sffan'utul.

"Yes," said Leon. "While my father educated me in mathematics and the sciences, my mother tried always to interest me in our history and culture. As I recall, these are the House of Aljt'in, the House of Ti'emir and the House of J'ak'ut."

"That is correct, Leon," said Sffan'utul. "Your mother has taught you well."

"Yes, three of the original ruling houses survive. In name, at least. Today, their bloodlines are represented by their descendents. Amongst them, are three existing councillors."

"And one of them is High Councillor Smiall'kes'hep?" asked Mr Knutt.

"Yes," said Sffan'utul. "He is of the House of Aljt'in, the most influential of the old families."

"Tell me," said Mr Knutt. "You said that only a few were capable of translating the inscription at Cydonia?"

"Yes," said Sffan'utul. "And you are about to ask me if Smiall'kes'hep is one of them?"

"Yes."

"Yes, he is. As was his father before him."

"Of course," said Mr Knutt. "And Jziee'ekkkzoor'sup? Did he also belong to one of the ancient families?"

"Jziee'ekkkzoor'sup was of the House of J'ez, the least of the five families of the southern hemisphere."

"Oh," said Mr Knutt.

"Yes, Jziee'ekkkzoor'sup was neither high-born nor well known to begin with. But he was passionate about achieving peace. The House of Aljt'in initially opposed him when he tried to gain support to forge a truce. Eventually, under growing pressure even from its own side, it was forced to concede to Jziee'ekkkzoor'sup's settlement and his leadership. And, accordingly to what has been passed down to us, it was Aljt'in that was instrumental in raising Jziee'ekkkzoor'sup's grand memorial at Cydonia after his death."

"Hm," said Mr Knutt. "Perhaps, then, we should press on and view the content of Kindlebir's papers before we go forward – or before Smiall'kes'hep's police come for us?"

19 - THE COUNCIL

"**W**hat is it?" asked Mr Smiley.

"The comportal network is functional," replied Mrs Sparks.

"Oh, when?"

"Thirty minutes ago."

"Oh?" said Mr Smiley.

"There was little point in alerting you until I had something more to report."

"And now you have?"

"Yes."

"Fred?"

"No," replied Mrs Sparks. "I have tried to contact him. There is no reply. But I have received the copy of my grandmother's diaries, and a copy of Herbert Wells's letter."

"You've read it?" asked Mr Smiley. He took a seat beside her.

"Yes. But, please. Read it yourself," said Mrs Sparks.

Mr Smiley took a few moments to read it. Then he said, "Wow."

"And there is much more," said Mrs Sparks. "Besides my grandmother's diaries, there is a copy of Mr Wells's journal from his time on Mars. It describes, amongst other things, precisely how he gained entry to the archives.

"And there are the two ancient prisms..." Mrs Sparks paused, taking a deep breath. "... which, as my grandmother's letter indicate, document the last war and the fall of Ti'aransc."

Mrs Sparks's complexion had grown paler than was normal for her.

"Are you alright, Wilma?" asked Mr Smiley.

"Yes," replied Mrs Sparks. "It is just a... shock to fully realise that this is all real."

"I know. I'm sure I would react in a similar way," said Mr Smiley.

"You may yet have that opportunity, James. I suspect that the second prism records the destruction of the civilisation on your own world long ago."

"Hm," said Mr Smiley. "What can we do, Wilma?"

"My grandmother said that she could not access the prisms. They are too old," said Mrs Sparks. She swiped a hand across her screen and the view on her monitor changed to an image. Mr Smiley leant forward to examine it. It was a sketch of a prism, but unlike any that either of them was familiar.

"A sketch, from Mr Wells's notebook," said Mrs Sparks, anticipating Mr Smiley's next question. "Neither grandmother nor my husband could read them. But Mr Wells evidently could. At Cydonia."

"You believe there's a chance the original device could still work?" asked Mr Smiley.

"It was operational a hundred of your years ago, after countless centuries," said Mrs Sparks. There is reason to believe it should remain so today."

"And if we could somehow get the prisms back to

Cydonia?" asked Mr Smiley.

"You are thinking that Leon and his party might be able to try?"

"It crossed my mind," admitted Mr Smiley. "Not that I wish them to get into danger. But it's likely they had something to do with getting the comportal network back up. Which means they're probably safe. And I believe they can pull it off. So, where would they likely be right now?"

"My husband was to go to Cydonia with Councillor Sffan'utul. If he is not also indisposed, I believe they and the Councillor will seek out one another."

"Do we risk trying to contact them?" asked Mr Smiley.

"Communications have been steadfastly regarded as private in our culture. But we must accept that this may have changed. And *I* will have to battle my respect for our traditions and my concerns for my son if I am to send him to complete my grandmother's work."

2

"What's that?" asked Dominic.

"Hm?" asked Lucy.

"That buzzing sound," said Dominic.

Leon put his drink down and reached for his belt.

"It is my comportal," he said. He raised the device and squeezed its sides. A holographic display popped up. "It is my mother!"

"Leon. At last," said Mrs Sparks, initially in Martian. "We have not much time. Go to speaker; speak in English. This is for everyone."

And that was it. No 'How are you?' or 'I'm glad

you're safe'. Just straight to business.

Leon did as he was told. The small holographic head of his mother looked around the room. As the assembled could make out Mr Smiley in the virtual shadows behind her image, so too could she see everyone here.

"Councillor Sffan'utul. Good. I have been unable to contact my husband. Your presence fuels my concern."

Sffan'utul made the customary Martian greeting to Mrs Sparks. "Yes, Kimb'bul'bir. However, I do not believe he will be harmed. I go to Cydonia, where I shall demand his release before the Council."

"The Council meets?"

"I have sent the signal to recall it, on my authority as a su'rmat'ata."

"A what?!" whispered Emily.

"Respected father. An elder," whispered Leon in reply.

"At which occasion, we shall also denounce Smiall'kes'hep's leadership and actions," said Sffan'utul.

Another face appeared besides Mrs Sparks's in the holo display.

"'We'?" asked Mr Smiley.

"Myself, accompanied by Mr Knutt. Plus those of my colleagues whom I can persuade to align with us."

"Councillor," said Mr Smiley. "With the greatest respect, sir, is that wise at this time? Can it wait until we – until the OPP – can get there to assist?"

"Time is our enemy, James. If we are to excise this pernicious influence from our society, we must act quickly, if uncertainly. But your assistance is welcome, as soon as you are able. We are sending a pod back for you."

"And the children? They are coming back?"

"No," said Sffan'utul, looking at the tired-looking group of youngsters sprawled about his living area. "Not immediately. Our plan requires their help – unless there are any objections from parents or guardians?"

Mr Smiley's image turned to Mrs Spark's.

"You hearken to the words of Jziee'ekkkzoor'sup?" asked Mrs Sparks.

"We do," replied Councillor Sffan'utul. "And Mr Wells himself shall be our guide."

"Then Leon will do what he needs to do," said Mrs Sparks. "But I cannot speak for his friends."

Murmurs arose from the children.

"We're going, aren't we?" called out Dominic.

"But we do not know what it is we are to do," said Camille.

"Doesn't matter," said Dominic. "We're all in this together, remember?"

Lucy and Emily nodded.

"I'll handle that," said Mr Smiley. "I'll talk to their parents. You'll look out for them, Howard?"

"Of course," said Mr Knutt. "Mr Flynn too."

"Great. Look, you better get going soon. They will be onto you – if they're not already."

"Yes," said Sffan'utul. "We depart soon. Already many of my fellow councillors are responding; some attempting to contact me. Smiall'kes'hep will be aware too."

"Leon."

"Yes, mother," replied Leon.

"Do you know what needs to be done?"

"I do," said Leon.

"And the way in?"

"Councillor Sffan'utul has explained the interpretation."

"I am sure he has. And you have your great grandmother's effects?"

"Yes."

"Good. Then pay special attention to Mr Wells's notebook, pages thirty-four to forty."

"We will," said Leon.

"Good. My blessings," said Mrs Sparks.

"Good luck everyone," said Mr Smiley.

3

Smiall'kes'hep's narrow face filled the display.

"So, they dared take refuge with Sffan'utul."

"Yes, father," replied Skiel'aeljtın.

"It should have been anticipated. You have moved to arrest them?"

"Yes, but they have escaped. Again. Their pod has been detected leaving the atmosphere – for Earth, we believe."

"It is of no consequence. We have other concerns."

"Councillor Sffan'utul's pod is on its way there."

"Yes, I know."

"Shall we intercept him?"

"No!" said Smiall'kes'hep. "That opportunity has passed. He has evoked the right of the su'rmat'atae to summon the Council. He travels in the knowledge of that privilege. He cannot be touched. His foolish idealism will be his undoing.

"Now, daughter. Come to me. And have that traitor, SShieekk'ssup'pl brought to Cydonia."

4

"How are our environmental suits and bracelets?" asked Mr Knutt. "Everyone, please check your bracelet phials and change the capsule if it less than half depleted."

"How long now, Councillor?" asked Mr Knutt.

"We shall arrive in seventeen solminutes. We are running cloaked. I will set the others down at the head of the monument. There is a small crater nearby. It is but a short walk from there. You and I will then come around and land as expected near the transit station."

"Mr Flynn, are you up to the walk, and the climb?"

"Yep, h'edmaster. I 'aven't brought me 'iking boots, though. How 'igh we gotta go up again?"

"Approximately two hundred and seventy feet," said Leon.

"An' that's where his lug-'ole is?"

Leon looked blankly back.

Dominic chuckled.

"His ear-hole," explained Lucy.

"Oh," said Leon. "Yes. Mr Wells was exploring the face and had climbed the mesa to its first level to take in the view. In his notebook, he describes how he stumbled upon an opening that had been exposed by a landslide."

Lucy held the open notebook before her. "Here it is," she said. And she started to read:

Here, in the midst of an outcrop that forms the left ear of the effigy, a landslip had exposed a narrow shaft that appeared constructed. I ventured inside, carefully, expecting to lose the daylight behind me with every step. But the stones seemed to hold a light of their own, a phosphorescence like moonlight, so that, for the most part, I did not need to use the light stick. The faint light showed the way ahead along a narrow triangular corridor, shaped so that I might have difficulty passing someone coming out. Many of the stones hold markings. Some I recognised as characters of the ancient written language!

The corridor leads deep inside the structure, and descends to an open space, a vast round room supported by a stone pillar, which I judge lies directly beneath the Council chamber itself. And here it was, bathed its own gloomy light, the great Hall of Records, like the legendary cache of Thoth beneath the paws of the Sphinx!

"It goes on to describe his discovery of the prisms, and the ones that he found from the earliest times. There are sketches of the chamber and the prisms – the ones we have. Look," she said, holding the notebook up."

"Thank you, Lucy," said Mr Knutt. "So, Leon, do you think you will be able to lead the way there alright?"

"I believe we have the right co-ordinates, Mr Knutt."

"And you have the prisms, of course? And your comportals?"

"Yes." Leon had his own comportal, while Dominic held onto the one captured from the guard at Ares.

"Good. Now, it may be that the entrance has

become covered again. If so, make your way back to the crater and... Councillor Sffan'utul and I will try to work out what to do next.

"But, if all goes well, we will meet up again soon in rather less fraught circumstances, I hope. Good luck everyone."

5

Mr Smiley addressed Mrs Sparks and Caroline Miller.

"I've spoken with HQ. We have no craft capable of getting to Mars within weeks. We'll have to wait for the return of the pod. How long until it gets here?"

"Twenty hours," replied Mrs Sparks. "Without passengers, it can achieve maximum speed. But that means we cannot get there for almost two days."

"Then I guess that will have to do," said Mr Smiley. "See if you can find a way to follow Councillor Sffan'utul's mission. Meanwhile, Caroline and I will try to find out what's going on via the official OPP channels."

6

Mr Sparks was ready when the door to his secure quarters opened. Skiel'aeljtın stood in the doorway flanked by two guards.

"Do not even think of it," said Skiel'aeljtın. "They are authorised to take whatever action is necessary if you show any resistance. You will accompany me to Cydonia, where you will stand before the Council."

Inwardly, Mr Sparks was pleased. He could tell from Skiel'aeljtın's demeanour that all was not well. It could only mean that Leon and his friends had been successful in their task and contacted Sffan'utul. The Council had been summoned to meet again.

"As a Councillor, you must know that it is my right to take my normal place at the Council."

"A *disgraced* Councillor. You go to stand trial."

7

Leon and the others looked up as Councillor Sffan'utul's pod lifted skyward and vanished – literally – as it re-cloaked before it cleared the wall of the crater, the crest of which reflected back the first rays of a new day. They hadn't slept properly – well, hardly at all since arriving at Mars. And for the first time, they were not together, and without transport and the protection offered by a pod. Not to mention Mr Knutt.

But they did have Mr Flynn, who looked especially out of place in his baggy environmental suit and clutching his favourite garden rake.

"Righ', young Leon. It's all up t'you now. Lead on."

"Thank you, Mr Flynn." Leon held out his comportal. The display showed a map of their location. "That way," said Leon. He pointed to a spot on the crater wall where a fissure split its rim.

As they started to walk, Emily spoke to Leon. "What are we really doing here, Leon? We don't have the foggiest idea how to play these prisms, even if we can find our way inside."

"We have Mr Wells's notebook," replied Leon. "And Councillor Sffan'utul and I have spoken about it."

"I estimate we have only six hours of oxygenator left," said Camille. "I hope the climb will not be too exhausting."

"We've got some oxygen left in our suits," said Dominic. "Let's face it, if we don't get this done in the next couple of hours, it's not going to happen at all. We'll be in prison. Or dead."

"Always the optimist," said Lucy, not unkindly.

"Now then," said Mr Flynn, who, as they started up the crater's inner slope, was already beginning to puff, "If we do as Councillor Snaffatol and Mr Knutt told us, we'll be fine."

"Don't you mean 'Councillor Sffan'utul'?" said Emily.

"Tha's what I said," said Mr Flynn with an unseen twinkle in his eye.

8

Sffan'utul's pod swept silently over the ruined city complex of Cydonia. Mr Knutt peered with fascination at the destroyed structures below, which looked even more mysterious in the burgeoning light and long shadows of morning.

Much had be written about these forms on Earth, which some had argued were evidence of a past high civilisation on Mars. The official view was that they were merely natural landforms, thrown into patterns by *pareidolia*, the tendency of the mind to find shapes and meaning in clouds and other natural phenomena. Now, Mr Knutt could see that, in fact, both were true.

The face itself came into view. From this angle and height it was an impressive mesa that soared to almost their cruising height. The monumental but much degraded likeness of Jziee'ekkkzoor'sup himself stared up at the sky out of the flat surroundings of the plain.

Near the foot of the monument, near to what must be the transit station that Sffan'utul had spoken about, there were already around thirty other pods of various designs and sizes, plus a number of smaller vehicles that may have been surface vehicles.

Sffan'utul waved a hand and their pod began its descent.

"When we land, follow me. Stay one pace behind, please. Say or do nothing without my instruction."

The pod came into land between two other craft, its magnetic field pulling a whirling cloud of dust up to meet it. The dust settled quickly in the thin atmosphere. A ramp appeared beneath the pod and two figures walked down from it. Four other figures approached them.

"Councillor Sffan'utul. Welcome," said the leading figure, who was dressed in the blue robes of a councillor of the North. If he had been an Earth man, he might have been judged to be around sixty years of age. Which made him about twice that in Earth years. He gave the customary hand gesture, which Sffan'utul returned.

"Councillor Skep'hol," said Sffan'utul.

Behind Skep'hol stood Smiall'kes'hep, flanked by two Council guards. Smiall'kes'hep stared at Sffan'utul and Mr Knutt but said nothing.

"You have called the Council, Sffan'utul. You are aware that only the High Councillor is authorised to summon the Council. You are aware of the penalty if found to be unwarranted?"

"Of course, Skep'hol. But allow me to remind you of the Council law that you also know well: that any member of the su'rmat'atae may call the Council whenever it is believed that grave injustice or danger presents itself. Wherever it is found," he added, looking past Skep'hol to Smiall'kes'hep.

"And your right is respected. For now," replied Skep'hol. "But that privilege extends to you only. Not to non-Councillors, nor humans, and especially not to renegades sought for subversion and sabotage. Where are the other humans?"

"This is Mr Knutt, who assists me. The others are children and not your concern. Mr Knutt is guilty of nothing besides helping our people come to the truth. There are no restrictions as to whom a su'rmat'ata selects for his personal council."

Smiall'kes'hep spoke for the first time. "But there *are* regarding who is permitted into the Council chamber."

"Except by the majority vote of the Council, or by the order of the High Councillor."

"He remains in the outer chambers. Until this is over, old one," said Smiall'kes'hep.

Sffan'utul bowed his head. "And I also request that Councillor Shieekk'ssup'pl is permitted to join my team."

"He is under arrest," said Skep'hol.

"Until tried and found guilty, he remains innocent and worthy of the full respect of his position. I demand he is set free."

"You stretch the boundaries of su'rmat'ataial privilege, Sffan'utul," said Smiall'kes'hep.

"Such a call can be made only once in a lifetime, High Councillor. Is it too much to ask?" Sffan'utul said softly.

Smiall'kes'hep considered for a moment. Then he said, "Very well. He will be released. But after this unprecedented hearing, Sffan'utul, you shall all receive your just rewards."

At that, he turned and walked away. The two guards followed, leaving Skep'hol behind.

"Allow me to escort you to your chambers," said Skep'hol.

Sffan'utul nodded at Mr Knutt to follow.

9

"How much further?" asked Emily.

"Almost there," said Leon. He glanced at his comportal. "Up there."

They stood at the base of the mesa. The sloping base of the structure, like a great slab on which the face sat, rose to a hundred metres or more above them.

"Oo-er," said Emily. "We've got to go up there? It looks so steep."

"If old H.G. Wells got up there, I'm sure you can," said Dominic. "It probably looks worse than it is."

"We need to zig-zag up," said Lucy. "That way, it won't seem so steep. Can you manage it, Mr Flynn?"

She turned. "Mr Flynn?"

"He has already begun," said Camille. She pointed to the slope. Mr Flynn was already twenty feet up and using the shaft of his rake to support him.

"What are we waiting for?" said Emily, and one by one, they set out after Mr Flynn, following his path up the rubbly face.

Mr Knutt followed Councillor Sffan'utul down the processional pathway that led to the monument, staying always one step behind as instructed.

Despite the sense of danger in their situation, he was aware of the importance of this event, which was supported by the increasing numbers of robed officials and their aides that joined them on the path. Overhead, pods and shuttles arrived from every direction – except, he noticed, from directly over the monument. That was just as well. Leon and the others should be there any time soon.

Few who lived today could remember the last time the Council had been called by anyone other than the High Councillor. Even when the young Kindlebir had called the Council a hundred and twenty years ago to hear the words of the men from Earth, it had been with the acquiescence of the High Councillor and a Council majority.

Mr Knutt was beginning to understand the boldness, and the risk, of Sffan'utul's move. His call amounted to a direct challenge to the High Councillor himself. There could only be a clear winner, and a clear loser, in this contest. And if Sffan'utul were to emerge the loser, the implications did not bear thinking about.

Presently, they arrived at the huge stone entrance that led into the monument. It wasn't very long before Sffan'utul led Mr Knutt off the descending tunnel and into an oval-shaped hall. The light was dim but adequate. He could make out a number of stone walls and alcoves that had been cut into the base of the rocky walls, so that each recess was its own open chamber, with rock-hewn benches and tables for the delegates to rest and prepare. Without a word, Sffan'utul led Mr Knutt to his own alcove, where a single spot of light shone down where a Council attendant placed a tray of refreshments.

"Mr Knutt, please wait here. I go to find out where my friend Shieekk'ssup'pl is – whom you know as Mr Sparks. Then we shall go to the chamber together."

"But –" began Mr Knutt.

"I shall call for you shortly," said Sffan'utul.

20 - THE MONUMENT

Mr Flynn may have been the first to start the ascent, but he was not the first to reach the top. Then again, he wasn't the last either. Dominic held that dubious honour. Flintworne's erstwhile Year 5 football team captain hadn't exercised as much after the football season had closed and after Leon left the school, and, frankly, he had seen rather a few too many sweets, chips and burgers since the Summer holidays had begun. And this was in one-third gravity. He flopped down at the top of the slope besides the others.

Here, they were safely out of direct view of the gathering of pods and officials at the main entrance to the Council chambers. Councillor Sffan'utul had told them it was unlikely that guards would be posted on the monument itself, since this was forbidden, but it would be as well to be wary all the same.

Sffan'utul had also provided them with some provisions, and backpacks and waistbands to carry them in. There was Tharsan honey, which was actually a concentrated dry solid, quite dry and crumbly like dark Muscovado sugar, that was produced in rock crevasses by termite-like insects. Lucy handed out pieces to everyone. They ate and rested quietly, gathering their strength and bearings.

"A nice cup o' tea would've washed that down nicely, young Lucy," said Mr Flynn.

"There's water, or juice?" offered Lucy.

"No, tha's alright," said Mr Flynn. "Jus' kiddin'. Now, young Leon, where's this rabbit warren we're supposed to be lookin' for?"

"It should be near that projection over there," said Leon. He pointed across the rocky table on which they sat to where the ground rose again (which eventually peaked as the effigy's mouth or nose).

"Well, what are we waiting for?" said Mr Flynn, and he was on his feet again and leading them onwards.

2

At the base of the landform – which from close up, hardly resembled a carved structure, a representation of the ear of Jziee'ekkkzoor'sup – there was a scree of debris. Leon took out Wells's diary and found the right page. Yes, this seemed right. But where was the entrance?

While Leon studied Wells's sketch, Mr Flynn studied the scree itself. Then he took his rake and carefully made up to a point about half-way up the slope and began to sweep the loose debris behind him. The children stood back as the loose material trickled and bounced down the slope, sending up puffs of dust. When it settled, it was apparent that Mr Flynn had found something. He stood, resting on his rake, looking at a dark triangle at his feet.

"Is that it?" called Emily.

"I'd say so," said Mr Flynn. "Now, are any of you

youngsters gonna 'elp me clear the rest of it?"

3

At last, the tunnel entrance was fully exposed. It was in the shape of an isosceles triangle, tall and narrow, approximately two metres high by sixty centimetres across the base. Apart from where the early light penetrated the entrance, it was completely dark inside. Carved symbols in the stone near the entrance added to its sense of foreboding.

"Eugh," said Emily. "I'm not sure I want to go in there."

"Especially when it forces us to proceed one after another," said Camille.

"It is an effective defensive design," agreed Leon. "Only one person can enter at a time."

"And you can't bring your arms up 'cept sideways," said Mr Flynn. "Now, young Leon. What says you if I take the lead and you be behind me to let me know what to expect? And we'll have young Dominic at the back?"

Leon and the girls nodded their agreement.

Only Dominic seemed less sure to be bringing up the rear.

"What if someone follows us in?" asked Dominic, trying to keep the concern out of his voice.

"Then you'll be the first to know and tell us," said Mr Flynn.

"Yeah, but –"

"Don't be such a wuss, Dom," said Lucy. "It's usually Emily that's the wimpy one."

"Oi," said Emily.

"Sorry," said Lucy.

"That's alright," replied Emily. "It's true."

"At least you will be the first one back out?" suggested Camille diplomatically.

"Only if we turn around now," said Dominic. "Not if we come out the way we went in."

Finally, Leon spoke. "We are wasting time. This is the best arrangement. Please follow."

4

Mr Knutt sat somewhat impatiently in the side chamber. On Earth, it might have been called a green room, a lounge area where performers or guests wait to be called to the stage or arena. He ignored the refreshments on the table as he watched growing numbers of robed delegates and their aides drift down the main corridor towards the underground Council chamber.

Eventually, the flowing crowds slowed to a trickle until, finally, he found himself virtually alone. He rose from his place in the alcove and wandered towards the doorway to the main corridor, where he almost bumped into two figures.

"Ah, Howard. Good." It was Councillor Sffan'utul. And with him was Mr Sparks, Councillor Shieekk'ssup'pl.

"Fred! How are you?" said Mr Knutt.

"I am well, Howard," replied Mr Sparks. Except, with his Martian pronunciation, it sounded like *Haw'udd.*

"We must proceed. It will not do to be late for our own party," said Sffan'utul.

Mr Knutt found a small smile.

"Please, put this on," said Sffan'utul. It was a gold and blue robe with a purple waistband. Mr Knutt took it from Sffan'utul. He noticed it was similar to the one worn by Mr Sparks.

"This marks you as one of my aides for this hearing. You cannot be denied entry to the chamber, despite what Smiall'kes'hep has said."

"Thank you," said Mr Knutt. "If it is your wish, and it is permitted, then I am honoured."

Sffan'utul nodded graciously.

Mr Knutt shed his jacket and slipped on the robe.

"You are tall," said Sffan'utul. "It is the best we can do."

"It's fine," said Mr Knutt politely, even if he did feel like he was dressed up in a colourful bathrobe. Despite the seriousness of the event of which he was now a participant, he couldn't help feeling grateful that his former pupils were not present.

"You will need these also," said Mr Sparks, and he handed Mr Knutt a small device that looked like a hearing aid, plus a silver wristband.

"A translator," explained Mr Sparks.

So, it *was* a hearing aid, of a kind.

Mr Knutt put them on.

"Now, please," said Sffan'utul. "Follow me as before."

5

Leon paused in the long corridor. Mr Flynn had walked on a few paces before he realised that Leon had paused. He stopped and turned back to where Leon held H.G. Wells's notebook under a light emitted by his comportal. Mr Flynn lowered his own pocket torch.

"What is it, lad?"

"According to Mr Wells, we should be on what he calls the path of the three ways by now."

The others held single file behind Leon.

"What's that?" asked Lucy.

"This path should be descending," said Leon. "If it is to lead beneath the council chambers."

"Perhaps it is, but we haven't noticed?" offered Emily.

"No, it is not," said Leon. "Look." He pointed his comportal at the floor and a shimmering blade of orange light appeared, which ended in a narrow laser-like line on the granular surface of the tunnel. Holographic symbols either side of the glowing line changed as Leon moved the device. "See, it is level."

"OK, so we need to keep going?" said Camille.

"Yes, but we must proceed carefully. The notebook suggests the path soon divides into three. Only one leads to the hall."

"And where do the others go?" asked Lucy.

"I do not know," replied Leon. "They simply stop. Mr Wells just marks an arrow, but it is not clear which way it refers to."

"I see what he has done," said Camille.

"What's that?" asked Lucy.

"If anyone were to have only his notebook, they could not tell the right path."

"Meaning?" asked Emily.

"Meaning that you need to be here. I believe he left a mark here."

"So we're looking for an arrow?" asked Lucy.

"Yes, that makes sense," said Leon.

"Are we ready to get along, then, Leon?" asked Mr Flynn.

"Yes, I think so, Mr Flynn. But please tread carefully."

After a while, it became increasingly obvious that they *were* now descending. The air became steadily warmer and the pull of even Mars's weak gravity became apparent. The light from Mr Flynn's torch bobbed and danced ahead of them, and his own shadow, created by the light on Leon's comportal, preceded him.

It wasn't long before Mr Flynn stopped. They gathered behind him.

"What is it?" asked Dominic from the back.

"The tunnel has divided into three," said Lucy. She shuffled forward, and found she could now stand beside Leon in a circular space that accommodated the three ways.

"Which one do we take?" asked Emily from behind Lucy.

"I suggest you all sit tight while me and young Leon have a closer look," said Mr Flynn. "Right, lad?"

"Of course," said Leon.

The two of them moved forward, Mr Flynn towards the left tunnel; Leon towards the middle one.

"We're lookin' for an arrow, you say?" asked Mr Flynn.

"I believe so," said Leon.

They each began inspecting the walls of their tunnels, moving slowly into them. After a short while, Leon came back out.

"The walls are decorated with the same ancient

symbols, but I can see no sign of an arrow amongst them."

"How are you doing, Mr Flynn?" called out Lucy. The sound of her voice echoed off the walls of the confined spaces.

"Nothin' down this one," replied Mr Flynn. They could hear him making his way back.

Leon was already moving to the third tunnel. He started again by exploring just inside the entrance, then moved deeper inside. It *must* be in this one.

The others waited patiently outside, now in the dark apart from the light reflected back from Leon's comportal and Mr Flynn's torch, plus a faint phosphorescent light that was only now noticeable. Mr Flynn rejoined the others, who huddled together in the open space.

Suddenly there was a yelp, which echoed loudly in the void, and was followed by clatters and thuds that came from further and further away.

"Leon?" called Emily.

No reply.

"Leon!"

Mr Flynn hurried towards the tunnel.

"Be careful, Mr Flynn," said Camille.

Mr Flynn looked into the tunnel. His torch picked out... nothing. His heart leapt into his throat.

Then a bluish light appeared. It swelled to fill the space with cold light. Oddly, it seemed to be coming out of the floor a dozen steps along the tunnel.

"Mr Flynn."

It was Leon. Mr Flynn was stunned into inaction. "Wha–"

"Stay back."

Leon's face appeared above the side of what was now clearly a hole in the pathway. Then the rest of him came into view as his anti-grav boots raised him clear and he could set foot back on the solid tunnel floor.

Mr Flynn was shaken. So, clearly, was Leon. He was breathing rapidly.

"I was examining the walls as I moved along. I took another step and I found myself falling. I managed to activate my shoes. But I have lost my comportal."

"Thank goodness you managed that, lad," said Mr Flynn, who had now found his voice. "Anythin' else lost – apart from your comportal?"

"No. The prisms are safe, as is Mr Wells's notebook. Luckily, I had just moved it to my pocket."

"Good," said Mr Flynn. "Let's get of 'ere, shall we?"

"Wait," said Leon. "Can I have your torch a moment?"

Mr Flynn handed it over. Leon pointed it down the tunnel. The hole was barely visible unless one stood right over it. It stretched from wall to wall, but on its other side, the tunnel continued on as normal – at least as far as they could see.

"What happened?" came a voice from behind.

Leon and Mr Flynn turned to see the other children crowded into the tunnel entrance.

"Leon fell down an 'ole –"

Emily gasped. "He *what?*"

"He's alrigh', though, thank 'eavens. Aren't you, Leon?"

"Yes. Some scratches and bruises, and now no comportal. But I am alright."

"Oh," said Dominic. He opened a pocket on his waistband and retrieved the captured comportal. "I forgot I had this."

He passed it forward to Leon, who turned on its lamp. The tunnel became lighter so that they could now see one another properly.

"Can't we climb down to get your comportal?" asked Dominic.

Leon shook his head. "I fell sixty metres before I could activate my boots. It is much deeper than that. It is gone."

"This can't be the tunnel," said Lucy. "Perhaps you missed the mark in one of the others?"

"Or there is no mark, after all, in any of them?" suggested Camille.

"Could it still be this way?" suggested Emily.

"Don't be daft," said Dominic. "Don't you think old H.G. might have mentioned a bloomin' big hole in the floor?"

"Unless it has collapsed since his time?" said Lucy.

"No. It is too regular, and there are symbols carved on its wall," said Leon. "It is purposefully made."

Leon took the guard's comportal and shone its light back on the walls nearest them. The embossed symbols of another age seemed to come alive as their shadows moved under the shifting beam.

"It could have been crossed using a bridge or antigravity technology," said Leon. "It would only keep the unwary or the unsophisticated out."

"Like us," said Lucy.

"I have another idea," said Leon. He pointed the comportal at the roof of the tunnel. The carvings that adorned the walls were absent here. There was just bare, unmarked stone.

Leon lowered the comportal and moved towards his friends.

They stepped back to let him through, then followed him as he made his way back to the first tunnel – the one Mr Flynn had inspected. He shone his light up at the roof. After a few moments, he came back out. Nothing. Finally, he entered the middle tunnel. He raised the comportal again and, this time, he saw something – a faint, but definite arrow scratched into the stone that pointed down the tunnel. He came back out.

"It is this one," said Leon, finding a faint smile for the first time.

"Really?"

"Woo-hoo," said Emily.

"W'as that?" asked Mr Flynn, who had just joined them.

"Leon's found it!" said Lucy excitedly.

"Where?" said Dominic. "Let me see."

Leon stepped back into the tunnel, where he pointed his light for Dominic and the others to see."

"What was he playing at?" said Dominic. "Wells. Why didn't he just say so in his book? You could have been killed!"

"As Camille said before, I believe Mr Wells was simply being cautious," replied Leon. "Helping to ensure that only serious and knowledgeable seekers could find their way to the archive itself."

"Well," said Mr Flynn. "Tha' being the case, we'd better be gettin' on."

6

By virtue of his height, Mr Knutt attracted some attention as he, Mr Sparks and Councillor Sffan'utul made their way into the Council chamber. But, with the hood of his robe up, not nearly enough to be of concern.

They took their seats: Councillor Sffan'utul on one row; Mr Sparks – Councillor Shieekk'ssup'pl – and Mr Knutt on the next level behind him.

The benches on both sides of the auditorium were full: a sea of blue on the far side; a sandy expanse of the southern hemisphere delegates on this. Three hundred and sixty councillors plus their aides.

Mr Knutt studied High Councillor Smiall'kes'hep, who appeared quietly composed and confident. Seated behind him, beside the rounded stone structure that represented Phobos, were Skiel'aeljtın and, surprisingly, her daughter Aurore.

Were children permitted at the assembly? If they happened to be a grandchild of the High Councillor, the answer appeared to be 'yes'.

Gradually the hustle and noise died down and Smiall'kes'hep rose to his feet. He tapped his wristband. After a moment, he spoke.

"Esteemed colleagues. I welcome you again to another extraordinary meeting of this Council.

"For the benefit of those amongst you who may be unclear regarding the events that have led to this gathering, I shall summarise for you.

"You will be aware of the recent failure of the comportal network. You may *not* be aware that the gatekeeper sentinel on Su'umka'r, that coordinates our planetary defence systems, has also been disabled."

Murmurs rippled through the assembly. Smiall'kes'hep allowed the sound to continue for a few moments. Then he raised his hand to call for quiet again.

"The two are related."

He raised a hand and a holographic image appeared in the central space of the auditorium. After a moment, Mr Knutt realised what they were seeing. It was a recording of their mission at Su'umka'r, from the perspective of the monolith itself. Their pod was visible in the background and, in the foreground, Mr Flynn, who was reaching inside a pocket of his environmental suit. As they watched, he threw an object over his shoulder. It flew towards them, growing in size until it vanished past whatever recording equipment the monolith possessed. Then was a flicker of black light, a flash of green, and the image faded.

Smiall'kes'hep pointed directly across to where Mr Knutt, Mr Sparks and Councillor Sffan'utul sat.

"Yonder, on the benches of our colleagues across this chamber, sits one of the saboteur humans himself! Here, with us, in these hallowed chambers; invited in by his sponsors, one of whom is himself accused of subversion!"

The murmurs rose to a rumble of exchanged and indignant comments that reverberated around the amphitheatre. A number of the delegates on the northern benches stood in protest.

"They are no friends of the people of Oztzıldıj!" exclaimed Smiall'kes'hep.

Councilor Skep'hol raised a hand and several of the Council guards that stood around the upper perimeter of the amphitheatre began to move towards Sffan'utul's party.

Councillor Sffan'utul rose calmly from his place. All eyes turned on him. Many knew that it was Sffan'utul who had taken the unprecedented step of calling the Council.

When one speaker rose to speak, it was usual for the other to concede the floor and sit out of respect. Eyes watched expectantly to see if Smiall'kes'hep would yield. At last, he did.

Sffan'utul touched his own wristband.

"High Councillor, thank you. Esteemed colleagues," he said calmly. "It may first serve to remind this Council of the proper protocols to be followed in these proceedings, rare that they are.

"It is customary, is it not, High Councillor – and no small matter of respect – to permit the one who has called the Council to address it in the first instance, thereby setting the agenda for the debate? And with it, the expectation that it will run its natural course? May I be afforded that courtesy?"

The chamber fell silent. In the tense stillness, Smiall'kes'hep stood again. His expression was steely. He eyed Sffan'utul intensely. "Proceed," he said curtly. "But on its conclusion, Councillor, those responsible for these outrages shall face justice." He sat down.

The Council guards likewise stood down and returned to their posts.

"Thank you," replied Sffan'utul. "I certainly hope so," he added.

He turned to address the audience.

"Esteemed colleagues, friends. You have heard the words of our High Councillor. I do not dispute the essential facts of what he has said."

The whispered undertone of the crowd threatened to rise again. Sffan'utul raised a hand.

"To which I shall return. But I *do* dispute their

attribution. There *is* indeed a pernicious force at work within our society. But it is not the humans. Rather, it is a force from within – one represented and wielded by a small but influential clique amongst us."

Sffan'utul continued through the tide of protests that lashed at him from across the auditorium.

"This inner circle of privilege and power has been adept at hiding itself and its secret agenda from us for aeons. So much so, that even to contemplate its existence will be an affront to the dearly-held beliefs most of us hold regarding our heritage, and of ourselves as a peaceful and benevolent species. As long as we are ruled by a secret faction that is motivated primarily by its own interests, we cannot embrace this ideal.

"Its exposure is the reason that I, Sffan'utul of Tharsis, have taken the decision to evoke the right of the su'rmat'atae to bring you here today. Those that know me – and that is a great many of you – know I do not do so lightly. You shall be presented with the evidence, much of which was compiled by my late, great friend, Kindlebir of Solis. I urge you to have patience and to suspend judgement until this presentation concludes.

"If I fail to convince you of my argument; if you elect to remain with a comfortable lie over the unpalatable truth, I shall accept without protest the due penalty imposed by this Chamber."

Mr Knutt noticed that, at the mention of Kindlebir, Skiel'aeljtın had stepped down and whispered in her father's ear. Smiall'kes'hep nodded.

The atmosphere in the auditorium had changed noticeably, from animated hostility on one side and disquiet elsewhere, to curiosity. Subdued conversations broke out around the arena.

Sffan'utul produced a prism from within his robe and inserted it into a slot beside his seat. "We will begin with the events of two days ago," he said.

Mr Knutt turned to Mr Sparks. "Do you think they can make it in time?"

Mr Sparks maintained his forward gaze. "Leon will not fail us."

21 - THE HALL OF RECORDS

"**H**ow much further?" asked Emily.

"I believe we are almost there," replied Leon from the front.

They had taken the tunnel marked with the arrow, which had descended steadily at a comfortable angle. At one point, it deflected slightly to the right then continued straight again. The deeper they went, the warmer it became and the tunnel itself widened and levelled out. Leon checked it with the spare comportal. Yes, it was now perfectly level.

A little further on, they emerged into a large semi-circular chamber. It held a smoky greenish-grey light, supplementing the light from the comportal and Mr Flynn's torch, which showed walls constructed of what looked like bronze and adorned with a honeycomb pattern that contained numerous symbols and designs.

Directly ahead stood two huge statues. They stood side by side, each with their right leg extended that made it look as if they had been frozen in the act of stepping out of the wall itself.

The one on the left was attired in a long robe carved from sand-coloured stone and patterned with a circular design laid out in a polished blue metal. It had a four-pointed star set uppermost above a central embossed circle and a crescent below it. Other patterns swirled off the main design, some disappearing into the carved folds of the fabric.

The figure stared down at them with the baleful glare of a bird of prey. In its left hand it clutched a long staff, and in its right, a four-pronged star.

Its companion was a mirror image, with the exception that its cloak was of blue stone overlaid with designs in gold, and the star and the crescent were in opposing positions. In its left hand it clutched a golden crescent.

"Is this it?" whispered Lucy.

"No, I believe it is through there," replied Leon. He too found himself whispering. The imposing figures, the sheer weight of time and the idea of the secrets they guarded demanded a hushed, respectful tone.

Dominic looked at Leon, then at the wall between the two figures. He frowned. "What, through the wall?"

Leon stepped between the figures and began studying the wall, examining the pattern of hexagons.

Dominic stepped up next to him. "What are we looking for?"

"This," said Leon. He held Mr Wells's open notebook up. Dominic found his mobile phone and turned its torch on. Leon's thumb was placed beneath a sketch of several joined hexagons. All were blank except one, which had a circle drawn in the centre, surrounded by three small shapes, a crescent and two stars.

"He does not state precisely where it is," said Leon.

They began to pore over the wall, and soon Dominic announced he had found it. Leon came over. It was midway along the lowest row of hexagons, and so faintly inscribed it was barely visible.

Leon reached out and pressed it. It yielded by a few

millimetres. Then something took over and it sank further into the wall. Then the others around it did likewise and began to slide sideways, until an aperture appeared. It was perhaps a metre high. Behind it was darkness.

"That's a door?" asked Dominic. "It's too small."

"It reminds me of the entrance to the Great Pyramid in Egypt," said Camille. "It forces visitors to bend low; perhaps to be humble. It could be similar in purpose?"

"Or invaders," said Dominic. "You can't fight bent over," said Dominic.

"Who's going first?" asked Emily.

"I think that's me," said Mr Flynn. "I'm suppose' t'be lookin' after you lot."

No-one protested.

Mr Flynn approached the aperture, which wasn't completely dark, but glowed with that same ashen light like faint moonlight. He pointed his torch and stooped to look inside. Then, with the barest hesitation, he disappeared into it.

"Oomph."

"Mr Flynn?" called Lucy.

"S'alright, Lucy," he called back. "Just me back playin' up a bit."

There was a few moments' pause, then they heard Mr Flynn call out, "Er, it's a short tunnel, but there's jus' a wall at the end."

Leon bent forward and vanished inside. Dominic followed him in.

The inside of the passage was of plain, unmarked stone. Leon and Dominic began to examine the walls and the roof in the cramped space.

"Nothing," said Dominic in frustration. "What do we

do now?"

Mr Flynn was wedged in the corner, his back to the end of the passage and its left wall. His torch beam was aimed at the floor, but the perspiration on his brow was visible in the reflected light.

"Mr Flynn, could you step away, please?" asked Leon.

"Eh?"

"He wants you to get behind us," said Dominic.

"Oh. Right you are," said Mr Flynn. He shuffled out of the way.

Leon moved into the space. And immediately saw it, a simple hexagon on the side wall near to the end wall. He looked at Dominic.

"Yes!" said Dominic.

Leon studied it for a second. Then he pressed it. As before, it sank evenly into the wall. A whoosh of air met them as the wall began to move. It fragmented into hexagons that moved outward and sideways, leaving, as before, an opening. The space beyond was lighter than the either the passage or the chamber behind them. Leon and Dominic stepped forward to peer out.

Mr Flynn meanwhile called back to the girls. "Alrigh', you can come through. Mind 'ow you go."

One by one, the others ducked under the entrance and made their way along the short tunnel to emerge alongside Mr Flynn, Leon and Dominic in a large hexagonal chamber. The light here, whatever its source, was stronger; like the cool grey light of dawn. It revealed a space the size and majesty of a cathedral's crossing.

They stood on a stone ledge that ran both ways

312

around the space to form a ring. Before them, simple stone-cut steps descended to a dust-laden floor. A narrow fissure in the floor ran towards the rear of the chamber, where it ran up a thick column of rock that spread upwards to merge into a high vaulted roof. Cut into the base of the column was a semi-circular recess, and within it stood a decorated stone dais. On it lay a prone figure, carved in stone.

"Could that be *Jez...thingummyjig*?" whispered Lucy.

Leon didn't respond, not immediately. He stared at the statue in disbelief. Could this be where the great, the revered, Jziee'ekkkzoor'sup was buried? He had temporarily forgotten their mission.

All around the inner wall of the ring of stone on which they stood were hundreds of prisms of the same kind that they carried back here. The walls were patterned with the same honeycomb design they had seen in the antechamber, and each hexagon seemed to hold five prisms, which sat in pockets so that around half their length projected out like rows of teeth.

In the middle of the floor space, which continued the hexagonal theme, stood a structure that resembled a large prism; one made of solid bluish-green crystal. Inset into its angled top, were two shallow circular depressions with hexagonal holes in their centre, one at top centre; the other near its base. Scattered around the dusty floor at its base were a number of broken prisms.

"That must be the control panel?" asked Lucy.

Leon nodded. It matched the view sketched in Mr Wells's notebook. But *that* hadn't included the tomb of Jziee'ekkkzoor'sup (if that is what it was), which puzzled him.

"Hadn' we get on?" said Mr Flynn. "The councillor and your dad will be expectin' us to do our bit soon, won't he?"

Leon didn't answer. He had his head cocked to one side. Then his eyes widened.

"Quickly, hide!" he whispered.

"What?" said Emily.

"Someone is coming," said Leon.

"I can't hear anything," said Dominic.

"Wha' is it?" asked Mr Flynn.

But Leon was already looking for somewhere to hide. Lucy and Emily and Camille followed him.

Then Dominic could hear it too, a faint sound like footsteps on crumbled plaster or fine gravel; getting closer. Then he noticed a faint flickering glow from the other side of the raised tomb, coming from inside the recess.

He glanced around and saw that the others had huddled behind a long, solid stone bench on the edge of the ring platform. He hesitated for a second, then made his way to it as quickly and quietly as he could. He squashed in beside Emily and Camille and pulled his knees towards him, trying not to breathe heavily, just as the glow from the recess brightened, casting shifting shadows around the chamber.

Dominic couldn't resist taking a peek. He twisted to peer around the corner of the bench to see three robed figures appear from behind the tomb structure. They barely came to half its height, giving its true scale. Two of the figures were dressed in blue; the other – a shorter, squatter figure – in gold.

"That's High Councillor Smiall'kes'hep," said Camille

314

in barely a whisper. *"And Councillor Skep'hol."*

"You know them?" whispered Lucy.

Dominic looked around to see Camille and the others looking through narrow letterbox-like slits in the back of the bench. He looked above him and saw one there. Already, Emily had positioned herself to look through.

"Yes," I have seen them at Aurore's home," said Camille. "I do not know the other one."

Dominic turned onto his knees and, finding his mobile phone, he positioned the camera eye before the slit.

"What are you doing?" said Emily.

"What's it look like?" said Dominic.

"No – it might light up!"

"I've disabled the light," said Dominic. He started to record. "Flippin 'eck. Girls," he muttered under his breath.

"Sshh over there," whispered Lucy.

2

Smiall'kes'hep led the others towards the control panel in the centre of the arena. He stopped, and for a few moments he looked around the hall. Studying it.

Behind the bench, the children ducked away from the eye-slits. In the silence, they could almost feel Smiall'kes'hep's gaze penetrating the stone. Only Dominic's phone remained in place, continuing to record. Dominic held it as still as possible, until his hand began tremor and his brow broke out in beads of sweat.

After what seemed an age, Smiall'kes'hep dropped

his gaze and turned to his fellow councillors.

"Where did that old kes'eldril obtain that imagery?" asked Skep'hol, who was attired in the same colours as Smiall'kes'hep, which denoted him as a fellow councillor of the North.

"From the same source that thwarted the attack on Earth," replied Smiall'kes'hep.

"Your daughter's pod – the humans?" asked the other councillor. He was smaller and stouter than either of his companions, and dressed in gold rather than blue.

Smiall'kes'hep nodded.

"It is of little consequence," said Councillor Skep'hol. "It shows nothing but an asteroid swarm, with unfortunate strikes on the Earth and its satellite."

"That also happened to destroy the orbital Sentinel," said the other councillor, whose name was Jzke'el'hep. "The very device emplaced by our ancestors to protect the humans from such chance events. Already my colleagues are clamouring for you to account for the full complement of sentry engines."

"And I shall do so," replied Skep'hol. "There remain, as always, six in orbit. And, as far as they are concerned, there are still eight stationed at the asteroid belt. By the time they discover otherwise, it will be too late."

Smiall'kes'hep raised a hand. "It is sufficient that Sffan'utul raises doubts. He risks much by summoning the Council. But he is widely respected. His word may carry beyond what he can prove.

"So, we must fight fire with fire. We have shown the humans had the capability to disarm the Gatekeeper. It has already been suggested that they – with the help of their traitorous Martian accomplices – neutralised the comportal network. It is but a small stretch to suggest that they also destroyed the Sentinel as a prelude to an attack on our world.

"But we must press the advantage. And soon, Skep'hol. Sffan'utul will not have come here only with weak evidence and hearsay. I need you to move quickly to end this charade. On my cue, move to arrest them and let us put an end to this before it has even begun."

"But what of Kindlebir? Is it possible?" asked Jzke'el'hep.

"That they might have the missing prisms? What of it?" said Skep'hol. "It will prove only that Kindlebir discovered Jazu'ul'ard'zahl and the resting place of Jziee'ekkkzoor'sup. She kept both a secret and stole away the prisms. Her reputation and that of her followers will be sullied forever."

"There is something else," said Smiall'kes'hep. "The prisms preserve the identity of every person ever to have accessed their information. Sffan'utul himself may not know this, but we cannot risk any chance that he does."

Smiall'kes'hep's companions looked at him fearfully.

"*Every* person?" asked Jzke'el'hep. "But –"

"Yes, my dear Jzke'el'hep. Even yours. And mine. Ah, Sffan'utul! Note the cleverness of his scheme!" said Smiall'kes'hep. "*If* he possesses the prisms, he has successfully drawn us all to the only place that they can be viewed."

"But did you not say that they can only be read here, within Jazu'ul'ard'zahl itself?" questioned

Skep'hol.

"That is true," replied Smiall'kes'hep. "The ancient prisms are unique. They cannot be read or copied by our technology. They can be read only here at this panel. But, their content can be projected into the chamber above."

"How do you know this?" asked Skep'hol.

"I have seen it. Long ago. With my father."

Smiall'kes'hep stepped away from them. He carefully surveyed the hall again. With his back to them, he said, "Skep'hol, post additional guards at every known point of entry."

"I shall employ my personal guard," said Skep'hol.

Smiall'kes'hep turned around. "Are they trustworthy?"

"They are sworn unto death."

"My friends," said Jzke'el'hep. "I have word that recess has ended. The council is reconvening."

3

From their hiding place, Mr Flynn and the children watched as the three councillors left the way they came.

Mr Flynn was the first to stand. He used the back of the bench to get to his feet. "Oof," he said, holding his lower back. "'Aven't 'ad to sit on the floor in years."

He looked out over the chamber before he permitted the others to get up.

"Right; s'all clear."

Leon was the first up. He made straight for the stairs and was soon standing beside the tomb of Jziee'ekkkzoor'sup.

He stared up at the sarcophagus in awe. The upper and lower portions were decorated with strange symbols, while a central band displayed a carved frieze depicting a series of events, much like a Roman victory frieze. Leon walked around it, examining the full story, which ended where it began, on the side facing the arena, with a figure seated on a throne.

The others waited by the control panel – except Dominic, who had trotted over to see where the councillors had gone. There, he found an archway in the rock and the start of a stone ramp. He ventured a little way into it. It rose and curved to the right into a spiral. He rounded another bend and found himself on a level platform, like a stair landing. The ramp continued on up to his right, while to his left and straight ahead there were two new arches that led to goodness knew where. Satisfying himself that there was no-one there, he made his way back down.

"All clear," he said to the others.

"Good," said Lucy. "Keep an eye out. Oh, here," she said. She handed Dominic a small silver device.

"What's this?"

"Translator. One each from Mr Sffan'utul. To help us understand some of what we might find. Pop it in your ear. It'll do the rest."

Lucy turned her attention to Leon. "Now, Leon, we've got to hurry. Can you operate it?"

Leon was studying it. "I believe so," he said. He reached out and drew his hand over the central space of the panel. Emily, standing to the side, noticed that his gesture retraced a faint pattern already marked in the dusty surface.

He took out the first prism and checked its

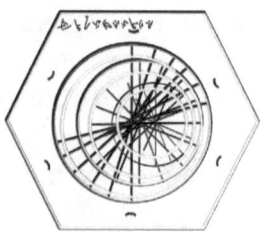

flattened end.

"I believe this is the earliest one," he said. He placed it over the nearest hexagonal depression and carefully inserted it.

On contact, the prism was drawn in as if by magnetic attraction. Two-thirds of it still sat proud of the panel, but its effect was immediate. Its top lit up with a glowing pattern of fine criss-crossing blue filaments. They spread rapidly down into the crystal body of the panel, forming a complex lattice that bathed them it its cool light and threw their shadows across the hall and onto its walls.

They all took a step back. The panel swirled with blue energy.

Then the panel itself sent out larger tendrils from its base, flooding the joints in the floor like molten metal giving off blue flame. The effect spread up the walls until the whole chamber glowed within a grand web of electric blue light.

Then, just as suddenly, it began to fade away, leaving just a faint blue glow. Or was that just an after effect left on their retinas?

"What's up?" asked Lucy.

"I do not know," said Leon.

"Here, let me see," said Camille. Leon stepped aside to let her through.

"In his notebook, Mr Wells sketched the prisms," said Camille, "with marks that suggested to me that they must rotate."

"Oh," said Lucy.

Camille grasped the prism and twisted it slightly to the right.

Nothing.

Then she rotated it back and around to the left.

Again, nothing.

"It's not working?" said Emily.

Camille said nothing. She twisted the prism around in the other direction, past where she had before and, finally, it dropped down a notch. The panel lit up again.

Camille looked up, almost as surprised as everyone else. But she continued the random turns on the prism. "It is like a combination lock," she said.

Immediately a cone of light appeared in the space above them.

"Woo-hoo," said Emily. "We're in!"

A holographic menu formed above them. On its left was a column of images of six individuals, each framed in a different geometric shape. At the top was Camille, now forever captured in the memory of the prism. Beneath her was a young Martian female with bright, intelligent eyes. Beneath her was an image of a human, a young man sporting a significant moustache. And beneath him, three formal-looking Martians attired in the blue robes of the North; one in the robes of the High Councillor.

"The most recent ones to have viewed the prism," said Leon. Including my grandmother."

"Huh?" said Lucy.

"That's Councillor Kindlebir?" asked Emily.

"Yes. It has to be. It appears she did come down here after all," said Leon.

"And that must be that Wells fella," said Mr Flynn. "So, who are those fellas underneath?"

"I cannot read the symbols," said Leon. "But my guess is that one of them is Councillor Smiall'kes'hep's father."

"How do we access the data files?" asked Camille.

Leon stepped forward again. He moved a hand over the symbols arranged on the right. With a flick of his hand, the topmost symbol unfolded to form a list of other options. The top one was illuminated.

Leon twisted the prism and it scrolled through them. A series of thumbnail images flickered before them, showing scenes of angry crowds and heated exchanges in the chamber above, then images of armies and fearsome weapons that emitted searing beams of destructive energy that H. G. Wells had described in the only way he could comprehend – as deadly heat rays.

Leon stopped on a row of symbols towards the bottom of the list. He touched the top of the prism and that line flashed, then exploded outward in a holographic projection that, this time, filled the entire space above them.

"Whoah! That...is...epic!" exclaimed Dominic.

"How did you know which line to pick?" asked Lucy.

"Mr Wells. I memorised the symbol pattern in his book," said Leon.

"How did *he* know which one it was?" asked Lucy. Her question went unanswered.

Above them, around them, behind them, the

hologram was of perfect fidelity – better than the sharpest, most vital three-dimensional movie on Earth.

"This should show the collision with Ti'aransc," said Leon.

And so it did. It began with views of life on the surface, aeons ago. The land was clothed in green; the sky blue and studded with puffy white clouds. The city around them was filled with large, tasteful buildings of stone and glass. Clean open spaces, punctuated by trees and fountains, were sprinkled with gowned figures that moved slowly but purposefully through it. If it were not for the people – thin hairless figures with large almond-shaped eyes – it might have been mistaken for any modern new city on Earth. But no, it had a quality beyond these – of elevation, of grace and harmony and peace.

Then, a view of the sky. Overhead, a bright streak appeared, orange turning to yellow, growing longer and brighter. The people in the plaza began to flee, to take cover as the brightness of the moon's steep descent into the atmosphere increased rapidly, changing to an impossibly bright white globe. In an instant, it exploded.

The view switched to one from orbit. The asteroid moon Ti'aransc shrank in the centre of their view, falling in a tight arc towards Mars. Two objects, like bright greenish-blue dots, flared bright from its surface. Another followed the asteroid on its fiery plunge. It accelerated towards the falling moon, joining the other two already on its surface. It too flared brightly with sickening green light as it applied its fatal thrust to the doomed moon.

Their viewpoint evidently was from a fourth zero-point engine. Ti'aransc fell into the atmosphere, becoming superheated before it exploded with unimaginable ferocity, spraying a huge cone of debris-laden atmosphere into space and sending shock waves sweeping around the planet, and sending their viewpoint tumbling over and over out into space. The scene ended abruptly.

Leon took a deep breath. He had just viewed the destruction of his home world, its reduction from a vital living one to a dying ball of dust. This time, he knew that the imagery was real, captured all that time ago; not a simulated reconstruction his mother had shown them in her lecture a few days ago.

"Then it *was* deliberate," said Camille.

"So, what's this got to do with that Smiall'kes'hep bloke?" asked Dominic.

"Planetary defence is under the direction of the North's leaders. It has always been so," replied Leon.

"And?" said Dominic.

"Don't you get it, Dominic?" said Lucy. "Someone tried the same kind of thing a couple of days ago. On Earth."

"And do not forget the other prism," added Camille. "Mr Wells claimed it records a similar attack on Earth thousands of years ago too. Or the others he noted down in his book."

Emily nodded in agreement. "We must look at them," she said. "But we have to be quick. How will we know what to do and when to do it now that we've lost Leon's comportal?"

"I've been working on that," said Dominic. "With this." He held up the guard's comportal. "I've been trying to find Councillor Sffan'utul on it."

"Any luck?"

"Not yet," replied Dominic.

"He was going to send us a signal on my comportal when they were ready," said Leon.

"Well, tha's outa the question now, in't it, lad?" said Mr Flynn. "We'll 'ave to find another way. First, though, 'adn't we better get on an' find out 'ow to send some of these pictures upstairs?"

22- SMIALL'KES'HEP

Councillor Sffan'utul sat back down. On the other side of the chamber, High Councillor Smiall'kes'hep rose to speak.

"Esteemed colleagues, honoured guests," he began. "Do you not grow as weary as I at the baseless ramblings of our venerable colleague?

"Like me, do you not feel *offended* to have been summoned here today on account of mere conjecture and questionable 'evidence'?

"Do you not likewise find it *repugnant* to hear him make false accusations about his fellow councillors and their ancestry."

Aside from the sound of uneasy shiftings in seats, the chamber was quiet.

Smiall'kes'hep continued. "My friends, of the North and the South, let us examine again the claims made by our esteemed colleague:

"He claims that asteroids were intentionally guided towards Earth. This is untrue. My colleague, Councillor Skep'hol, can demonstrate that all of our defensive sentinels are accounted for and remain where they should be.

"He claims that thousands of humans perished on Earth as a result of this 'attack'. We cannot verify this. But if this proves to be the case, we shall sympathise with our human neighbours in their sufferings at the hand of Nature.

"He further claims that the destruction wrought on our world by the fall of Ti'aransc at the end of the First Age, plus a purported event of a similar nature on Earth aeons later, were likewise intentional attacks. And in relation to these, he has the breathtaking audacity to cast aspersions on the characters and lineages of several prominent persons present in this chamber today, including your High Councillor.

"And all of this rests on the word of a single human, who visited our world briefly long ago; who was welcomed here as a friend but proved to be no friend to us after all.

"So, let us take a look at this 'trusted source', this *Mr H.G. Wells*, who came amongst us at the invitation of our late friend and colleague, Councillor Kindlebir.

"Mr Wells. The writer of fiction! The dreamer and fantasist! A man who dedicated his life to the concoction of tales for the diversion of the idle! A man who portrayed our species as hostile to humans, with designs on their world; whose work inspired fear and encouraged others in the invention of weapons for the conquest of *our* world – copied, it was said, from weaponry first developed by us. *Us!* The people of Oztzıldıj, who for millennia have cherished peace above all else!

"I tell you, Councillor Sffan'utul's information is wrong; his claims fanciful!

"As for Jazu'ul'ard'zahl, the famed lost archive of our world? It is a fantasy! Do you think that scholars over the centuries have not searched for it? It is a myth, born of wishful thinking. It does not exist.

"On Earth, they have a saying: *Fake News*. This is all fake news. And lies. Lies intended to undermine our established order. Lies intended to undermine the position of the High Councillor and to further his own ambitions.

"I therefore challenge him again: produce the evidence he claims. Or desist and submit to the justice of this Council."

Smiall'kes'hep sat down.

Behind Sffan'utul, Mr Knutt leaned closer to Mr Sparks. "Now would be a good time to establish contact?"

"I have been trying, Howard. But it is odd. The device is active, but there is no response."

"Perhaps you should keep trying?" suggested Mr Knutt.

2

Thirty metres below where the Council sat, a blue light pulsed in the darkness. The guard made his way cautiously towards it along a long passage that led into the interior of the monument. Ahead, it appeared like a glowing blue square on the floor of the tunnel. As he got closer, he realised the light was coming out of the floor.

He arrived at the edge of a deep rectangular pit. A flickering blue light bounced off its walls and rebounded from the roof above him. Peering over the edge, he saw a pinprick of light at its bottom. He reached for his belt and removed a small device. With his other hand, he activated his comportal, and its light joined the first. At the same time, the other device, like a small rugby ball lit up and floated away from him. With his comportal, he guided the device down the shaft towards the object. Presently, it came to a stop above the source of the light, which by then had grown dim. On his comportal's display, the guard could make out the skeletal remains of two individuals, whose degraded and debris-encrusted bones had become virtually unrecognisable over time. And lying between them, a comportal; a modern one. He used the device to retrieve it, and soon he held it in his hands.

Even before he had raised his own comportal to sound the alarm, a thin blue band appeared around the middle of the other device.

3

Councillor Sffan'utul had hardly begun his reply to Smiall'kes'hep when Mr Knutt noticed a guard approach Councillor Skep'hol from above. Skep'hol appeared to listen for a moment. Then, abruptly, he got to his feet and left the auditorium.

Smiall'kes'hep looked after them with a flash of concern that was not lost on Mr Knutt or Mr Sparks.

"I hope that doesn't mean trouble," said Mr Knutt.

4

Outside, in the assembly chamber, Skep'hol confronted the guard. He held Leon's comportal in his hand.

"Where was this found?"

"The pit in the western tunnel. Eight solmins ago,"

Excellency."

"Who does it belong to?" asked Skep'hol.

"We have not yet determined that. But it was responding to a signal from another device when it was found."

Skep'hol straightened. "Oh? From where?"

"It stopped before it could be traced. But there is more, Excellency. A different signal. It has the signature of an Ares security comportal."

"*Ares?* Are you sure? You have identified its source?"

"Yes. This one originates from inside the... forbidden hall."

Skep'hol's jaw clenched visibly. Then he said, "Secure all entrances; all passages; all chambers. Immediately. Take your most trusted sentries and search the hall."

The guard's eyes widened. "Excellency, you know it means death to enter there!"

"Only for those that violate it, Kiel'er'ol, not its defenders. You have my order and my assurances. Be quick. Bring them to me here."

Skep'hol started to turn away.

"Who are we searching for, Excellency?"

He turned back. "A very foolish child. And his human associates."

5

"Give up on that, Dominic," said Lucy.

Dominic lowered the comportal. "Just trying to get some help," he said.

"Well, it's not working," said Emily.

"Nor's that thing," replied Dominic.

Leon and the girls were gathered around the control panel. Leon said nothing. He was concentrating on the menu.

"We're trying to figure it out, Dominic," said Lucy impatiently. "Go and... go and stand guard or something."

Dominic hovered for a second, unsure what to say or do. He had never been told off by one of his friends before. Then he said, "Alright, I will. Here then, take this," and he handed Lucy his comportal.

Lucy took it from him. "What am I going to do with it?" she asked.

"In case there's a call. Or you need to use it. You remember how to shoot a comportal, don't you?"

Lucy nodded. "Of course."

Leon's father, Mr Sparks, had shown Dominic, Lucy and Emily how to fire a comportal to stun someone in self-defence last year, but only Dominic had been comfortable using one.

"Good," said Dominic. "I'm gonna go see if I can find another way out of here."

Mr Flynn was over by the sarcophagus of Jziee'ekkkzoor'sup, if that is what it was. As he said, he couldn't be of much help with computers and the like.

Dominic headed for the passage that Smiall'kes'hep and his associates had left by. Soon he was mounting the spiral pathway that led him out of sight and sound of his friends.

He arrived at the first platform after the first full turn of the ramp. It was gloomier up here, but still there was the faint light that made it possible to navigate without artificial light. As before, straight ahead of him, there was a passage that extended for perhaps ten metres before being lost in the smoky gloom. To his left, another passage formed another dark void in the wall.

Which way had Smiall'kes'hep gone? It was impossible to tell. It was easy to become disorientated down here. They were supposed to be beneath the main council chamber. Perhaps the spiral led up there? He crept around the bend, peering up as he progressed. Before he quite realised it, he had made another full turn and found himself standing on another level area. This too had two passages off it, and itself continued upwards. He carried on.

He reached another level. It was dead quiet, save for the sound of his own breathing. He took his phone out and tapped on its torch. The harsh light threw his shadow backwards onto the wall and suddenly made the deep recesses all the more threatening in contrast to the light. He checked his oxygenator capsule. Hm. It was going down.

By now he was feeling a little spooked. He decided to keep his torch on. Just one more turn, he told himself.

The next flight had only one passage leading off it, but the spiral path continued on up. But he had decided already that this was far enough, at least on his own. Time to go back. He turned and started back down. And if truth be told, he couldn't wait to get back to the company of his friends.

He hurried around one bend, then another. And almost ran headlong into something blocking his way.

Or rather, *someone.*

"To'k'utu! Kı'mıl'ap at'pae't!"
Halt! Move and I will shoot!

Dominic stopped dead. He panted on the spot, his eyes wide and darting about as his shocked mind tried to process the sudden change in his situation.

The guard stared at him. Then he leaned back a little and called out:

"Kiel'er'ol! B'ul'jorg. M'n'alard'jo'k'mu'un."
Kiel'er'ol! Down here. I have discovered one of them.

Without thinking, Dominic took his opportunity to make his escape. He thrust forward and rebounded off the figure and dashed down the passage as fast as he could.

6

Down in the hall, the children were still at the control panel. Leon had removed the prism from the panel, unsure what to do next.

"It can't be that difficult," said Lucy. She twirled her fair hair unconsciously. "We must be missing something," she said.

"Yes," said Camille quietly. "Maybe the obvious."

"What do you mean?" asked Emily.

"Er, I –"

A sound interrupted them, a rapid thuddering. In a blur, Dominic shot out from behind the sarcophagus.

Behind him, a figure appeared in pursuit.

"The comportal!" yelled Dominic. "Luce, chuck me the comportal!"

But before Lucy or any of them could react, there was a flash and Dominic slumped to the floor and rolled over.

"Dominic!"

The guard entered the space. He slowed, glancing around the hall, taking it all in.

There was another flash as a fine white beam shot across the hall.

This time, it was the guard that crumpled on the spot and lay still next to Dominic.

Lucy looked with surprise at the comportal in her hand.

"Great shot, Luce," said Emily.

"Thanks," replied Lucy.

But their focus was on Dominic. Leon and the girls ran over to him.

"Is he... er... *dead*?" asked Emily.

23 - DISCOVERED

"No, he's breathing," replied Lucy.

"Thank goodness," said Emily, exhaling in relief.

Camille looked over in concern, her attention divided between the situation at hand and their unfinished task. She glanced at the panel and noticed that Leon had left the prism on it. She picked it up, and acting on her earlier hunch, she moved it to the top aperture and dropped it in. The panel took hold of it and a flicker of light appeared in its body.

"Storppp righyyertlerrrr."

Stop right there.

Camille froze.

Kiel'er'ol stepped past her. He was flanked by two of his guards. He looked over to where Lucy, Emily and Leon huddled over Dominic. On the other side of them lay his other guard.

"Seize them," he said.

Leon was already to his feet. The guards moved as directed. They both had comportals raised and directed at them.

"Come with us," commanded one.

"*But our friend,*" appealed Lucy.

"Leave him," said the other in fractured English. He aimed his comportal forcibly at Lucy.

Reluctantly, they stepped away from Dominic. Emily glanced back at him. He was lying on his side, one arm trapped beneath him.

The guards marched them past Camille, who was prodded to join them.

"Wait," ordered the senior guard. "Where is the other one – the old man?"

"He went back to Earth," said Lucy.

"Lies!" He turned to his guards. "Take them. Then come back and search for him."

"And Sl'ekep'el and the boy?" asked one guard.

"They will awaken by the time you return," answered Kiel'er'ol."

The guards nodded and escorted the children from the hall.

"Where is Mr Flynn?" whispered Emily as they walked.

Leon looked at her and shook his head.

2

Kiel'er'ol looked around the hall. Like Leon, he was drawn to the effigy of Jziee'ekkkzoor'sup and he found himself trembling, simultaneously awed at the realisation as to where he stood and, despite Skep'hol's reassurances, overcome with trepidation.

He turned to the panel and looked at the prism that he had seen Camille insert into the device. He took hold of it and withdrew it. At the foot of the panel sat some of the Earthlings' possessions. One was Leon's rucksack. He bent to search them, and found the second prism. He put both inside his uniform and left the hall.

Mr Flynn peered out through a small spyhole in the wall of his hiding place, where he had been when the Council guards had shown up.

While the children had tried to get the projection panel to work, he had explored the prism banks and the tomb of Jziee'ekkkzoor'sup. At the end of the tomb nearest the wall of the chamber, he had noticed a crack that ran down its corner, forming an opening approximately a centimetre in width. Inquisitive, he had shone his torch into it, and his eyes had widened in surprise.

Stepping back to examine the wall of the tomb, he had noticed a panel in its lower half, which was decorated with a scene that looked like a coronation of sorts. It looked curiously like a door. Projecting from it was a stone star, which was surrounded by seven smaller stars. When he touched it, it twisted beneath his hand and he felt something release behind the panel. Cautiously, he had pushed it and the door swung inward without a sound.

Inside he saw, not the remains of the revered leader of ancient Mars, but what could only be described as a library and a meeting room. And it had all the signs of having been recently occupied. He had sensibly wedged his garden rake into the doorway to prevent it locking behind him and stepped inside.

Now, through the discovered spyhole, he saw the last guard leaving the hall. As soon as he judged it was clear, he crept out and hurried over to Dominic.

The boy was breathing but still unconscious. He looked over to see their rucksacks on the floor by the control panel and went over to collect them. He slung them over one arm then went back to Dominic.

The guard was still unconscious too. He stooped quickly to take the guard's comportal and then carefully lifted Dominic from the floor and carried him to the hide. He lay Dominic on a long couch there and dropped the bags on the floor before checking the inside of the door before he removed his rake and gently pushed the door closed. He felt it lock before he returned to Dominic.

4

"So," said Skep'hol. "These are the Earth children who would meddle in the affairs of our planet?"

Leon, Lucy, Emily and Camille stood before him, flanked by his guards. None spoke. They couldn't help notice the two prisms he held in one hand. On the table behind him, between the two guards, lay H.G. Wells's notebook and Leon's comportal.

"And you," he continued, looking intently at Leon, "must be Shieeekkksssup, son of Councillor Shieekk'ssup'pl? Also known as *Leon Sparks*, darling of the humans' Controlled Contact programme? How charming."

He turned to one of the guards. "You, go and wait by the entrance. See no-one disturbs us."

He returned his attention to the children. His gaze stopped on Camille.

"I have seen you before. You are the friend of the High Councillor's granddaughter?"

Camille looked into his eyes. She nodded. She hadn't been keen on him when they had met at

Aurore's home at Ares. Now he seemed cold and dangerous.

"Unfortunate," he said.

He held up the prisms. "Where did you get these? And what did you intend to do with them?"

No-one answered.

"I needn't remind you, young Shieeekkksssup, that under our law, your presence where you were arrested carries the penalty of death."

Leon flinched.

Then he spoke, in Martian. "Then, sir, both you and the High Councillor should be dead already," he replied.

"Impertinence!" shouted Skep'hol, and he reached out and struck Leon across his cheek.

Leon's eyes flared in shock, but he kept from showing it by crying out.

"Did you really think that you – mere *children* – could overthrow a great dynasty of our world, which has existed longer than human civilisation? No, of course not. You have not succeeded. Nor will Sffan'utul, or your father, Shieeekkksssup.

"Kiel'er'ol, hold them somewhere out of sight until I can consult with the High Councillor as to what we do with them."

5

"Sshh."

Dominic regained consciousness to see Mr Flynn leaning over him, his forefinger held against his mouth.

Dominic sat up, rubbing his head.

339

"Where are we?" he croaked.

"Quiet," whispered Mr Flynn. *"Safe. For now."*

Mr Flynn left him to look through the spyhole.

Dominic looked around the space they were in. It was gloomy but, like other spaces down here, not completely dark. This one had a rusty red light, like that of oil lamps reflecting off old velvet.

Out in the hall, Mr Flynn watched as two guards helped their colleague to his feet. He could see them conversing, but couldn't hear what they said. Then they began to search around the floor. The stunned guard's missing comportal. Mr Flynn patted his belt, where it now hung. Then they split up, the other two with comportals raised, to search the hall.

Mr Flynn returned to Dominic again. He whispered, *"Guards."*

Dominic nodded.

Mr Flynn gave it five minutes. Then he returned to his spyhole, just in time to see the backs of the guards leaving the hall.

"Alrigh'," said Mr Flynn. "We're inside tha' tomb – Jazzy's or whatever 'is name is."

Tomb?

Dominic looked suddenly uncomfortable.

"S'alrigh', lad. No bones 'ave been 'ere for goodness knows 'ow long."

"Now, listen. They got Leon and the girls. It's up to me and you now. Go and look through that 'ole over there. I'll check the door – see if we can get out."

Dominic looked at him with horror.

"Jus' kiddin'," said Mr Flynn.

Dominic hurried to the spyhole. "All clear this way."

Behind him, he heard a dull click and a band of cooler light swept into the room.

6

Leon and the girls sat disconsolately in the alcove of the High Councillor's green room. The two guards stood nearby.

"What do you think will happen to us?" asked Emily.

Leon decided to answer honestly. "I do not know. We can only hope that Mr Flynn can still do something."

Camille shook her head. "But he does not have the prisms."

"They are not the only prisms there," said Leon.

"But Mr Flynn didn't pay much attention to what we were doing," said Emily. "I'm really scared. They're not going to kill us, are they?"

"Of course not. They wouldn't dare," replied Lucy, attempting to reassure her friend. She glanced at Leon. But his expression failed to find the reassurance she herself sought.

7

Councillor Sffan'utul looked around the chamber.

"Esteemed colleagues. Friends. I confess that I am disappointed that the further evidence I hoped to present to you today has not materialised. I gambled, and I have lost.

"So, unless I lead you myself into the sacred hollow beneath our feet – which the Council chair, I am sure, will not permit – I have little choice but to stand down."

He looked to Mr Sparks, who now stood with him on his right. He appeared downcast.

Behind him, Mr Knutt stared at the floor, hiding his worry. What on Earth had happened to Leon and the others?

"I therefore plead the forgiveness of my fellow councillors," continued Sffan'utul. "As I do of the High Councillor."

He looked across the auditorium to Smiall'kes'hep. While Smiall'kes'hep nodded graciously, his general demeanour barely concealed his sense of triumph.

"As is the requisite penalty in actions such as mine," continued Sffan'utul, "I hereby resign my commission as a member of this chamber. Additionally, I surrender my property and estates.

"If the Council will permit, I shall depart to pass the remainder of my days in quiet retirement. I shall be of no further trouble.

"In this, I take full responsibility. I ask only that my friends be permitted to go on their way."

8

"Righ', young Dominic," said Mr Flynn. "There's only one thing left to try."

They stood out in the hall, at the control panel. Mr Flynn held a prism in one hand.

"What's on that one?" asked Dominic.

"Don' know. Found it in the tomb. Let's see what them fellas were lookin' at, shall we?"

Mr Flynn reached to place the prism in the top slot.

"And if this doesn't work?" asked Dominic.

"Well, we'll go up there anyway, didn' we say?"

Dominic nodded.

"Alrigh'. 'Ere goes."

Mr Flynn inserted the prism. It engaged and the panel lit up as before. But this time, the light it emitted had a slight golden tone.

Dominic looked at Mr Flynn, who nodded. Dominic took over. He rotated the prism and it dropped in a notch and stopped. He twisted it again and a cone of light appeared above them, projecting a menu into the space above their heads.

On its left were the images of the previous viewers.

Dominic drew in breath. "The top one – that's Smiall'kes'hep!"

"Thought as much," said Mr Flynn. "An' that fella at the bottom – his face rings a bell."

"The one with the big collar? Hey, he was in the other prism, wasn't he?" said Dominic.

"And there's Mr Wells again!"

The image of H.G. Wells sat above the familiar Martian's.

"And another human!"

Above Wells, there was the likeness of another human, a man who sported dark hair and a moustache.

"Who's that?" asked Dominic.

"Don' know, lad. Let's 'ave a look at one of them records," said Mr Flynn.

The menu lines were, of course, meaningless. Dominic twisted the prism to start it scrolling through them. Vivid thumbnail images blurred across their vision.

"Hol' tight," said Mr Flynn. "Go back a bit. Yep, there. That one."

Dominic tapped on the prism and the selected line flashed and immediately the hall became flooded with golden-greenish light and holographic images began to play within a bubble of light above them.

In the image field, crab-like machines crawled across a landscape strewn with smoky ruins. Searing white beams shot out of the heads of the machines, ripping up the ground before them and sending clouds of debris and white steam into the air. Overhead, blips of energy, like molten missiles, flew across the landscape, destroying buildings and levelling hills.

"Looks like a war," said Dominic.

"Yup, it does," agreed Mr Flynn.

"Now, I want to try somethin'."

Dominic stepped aside to let Mr Flynn get to the panel. He took hold of the prism and started to push on it, side to side and back to front. In the process, he twisted it, and the imagery above them speeded up, then slowed down.

"What you doing?" asked Dominic.

Mr Flynn stopped. "Ah, there we go."

Within the crystal body of the panel itself a new image formed. It was the shape of a diamond, but one divided into two colours. The top half, forming a triangle, was coloured green; the lower half, gold.

Mr Flynn reached out again and pressed the green triangle. Immediately, the projected image rose higher into the air.

"Oh," exclaimed Dominic.

"Got it," said Mr Flynn. "Let's try it a bit more." He touched the green triangle again and the image bubble was propelled upwards and vanished into the roof of the chamber.

"I reckon the telly's come on upstairs, don' you?" he said impishly.

"That's brilliant, Mr Flynn!" said Dominic.

"Shall we go see?" he replied.

"They'll gonna know we're here now, anyway, aren't they?" said Dominic.

"Good lad. Lead on."

Dominic started to move towards the spiral passageway.

"Oh, you better take this," said Mr Flynn. He handed Dominic the captured comportal. "You'll know 'ow to work it. I'll stick with me garden rake," he said.

24 - SKIEL'IEL'KOR

In the Council chamber above, Smiall'kes'hep was on his feet. He paused to listen to something said quietly to him by Councillor Skep'hol. He nodded, then straightened, making himself tall.

Behind him stood his daughter, Skiel'aeljtın, and his granddaughter, Asıl'el'tassz, known to the Earthlings as Aurore.

When all was quiet, he began to address the assembly.

"Esteemed colleagues, you have heard the concession of our respected friend and colleague, Sffan'utul of Tharsis. In deference to his long service and his wise council and judgement in times past, we harbour no ill will towards him in this matter, serious and misguided though it was. But the law must be obeyed, and we therefore accept his resignation and the due confiscation of his properties in accordance with its statutes. We further –"

He was interrupted by a greenish-golden glow that emanated from the floor of the auditorium. Before he could make sense of it or utter another word, it swept upward and unfolded into holographic scenes of war and destruction.

Startled cries erupted from both sides of the auditorium, followed by a rising babble of conversation that swelled like a tide.

"What is the meaning of this?" demanded an elder councillor on the northern benches.

Sffan'utul breathed a sigh of relief. He stood and touched his wristband. "That, I believe, is a projection from our lost archive of Jazu'ul'ard'zahl."

"Impossible!" exclaimed Smiall'kes'hep.

"No, it isn't!" came another voice, this time in English. "You've been there yourself."

Dominic appeared from behind the stone pulpit on the northern side of the auditorium.

If it had been on Earth, a wave of muttered comments might have arisen at the appearance of a human child in the midst of Council. As it was, the assembly fell quiet. So, when Mr Flynn also appeared, red-faced and huffing and puffing, everyone's attention was focused on him.

"S'true enough," said Mr Flynn.

"And we can prove it!" said Dominic.

"This is outrageous!" cried Smiall'kes'hep. "These are more of the human renegades! Arrest them! Arrest them all!"

Council guards began to descend from the outer ring of the amphitheatre.

"No!" called the senior Councillor on the North's benches, whose name was Skiel'iel'kor, who had seen Dominic and Mr Flynn emerge from the stone pulpit.

"Let the boy speak."

"Objection!" protested Skep'hol.

"Shall we put it to a vote, Councillor?"

He addressed the assembly. "Esteemed colleagues, please."

A dull red glow lit up the chamber as hundreds of

wristbands were activated.

Skep'hol lowered his head, giving way.

"Thank you," said Skiel'iel'kor. He addressed Dominic directly: "What is the nature of your proof, child?"

Child? Dominic winced.

"Step up to the stand and speak."

"Go on, lad," said Mr Flynn. "Tell 'em the way it is."

Dominic took a few tentative steps forward. There was a short staircase with worn and repaired steps that led to the top of the stone mound. He trotted up them and stepped onto its level surface.

The space was surrounded by a low wall, and in the midst of this stood a lectern carved from the same stone. He stepped up to it, and from his new vantage point, the full seated areas of the auditorium came into view. More than four hundred eyes regarded him in quiet anticipation. Across the chamber he knew that Mr Knutt would be seated with Councillor Sffan'utul and Mr Sparks. That thought encouraged him to speak. He took out his mobile phone and held it up.

"I videoed them on this when we were down there," began Dominic.

"Down where?" asked Skiel'iel'kor. "Please explain."

"There's a big chamber under here, about the same size as this one," replied Dominic.

"And what is down there?" asked Skiel'iel'kor.

"Councillor," intervened Smiall'kes'hep. "I believe –"

"High Councillor," replied Skiel'iel'kor. "Must I too invoke the rights of the su'rmat'atae? Please, let us hear what he has to say."

Smiall'kes'hep deferred, but he stole a heated glance at Skep'hol as he retook his seat.

"Continue... what is your name, child?"

Dominic winced again. "Um, it's Dominic. Dominic Addison."

"Please continue, *Domi-neeek Adtiiisornn*," said Skiel''el'kor.

"Well," said Dominic, "there's, like, loads of crystals around the walls, and in the middle is a machine you can put them into to play, well, tapes like the one here." He looked up to see that the holographic film had stopped.

"And how did you gain entry to this chamber?"

"We came up the ramp and some stairs. Underneath here," said Dominic.

A low sound of disquiet rippled around the amphitheatre.

"And have you any of the prisms – the crystals – that you saw?"

"We did – but *he* took them. When he took my friends," replied Dominic. And he pointed to Kiel'er'ol.

The ripple of unrest became an audible shuffle. Kiel'er'ol was well known as the chief of Councillor Skep'hol's personal guard. And Skep'hol himself was close to High Councillor Smiall'kes'hep.

A pinging noise drew everyone's attention across the chamber to where Councillor Sffan'utul had tapped his wristband.

"Councillor Skep'hol, is this true? I demand that they are delivered to us at once."

Skep'hol hesitated. He looked at Smiall'kes'hep, who sat tight-lipped and unmoving. Then he said, "The renegades are in our custody, for acts of sabotage and trespass and as a security risk to this gathering."

"You are protecting us from children, Skep'hol?"

asked Skiel'iel'kor. "Why, *thank you*."

"Councillor, may I remind you that these *children* disabled the gatekeeper sentinel on Su'umka'r?"

"Ahem."

Dominic looked round. Mr Flynn stood behind him. There was something here that projected one's voice, like an invisible microphone or something.

"Er, no. That was me. It was a haccident, really," he said. "Well no, it was litterin', if I'm tellin' the truth. Somethin' I wouldn' do at 'ome, you understand."

Across the chamber, Mr Knutt couldn't help but smile. *Ah, the inimitable Mr Flynn.*

"That aside," continued Skep'hol, "are we not gathered here today on account of them?"

"No, my esteemed friend, we are not," replied Sffan'utul. "We are here today because of *you*. Now, please, release our friends."

Skep'hol looked again at Smiall'kes'hep, who failed to respond to him.

Instead, Skiel'aeljtın stood and said, "May I remind the Council that children are not permitted in these chambers. Especially children from Earth."

"That rather overlooks the fact that one is already here. And the presence of your own offspring, madam Skiel'aeljtın," said Skiel'iel'kor. "Please bring them in."

Skep'hol nodded at Kiel'er'ol, who in turn nodded at another guard, one of the regular Council security, and they left together.

Skiel'aeljtın stepped down to talk to her father. Skep'hol and two other councillors from the northern side joined them in a huddle.

Skiel'iel'kor looked away from them to the assembly.

"Now, perhaps it is time we viewed the evidence the boy claims to possess."

The fire of bracelet lights gave the assembly's assent.

"Hold your device over the stand in front of you, please, Domi-neek."

Dominic started to bring his mobile up, then he hesitated. "I'd better find it first," he said.

But whatever was scanning his phone was already extracting its files and was projecting them into the air before them. As two-dimensional images, they were automatically mapped onto the sides of an invisible hexagonal prism to enable everyone to see.

"Ah... wait... um," said Dominic as he saw his photos and videos projected up there for everyone to see. They followed one another in rapid succession – photos of Benji, his dog; of a football match at school; a selfie with his friends Leon, Lucy and Emily. Then a video selfie in which he contorted his face in various ways, scrunching up his nose and poking his tongue out.

Dominic turned away in embarrassment, trying to turn his phone off, but to no avail. He looked at Mr Flynn, who shook his head slightly as if to say 'don't worry about it'. At least his friends weren't here to see it.

Then the images were replaced with another, the most recent record, a video file, which began to play. Almost immediately, the volume of noise from the assembly increased and for the first time was joined by audible gasps.

On the screens above, in the grainy imagery of human technology, High Councillor Smiall'kes'hep,

Councillor Skep'hol and Councillor Jzke'el'hep conversed in a space that agreed with the description the human child had given just minutes before. Moreover, they did so in the same official attire that they now wore.

Across the auditorium, Councillor Sffan'utul and Mr Sparks were as engrossed in the imagery as everyone else. It was their first view of the legendary Hall of Records.

As it played, quietly and unnoticed, Council guards filed in from the back of the chamber to surround the space; while in its midst, a small escort of Skep'hol's own guards entered with Leon and his friends. Mr Knutt spotted them and nudged Mr Sparks, who saw his son in person for the first time in weeks.

The children made their way around the auditorium, passing Smiall'kes'hep and his entourage, until they were made to wait at the base of the pulpit mound that represented the principal moon of Su'umka'r, the symbol of the northern hemisphere.

Aurore, whose Martian name was Asıl'el'tassz, left her mother's side and, despite her mother's protests, went down to greet her friend, Camille. The pair hugged and they stood together with Leon, Lucy and Emily.

Up on the screen, the councillor known as Jzke'el'hep was saying, *'But what of Kindlebir? Is it possible?'*

'That they might have the missing prisms? What of it?' asked Skep'hol. *'It will prove only that Kindlebir discovered Jazu'ul'ard'zahl and the resting place of Jziee'ekkkzoor'sup. She kept both a secret and stole away the prisms. Her reputation and that of her*

followers will be sullied forever.'

The noise from the assembly grew more pronounced.

The resting place of Jziee'ekkkzoor'sup?

This was more shocking, more extraordinary, more enthralling than the discovery of Jazu'ul'ard'zahl.

But the ancient law also said that the death penalty awaited those who disturbed the grave of Jziee'ekkkzoor'sup.

Smiall'kes'hep and Skep'hol were staring at the floor. On the southern benches, Councillor Jzke'el'hep, rose quietly from his place and began to make his way out of the chamber. A Council guard stepped forward to block his way.

On the screens above, Smiall'kes'hep said, *'The ancient prisms are unique. They can only be read here at this panel. But, their content can be projected into the chamber above.'*

Skep'hol said, *'How do you know this?'*

'I have seen it. Long ago. With my father.'

2

The video finished, leaving the Council in stunned silence. The damage to High Councillor Smiall'kes'hep had been done. And if the structure they had seen within the hall beneath their feet *was* the tomb of Jziee'ekkkzoor'sup, there were serious consequences awaiting all. Potentially for the humans too.

"High Councillor," said Skiel'iel'kor. "Have you anything to say?"

Smiall'kes'hep rose wearily to his feet. He glanced around at his daughter and his granddaughter.

Skep'hol rose with him.

Smiall'kes'hep led his colleague up to the stone platform where Dominic stood. They passed Leon and the girls, paying them no attention, and Smiall'kes'hep stepped past Dominic and Mr Flynn with the same indifference.

He stood for a moment, looking over the full Council assembly, before speaking.

"Esteemed friends and colleagues. It is the preserve of the leaders of the territories of the North to defend our planet. It has always been so. Sometimes the nature of the threat is not obvious, or immediate.

"The burden of this duty has fallen on a select few, who have shouldered it through the generations so that the majority of our people can exist in safety and peace. It is a responsibility few can carry. It requires discipline. It requires resolve. And the willingness, when it is demanded, to make the difficult decisions in the interest of preserving our race.

"To this end, it was vital that the existence of Jazu'ul'ard'zahl remained a closely guarded secret – for the protection of this generation and all those to come. And, regrettably, with it, the tomb of our revered father, Jziee'ekkkzoor'sup, even though it has been empty since time in antiquity.

"The Hall of Records preserves the high knowledge of the people of Oztzıldıj; everything we need to assist our survival. It must not be squandered, less risk it falling into the hands of the humans."

"Indeed, it was the betrayal by one human, and the misguided invitation to the others that followed, that has led to the humans posing a substantial threat to us today! All of this I have set out before you previously."

Leon, who stood below with the girls, could stand it no longer. He leapt up the steps to the platform. With the briefest acknowledgement of Dominic and Mr Flynn, he strode up to Smiall'kes'hep.

"And that justifies the murder of thousands of people on Earth?" he asked.

Smiall'kes'hep regarded him with something bordering on contempt.

"Ah," he said quietly. "If it is not our little friend, the celebrated *Leon Sparks*, son of our dear friend, Shieekk'ssup'pl."

"May I say something?" asked Leon. He looked from Smiall'kes'hep to Councillor Skiel'iel'kor. The two exchanged looks before each nodded to permit Leon to speak.

"The floor is yours, Mister *Sparks*," said Smiall'kes'hep. He turned to the assembly again. "I have no more to add." He withdrew and returned to his seat. Skep'hol remained close by.

"Thank you," said Leon. "Ah, I am not accustomed to challenging my elders, less so our leaders," he said. "My father and mother raised me to respect those older and wiser than I. But what I have to say must be said, because it is true."

He held the notebook of H.G. Wells high in his left hand.

"A hundred and twenty Earth years ago, Mr H.G. Wells, a human guest of my great grandmother, Councillor Kindlebir, secretly discovered the hall of records in this place. In it, he discovered the lost history of our race. He also uncovered some truths that my great grandmother could not then accept. She locked them away in her private files for my mother to discover when she came of age.

"One of the prisms that Mr Wells discovered – which we tried to show you today until they were confiscated – records the virtual destruction of our civilisation long ago by the impact of Ti'aransc. There is evidence that it was *directed* to crash into our own planet, and it came down in our southern hemisphere."

The chamber reverberated with the sounds of disquiet, which included the unearthly wailing of numbers of shocked and wounded delegates.

"The other prism shows the destruction of Earth's civilisation thirteen thousand Earth years ago, also by an asteroid impact.

"Only two days ago, similar events befell Earth and its moon. My friends and I witnessed that attack and the destruction of the Sentinel in Earth orbit.

"These are not a coincidence. In each, there is evidence that Martian zero-point technology was involved – a technology that the High Councillor has confirmed has been always at the command of the ruling families of the North.

"Mr Wells found that whenever human society reached a given technological capability, it had been ruthlessly suppressed. And he discovered evidence of a fresh plot to launch a new attack in his time. Since the Sentinel protected Earth against threats from asteroids, the plotters came up with an alternative plan, employing weapons first developed during the ancient wars of our world.

"When Councillor Kindlebir declined to reveal this discovery, Mr Wells resorted to the only way he knew to warn the peoples of both planets, by writing what became his most famous work.

"The attack did not materialise. High Councillor Siall'kebs'hep, the present High Councillor's father, stepped down and Councillor Skallir'rir became the new High Councillor, who presided over us until his death this year.

"And with his death, came the election of High Councillor Smiall'kes'hep, and the shelved plan was reactivated. Only, now, Earth's defences were capable of intercepting the old missile technology. They needed something that could not be stopped, as they could not thirteen thousand years ago."

"Objection!"

Leon stopped. It was Skiel'aeljtın.

Skiel'iel'kor turned to her. "What is the nature of your objection?"

"This is baseless speculation, unsupported by evidence."

"This chamber shall examine all claims and evidence in due course, madam," replied Skiel'iel'kor. "But based on the direct and worrying circumstantial evidence presented thus far by our guests, the weight of favour is with them. We shall hear the remainder of the argument."

He turned to Leon. "Please proceed, master Shieeekkksssup."

Leon nodded. "Thank you. I shall not be much longer."

"Take your time," replied Skiel'iel'kor.

"There is something else I believe should be made known today. There was something in this beyond protecting your own position and interests, wasn't there, High Councillor? For you, there a very personal agenda too?

"In Earth's year 1897, during an expedition to Earth, Councillor Kindlebir's assistant, Tek'tu'jan, died at the hands of humans. She was buried on Earth. Her unborn baby survived. He was rescued by Kindlebir and returned to his father on Oztzıldıj. That baby was you, High Councillor, wasn't it?

"Your father retired from office, having developed a growing hostility towards humans and to Councillor Kindlebir's programme of contact.

"Deprived of his mother, and infected by his father's bitterness, the young Smiall'kes'hep grew up with an instilled animosity towards humans, turning a personal tragedy into a genocidal hatred of a fellow species. And in turn, his hatred poisoned his own daughter, who stands beside him and whose own betrayal of the controlled contact programme led to me and my friends being brought against our will to Oztzıldıj."

"Enough!"

Skiel'aeljtın was on her feet, her face taut with rage.

"You dare take the word of a child over those of your High Councillor and Chief?!"

"Skiel'aeljtın..." began Smiall'kes'hep.

"No, father! I will *not* permit them to treat you this way. You have held nothing but the best of intentions for our people."

"I believe," said Skiel'iel'kor, "that there is cause to draw this hearing to a close? Councillor Sffan'utul? If there is anything else?"

Sffan'utul bowed. "No. Thank you," he said.

"Then it is settled," said Councillor Skiel'iel'kor.

"What do you mean, *settled*?" called Skiel'aeljtın.

"A court of elders shall be convened to examine the evidence in more detail. In three days it shall present its verdict.

"High Councillor Smiall'kes'hep, Councillors Skep'hol and Jzke'el'hep, please prepare yourselves to be sequestered for the hearing."

"What?! No!" screamed Skiel'aeljtın. Suddenly, she raised her comportal and, aiming it at Leon, she fired.

An orange-red beam crackled through the air towards the platform. The stone lectern exploded into a shower of debris.

"Get down!" exclaimed Dominic as he instinctively ducked. "It's set to kill."

No sooner had he said this than another searing bolt flashed out. He felt its heat and smelt his singed hair as it whizzed over his head. He dropped down again, aware only that almost everyone around him had done the same.

In the commotion that followed, Skiel'aeljtın left her place and was joined by Councillor Skep'hol, whose personal guard rushed in to form a protective ring around them. Comportal beams flashed out from them, maintaining a barrage of fire as they moved towards the beehive-shaped pulpit.

Above them, on the platform, Dominic saw them move and realised what they were trying to do. He shuffled on his stomach to the top of the short staircase and aiming, he fired his comportal at the group. The beam shot over the head of Councillor Skep'hol and struck one of his guards. The guard sank to the floor.

The group stopped immediately. Another searing beam shot towards Dominic. It strafed up the staircase, unzipping its stone casing. Dominic rolled out of its way.

The guard who had fired it re-set himself as Skiel'aeljtın paused to seize her daughter. She spoke rapidly in Martian as she dragged Aurore away from her friends. Aurore protested as she was pulled away.

Councillor Skep'hol uttered something and two other guards prodded Lucy, Emily and Camille, forcing them to follow.

Dominic fired again, narrowly missing Skiel'aeljtın. His shot struck another guard.

On the platform behind, Council guards had closed in and surrounded Smiall'kes'hep. They fired their comportals at the departing group.

Dominic picked himself up. Leon joined him. Leon winced as the guards' beams – although set on stun – lanced uncomfortably close to his friends. Another of Skep'hol's private guards fell.

"They're heading down to the tunnels," said Dominic. "We've got to get after them!"

"Wait," said Leon. "They are too many. The Council guards can –"

"But they've got the girls!" said Dominic.

He scampered down the steps after them, disappearing to the left, to where he knew the secret staircase beneath the platform was located.

Leon looked around. The chamber was in still in confusion. Delegates were attempting to leave the arena or were emerging from where they had taken cover in the comportal fight. On the benches on the other side, his father and Councillor Sffan'utul and Mr Knutt were starting to make their way down.

Torn between waiting for help and the plight of his

friends, he made his way down the steps. Two of Skep'hol's guards lay nearby. A comportal of one lay at his side. Without further thought, he snatched it up and hurried after Dominic.

25 - DOMINIC

Faint sounds of movement and voices met Leon's ears. Overlaying these, closer, was the sound of scurrying.

Dominic.

He switched the comportal's light on. It revealed an ancient-looking staircase, worn and polished with age, which curved around to the left in a descending corkscrew. Leon set out after Dominic. After a while, the steps ended and the way down continued as a spiral walkway.

2

Far below, Skiel'aeljtın, followed by Councillor Skep'hol, led the group purposefully down to the Hall of Records. At each level on the descent, a guard stayed behind to cover their escape.

3

Dominic rounded the bend warily, trying to keep his breathing as quiet as possible. A faint shadow from the strange phosphorescent light moved on the back wall. At the same time he became aware of it, the shadow began to move more rapidly. In an instant he knew what this meant. He rushed forward and ducked under the arm of the guard, who held a comportal before him.

Dominic rebounded off the outer wall and fired his comportal. The area lit up in a lightning flash and the guard dropped. Almost immediately, he heard sounds from below.

Another guard?

His heart pounding in his throat and his thoughts racing at supercharged speed, Dominic squatted down against the wall and pulled the guard's unconscious body upright in front of him.

Thank goodness for Martian gravity, he thought abstractly.

The other guard's torso appeared at the bend below. He approached cautiously, his comportal aimed ahead. At the sight of his comrade sitting against the wall, his own arm pointing in his direction, he relaxed momentarily, uttering something in Martian that, despite his translator, Dominic couldn't understand.

Another white flash lit up the space and the guard collapsed and rolled backwards down the passageway.

Dominic lowered the other guard's arm, beneath which he held his comportal.

"Cor, that worked better than I expected," he said to himself.

He pushed the guard aside and scrambled down the remaining flight to the hollow that led out into the Hall of Records. All was quiet here. He placed his feet carefully, quietly as he edged towards the open space of the hall.

Something grabbed him from behind. A hand

fastened over his mouth, while another twisted the comportal out of his hand. Dominic found himself pushed to the floor. When he turned over, a guard stood above him, and approaching from the hall was Councillor Skep'hol.

Skep'hol looked down at him. "Your foolishness outweighs your bravery. Come and join the others, *Domi-neeek.*"

4

Leon saw the reflected flashes and heard the echoing zap of two separate comportal blasts. Every time he rounded a bend he expected to see Dominic lying on the floor. Instead, he came across one unconscious guard, then another. Stepping past them, he soon emerged at the foot of the passageway where Dominic had been apprehended just minutes before.

The hall initially appeared empty, but then Leon discerned figures gathered outside the tomb of Jziee'ekkkzoor'sup. He could make out Skiel'aeljtın and Aurore, plus Lucy, Emily and Dominic, who was being held by a guard. Two other guards were visible, but Skep'hol was not.

Leon glanced behind him. No sign of any help. When he looked back, Skep'hol had appeared from around the side of the tomb with two other guards. They all carried articles removed from the structure. He could see prisms and scrolls and other artifacts. No doubt they were planning to escape with other recriminating evidence. And what they had in mind for his friends could only be guessed.

It was now or never. Leon stepped out in full view of

them.

Immediately, two of the guards detached themselves and stepped forward to confront Leon.

"Leon!" called Emily.

Leon pointed his comportal their way. "Let my friends go," he said.

The guards stopped in their tracks.

Skiel'aeljtın smiled sparsely. "I think not," she said. "Call them an insurance policy against... overzealous actions. Perhaps you will prove useful in bargaining for the release of my father."

Leon stared past the guards. Skiel'aeljtın stood with Aurore on one side and Dominic on the other. Emily stood to Dominic's side, and Camille and Lucy stood behind.

Leon was outnumbered. He had fired his comportal only once before, when, the previous year he had stunned a human that threatened the safety of his friends. The question now was: could he take one or two of the guards out before he was shot down, stunned, or...

The two nearest guards moved towards him. The closest one spoke to him in Martian, ordering him to place the comportal on the floor. Leon slowly did as instructed – Until the comportal was almost in contact with the floor, when he suddenly aimed it upwards and fired at the guard.

The guard crumpled. The second fired his comportal, narrowly missing Leon before he was himself felled by a white beam that came from over Leon's shoulder.

The rest happened fast, almost too quickly to follow. Suddenly, both white and red comportal beams were flying over his head. Leon kept low as he realised what was happening. Council guards had arrived behind him and were fighting it out with Skep'hol's guards.

He became vaguely aware of another form, a familiar one, across the hall, coming up on Skiel'aeljtın and the children. It was Mr Flynn! He prodded Skep'hol out of the way with his rake, then twirled it around and swept the guard who was holding Dominic off his feet.

The guard toppled backwards, his comportal firing its red beam towards the roof. The beam found the column of rock above their heads, which was faulted and cracked from some past disturbance. Loose debris began to rain down on them.

Seeing the guard down, Skiel'aeljtın pressed forward and grabbed Dominic by the arm.

From overhead, there came a resounding *CRACK*.

Mr Flynn looked up, shielding his face with a raised arm. His eyes widened. Immediately, he brought up his rake and rushed at the children and swept them out of the way just as part of the roof came down. They all landed together in a heap as rocks and masonry exploded in a thunderous barrage around them.

When all was still again, it became evident that the short battle was over.

Leon got to his feet, wiping dust from his face.

Skep'hol's guards lay about, either stunned or dead. One had been struck by falling rock. Leon looked quickly away.

As fresh Council guards flooded the room, Leon looked for his friends. The space where they had stood was occupied by a loose mass of rocky debris. His heart leapt as he tried to make sense of what he was seeing.

To the right of the pile, between it and the tomb, a moving mass resolved itself into several figures getting to their feet. With relief he rushed forward and helped Mr Flynn to his feet. Then there was Lucy and Emily, and Aurore and Camille – all dusty; a few scratches and bruises but, on whole, unhurt.

"Where's Dominic?" asked Lucy.

Dominic. Yes, where was he?

Leon had last seen him beside Skiel'aeljtın. They all turned to the pile of debris that littered the smashed floor of the hall. Skep'hol lay nearby, unmoving; his body contorted into an ungainly position. There was no sign of either Dominic or Skiel'aeljtın.

"They were right there," said Leon, who was staring at the mass of debris.

"Mother?" called Aurore. She broke away from Camille's side and rushed forward. *"Mother?!"*

"Dominic?" said Lucy. She looked at Leon, who wore a pained expression, unlike anything she had seen him display before.

"You don't mean Dominic... might be...?" asked Emily.

The girls and Leon and Mr Flynn rushed over to where Aurore was frantically pulling at the rocks.

"Wai' a minute," said Mr Flynn. He stepped in and, positioning his rake, he tried to lever some of the larger rocks aside.

Unnoticed by them, Councillor Sffan'utul and Mr Sparks and Mr Knutt arrived.

Mr Knutt, noticing Mr Flynn busy at the rocks, approached Leon. Leon didn't seem surprised to see him.

"Leon, what's up?"

Leon looked up at Mr Knutt. "Dominic," he said quietly.

Mr Knutt looked from Leon to the rock pile then back at him. "You mean...?"

Leon nodded.

"Why don't you go over by the exit and wait there?" suggested Mr Knutt. Then he took Mr Sparks aside by an elbow and spoke to him quietly. The pair of them then moved forward, telling the children to step back so they could assist Mr Flynn.

Eventually, their efforts revealed something other than rock. Mr Knutt looked around to check on Aurore's whereabouts. She stood with the others, keenly following what they were doing.

Mr Sparks bent down to examine the exposed clothing and flesh that lay quite still beneath a sparse layer of rock fragments and dust. He stood up and shook his head at Sffan'utul and Mr Sparks. Mr Flynn lowered his head.

Aurore, who had followed their every movement, did not miss the gesture. She ran forward, and catching a glimpse of the still form of her mother, clutched and writhed in Mr Sparks's arms in the agony of her loss.

Then Skiel'aeljtın's right arm twitched. Mr Flynn saw it first. Then it bent at the elbow, and it was evident that something beneath had moved it. Another hand.

Mr Flynn moved forward and carefully levered a slab of masonry that pinned Skiel'aeljtın's body until it fell clear. Mr Knutt stepped in and helped him gently tilt Skiel'aeljtın's lifeless form to one side. Beneath her, partly enclosed by two large rocks, lay Dominic. His eyes were closed and covered in grime and dust, but his expression flickered, and with the weight of Skiel'aeljtɪn removed from him, he took a deep breath.

"S'alright, lad," said Mr Flynn. "We got you now."

Dominic spluttered and Mr Knutt found a handkerchief, which he used to wipe Dominic's face and eyes so that soon he was able to open them and look up at his rescuers.

"Mr Knutt," he croaked.

"Lie still a moment, Dominic," said Mr Knutt, "until we can check you over."

Dominic nodded. "What happened?" he whispered.

"It's all over," said Mr Knutt.

After a few minutes, it was evident that, by a miracle, Dominic had not been badly injured. Two boulders had rolled together, trapping him. Skiel'aeljtɪn had been struck, and she had fallen onto him, winding him, but protecting him from the fall of other debris.

Soon he was sitting up; then he found he could get to his feet with assistance and join the others.

His friends rushed over to greet him. Lucy and Emily threw their arms around his neck.

"Ooh, careful," said Dominic.

"Oh, sorry," said Lucy.

"We really thought you were dead this time," said Emily.

"You can't kill me that easily," replied Dominic. "What happened?" he asked.

"Part of the roof collapsed," said Leon. "Miss Sky and Councillor Skep'hol are dead."

"Good riddance, I say," said Dominic.

"Dominic!" exclaimed Lucy. "Don't forget Miss Sky

is Aurore's mum!"

"Oh, yeah. Sorry," said Dominic.

"Where is Aurore?" asked Emily.

"Over there," said Lucy. She nodded towards where Camille was comforting her a little way off.

They all fell silent, and in that silence and the release of tension, hunger and fatigue descended on them. Suddenly they looked like school children again: weary, a little grubby, a little vulnerable.

"Well done all of you," said Mr Knutt. "Now, I believe we have all had enough for one day, don't you?"

He turned to Mr Flynn, who was perched on a nearby boulder, his rake held vertically in front of him.

"Mr Flynn."

"H'edmaster?"

"Well done to you too."

"Than' you, h'edmaster."

"Would you mind leading the children out; find them somewhere to wait; perhaps some refreshments?"

"O' course," said Mr Flynn. "Are you comin' as well, h'edmaster?"

"Yes. Once we have taken care of Aurore."

26 - HOME

"OK. The pod's loaded and ready to go," said Mr Smiley.

"Already?" said Dominic.

"I'm afraid so," said Mr Knutt. "Your parents are waiting for you at Tsiolkovsky."

Two days had passed since the Council meeting. Dominic, Lucy and Emily had stayed at Leon's home, while Mr Knutt and Mr Flynn had lodged with Councillor Sffan'utul – or rather, High Councillor Sffan'utul, as he now was. The previous day he had been unanimously voted by the Council as the successor to Smiall'kes'hep.

Smiall'kes'hep himself was now under closely guarded arrest at Cydonia awaiting a special court to be convened for his trial. He had offered no further resistance, especially after learning of the death of his daughter, Skiel'aeljtın.

Thirty-three other councillors and citizens had since been identified and arrested in connection with the attempted seizure of complete power.

Aurore had visited her grandfather only once, and she was now at her own home, accompanied by Camille.

Mr Smiley had arrived in the pod the previous day,

by himself. After a brief meeting with Mr Sparks and Mr Knutt, he had spent his time consulting with Councillor Skiel'iel'kor and Sffan'utul, so the children hadn't seen much of him until now.

Likewise, they had seen Sffan'utul only briefly since his election as High Councillor, which he felt honoured and duty-bound to accept, even though – as he had confided to them – he would rather be quietly exploring the historical treasures of the Hall of Records with the other scholars.

And so, after Dominic had been checked over and what turned out to be a fractured shoulder had been rapidly healed by the wonders of Martian technology, the children had spent their time eating and resting, and playing with Leon's pet, Shheikspule, or exploring the canyons near his home.

But, finally, even they had to admit that it was time to go home.

Lucy and Dominic and Emily looked at one another, then at Leon.

"We're saying goodbye? *Now?*" asked Emily. She had promised herself that she wouldn't become upset, but she couldn't now prevent a lump forming in her throat.

Lucy and Dominic too had grown quiet and serious. They had reached that moment. Again.

"No," replied Mr Knutt. "We must pick up Camille, then proceed to Cydonia to say our goodbyes to Leon's father and High Councillor Sffan'utul. Leon is coming along with us."

"Really?" said Lucy.

"Yes," said Leon.

"Oh, good," said Emily.

2

When they arrived at Aurore's home in the Valley of Ares another surprise awaited them. Aurore had decided to go with them.

"If it is alright?" asked Camille. "I have invited Aurore to stay with me and my mother in Paris for the rest of the holidays."

Mr Smiley glanced at Mr Knutt. "I guess that's OK?"

Aurore looked up with her large liquid eyes. "I have nowhere else to go," she said.

Camille bit her upper lip.

"Of course," replied Mr Knutt. "We will see she is alright."

3

They were met at Cydonia by Mr Sparks and High Councillor Sffan'utul himself and escorted into a building near to the transit station. It was of modern construction, airy and light (as it gets on Mars), and a far cry from the gloomy halls of the Council chambers a mile away.

Sffan'utul addressed Aurore directly in Martian.

"Would you like to see your grandfather before you leave?" he asked gently.

Aurore shook her head. "Only my mother," she said. She looked up at him with sad eyes.

"We shall see to it that you have all the support you need on your return," said Sffan'utul quietly.

Aurore nodded, forcing a small smile.

"Thank you, High Councillor," said Mr Sparks.

He turned to Mr Smiley. "James, we have much to

discuss," he said. "Howard, you too. Will you remain behind for a short while to assist us?"

"Oh," said Mr Knutt. This was quite unexpected. "Ah, I would be happy to. But –"

He looked at the children.

"But, I need to ensure the children get back home safely."

"Well, Howard. We've kind of prepared for that," said Mr Smiley. "Leon, can you handle it?"

Leon straightened. "Yes, Mr Smiley."

"Handle what?" asked Dominic, suddenly interested.

"With his father's blessing, Leon is to be permitted to pilot you all back home. Your parents and Leon's mother will be waiting for you on the Moon."

"Epic!" said Dominic.

"Leon, you could have told us!" said Lucy.

"I did say I would go with you, did I not?" smiled Leon.

""But, without Mr Knutt?" asked Emily.

"Leon was always the pilot on the journey here," said Mr Knutt, who was warming to the idea of a peaceful extension to his stay on Mars. "With Aurore's assistance, of course. Mr Flynn and I were really along for the ride with the rest of you. And Mr Flynn will be returning with you."

"Leon," continued Mr Knutt. "The inaugural Space School turned out to be rather more than anyone could have expected. I haven't had much of an opportunity to congratulate you on your impressive speech to the Council."

"Thank you, Mr Knutt," replied Leon modestly.

Mr Sparks stepped forward. It had always been a

rather uneasy relationship between father and son – which wasn't unique to Leon and his father. All Martians were rather emotionally distant from one another, unaccustomed to easy social contact – which was one of the major reasons that the Controlled Contact Programme had been established in the first place.

"Indeed," said Mr Sparks. "You accomplished your tasks very well, my son."

"Thank you, father," replied Leon.

"You will spend some time with your friends, and return with your mother in four weeks?"

"Yes, father," said Leon.

"Very well. I will see you then. Ah... enjoy yourselves."

"I am sure we will," replied Leon with a smile.

"Call us when you are ready," said Mr Sparks, and he handed Leon his own comportal.

Leon's eyes lit up, elated that he'd got it back.

"Well, good," said High Councillor Sffan'utul. He brought his hands together before him and the motion of the long sleeves of his ceremonial gown sent ripples down its length. "Then we shall delay you no longer."

He turned to address them all.

"Children, of Earth and Mars. On behalf of all of our people, thank you, thank you. Thanks also to you, Mr Flynn."

"'Appy to 'elp," replied Mr Flynn.

Sffan'utul made the customary gesture that meant goodbye. Leon and Aurore, of course, returned it perfectly. The other children and Mr Flynn did the best they could.

"Time to go, I s'pose," said Dominic. "What are we

going to do when we get there, then?"

"I will tell you on the way," said Leon.

Leon and Dominic moved forward together. Mr Knutt and Mr Smiley offered their hands. Leon and Dominic took them and they shook.

"Don't get lost," said Mr Smiley.

"I will try not to," said Leon.

"I will see you all back home soon," said Mr Knutt.

Lucy and Emily rushed forward and Mr Knutt found himself in the centre of a ring of hugs.

"We'll miss you, Mr Knutt," said Lucy.

"Ah, thank you, Lucy. Thank you, Emily. Have a safe journey."

Then it was Camille's and Aurore's turn, who shook hands with Mr Smiley and Mr Knutt. Then, finally, Mr Flynn.

"You're in charge now, Mr Flynn," said Mr Knutt. "I'm relying on you to keep them out of trouble."

"I'll do me best, h'edmaster," replied the older man.

"I know you will. See you when I return," said Mr Knutt.

4

It took only fifteen minutes to prepare for departure. With Aurore's help, Leon programmed the entire journey from lift off to landing back at Tsiolkovsky in a day's time. They could all sit back and enjoy the ride and their time together.

"OK everyone, prepare to say goodbye to Mars," said Leon. He waved his hand and the shell of the craft turned transparent. In the rusty light, they could see the transit station and nearby buildings. Across the plain to their left stood the rounded mesa of Jziee'ekkkzoor'sup's likeness and its Council chambers and Hall of Records.

"Here we go," said Leon.

The scenery around them fell silently away, tilting as it shrank from view.

"Did you see them?" asked Emily excitedly.

"Yes, yes," said Camille.

"Me too," said Lucy.

"No. See what?" asked Dominic.

"It looks like everyone in the Council came out to see us off," replied Emily.

5

Their pre-programmed trajectory took them out of Mars's atmosphere in a sweeping curve that overtook Phobos in its orbit. They watched it and Mars itself recede as the pod raced towards the Sun. Leon made two gestures; one to turn the pod's walls opaque; the other to step down the Sun's glaring brightness on the forward monitor.

"So," said Dominic, "you staying on the Moon when we get back?" he asked Leon.

"To begin with," replied Leon. "We will see my mother, and all of your parents. Oh, I'm sorry, Aurore. I did not think."

Aurore looked down and away. "It is alright," she said.

Camille placed a hand on her shoulder.

"Then what?" asked Lucy, keen to press Leon past his momentary embarrassment.

"Actually," continued Leon, "I would like to see

Paris, if it is possible. I have not visited an Earth city. I wonder if Camille and Aurore might show us around?"

"Us?" asked Emily.

"Yes. I hope you can all come. Then perhaps we could spend some time together somewhere else on Earth before I must go back?"

"Disneyland!" blurted Dominic.

"We have one at Paris," said Camille.

Dominic shook his head. "No offence, but I was thinking California."

"Well," said Lucy diplomatically. "We'll work it out. What do you think, Mr Flynn?"

"Jus' drop me off back 'ome on your way, Lucy. I expect the grass'll be needing a cut at the school."

6

Mr Flynn awoke first. He was slumped in his chair. He reached up with one hand and rubbed the back of his neck. Then he realised that he had dribbled in his sleep and wiped his mouth with his sleeve. He looked around. All of the children were asleep – Leon in his chair, while the others had found a place on the floor of the cabin to stretch out.

Leon had left the navigational display active. Just over two hours remaining. He yawned, looking around the cabin again, then back at the viewing screen. They were heading, it appeared, directly for the Sun. Its brightness had been dimmed down automatically by the pod's sensors. Somewhere in that field of view – now quite invisible – would be the Earth and its Moon. The Earth. Our planet. The whole world. Home.

Mr Flynn frowned. There was something not quite

right. He stared at the display. Then it dawned on him what it was. The Sun's disc had a dark smudge on its lower left edge, as if someone had taken a bite out of it. Before he could ponder it longer, from somewhere an alarm sounded.

7

Smiall'kes'hep was led out of the security area escorted by six formidable-looking Council guards and Councillor Skiel'iel'kor. They led him down the tunnel beneath the face of Jziee'ekkkzoor'sup towards the Council Chamber. He was attired not in the ceremonial robes of a councillor, but the plain robes of an ordinary citizen.

In the Council Chamber, High Councillor Sffan'utul waited with the special court of twelve judges who had been selected from both sides of the house.

The chamber fell quiet as Smiall'kes'hep entered. Smiall'kes'hep paused as he took in the panel of judges who sat on the northern benches, where only days ago he had presided as High Councillor.

To his left, he noticed Mr Smiley, who stood with Shieekk'ssup'pl of Solis, and he stopped to look their way.

"Is this your victory, Shieekk'ssup'pl?"

"It is justice, Smiall'kes'hep," replied Mr Sparks.

"Do you believe it ends here? It does not," said Smiall'kes'hep.

He looked at Mr Smiley. "When you reach home, you will discover that it is not as you left it."

Mr Smiley eyed at him warily. "Earth? What have you done?"

"Did you think we would not have an insurance

plan in the event of first failure?" said Smiall'kes'hep.

His smile was tight, spiteful.

"You are fond of naming objects and places in our planetary system after your mythological personages and realms. You may think to rename it... *Tartarus*."

The guards nudged Smiall'kes'hep forward. The assembly was waiting.

"Let it be known, Shieekk'ssup'pl, that the moment this charade is over, I wish to see my granddaughter."

"That won't be possible," replied Mr Smiley.

Smiall'kes'hep stopped. His expression grew darker. *"Do not contend with me, human."*

"She is not here. She left," replied Mr Smiley.

Smiall'kes'hep's expression turned to puzzlement. "For where?"

"In not many hours, she will be on Earth," said Mr Sparks.

Smiall'kes'hep's complexion, as pallid as it was, grew paler still.

8

"Smiley to Pod Nine. Pod Nine, come in. Leon, are you reading? Over.

"Leon –"

"Yes, Mr Smiley, we're reading you."

"Leon. Good. Please listen. Your father and Mr Knutt are with me. Something else may be happening at Earth."

"We are following it now, Mr Smiley."

"You're what?"

"The proximity sensors broke us out of our programmed course. We are now following a large asteroid."

Back on Mars, Mr Smiley exchanged alarmed looks with Mr Sparks and Mr Knutt.

"Leon, your estimates, please: size, velocity, trajectory," said Mr Sparks.

Onboard the pod, Leon nodded at Aurore.

"Hello. This is Aurore. Its dimensions are approximately 11.6 kilometres by 7.9 kilometres, with a velocity of 20.6 kilometres per second. I'm sending you the data now, but its trajectory suggests an origin in the asteroid belt. And…"

"And?" repeated Mr Smiley.

"And a direct collision with Earth."

The airwaves were silent for a few seconds.

Then Mr Smiley said simply, "Copy. When?" The strain was evident in his voice.

"Sixteen point two hours," replied Leon.

"Insufficient time for us to be of assistance," observed Mr Sparks.

"Leon, have you detected any zero-point engines on or near it?" asked Mr Smiley.

"No, Mr Smiley," replied Leon.

"And no other craft?"

"No."

"OK, OK. One moment," said Mr Smiley.

There was silence for another short period. Then Mr Sparks was back on the comms.

"Leon."

"Yes, father?"

"There is but one course of action open to us. You must repeat the manoeuvre taken with the asteroid that threatened Tsiolkovsky."

"But father, this is larger by an order of

magnitude," said Leon.

"I know," replied Mr Sparks. "But you have to try. The smallest alteration in its trajectory may make the difference. We cannot delay."

"Yes, father," said Leon.

On Mars, Mr Sparks was looking at his comportal and the data sent by Aurore.

"You will need to make a transverse approach, retrograde to the Earth's orbit. I calculate that an angular change in trajectory of 54.7 arcminutes at your present range should be sufficient. Based on an estimated mass for the asteroid of 1×10^{12} tonnes –"

"A trillion tonnes? Hurtling in at more than twenty times the velocity of a bullet," they heard Mr Knutt whisper from close by.

Mr Sparks continued: "I estimate you will need to apply full thrust for ninety-three point six seconds. Seek Aurore's help as before. Aurore, do you concur?"

"Yes, Councillor Shieekk'ssup'pl. I calculated ninety-four point one seconds."

"Good," replied Mr Sparks. "Now, there is no time to be lost. Proceed."

"Good luck," said Mr Smiley.

9

"So, what are we trying to do again?" asked Emily.

"We're going to try to push the asteroid off course," replied Dominic.

10

On Mars, Mr Smiley turned to Mr Sparks.

"Fred, can we trust Aurore to do the right thing? After all, her grandfather is the one who set this thing in motion."

"Do we have any other choice, James?" replied Mr Sparks.

11

"Aurore, are you ready to do this again?" asked Leon.

"I believe so," she replied.

Leon vacated the command seat for her. She immediately started to programme the pod.

"We may need to press the drive's capacity through maximum tolerance in order to affect such a mass," she said.

After a few more seconds, she left the seat and Leon resumed his place.

"This time, the rotation of the asteroid is negligible. I have programmed our course to approach it at its centre of mass."

"Thank you," said Leon. "Right, everyone. Seats and lap-belts, please. We need to do as before and use our force-field to drive into the asteroid. It may be a little bumpy."

Leon waved his hand over the chair arm, and the walls of the pod faded away.

"Ready, three, two, one."

The pod whisked forward, silently and with only the barest sensation of movement. The asteroid grew rapidly in their view, looking like a huge irregular hole in space that swallowed even the Sun as they made their own eclipse.

The pod's course took them within a kilometre of

the surface. They emerged from its shadow and the Sun's rays began to pick out its rugged form. Its true size became awfully apparent.

"It will be like a flea biting an elephant," said Camille.

"Or a flea on the flea," suggested Lucy, who was awestruck by the rolling mountain above them.

From their new vantage point, they could at last see the Earth and the Moon, a pair of thin crescents near to the Sun.

As before, Leon manoeuvered the pod closer to the asteroid's surface by looking at it through the pod's ceiling. From the outside, it would have looked like he was attempting to land it on its roof.

"Twenty metres," called Aurore.

"Autopilot on," said Leon. "Force-field coming up to full power."

A rumble of power reverberated through the craft. A hint of a greenish glow became evident around the pod's exterior.

Leon moved his hand away from the control arm to allow the pod to follow Aurore's programming.

"Five metres," called Aurore.

"Brace, everyone," said Leon.

Already, the pod's force-field was drawing surface debris off the asteroid. Dust and rocks flew past the pod or slammed into the force-field, sparking orange and yellow as they were superheated and destroyed by the strength of the field.

The pod shuddered and rocked. Inside, the children instinctively ducked from the shower of debris, which began to flow around the craft, as if an invisible umbrella was held open over them.

"It didn't do this last time," said Emily. "Are we alright?" she asked shakily.

"We require much more power this time," explained Aurore. "But we must take care not to push too hard, or we risk simply drilling into the surface. It should stabilise soon."

Sure enough, the debris began to abate as the pod's force-field found a firmer footing. They had formed their own crater in the asteroid's surface.

Aurore explained the next phase of their mission.

"The pod is now increasing power to try to divert the asteroid. The force-field will spread out like a web. It will create new clouds of debris. Do not be alarmed."

"It may become a little bumpy again," said Leon.

He waved a hand to make the pod's walls semi-transparent. Then another wave brought up a display that showed the velocity and trajectory of the asteroid.

Beside these were other values and symbols. One read: 93.2 (sec); another: 54.7'.

"What are we seeing?" asked Lucy.

"Our target countdowns," explained Leon. "Seconds, and minutes of arc – an angular measure of the asteroid's deviation from its present course."

Mr Flynn spoke up: "As I keeps tellin' yer, lad, give it to us in plain English."

"I am sorry," said Leon. "When both reach zero, we shall know we have done enough. The asteroid should miss Earth."

"Good," said Mr Flynn. "Jus' make it work, lad."

12

Leon and Aurore monitored the data on the pod's

performance. They spoke rapidly in Martian as the other children and Mr Flynn could only watch helplessly as the pod jumped and rocked as it pressed itself deeper into the asteroid's surface.

"Flippin 'eck!" exclaimed Dominic. "Thought you said it'd be a *little* bit bumpy!"

With each surge, the force-field glowed brighter and the sound of the pod's drive became audible, getting louder.

"Is it me, or is it getting warm in here?" asked Emily.

"Yes. It is much warmer than before," said Camille.

"The pod's drive is maintaining at ninety-eight percent," said Leon.

Lucy looked at the display. The seconds counter showed that thirty-three seconds had already elapsed, more than a third of the way into the countdown. Yet the arcminutes value was still high, at 39.7.

"It's not going to be enough, is it?" she asked.

Leon and Aurore looked at another. Then Leon said, "We must have miscalculated. We shall have to increase thrust."

"No, we cannot," replied Aurore. "Not without widening the field. Or we will succeed only in burying ourselves."

Leon was quiet for a second. He lowered his voice. "But we cannot increase thrust *and* extend the force-field," he said. "Not for the necessary duration. Not without a risk of overtaxing the drive generators. There is a chance it could explode."

Leon glanced around the cabin, for fear he may have been overheard. But there was no need to worry. The noise in the cabin was growing steadily louder, a combination of a rising electrical cackle and random creaking sounds that grabbed everyone's attention when they happened.

"We have to try," said Aurore. "At least we will take the asteroid with us," she added.

Leon's eyes widened more than normal.

13

"Hold on, everyone," called Leon. "Increasing power through a hundred and twenty percent."

The noise and vibration ramped up significantly as the pod's power output passed its normal operational limits. A dull but urgent alarm joined the cacophony of sound until the strain could be heard and seen and felt all at the same time.

"What's happening now?" called Emily in a wavering voice.

There was no time to explain. Leon's and Aurore's eyes were fixed on the display: 41 seconds elapsed; 28.4 minutes of arc.

No-one now could speak. The vibration and the noise cancelled out any attempt. All they could do was ride it out.

All eyes were now on the countdown readouts:

32 seconds; 19.6 minutes of arc...

28 seconds; 19.3 minutes...

"Come *on*, come *on*," called out Dominic, who was rocking in his chair.

24 seconds; 20.4 minutes of arc...

21 seconds; 20.7 minutes...

"Wait! What's happening?" exclaimed Lucy. "The minutes number is *increasing*."

"We are encountering resistance," reported Aurore. "The asteroid is trying to steer back."

"How can that be?" asked Leon.

"I do not know," replied Aurore. "But we are running out of time. We need all of the power we can get. *Now!*"

Leon managed to wave a hand over his armrest. Another value appeared on the forward screen.

137 percent.

The pod's drive was already in the critical zone.

11 seconds; 20.8 minutes...

"We need more," said Aurore.

Leon nodded.

Aurore took over again. "I am increasing it to one hundred and fifty percent."

Leon looked anxiously about. The noise and vibration grew rapidly, threatening to shake the pod apart. Through blurred vision, he saw his friends hanging on for dear life. Mr Flynn, usually unflappable, struggled to hold himself upright in his seat, a look of painful concentration on his face.

Leon looked back at the countdown display. The readouts jiggled and bobbed, making them virtually impossible to read. 4 seconds; 20.2.

20.2? It was working again!

1 second remaining; 19.8 arcseconds.

"Keep going," said Aurore.

Leon started to protest, but she cut him off.

"A few more seconds."

Then, suddenly, the lights in the cabin dimmed, then came back again, and the sound from the drive became a whine that rose to high pitch before fading off just as quickly.

Leon and Aurore exchanged wide-eyed glances.

Then, all at once, like a light bulb about to blow, the cabin lights and the light given off by the pod's force-field grew intensely bright. Then they felt a huge wrench and the artificial gravity fail as the pod's drive finally gave out and they were plunged into silent darkness.

27 - THE SPEAR OF ARES

Dominic found himself floating in a void. At last, there was stillness and peace. The dizziness and nausea produced by their ordeal had vanished. He couldn't feel his body; just a tingling awareness of it. He opened his eyes. It made no difference. It was still pitch black.

Then a horrifying thought struck him.

I'm dead.

It coursed through him like cold electricity.

"Am I dead?"

This time he said it aloud.

The darkness and the silence swallowed his question.

Then a faint sound. Like rubbing. And another voice.

"Course yer not dead, lad."

Mr Flynn.

With their movement, a light came on somewhere, followed by a sprinkling of other lights, and then the main cabin lights and the artificial gravity were restored. They were all forced down in their seats.

Mr Flynn was rubbing his neck.

"Mr Flynn! Phew, I thought I was um..." said Dominic. "What happened?"

"Dunno, lad," replied Mr Flynn honestly. "Must 'ave

blacked out or somethin'.""

Around the cabin, the others were still in their seats and now coming to. While they regained their bearings, the pod's artificial gravity re-established itself and the pod began to hum perceptibly.

As soon as Leon and Aurore were alert, they set about examining the pod's systems.

Leon called up the forward view screen and display. "We are on back-up power. The main drive is offline, probably damaged."

"What happened?" asked Emily groggily.

"There was a surge of power just before," commented Camille, who was rubbing her own neck. "Perhaps we were blasted away from the asteroid?"

"Yes, I think so," said Aurore.

"Where is it – the asteroid?" asked Lucy.

The view screen showed only empty space.

Leon checked his readings and frowned.

"What's up?" asked Dominic.

"The navigational system must be in error. I cannot fix our position or timeline," replied Leon.

Leon swiped his hand and the pod's walls faded away.

"Whoa!" exclaimed Dominic.

The Earth loomed huge before them.

Aurore studied the display data. "And the asteroid?"

"I believe it is that, there," said Leon, who pointed to a bright star near to the upper limb of the Earth.

"It is not possible," said Aurore.

"We must have been unconscious for longer than we thought," offered Lucy.

"Not for sixteen hours," replied Leon without looking away from the display.

"It is two thousand, six hundred kilometres away," he said.

"*Two thousand?*" repeated Emily.

"How long until closest approach?" asked Aurore.

"Twelve minutes, twenty seconds," replied Leon.

"Can we get closer, to observe it?" asked Camille.

"If it hits, we don't want to be anywhere near it," said Dominic.

"I do not believe it will," said Leon. "But it is going to be very close." He looked at Aurore.

But they agreed to move closer. Leon sat back and changed the display. He waved his hand over his chair arm, and the pod turned in the direction of the asteroid. All but the forward portion of the walls turned opaque. "We need to conserve power," he explained.

Soon their quarry changed from a bright star to a discernable shape, and then a rocky mass, uncomfortably close to the Earth.

"I wonder if they're tracking it down there?"

"If they are, lad, there's nothing they can do," said Mr Flynn. "Nor can we. Now."

There was no disputing Mr Flynn's assessment. All they could do now was to watch and wait in sober anticipation. The asteroid looked small compared to the Earth, but no-one needed reminding that it was capable of devastating virtually all life on the planet.

After what seemed an eternity, something began to happen.

"Look!" said Dominic.

On the screen, the asteroid was beginning to glow along one edge. The glow quickly grew brighter and lengthened into a long tail, so that it resembled a sharp weltering scratch on the limb of the Earth.

"Whoa!" cried Dominic again.

"Is it crashing?" asked Emily.

"No. Look," said Aurore. "It is fading already."

And indeed it was. The bright head faded away, followed by the tail, until there was no trace of it.

"What happened to it?" asked Lucy fretfully.

"I believe it has skipped off," said Aurore.

Leon let out a long sigh of relief. "Yes, I'm picking up its trajectory."

"So, it missed?" asked Emily anxiously.

"Yes. But it was very close," replied Leon. "It brushed the upper atmosphere and it has returned to space."

"Congratulations, Leon," said Aurore.

"Thank you," he replied. "But we really could not have done it without you, Aurore."

They exchanged smiles.

"So, Earth is safe," said Camille. "Magnifique!"

"Whoo-hoo! We did it!" said Emily.

"Well done, both of you!" said Lucy.

"I second tha' – great job, lad! And lass," said Mr Flynn.

"Right," said Dominic. "Now, can we get to the Moon? I'm starving."

"Of course," replied Leon. "But first, I must report to my father and Mr Smiley."

The children sat back, buoyant at the successful completion of their mission.

2

It didn't take long to realise that something was amiss.

Lucy picked up on it first. Leon had switched his attention from the pod's systems to his comportal.

"What is it, Leon?"

Leon looked up. "I cannot contact my father. Or Mr Smiley. Nor am I detecting any response from Tsiolkovsky, or my mother. In fact, I am getting... nothing."

"Can't you try again?" suggested Lucy.

"Well –" began Leon.

"Guys."

It was Dominic.

"Guys. Don't wanna worry you. But there's something else."

They all looked his way.

"What is it?" asked Emily.

"The Earth. The continents – they look... *wrong*."

THE END